ULTIMATE
RIDE

A YOUNG TROPHY WIFE, A CRIMINAL
AND THEIR DANGEROUS AFFAIR

C H LEE

ULTIMATE RIDE

A YOUNG TRIP WITH ADRENALINE
AND THE DANGEROUS AFFAIR

C H LEE

ULTIMATE RIDE

A YOUNG TROPHY WIFE, A CRIMINAL AND THEIR DANGEROUS AFFAIR

MEREO
Cirencester

Mereo Books

1A The Wool Market Dyer Street Cirencester Gloucestershire GL7 2PR
An imprint of Memoirs Publishing www.mereobooks.com

Ultimate Ride: 978-1-86151-036-5

First published in Great Britain in 2015
by Mereo Books, an imprint of Memoirs Publishing

The address for Memoirs Publishing Group Limited can be found at
www.memoirspublishing.com

The Memoirs Publishing Group Ltd Reg. No. 7834348

The Memoirs Publishing Group supports both The Forest Stewardship Council® (FSC®) and
the PEFC® leading international forest-certification organisations. Our books carrying both the
FSC label and the PEFC® and are printed on FSC®-certified paper. FSC® is the only
forest-certification scheme supported by the leading environmental organisations including
Greenpeace. Our paper procurement policy can be found at
www.memoirspublishing.com/environment

Typeset in 11/14pt Plantin
by Wiltshire Associates Publisher Services Ltd. Printed and bound in Great Britain by
Printondemand-Worldwide, Peterborough PE2 6XD

PROLOGUE

Birmingham, September 2004

With music blasting from the radio, the silver Audi coupé sped into the drive and screeched to a halt outside the detached Tudor-style house, the driver's mouth set firm with determination.

Soon they'd all be on his case, he thought bitterly. Hounding him with their demands, crushing him, stifling him; his wife, his MD Louis, the production team. And not forgetting Penny, his devoted secretary and mistress. Ah, Penny... tall, blonde and beautiful, always eager to please. Maybe a little too eager, although she was the only person that had kept him sane through all of this.

He gave a long drawn out sigh. Johnny Ricci, the kid from the slums of Birmingham who used to dream that one day he'd become rich, thinking that money and possessions were the keys to happiness.

Jeez! If only he could turn back the clock, he'd be willing to give up this whole freaking lot.

But there was one possible solution...

Making his way into the house he held his breath for a second. Reaching for his suitcase and passport, he began to plan his escape.

CHAPTER ONE

Birmingham, 1984

"Have you ever had a special dream, Johnny?" the girl in knee-high socks and mini skirt asked the young boy who was lounging next to her on the green near the council estate. "Like something you wish you could make happen?"

He felt like saying he'd dreamed of killing his parents – especially his father, who scared the hell out of him. Instead, he gave a shrug. "I guess I'd like plenny of cash. Buy a fast car- a mean sports job with a mega bass. Maybe become the next great train robber," he added half jokingly.

"Cool," she replied. "I guess when I leave school I'd like..." she paused for a moment. "Promise you won't laugh?"

"Nah – course not."

"Cross your heart?"

"Cross my heart."

"Well... I've always had this thing about becoming a model – someone famous like Christie Brinkley."

"Model?" he sniggered.

"Stop laughing," she cried, grabbing hold of him in an attempt to pin him down.

In one swoop he had her locked in his grip. "Gotcha! – now you can't escape."

"Johnny… pleease!" she squealed.

"Not until you beg for mercy," he teased.

Giggling, they rolled across the grass and held each others glance for a moment before she became serious. "Have you ever… you know?"

"Have you?" he asked, although he knew for a fact that she hadn't. Word on who was easy travelled fast in school.

She shook her head, her eyes glistening brightly. "Do you wanna?"

Did he want to? Holy Mother! Sex was something he'd only had smutty conversations about with his pals, although he'd often fantasized about it but never dared push his luck. Now he had the chance with a real girl - not just his hand and some dirty magazine.

"Well - do you?" she urged.

"Um… yeah," he mumbled, trying to appear casual in spite of being a nervous wreck. But hey – he was cool. A man had to be cool, especially in front of a girl.

Today was about to mark the most important day of his life. He was finally going to lose his virginity and, at the ripe old age of twelve, Johnny Ricci couldn't imagine a greater triumph.

Seven years later - April 1991

"Ooooooh Johnny…you're simply wiiiicked!"

From the old broken-down camper van the girl's gasps were shrill and breathless, becoming frantic squeals of ecstasy.

Wicked! Fantastic! Yeah, so they kept telling him. Scoring had never been a problem, and at nineteen his track record for bedding girls was unrivalled. Now if only he could get the rest of his life to run in as smooth and uncomplicated a way.

Miss Whatever-Her-Name finally shuddered with satisfaction. She was about seventeen, pretty with brunette hair and freckles and quite petite in comparison to her exceptionally large breasts. He'd known her just a few hours after chatting her up on the High Street, where she worked as a junior receptionist. She may have mentioned her name, who cared? He was never around long enough to get involved. Relationships? Forget it. He had no intention of landing himself in some dead-end marriage like his parents.

Johnny Ricci - medium height and skinny, wildly good-looking in a craggy type of way with jet black hair curling just a tad over his collar and falling in an unruly wisp on his forehead. A straight nose and defiant mouth, which set in a firm jaw gave him his tough-edged appeal. But it was his eyes, so dark and intense they could mesmerize at a glance.

"Is it just cars you repair here?" the girl asked, primly adjusting her clothes.

"Nah, we cut up bodies and store their parts for the black market," he teased, pulling up his jeans.

The rust-ridden camper van had long been immobile and stood decaying in the yard of a run-down garage. It was by no means the best of accommodation, although it did have certain advantages.

"Cum on - betta make a move," he said, grabbing his black leather bomber jacket, now eager to get rid of her.

"How do you fancy tomorrow night?" she suggested, scrambling down from the van after him. "We could always get a video and go back to my place."

"Can't make tomorra," he fibbed. "Like I'm gonna be working late."

"Well - maybe another night?"

"Yeah – whatever," he agreed, keeping her sweet. "Listen – if the coppers or anyone else asks, you were here with me last night. Got that?"

He walked her to the bus stop and they parted with a peck on the lips.

Setting back to the yard, he retrieved a battered joint from his pocket and tried to figure out exactly where his life was going. He certainly hadn't figured on things turning out as bad as they now were.

The night before came flooding back. He pictured the old man sprawled helpless on the floor, a pool of blood oozing from the gash in his head.

And once more the nightmare returned.

Only dreams weren't for real.

Were they?

It had been approximately 10.55 the previous evening when the Ford Transit had rammed its way into McKays' electrical wholesalers. The warehouse, crammed with software, was conveniently tucked away in a side street, close to the city centre.

There were four of them: Johnny, Mickey Brennan, a black kid named Lenny Morgan and a fourth accomplice known as T Bag, who would be waiting with a stand-by truck ready to shift the stuff up north.

Mickey Brennan had assured him it was a cinch. But nicking lager and fags was one thing. Knocking off a load of software was a totally different ball game.

Johnny had been just ten years old when he and his family had moved to a council estate in south-west Birmingham. He'd clicked immediately with Mickey

Brennan, two years older and incredibly streetwise. It hadn't taken Johnny long to realise it was far easier to go out and steal than beg for pocket money.

Meanwhile, life at home was intolerable. His father was Italian. His mother, although born in England, always insisted she was Irish. Almost every night he would have to put up with them fighting like a couple of mongrels in a junk yard – his mother's fiery temper and his father babbling away in Italian.

Happy days. Happy childhood.

As for school, forget it. He'd forged more sick notes than he'd had hot dinners. Fast cars and experimental sex sure beat the hell out of arithmetic.

It wasn't long after his fourteenth birthday that he was caught in possession of an XR3i Escort.

"What's wrong with you, Johnny?" the head teacher had scolded. "You're a bright intelligent boy. Why spoil yourself doing these dreadful things?"

Rebellion? Frustration? A lousy home life? All he knew was he got a buzz out of it.

At fifteen he was expelled from school. His parents hit the roof and he moved out to live with Mickey and his drug-addicted mother. Most of the time she was too spaced out to know what day it was, so girls came and went freely. By the time he reached sixteen he had been given the news that his father had been killed in an accident at work. Out of respect he went to the funeral. His mother snubbed him, apart from telling him what a useless waste of space he was.

As if he cared.

Eventually, Mick obtained a rundown garage, where he'd taken to running a dodgy car business - among other things - and where they shared the old clapped-out camper van. He didn't know which was worse – the stink of rot and decay from the van or Mick's bad odours. Either way, Mick had some pretty filthy habits, one of which was cocaine and at fifty quid a gram he'd turned to other resources to feed his addiction. He was stockily built with greasy brown hair and acne and although he didn't say it, he envied Johnny's good looks and popularity with the girls.

"There's this warehouse crammed with software – it's a cinch," he'd said persuasively, "Five grand a piece. You, me and the Costa Del, with plenty of hot pussy."

Nudge, nudge. Wink, wink.

That wasn't quite what Johnny had in mind. He'd had enough of this lousy existence. He was desperate for money and maybe if he went on this job he could start afresh somewhere and cut all ties with Brennan. And who was gonna miss a few computers?

"Count me in 'n all," Lenny piped up.

"No chance," Johnny said, reluctant to take responsibility for the kid. "It's too dangerous."

"Hey, c'mon man, I'm not askin' for a cut," Lenny begged, eager for excitement. He was just sixteen and wore hip-hop trainers, baggy pants and a baseball cap. His parents were Jamaican and apart from his Rasta-Blaster, he thought Johnny was the coolest thing on the planet.

"The kid's crazy," Mick said. "Tell you what – you can keep guard from the van. Watch out for anyone suspicious."

Johnny took control of the driving; he'd always been pretty cool at handling cars. All was going according to plan when a security man arrived on the scene and screwed up the whole operation.

"Move! Over 'ere where I can see ya!" Mick shouted at the old man. "C'mon - shift!"

The night watchman stumbled nervously onto a seat. In all his thirty years' service he'd never encountered or expected this. Another six months and he'd have retired with a decent pay-off.

Johnny was edgy. "You never mentioned any security," he said.

"It's no big deal," Mick shrugged. "Nothin' I can't handle."

Really? Those weren't the vibes he was getting. "This stinks," he said, wishing he'd never got himself and Lenny involved.

"Just shurrup," Mick growled.

Grabbing the guard by the scruff of his neck he led him over to the safe. "Open it," he ordered. "Cum' on open it."

"Just leave it," Johnny insisted. "Let's get the stuff shifted into the van and get outta here."

Mick ignored him, watching the guard fumble nervously with the dial.

"I don't know the sequence," the old man stammered.

"Then try a bit harder!"

Johnny shuffled. "Look – I don't want anyone gettin' hurt," he said.

The security man made a foolish move and reached for the panic button. The alarm went off, almost deafening them.

"You stupid ole fool!" Mick struck out and sent the security guard sprawling into a metal cabinet. The sharp corner of the unit caught him on the side of the head and he stumbled to the ground. A stream of crimson began to ooze from the gash. It didn't look good at all. The guard lay motionless.

Johnny stared in panic. He wasn't sure if the man was

breathing or not. He wasn't sure about anything any more.

"Don't just stand there, you prat!" Mick yelled. "C'mon – let's get the hell outta 'ere!"

"We can't just leave 'im!" Johnny screamed above the alarm. "Suppose he snuffs it?"

"Then he'll do us a favour," Mick snapped, making a beeline for the van.

"Great, so as well as attempted burglary we get done for murder."

Now he hated Mick. He never thought it was possible to hate anyone so much. Jumping in the van he started the engine and screeched out of the side road.

"Now listen – both of ya," Mick warned. "We're all in this together, so we stick to the same story – you got that?"

"There's no way I'm taking the rap for the old man," Johnny spat. "Why should I get busted cause of you?"

Mick made a grab for him. "You'd betta not open that trap of yours, I'm warnin' ya," he snarled.

"Get your lousy hands off me," Johnny yelled back, struggling to control the van.

Lenny's eyes darted nervously between them. There was gonna be trouble.

It only took a split second for the Transit to clip the curb and the brick wall to come looming towards them. The impact left Johnny dazed, but somehow he managed to gain control, slamming the gears into reverse and steering the van back into action.

Mick had hit the windscreen. His face was smothered in blood and he was barely conscious.

As he sped back to the yard Johnny tried to figure out his best move. A & E was far too risky. By the time they reached the garage he was tense and on edge. "Here, give us a hand," he yelled to Lenny, attempting to move Mick's bulky body out of the passenger seat. "I'm gonna make it look like he's had an accident under the car. Then I'm gonna fill T Bag in and dump the van."

"Is he gonna snuff it, an' all?" Lenny asked.

"No one's gonna snuff it, trust me," Johnny said, sounding a lot more confident than he felt. "Make yourself scarce – you haven't seen or heard anything of me – got that?"

"Cool, man," Lenny said, punching the air with his fist. He strode off with a chuffed grin. He was one of their gang and nothing could be more hip.

"Mick? Can you hear me?" Johnny said, shaking him. "I'm calling the medics - make believe the Jack gave way. OK?"

"The dope… " Mick whispered faintly.

"What about it?" If there were drugs lying around he had no intention of getting involved.

He thought of the old man. He was probably dead by now. Could he live with that?

So what had happened to his big plans? Heading in some positive direction?

He was heading somewhere all right, and it didn't look healthy one bit.

CHAPTER TWO

London, April 1991

Donna Deblaby woke in her luxurious satin draped four-poster bed and glanced at the unopened card and packet on the dressing table.

Shouldn't she be experiencing joy? Happiness? After all, today was her wedding anniversary. Her fifth, to be exact.

Life with Richard had kept her in the lap of luxury, if nothing else.

At twenty-five she had kept her girlish looks and had often been mistaken for Richard's daughter - quite understandable considering he was twenty years her senior.

She was five foot five, slim and exceptionally beautiful with honey-toned skin, a perfectly sculpted nose and her eyes a clear china blue, framed by long pale golden hair. She had everything a woman could possibly want; good looks, a wealthy husband and a magnificent home.

Everything except a happy and compatible marriage.

Donna was Doris and Jack Layton's first born, and the moment her father laid eyes on her he called her his doll.

They lived in a remote country village in Norfolk where they had a small detached house. She was the eldest of seven children, and the cramped ex-council house could barely accommodate the large family. Often she took responsibility for her brothers and sisters, especially Sarah Louise, the baby. Her father was a farm hand and though they hadn't been exactly poor, they'd had no such luxuries as a washing machine or telephone.

Her mother was plain in the sense that she never wore make-up, or took pride in her appearance. She never visited the dentist, her belief being that your teeth grew old and decayed with you. She was a God-fearing woman, taking them to church without fail every Sunday morning.

Her father drank, and with it came violence. Often she would hear his disgusting groans as he forced himself upon her mother.

Uncle Frank, as he was known, would bring them fresh meat and goodies. Sometimes he gave them sweets and ice cream. According to her mother, Uncle Frank was a good man who wouldn't harm a fly. But even as a child, Donna despised him. She'd notice the way he touched her when she sat on his lap. He would sometimes fondle her and as she grew older she began to avoid him.

At eleven, she was curious about sex. "Where do babies come from?" she asked her mother, dipping her fingers into the freshly prepared cake mixture. It seemed both parent and teachers were reluctant to discuss the subject, although Donna already had some secret knowledge, thanks to her friends.

"Daun't do thart filthy habit," her mother had scolded, smacking her fingers. "An' daun't ask such darft questions." The subject had been avoided once more.

"Uncle Frank keeps touching me," she complained to her mother.

"How dare you make up stories about Frank," her mother said. "It's very wicked to tell fibs."

Why did she bother?

Gran Watling paid her usual weekly visit and took the subject more seriously. "Time she knew the facts of life. Pretty young thing like thart'll be in trouble before you know it."

Gran was stout, with a large double chin and whiskers, her white hair scraped back with grips.

"Men are only interested in one thing," she added. "You've only to look at your father. Lust, my girl. That's what."

Her mother flushed uncomfortably. "Ere, make yourself useful," she said, thrusting a bag of corn in Donna's hand. "Go an' feed them there bantams."

Surely there was more to life than feeding a load of chickens?

And indeed there was.

On her fourteenth birthday, Donna was allowed to go to her first disco at the local village hall. Giggling over Cokes with her friends, she spotted a boy with black curly hair and a cheeky smile.

"Who's that?" she asked.

"Tony Philips," her friend replied. "Lives up at the farm by the old mill."

It wasn't long before she got to know him. She could hardly wait to meet him after school, where they would sneak off into the barn. It wasn't long before she allowed him certain privileges. She would let him slip his hand inside her school blouse and fondle her breasts. But when he tried to put his hand up her leg she swiftly objected. "You're a tease, Don," he'd complained, petulantly.

When she arrived home her father was waiting. "What time be this?" he demanded.

"I had to run some errands," she replied, squeezing past him without further questioning.

"That lass is up to no good," she heard him tell her mother. "She's gonna bring shame on this family."

Donna ignored them, turning her attention to Sarah Louise. She tucked her into bed and read her 'Little Red Riding Hood.' "Oh what big teeth you have Grandma, and what big eyes you have… "

Sarah giggled. "How do wolves wear glasses?" she asked.

"This is a special wolf - a really crafty one," Donna told her.

One day she intended to leave home. One day soon.

Just before her fifteenth birthday, her father summoned her. "Your mother an' I have some good news," he began. "I've managed to get you a job up at the poultry factory."

Donna pulled a face. "I don't want a job at the factory."

"You'll do as I say, lass," he scolded.

"Dolly," her mother cut in gingerly. "It's good money – £30.50 a week."

Why did her parents insist on calling her Dolly? They knew she hated it. And now she had to handle a load of dead chickens.

With her first week's wages she bought a lipstick before handing her pay packet over to her father.

"Where you off to?" he asked suspiciously.

"Um… I promised to run an errand," she lied.

"Just make sure you wash that muck off your face

before you go out," he grunted. "No daughter of mine leaves this house looking like a harlot."

She hated him. Most of all, she hated the way he treated her mother.

"Why do you allow it?" she asked Doris.

"It's a wife's duty," her mother had replied. "For better or worse, the good Lord tells us."

Her mother was pregnant yet again. She looked so old for her thirty-seven years. Hard work and child bearing had taken their toll.

Donna gave a sigh. If her mother was prepared to put up with him, then who was she to question it?

It was on her sixteenth birthday that her parents presented her with a dress ring. Nothing expensive, by all means, but to Donna it was the most precious thing she had ever possessed. She could hardly wait to show it off.

"I think my father's getting suspicious," she told Tony.

"I'll take care of you," he replied. "One day we'll get out of this village."

Sliding his hand beneath her sweater, he brought his lips down to her breasts and she sighed with ecstasy. Just the touch of him sent shivers down her spine.

"Come on, Don," he coaxed. "We've been going steady for almost two years. Everyone does it when they're going steady."

"I'm not everyone. You know how I feel about things."

He broke off with frustration and rolled away for a moment.

"Did you mean what you said?" she asked, "about leaving here?"

"Course I did."

"I wish we could run off now," she sighed.

"I need money first. As soon as I have enough we'll get married."

Her father was waiting when she finally arrived home. She'd never seen him look so angry.

"Where've you been?" he demanded.

"The farm," she said, avoiding his glance. "I've been helping out with their lambs... ouch!" She flinched at the sting of his rough hand across her face.

"You've done no such thing!" he roared at her. "I've been over the farm myself. You've been seeing that lad of theirs."

He pulled her hand down and removed the ring. "No lass o' mine brings trouble back 'ere," he snarled. "From now on you come straight home from work, you hear me?"

"Please mother!" she begged.

Her mother just stood there without saying a word, as timid as a mouse.

She was sent up to her room, the one she shared with her other three sisters. She retrieved the jar she'd hidden at the bottom of her mattress and counted the small amount of money she'd managed to save. Maybe it was enough to get her out of this village, and then she could try to find a job.

First, she had to discuss her plans with Tony.

"Are you going away?" Sarah asked, wide-eyed and innocent, watching her pack a few things into a plastic carrier bag.

"Sssh! Mother and father are not to know and you must promise me you won't tell them."

Sarah nodded. "Why are you going?"

"Because father is being nasty and spiteful to me."

"Can I come?"

"No, Sarah. There's your schooling and I have to find a job. But I promise I'll come back."

"Promise?"

"Yes. I promise."

The following morning she was ready to leave. Her father had set off for work and her mother had taken the children to Gran Watling's.

She collected her savings and put on two jumpers. She was about to leave when Uncle Frank arrived.

"Nice bit of beef, tender and succulent – just how I like my women," he said, placing the meat on the kitchen table.

His eyes roamed over her well-developed body. She was young and tasty, unlike that old worn-out wife of his.

"What are you staring at?" she screamed at him.

She knew that look only too well. She'd seen it enough times with her father when he'd come home drunk and abused her mother.

"You're a handsome lass," he said. "Bet the village lads can't keep their hands off you."

"Excuse me." She attempted to pass, but he blocked her path.

"Frankie's done you an' your folks a lot of favours in the past," he rasped, beads of sweat beginning to appear on his forehead. "Time you an' me came to a little arrangement."

She spotted the knife on the kitchen worktop. If she had to, she would use it.

"When you were a kid you used to love sitting on Frankie's lap - remember?" he said, undoing his belt.

"Get out of my way, or I'll scream," she warned.

"Yeah – And who's gonna hear ya - the chickens? I bet you love it, if the truth's known. Don't think I haven't noticed the way you an' that Philips lad carry on. Well he ain't got a patch on what I've got to offer."

She made a dash for the door. He seized her, pinning her down and shoving his hand up her jumpers, tore at her blouse.

"Let me go!" she squealed, attempting to struggle free.

"Now listen," he warned. "You stop fighting an' be a good girl, I'm not gonna hurt ya."

Holding her down with one hand, he managed to free himself.

"This is our little secret. No mention of this to your folks – understand?" He began to force his way between her legs. Somehow she managed to bring her knee up, winding him for a second. Then she grabbed the knife.

"Don't come any closer," she warned, her eyes staring at him like a wild animal.

He laughed in her face and made a further grab for her, and she felt the knife plunge into his side. She watched in horror as he staggered towards her clutching the knife. Oh my God!

She grabbed her bag and ran. No one would believe her. It would be her word against his. Suppose he died? She would be locked away, imprisoned for life. She had to get out. Leave the village for good.

If only she could see Tony. Explain what had happened. But he'd only make her go to the police.

No. The best thing to do was to get out - away from Frank, away from her father. Although her parents had warned her never to accept lifts, she thumbed her way south.

London was a vast cosmopolitan city Donna knew little about. It was big and scary, a maze of streets and shops. Busy, yet lonely. Where would she go now she was here? What about food? What about accommodation? The little money she had wasn't going to last very long in a place like this.

"Fifteen quid a night, luv - that includes breakfast," the landlord said. He led her up three flights of stairs to a creepy attic room where an old gas cooker stood, looking as if it had never seen a flannel. Her parents' house, although small, had always been scrupulously clean.

"The meter takes fifty pence," he told her. "If you need anything just give the old Dutch a shout."

She had just enough money to pay for three nights' accommodation, along with a writing pad. Tomorrow she would have to find work.

She sat and wrote Tony a letter.

"Please whatever you do don't let my parents know where I am as my father will have me arrested... "

She was careful not to mention Frank or the fact that she had no job. With no qualifications – not ever a reference - it had been impossible to find work.

She finally managed to get a job in a rundown restaurant. A sour-faced cook with grey hair and a double chin pointed her in the direction of a sink full of dirty plates. "Dishwasher's bust, so you'll have to use your hands," she snapped.

It was never-ending. As soon as she cleared one pile, another one appeared – and when a large furry rodent scurried past her feet she let out a scream and dropped the dish.

"That'll be deducted from your wages," the cook scolded. "Any more accidents and you're sacked."

She wished she could go back home. She missed Tony and her mother. But she could never face her father or Frank again. She could never return to that village, no matter what. In the meantime, she circled every possible vacancy she could find.

It was six whole weeks before Tony's long awaited letter arrived.

"Sorry it's taken so long," he began, "but I'm not much good at writing letters. I miss you something awful, Don. Wish you'd come back. Your father kicked up hell when he found you were missing. He came round the farm looking for you an' threatened my dad, blaming me for everything. I told him I knew nothing about you leaving, but I don't think he believed me.

I meant what I said about getting married, just as soon as I have enough money.

I can't think of any more news, but I'll write soon, I promise.

Love always Tony

XXX

P.S - By the way Frank's dead.

Dead! Oh dear God. She'd murdered him! Suppose the police questioned Tony and he gave them her address?

She had to get out and move on before they found her.

CHAPTER THREE

Midlands News, Birmingham

"Police were last night investigating an attempted robbery which took place on Monday evening in the Newtown area of the city, where a security man was attacked. His condition is said to be critical..."

At the fruit machine the girl approached Johnny. "Gorra fag on ya?" she asked.

Johnny glanced up briefly. It was Mick's missus and a right scrubber at that. The remains of yesterday's mascara was smudged around her eyes. She wore a baggy out-of-shape jumper, her bitten fingernails were stained with nicotine and her peroxide hair was tangled with black roots.

He ignored her in the hope she'd go away, and carried on playing.

"I've just come from the hospital," she began, as if for his benefit. "Mick may be out by the end of the week."

"Give him my regards," Johnny sneered, concentrating on the game.

"He wants to know if you've heard anythin?"

"Like what?"

"I dunno - you tell me."

Whatever Mick had put her up to, he was having none of it. "You can tell him I sold the old Escort for a hundred quid an' took fifty. I figured it's what he owes me," he muttered.

"Mick's got some bad debts, Johnny. I suppose you already know?"

He banged the machine with annoyance. "Mick always owes money –that's nothin' new."

"These geezers are dangerous – They'll stop at nothing."

He delved in his pocket for more change. "If Mick wants to get involved with scumbags that's his problem."

"You're his mate. At least you could try an' talk some sense into him."

He gave a short brittle laugh. "D' ya think I haven't tried?"

"I'm scared, Johnny."

"Join the club."

He hit the jackpot and the fruit machine juddered into action.

"You couldn't spare us a couple of quid for some fags, could ya?" she said. "Only I'm gaspin'. My nerves are in shreds."

He tossed her a couple of pounds in the hope of getting rid of her. But to his annoyance, it appeared to have the reverse effect.

"The name's Maggie, in case you've forgotten," she said, eyeing him up. "If you're stuck for somewhere you can always kip down at mine - while Mick's away."

She must think him desperate. He wouldn't touch her with a barge pole.

The stink of stale tobacco hit him as she edged closer. "Like you say –what Mick gets up to's his business."

"You've gotta to be kiddin," he snorted with disgust. "Ain't you ever heard of honour among thieves?"

"Don't give me that crap. You couldn't give a toss about Mick."

Too right.

He grabbed his bottle of lager and hastily escaped her company.

"See ya around, Johnny."

Not if I see you first, sweetheart.

He wandered over to the other side of the bar. It was three days since the break-in and events still haunted him. He wasn't sure about the old man. As much as he wanted him to pull through, there was also a nagging apprehension. Whichever way he looked at the situation there was no easy escape.

He headed back to the yard with a bag of chips. Despite everything he was still stuck in this God-forsaken hellhole. Was there no getting away? He made himself a mug of coffee and was about to sit down when he heard the roar of sirens.

Jeezus, the coppers!

Climbing out of the back window he scaled an eight foot wall and ran. He didn't stop running until he was as far away as possible.

Time to move on and put the past behind him. Where he was going was another matter.

***

The following morning Johnny was woken by a child's screams echoing down the concrete passageway. Not the usual sound he was familiar with back at the yard. And then he remembered - he'd picked up some girl at the take-away and spent the night in a high-rise flat. Finding accommodation for the night had been easy – maybe too easy.

She lay next to him, occasionally twitching in her sleep. The bright sunlight beamed through a gap in the curtains on her face. She looked kinda old, thirty if she was a day.

Maybe one of these days he'd have his own place. Yeah

– one day. And then he wouldn't have to rely on some dumb girl. They all had the same idea; move in with them, and they got this crazy notion they owned you. Before you knew it they were coming on strong with all that crap about getting hitched.

Responsibility! Marriage! Just the words sent shudders of despair through him.

He glanced at his Rolex. Eleven-thirty. He could kill for a bacon sarnie, but there didn't appear to be any offer of food around here.

He took a closer peep. Yeah… she was definitely a dog. This was one freebie he wouldn't be accepting in a hurry.

Very steadily, he eased himself out of the bed. He paused as she stirred with a groan and rolled over back to sleep. Catching sight of her bag open at the side of the bed he glanced in and was tempted to take the money, but decided against it.

That would only make him as bad as Mick.

Grabbing his clothes he crept quietly out towards the lift, where he attempted to get dressed. A scream of horror echoed down the passageway from a woman in the flat opposite.

"Wassamarra?" he shouted. "Ain't you ever seen a naked bloke before?"

"You filthy beast!" she screamed, scurrying to the safety of her apartment.

He sniggered and waited for the lift. When it finally arrived it was splattered in graffiti and stank of stale urine. He decided to use the stairs; all eight flights of them.

What had he been thinking, accepting an offer like this? From now on things would be different. Whatever the case, there was no going back. And then he thought about Lenny. Maybe he should have told him his plans. He felt kinda responsible for the kid. He was barely seventeen and looked up to Johnny as if he was an older brother.

Nah – he was just being over cautious. Lenny would be OK. He had a family to take care of him. Safe enough, he guessed. And when he got back to Birmingham he'd make it up to him.

He made his way to T Bag's. A scruffy four year old boy answered the door of the council house on tip toes, mucus streaming down his nose.

"Is your dad there?"

"No mister, so bugger off," the child replied, attempting to close the door on him.

"Who is it?" T Bag's wife appeared cradling a sobbing youngster as a third child screamed for attention from the hallway.

"Oh, hello Johnny."

"Is Tez around?"

"He's out somewhere." She glanced at him quizzically. "You don't know anything, do you? Only he's been acting strange lately. I know when he's pulling a fast one."

Johnny kept dumb. There was no way he was getting involved in a domestic.

The kid peered around the door wiping his nose on his sleeve then stuck his tongue out. If this was married life you could shove it up your jacksy.

"Come on through," she offered. "I'll make you a cuppa."

"Thanks, but I've gotta go," he replied. "Just tell him I'll be in touch."

Half an hour later he was on the motorway after being picked up by a lorry driver who seemed only too glad to discuss his matrimonial affairs with someone. It turned out his estranged wife had taken their five kids and run off with their eldest son's eighteen-year-old best mate.

"Twenty years we'd been married," he said. "And then she goes and pulls a stunt like that. I'll never be able to work out how a woman's mind works."

He wore a red and white check shirt and looked somewhere in his mid forties, with long greasy ginger hair receding at the front.

They pulled up at a transport café and ordered sausage, egg and chips. While they sat waiting, the driver was busy eyeing up the woman serving at the counter. She wore an apron and had massive breasts and frizzed brown hair.

"She's a little cracker," the trucker said.

Jeez, Johnny thought, anyone pulling that cracker would have to be nuts.

She brought their order and leaned over the table, her enormous breasts dangling in front of them.

"Can I get you anything else?" she asked, wiping her greasy hands down her apron.

"Two mugs of tea, luv," the driver said, ogling her assets.

He watched her walk off. "You don't get many of them to the pound. I bet she's a right little raver in bed."

Johnny picked at an over-fried, greasy egg. If she were the last woman on earth, he'd rather jerk off.

The driver finished his meal with a loud burp and lit up a cigarette. "So what's your plans, son?" he asked.

Johnny shrugged. "Maybe find some work, I guess."

"You shouldn't have much trouble, what with the summer season coming up. They're cryin' out for people." He sorted out his money to pay the bill and slipped Johnny a confident wink. "Watch this, son – I'll show you how it's done."

He swaggered over to the counter, purchased a packet of cigarettes and muttered something to the woman as he paid the bill.

"You filthy so an' so!" she cried, hurling his change at him. "Take your friend and get out."

Johnny looked on with a sneer. Yeah, he'd show him how it was done all right.

The driver finally dropped him off by the docks at some seaside resort. It was early evening, raining and miserable, and the weather did nothing to boost his already deflated ego.

He hung around for a while, then finally wandered into a casino. He had a few attempts on the fruit machines, and then went over to the attendant for change.

"Any jobs, mate?" he asked, slipping over his last fiver.

"Nothin," the man muttered, a cigarette dangling between his lips.

Johnny thought maybe it was for the best. Working in a gambling joint wasn't the smartest of ideas.

He spent the night on a bench in a bus shelter. He wasn't sure what was worse, lying in the freezing cold or being banged up in prison.

Either way he'd struck a pretty raw deal.

CHAPTER FOUR

"How old are you, kid?" the man asked Donna through a cloud of cigarette smoke across his desk.

"Eighteen," she lied. She'd responded to an ad she'd seen in the newspaper asking for models.

"And your name?"

"Donna," she whispered.

"Speak up, sweetheart."

"Donna."

"Have you ever done this type of stuff before, Donna?" he asked.

"Um… no."

"What are your bust measurements, sweetheart?"

"I'm not sure." And she wasn't. She hated the way he was undressing her with his glance.

He stubbed out his cigarette. "OK, if you'll just slip the sweater off for me."

"Pardon?"

"The jumper, babe. After all, there could be a multitude of sins hiding beneath that little lot."

Slowly she stood up and peeled off the two jumpers. His eyes feasted on her well-developed breasts. "Good, good," he kept repeating. "I think you're just what we're looking for. I'll briefly fill you in. I'm about to launch a new magazine. I'm looking for six or more models I can use on a monthly basis. Interested?"

"What about money?" she asked, business-like.

"It varies," he replied. "I pay roughly a hundred pounds

an hour depending on the work. A session can last anything from two to four hours. The rest of the time is all yours."

Sounded too good to be true. "What exactly will I be modelling?"

"This should give you a rough idea," he said, throwing a magazine in her direction. "Here – take a look."

Donna was horrified. Disgust and humiliation flooded through her. There were men and woman in all sorts of obscene positions showing off their private bits. There were even animals involved.

He read the shock on her face. "To most girls it's just another job," he said. "I wouldn't let your morals talk you out of making big money."

"I wouldn't want your money even if my life depended on it," she replied frostily. Grabbing her sweaters, she rushed out of his office. How could she have been so stupid?

Once outside, the tears flowed. And as if that wasn't bad enough, an old man stumbled into her path and muttered obscenities.

She fled to her accommodation. It was a basement flat she shared with two other girls. They seemed to have lots of boyfriends between them. One was just leaving as she arrived. He was middle-aged and well dressed – much too old for them, she thought.

Sal was sitting on the edge of the bed, pulling on a shabby old cardigan which barely covered her. "Landlord's been round," she told Donna. "He wants your rent money by tomorrow, or else."

She was now out of a job and had been there just a week. "I've only enough for food," she said, disheartened. "You couldn't lend it me? I'll pay it back as soon as I find work."

"And when's that likely to be?" Sal scoffed, lighting up a cigarette. "Sorry, luv. If you can't figure out a way to pay off your debts, then that's your problem."

Fine friends they'd turned out to be. They couldn't give a monkey's, either of them. Of course, this was all a chastisement. She was being punished for killing Frank.

And from the upstairs apartment, the Beatles played on. Help! I need somebody... Help! Not just anybody...

The following day she picked up her brown paper carrier bag, and was off on the road again. She made friends with a girl who was backpacking and who kindly let her share her sleeping bag and food. They would sit and talk for ages about things like Greenpeace and animal welfare, which the girl was into in a big way. Meanwhile, the search for work continued. It was always the same old story; 'too young - looking for someone smartly dressed with experience - not quite what they had in mind.'

Well now she was fed up with their feeble excuses. Fed up traipsing around being told this, that and the other.

When she spotted the notice in the window of the transport cafe, she didn't hesitate. She walked boldly up to the counter and dismissed the lewd comments and vulgar laughter from the truck drivers.

"I've come about the job," she said, addressing a thin elderly man in a white apron.

"It's been filled," he replied, not impressed by her appearance.

She hung around. She didn't see anyone in the kitchen.

"I cooked for my family - there were nine of us in all," she said, with a determined attitude.

He carried on serving a driver who requested two eggs with his meal. The driver looked her over with the same lust she'd seen in Frank's eyes. "Why don't you try your luck up Soho, darlin'?" he sneered. "You'll find plenny of work there."

"Soho?"

The owner slapped the two eggs onto a plate of greasy bacon and sausage. "Kids," he mumbled. What were they thinking of, leaving home? Surely they weren't all so hard done by? He noticed her bag and thought of his own children, all grown up now. Suppose they'd been in the same situation? It didn't bear thinking about.

"This ain't no place for a young girl," he told her.

"I can look after myself," she said, loud enough for the driver's benefit. She'd killed a man, hadn't she? What was to stop her doing it again?

The owner glanced at the slip of a girl. Despite her grubby appearance she had an honest face. He must be going soft in his old age, but he hadn't the heart to turn her back out on the street.

"You say you can cook?"

"Yes, my mother taught me. She was the best in our village."

"You can start by clearing the tables," he said. "But make sure you tidy yourself up first."

"Does that mean I've got the job?"

"It means you're on a day's trial. Any trouble and you'll be out on your heels. Is that understood?"

"Yes," she replied, excitedly. She had a job, and that was all that mattered.

She discovered that Ken had lost his wife a few years ago. He didn't appear keen to discuss the matter, so she let it drop.

It didn't take Donna long to draw up a menu. Less grease, more substantial meals, she'd pointed out.

"The drivers want their fry-ups," Ken argued. "They won't go for all this fancy stuff."

"Nothing fancy about my cooking," Donna said. "Just plain old-fashioned good food - and wait till they try my steak an' kidney pie."

It wasn't long before word got round. If you wanted decent home-made cooking, Ken's was the place to visit. And with Ken's watchful eye, Donna also gained respect from the drivers.

She worked for him for eighteen months, during which time he became like a father to her. Any problems and Ken would lend a sympathetic ear.

She thought often of her family back home. She longed to get in touch with them, especially her mother.

On her eighteenth birthday Ken had surprised her with a bonus. "Thanks for all your help," he began solemnly.

"Is something wrong?" she asked. She knew by the look on his face that it wasn't good news.

He sat down, his face solemn. "I have to give up the business on doctors orders."

"What will you do, Ken?"

"I have a pension. But you, my girl, have nothing to worry about. I'll see you get a good reference."

So she moved on and went to work for an elite restaurant. The little Spanish manager took a shine to her immediately.

It was a family-run business and Donna was thankful that his wife was never far behind, as Roberto had a habit of squeezing her bottom. She took wine orders and occasionally helped to cash up at the end of the night. She got on well with the Escandells, they were kind and considerate people. Roberto was a flirt, but it was nothing she couldn't handle.

Her employment came to an end when Roberto asked for her bank details.

"I haven't a bank account, Mr Escandell," she told him, thinking she could easily be traced. "Is there no way I could be paid cash?"

He looked shocked. "You ask me to... how do you say... fiddle the accounts?"

It appeared Roberto worked religiously by the book. She promised to open an account, but she left that evening and never went back.

And so she moved onto her next employment and after being given the number of the Alpine club she went along. It was a shabby-looking place, despite the recent coat of paint. She managed to grab hold of a skimpily-dressed girl. "I'm looking for the manager," she said.

The girl pointed her in the direction of an extremely fat man with ginger cropped hair and sagging jowls. She walked over to him. Mr O'Connor?" she began, handing him her reference. "I'm Donna. I called you earlier this morning about the job."

He glanced briefly at the note, took out a handkerchief and mopped his sweaty forehead. "Lap dancing, wasn't it?"

"No, waitress," she said, taken in by the seedy surroundings.

"Can ya lap dance?" he asked.

"Umm... no."

"Pity, we could do with a little excitement around 'ere." He broke off with a wheezy laugh and fragments of stale alcohol drifted towards her.

He held up his fingers to a coloured girl rehearsing with a pianist. "Melania – five more minutes." Turning to Donna he muttered, "That one you've gotta watch, she's an arsy piece – scratch yer eyes out if you so much as look at her."

"She sings well," Donna said, thinking she was too good for this place.

"Yeah well, don't let her hear you saying that. She'll demand another fifty quid outta me."

Donna wasn't sure about the job but no other work was on offer with cash in hand.

It wasn't a brilliant wage, but she made up for it in tips. Some of the regulars she got to know well. Others were just after one thing.

"Say – have you ever considered modelling?" asked a smooth-talking man whose order she was taking.

Now there was a question, if ever she'd heard one.

"I'm a freelance photographer," he added.

"That's nice for you," she replied, giving him a frosty glance and placing his drink on the table.

He looked at her as though she was mad. A girl not interested in modelling- Impossible!

"I'm serious," he said, handing her his card. "I work on the commercial side of things. I know a photogenic face when I see one. Think about it."

She did, and tore up his card. But a few nights later he was back again.

"I was expecting to hear from you," he smiled.

"Then you expected wrong."

He ignored her abruptness and smiled. "Sure I can't buy you a drink?"

She accepted a slimline tonic & ice.

"You say these pictures are purely commercial - for what?"

"Make-up, hair products - that type of thing."

He read her uncertainty. "I can assure you there's nothing tacky about them."

Why should he be doing her a favour? Men only did you favours for one reason.

"A portfolio is usually somewhere around two hundred pounds," he said. "But I can work you out a deal. I'll see it gets into the right hands – so to speak."

Modelling? It was tempting. Call it curiosity, but on her night off she went to his studio apartment, a very hi-tech affair with tubular steel furniture and a large black leather sofa.

"Drink ?" he offered.

"No thanks."

"You seem uptight," he said. "It will help you relax."

"I don't drink beer."

"There are shorts, if you prefer?"

She accepted a Napoleon with ice and he ripped open a can of beer and settled down on the sofa next to her.

"So tell me about yourself."

"What's there to tell?" she said. She took a sip of the brandy and it hit her stomach like red-hot coals. She coughed and spluttered. He watched with amusement.

"So how about boyfriends?" he asked. "You do have one, don't you?"

"Yes," she lied, thinking maybe it would stop him from getting ideas.

"What does he think about all this? Does he approve of you modelling?"

She shrugged. "How I make my living is my business."

"Smart girl."

She avoided his glance, staring into the contents of her drink and beginning to feel uncomfortable.

"Relax," he kept repeating. "I'm not going to bite."

She smiled sweetly. Just try it.

"The name's Leon," he said. "To achieve good shots, it's crucial that there's a good relationship between the photographer and the girl. You have the makings of a good model, Donna," he said, stroking her hair to one side. "Good bone structure, a great body – the boyfriend has a lot to be proud of."

She slapped his hand away. "I'd rather you didn't," she replied abruptly.

"Because of the boyfriend?"

"No - Because I don't want you to."

He smiled a sarcastic grin. "Most of the other girls in this business I've bedded. The majority of the time I don't even have to ask. They need work, Donna, which I can find them. And in return, they have something to offer me."

"I'm not the other girls," she replied curtly.

"Look Donna, all I'm saying is to work well together there are certain barriers that need to be broken down."

"And you think sleeping with me is the answer?"

He shrugged. "It puts ease between the photographer and the girl, and results in better shots."

The past came flooding back. Her father. Uncle Frank. The seedy little creep from the other modelling agency...

She slammed her glass down on the table so hard it spilt. "You know what you can do with your job," she snapped. She stood up, grabbed her coat and headed for the door.

Stepping out into the hustle and bustle of the city, she took a deep breath and smiled to herself. If she'd managed to survive three years in London, she could survive anything. She was at last in control of her life. And it felt good, to say the least.

CHAPTER FIVE

Hospitals gave Mick the creeps. The smell of antiseptic, the discipline and especially nutters like the one in the next bed who'd kept him up half the night hallucinating about cockroaches. He'd just managed to drop off when a black auxiliary nurse woke him with the six-thirty breakfast call.

"Cereal or prunes?" she asked, with a 'take it or leave' it attitude.

"Shove your prunes up your arse," he hissed.

By now the staff were well acquainted with Mick's aggressive behaviour – in fact, they couldn't wait to see the back of him.

By nine o'clock he was up and dressed, waiting impatiently to be discharged. Home, sweet home. Back to Maggie, who had kindly offered to pick him up in her brother's truck.

The old boy in the next bed continued to ramble on in confusion, his dentures floating unpleasantly in a glass of water at his bedside.

"Where am I?" he asked.

"Hospital, Granddad," Mick replied.

"Hospital?" he muttered in confusion. "What am I doing in hospital?"

Mick cringed. Five stinkin' days he'd spent in this dive, enough to send anyone mental. And what was all that crap about drugs rehabilitation? If he needed their help he'd ask for it.

Meanwhile, two blocks away in intensive care, the

security man continued his battle with the help of a life support machine. What did Mick care? Because of that ole fool he'd missed out on a few grand.

He finally got the all clear and while waiting for Maggie he rung the garage from the hospital call box. There was no reply.

Slamming down the phone, he spat. What the hell was Johnny playin' at? He was supposed to be takin' care of things back there. No doubt the tosser was too busy shagging some bit of skirt.

He was not in the best of moods when Maggie finally arrived. "Summat's up," he snarled, "Ricci would have got in touch by now."

"Maybe he's bin arrested," she suggested.

He manoeuvred himself into the truck, which wasn't easy with his leg in plaster.

"I'm goin' back there to see if everythin's OK," he growled.

"What, now?" Maggie complained.

"Nah – tomorra… Course now, you stupid bitch!"

Maggie drove into the yard and looked cautiously around. "There don't look like anyone's about," she said.

"You wait 'ere," he told her.

Hobbling his way into the garage, he was enraged to find there was no sign of Johnny. Then he checked the back of the sink where he'd hidden the cocaine, and saw it was missing.

Effing and blinding, he picked up the phone and rang T Bag. His wife's whiney voice answered.

"Let me speak to your ole man," he demanded.

"Who is it?"

"Tell 'im it's Micky. Ask him if he's seen anythin' of Johnny. Or had any trouble with the coppers."

"Why should Tez be involved with the police?" she asked.

Was this woman crazy or what?

"Just put yer ole man on – now!"

"I don't like your threatening tone," she snapped.

T Bag grabbed the receiver off her. "Everythin' OK, Mick?" he asked.

"Do I sound OK?" he spat. "Johnny's done a runner. You ain't seen 'im, have ya?"

"No. But the missus said he came round a couple of days ago."

"The coke's vanished."

"You don't think Johnny had anything to do with it, do ya?"

"I trust 'im as much as I trust a rattle snake," Mick snarled.

"Terry!" his wife yelled. "What's goin' on?"

"Nothin," he shouted back, hand over the receiver trying to be as discrete as possible.

"If ya see anythin' of Ricci let me know," Mick snarled. "I'm gonna strangle his fuckin' balls when I get hold of 'im."

He slammed the phone down and muttered more abuse, kicking an empty grease can lying on the floor with his good leg. He paced the garage anxiously for a few minutes before making another call.

"It's Micky," he said. "We've gotta problem – the coke's been nicked."

"You have the problem, not me," said the well-educated voice on the other end of the line. "Either you return my merchandise or you find the cash."

Mick gave a nervous chuckle. "C'mon – how long have we bin doin' business together? Have I ever tried to double cross ya? Just give me a couple of weeks. I'll find Johnny an' sort it out - trust me."

"Oh I trust you, Micky – I know how you value your life."

"Whatta ya doin?" T Bag screamed at his wife, who was cramming her belongings into a suitcase.

"Something I should have done years ago," she shouted back. "I'm packing my bags and taking the kids with me."

"What's brought all this on?" he said, trying to calm her down.

She slammed the case shut. "I don't appreciate your so-called friends threatening me."

"Mick?" he laughed. "Don't be stupid."

"You lied to me. You told me you were down the pub and all the time you were on some job."

"Come on, luv," he said sheepishly. "It ain't as if we took anything."

"Oh, and that makes everything OK, does it?" she shouted back. "I've had it up to here being a gangster's moll. I want a proper upbringing for my kids."

"And so they shall," T Bag replied.

"You're useless," she spat scornfully. "Just look at you. Why don't you get off your backside and get yourself a decent job. Instead you have to hang around with scumbags like that."

"I told ya, it's the last time."

"How many times have I heard that? It's always the last time – until the next and the next."

"I promise it won't happen again," T Bag pleaded.

"It's no use, Tez. I'm leaving an' I don't intend coming back. There's no way I'm struggling to bring up my kids while their father's in the nick. And don't say it won't happen because as sure as I'm standing here, it will." She gathered the children. "Come on, we're going to grandma's."

"I don't want to go," wailed one.

"I hate it there," screamed another. "She makes me eat yucky greens and I can't watch my programmes."

T Bag raised his voice above the commotion. "You can't do this," he yelled.

"Oh yes I blooming well can. You had your chance, Tez - and you've blown it."

CHAPTER SIX

Melania was as lithe and supple as a tigress and every bit as mean and quick tempered, as O'Connor had pointed out. Apart from her outbursts, she was a talented performer. She was semi-professional, tall and extremely attractive with long black scrunched hair. She also had a habit of turning up late; sometimes she didn't bother to turn up at all, which sent O'Connor into a rage.

When she finally arrived, he hit the roof.

"Where the hell have you been?"

"Trash," she hissed storming past him to her dressing room to pick up her belongings. "You can stuff your crummy job right up your fat white arse."

She slammed the door in his face and he banged furiously on it. "We have a contract- remember?" He turned to Donna. "Maybe it's the time of the month," he said. "You try an' talk some sense into her."

"Me?"

"Yes, you."

She tapped gently on the door. "Melania? It's me – Donna."

There was no response, so she walked in.

"What do you want?" Melania spat, ripping her clothes down from the hangers and hurling them into a case. "O'Connor put you up to this?"

"I, um… wondered if I could help in any way?"

"You can start by getting the hell out."

Donna stood in silence. Why couldn't O'Connor do his own dirty work?

"It's not that bad here. You do four nights a week and have your own dressing room."

"You call this a dressing room?" she yelled, flashing her wildcat eyes at Donna, as if it was all her fault. "There's hardly space to swing your tits."

"I really think you should consider it," Donna said.

"You do, huh? An' what gives you the right to tell me what I should or shouldn't do?"

Up close, Donna noticed the swelling under the girl's left eye.

"What are you staring at? Never seen a bruise before?"

"I know it's none of my business."

"Damned right it's none of your business," Melania cut in. "So just keep that pretty little nose out of it."

"Some man did this to you, didn't they?"

"Like I said, it's none of your business."

Donna stood her ground. "I had a father that abused my mother –he never hit her but he abused her in other ways. And all I felt was contempt for him. If you're foolish enough to let him do this, then you deserve no pity."

She expected the girl to hit back. Retaliate. But instead, Melania collapsed into a chair with a sigh of frustration. "He's just a bastard!" she said. "And I should have packed my bags a long time ago."

"So why haven't you?"

"You know, you keep telling yourself maybe they'll change. You give them one more chance. Then another, and another. And before you know it you're in one hell of a rut."

"Come on, Melania. You can make it anywhere. But not while he's dragging you back."

Melania gave a brittle laugh. "So what the hell are you doing in a dump like this?"

Melania's personal affairs didn't improve much over the months, although, as their friendship developed, Melania would confide in her more often. Winston Brown was a worthless piece of garbage who frequently beat her up whenever the mood took him – which was often.

One night in the club Melania was sitting with a smartly dressed businessman. She'd polished off almost a bottle of Martini when she beckoned Donna over to their table.

"Honey – this is Richard," she began, addressing a tall man in his early forties. She gave Donna a nudge. "He has no baggage, he's unattached – and loaded," she whispered discreetly.

Donna returned a wink of confidence. Anything had to be better than Winston Brown. She smiled sweetly at the man before quickly escaping their company.

She had almost forgotten the incident until a few nights later, when she received a call at the club. O'Connor was kind enough to let her use his office.

"Hello Donna – This is Richard Deblaby," the voice on the other end announced.

"Should I know you?"

"We met the other evening in the club... I was sitting with the coloured girl."

"Oh yes I remember."

There was a pause on the line. "Look, I know you're busy," he continued. "The reason I'm ringing is I thought maybe you'd care to have dinner with me one night?"

"I work most evenings," she said.

"What about your night off?"

His persistence annoyed her. "If you think I'm an easy touch, the answer's no."

"I don't think anything of the sort."

"Well I'm sorry, but I've already made arrangements."

"I take it this is a firm no?"

"I must go. I'm using the office phone," she replied, keen to get away.

Melania was surprised when she told her. "I don't know why you don't give the guy a chance, honey," she said, finding it hard to believe that Donna would turn down such an offer. "He's charming and absolutely loaded."

"So you've said... "

It suddenly struck Donna what she was getting at. "You were trying to match me up, weren't you? I thought it was you who was interested in him."

The following morning four dozen roses arrived on her doorstep with the message: Hope I didn't make myself too much of a nuisance. Fondest regards, Richard Deblaby.

It was a whirlwind courtship – six weeks to be exact. They were married on the romantic island of Bali, amid a clear blue sky and white sand. Only Melania and Richard's best man bore witness to what should have been the happiest day of her life.

"Was that good?" Richard asked on their wedding night.

"Yes," she lied, disappointment flooding through her. The earth never moved. Nor were there any of the thrills and shudders of excitement she'd felt when Tony had touched her.

It wasn't until they had married that Richard had made it quite clear that he didn't want children.

"It's not as if I'm in my twenties, Donna," he had said. "If we had a child by the time it was ten I would be in my fifties."

It was the first of many disappointments. Not only was their lovemaking a disaster but she also came to realise they had completely nothing in common.

She liked pop, Richard liked classical.

She loved dancing, Richard preferred golf.

She loved life. Full stop!

She had made a mistake. But it was too late.

She sighed and tore open the envelope and read the simple message inside the card.

From Richard

With love

She glanced at the small packet on the bedside table. She didn't want his jewellery or his expensive presents.

What had happened to Donna Layton – the young girl who had always been so independent and full of dreams? Suddenly she was left trapped with a man she knew she could never find true love with.

And all she wanted was to be happy – was that too much to ask for?

CHAPTER SEVEN

"Hi." The girl in the Fat Willy tee shirt hung around expectantly.

"Hi, whoever you are," Johnny replied, busy unloading a crate of dead fish. Even his filthy vest, splattered in fish gut, didn't put her off.

He had managed to get a job as a packer at the docks. Not quite the job he'd had in mind, but he was desperate. And anyway, it was only for a few months. By then maybe things would have settled down back in Brum.

"Doesn't it bother you working with dead fish?" she asked.

"Nah… I used to help out at a taxidermist," he replied, spinning her a yarn. "You kinda get used to their cold lifeless eyes staring up at ya."

She quickly changed the subject. "Do you fancy doing something later – maybe a drink?"

"I'm skint till I get paid," he replied.

She was only too willing to oblige, and they arranged to meet later that evening. She was nothing special, but a lay was a lay.

He met her at the docks and they headed off to a secluded spot on the beach.

"I can't do it here," she complained. "I'll get sand up me bum."

He obligingly took off his leather jacket and placed it on the damp sand beneath her.

"Is that OK?" he murmured.

"Hmmmm, fine," she sighed, wriggling beneath him.

No problems. As usual, it was easy.

Later, they headed off to a bar. It started out as a bit of fun – him, the girl and some middle-aged couple who had kindly invited them back to their house for drinks.

"I think we should def it," Johnny insisted.

"Come on," she giggled. "It's free drinks."

As they headed back to the couple's semi he still had bad feelings.

The three of them perched at the kitchen table, while the man's wife sat in the living room watching television, and hardly speaking a word.

He guessed they were somewhere in their mid-forties. Kind of a strange couple, he reckoned. The wife was no oil painting and the man was short and on the stocky side with a bald head. It transpired he worked the clubs as some kind of entertainer.

"Jot down a forwarding address before you leave," the man suggested. "When the next gig comes up I'll send you a couple of free tickets."

Was it Johnny's imagination, or did the bloke touch his leg under the table?

Seventies music spun from the stereo and after the third round of YMCA, Johnny began to get bad vibes. As soon as they had the chance to be alone, he nudged the girl. "Cumon – let's get outta here," he murmured.

"We can't just walk out – it looks rude," she said primly.

"So what? The bloke's a weirdo. He keeps giving me kinda strange looks."

She burst into giggles. "Maybe he fancies you."

"Is that supposed to be funny?" he snapped. Her attitude was beginning to piss him off. At the first opportunity he was dumping the dumb bitch.

He shot her a filthy glance as she polished off a glass of vodka. "I gotta be up in a few hours for work," he complained. "Are you comin' or what?"

"In a minute," she said, beginning to slur her words.

"Fine – do what you like." He was about to bounce out of the room when the man returned with a bottle of Jack Daniel's.

"If you're looking for the toilet, it's at the top of the stairs," he said with a glint in his eyes.

Johnny decided to use it as an excuse to get out. On the landing there was movement from the bedroom and he realised that the wife had already turned in for the night. So much for hospitality, he thought. He swilled his face under the cold-water tap and then he decided he'd sneak out. After all, he hardly knew the girl.

He crept gingerly down the stairs. Before he had chance to reach the front door the man caught him. "She's on the sofa - had a bit too much to drink," he said. "She'll be fine in the morning."

No frigging way was he stopping here until morning. He glanced briefly at the girl. It crossed his mind that maybe the slimy bastard had spiked her drinks.

"Wake up," he said, shaking her vigorously. She gave a grunt and slipped back into oblivion.

"You can use the spare bedroom," the man offered.

He had two options. Either he took up his offer or he left the girl there. Maybe not, he thought. Suppose the bloke raped her? Not that it was any concern of his.

The small room had a double bed with a large solid mahogany headboard. Sitting down fully clothed he eventually became drowsy. Within seconds he had fallen into a restless sleep.

At first he thought he was dreaming. Bad dreams... hands fumbling, groping inside his zipper.

He woke startled. "What the hell...?"

He quickly lunged for the light pulley over the bed and he found the man leaning over him, his pathetic erection poking through his Y Fronts.

"You pervert! You filthy stinkin' pervert!" He grabbed hold of the man by the scruff of the neck and began banging his head repeatedly against the headboard.

"You wanna play dirty games?" he yelled. "I'll teach you one you won't forget."

"Stop it! Stop it!" His wife burst into the room, wearing nothing more than a pair of red see-through knickers and a terrified expression.

"I'm calling the police," she said, dashing off down the stairs. "I'll have you arrested."

He raced down the stairs after her. "You ain't callin' no coppers," he yelled.

His wife picked up the receiver, about to dial out, and he snatched the phone from her. "Just unlock the friggin' door and let us out of here," he demanded.

There was a scream and Johnny swung round to face the man, who had grabbed hold of the girl, holding a Stanley knife to her throat. "Get your filthy grubby hands off my wife – or your girlfriend gets it."

"Please Johnny... help me!" she screamed.

Jeezus!

"Just put the knife down," he said, attempting to stay calm. "Just put the knife down an' let her go."

"Stay away, I'm warning you."

"The girl has nothing to do with it," Johnny said, attempting to edge his way closer. "Just let her go and I promise we'll leave quietly."

His wife stood with her hands trembling. "Gary – please luv - you can't keep doing this," she cried.

The man's red-painted lips quivered. "You're a nasty spiteful boy who can't be trusted," he hissed, jabbing the blade further into the girl's skin.

Johnny tried to edge his way nearer.

"Stay back..."

"Come on Gary, luv," his wife pleaded, holding her hand out to take the knife. "Just give it to me."

Slowly, very slowly, he handed her the knife and turning to unbolt the door, she gave Johnny a displeased look. "Just get out of my house," she said.

Quickly grabbing the girl he steered her out of the door. Once outside, she went berserk. "You bloody weirdo! You both want locking up!" she screamed through the letterbox.

"Just leave it," he said.

Before he knew what was happening, she'd picked up a brick and hurled it at the window. The shattering of glass shook the neighbourhood. A dog began to bark incessantly and the street lit up.

"You stupid bitch," he yelled as they legged it down the road. "What the hell you go an' do that for?"

CHAPTER EIGHT

Arriving back at the flat, Maggie had changed into a well-worn negligee and sprayed herself in cheap perfume ready to rekindle their relationship. Mick showed little concern, ripping open a can of lager and settling himself down on the sofa.

She came and sat on the edge of the arm beside him. "By the way," she began, "Johnny said to tell ya he'd sold the Escort for a hundred quid an' taken fifty."

Mick's eyes pinned her dangerously. "You never mentioned you'd seen 'im?"

"I forgot," she said, chewing on a well-bitten fingernail.

"You forgot – huh? So when was this?"

"A couple o' days ago."

"You've known for a couple of days an' you ain't said anything?" he snarled.

Maggie twitched nervously; she knew only too well when Mick was spoiling for a fight. "I didn't think it was important."

"He helps himself to fifty quid – an' ya don't think it's important?" he spat.

She glanced at him warily. "He said you owed 'im."

"I owe 'im nothin'. He had the use of the camper – what more did he want?"

Maggie continued to nibble on her nails.

"What else did he say?"

"Nothin," she replied, knowing it was in her best interests to keep quiet.

Mick stood up. "He must have said summat." He grabbed hold of her. "You an' 'im been havin' a cosy chat behind my back?"

Maggie flinched. "Course not."

"Lyin' whore. You're like a bitch on heat when he's around," he snarled, about to bring his hand up just as there was a knock on the door. "Who yer expectin?" he snapped.

"No one," Maggie replied.

Whoever it was had no intention of leaving and continued to bang on the door.

Mick crept to the window and peered round the curtain. "It's the coppers. Get rid of 'em."

"How?" she panicked.

"You ain't seen me or heard nothing - you got that?"

Gingerly she opened the door and peered at the two police officers.

"Maggie Thompson?"

"Yeah."

"Mind if we come in and ask a few questions?"

"It's a bit inconvenient," she said, pulling the thin worn housecoat around her scrawny body.

The lady officer glanced over her shoulder suspiciously. "We have reason to believe Michael Brennan may be staying at this address."

"I ain't seen 'im," she said, attempting to close the door.

"We have a warrant to search the premises," the sergeant said.

"You just can't barge in 'ere," she screamed at them.

Mick had every intention of running, but it wasn't an easy option with a fractured leg. Instead he acted the innocent.

"Cocaine was found at the garage," the sergeant said, surveying the empty food cartons and beer cans strewn untidily across the floor. "So how do you account for it?"

Mick shrugged. "Maybe the fairies were planning on havin' a party," he sneered.

"This is no laughing matter, Brennan," the sergeant snapped. "Where were you last Monday night between ten and twelve?"

"Last Monday.... now let me see. I may have bin right here shagging the missus. Or was I down the boozer?"

"Maybe a trip to the station will help jog your memory?" the sergeant said. "Read him his rights."

"Michael Robert Brennan," the female officer began, "I'm arresting you for being in possession of class A drugs. You do not have to say anything… "

"Yeah – yeah - I know all that crap," he snarled. He'd heard it enough times by now.

***

Chief Inspector Clements had not had the best of mornings. There had been an arson attack and some hysterical woman claiming her cat had got stuck up a tree. Now there was this cocky little bastard.

He sat facing Brennan in the interrogation room. He hadn't got a peep out of him, let alone a statement. Spread across the table were Brennan's files, with a list of offences as long as the day.

Narcotics at the age of fourteen
Burglary
Shoplifting
Car crime
And so on.

Clements stroked his moustache. He was in his mid fifties, stocky with wavy greyish hair. "Suppose we start with this," he said, slapping two and a half kilos of cocaine on the desk in front of Mick. "It was found at the yard."

Mick slouched in his seat, an arrogant smirk on his face.

"Who's supplying you?"

"No comment." As if he'd be mad enough to squeal on dealers.

"What about McKays'?" Clements asked.

"No comment - Sergeant."

"Chief Inspector, if you don't mind," Clements snapped.

He got up, walked round to Mick and breathed heavily down his neck. "I'm going to prove you did this, Brennan, and when I do I'm gonna bounce you by the balls so hard your feet won't touch the ground. What do you have to say to that?"

"Nothin', till I've spoken to a solicitor," Mick snarled.

"Have you fallen out with me?"

The girl was back. Johnny glanced at her briefly. "That was a stupid stunt you pulled last night," he said.

"I'm not fishing for compliments."

"Good, 'cause I don't have any."

She picked at a thread of cotton on her skirt. "I've decided I'm going to the police," she said.

"What the hell for?"

"I'm going to tell them everything that happened."

He glanced up at her. "An' who do you think they'll believe?"

Wasn't it bad enough he'd left Birmingham to get away from trouble?

She shook her head. "I don't care. I think they should know the truth. The quicker he's locked up the better."

"You think he's gonna own up? It's you they'll lock away. Damaging people's property is a criminal offence."

That shut her up.

"I told you it was a bad idea going back there," he snapped.

"So it's my fault?" she replied.

He ignored her and carried on unloading the crates. Suppose they did decide to press charges? And then it occurred to him – what if she'd given out his details?

"You never mentioned where I worked, did ya?" he asked anxiously.

"Why should I? Anyway, he hardly spoke to me - it was you he was interested in."

She hesitated for a moment. "Does this mean you don't want to see me any more?"

He ignored her and carried on working.

"You took advantage of me," she said, on the brink of tears. "You told me I was special and you cared."

"So I lied."

"I hate you," she snivelled.

"Shurrup!"

"No I won't!"

"Get lost," he spat.

"I hate you – I hate you!"

He watched as she ran off. Yeah, the feeling's mutual, sweetheart.

He leaned against the wall and lit up a cigarette. So here he was, stuck in this strange town with strange people. There wasn't much going on, in fact he'd seen more life in a graveyard. Apart from the casino on the sea front and a couple of pubs there was nothing apart from the nearest night club, which was five miles away, and which you needed transport for. He'd made pals with a kid on the docks. Maybe he could persuade him into driving down there?

At least he had a job - more than he'd imagined possible a few weeks ago, and if he stuck it out for the summer, things should have quietened down by then.

He vowed his life was going to change. Mick had led him into some pretty bad ways and he never wanted to set eyes on him again.

From now on he intended going straight, no matter what it took.

Attempting to snatch a quick lunch break, Clements received news of the security man's death.

"There's also a Mr Barking claiming his Porsche has been vandalised," the lady officer added.

"Well?" Clements snapped, inspecting a piece of wilting lettuce. "What's wrong with the front desk dealing with it?"

"Sorry sir," she began, "I thought you might be interested to know that the incident happened at Brennan's yard."

"Why the hell didn't you say?" he growled, pushing his plate to one side. "What in heaven's name was the man thinking of to take it there in the first place?"

"From what I can gather this bloke wasn't familiar with Brennan. Apparently, he was approached in the pub. Brennan said he could work him out a deal."

"I'll bet he did," Clements said derisively. "Well, if it's compensation he's after he's in for a bit of a shock. I doubt if Brennan's ever heard of an insurance company, let alone dealt with one."

Clements rose from the table. "Get it checked out. Maybe it's just some kids messing around. On the other hand it could be someone who knew exactly what they were looking for."

"Oh sir – the DNA tests are back."

"Good. Get them ready."

Marching back into interrogation, he slapped the details onto the desk. "Well, well, it appears we now have a murder investigation on our hands."

Mick remained silent, his solicitor now present.

Clements glanced at the details. "The name Mr Barking mean anything to you?" he asked.

Mick shrugged. "Why should it?"

"Well, he certainly knows you. He claims his car has been vandalised on your premises - turns out to be a costly insurance job."

"Is this really relevant?" his solicitor cut in.

"I'd say Class A drugs were very relevant. That's what they were looking for, wasn't it Brennan?" Clements said, raising his voice.

"I dunno what you're on about."

"No? Wasn't that the reason for breaking into McKays' – to pay for your filthy habit."

"Stuff you!" Mick spat back.

His solicitor shuffled uncomfortably. "You are distressing my client," he said.

"Well it's not exactly doing my blood pressure much good, either."

"Do you intend charging my client?"

Clements stroked his moustache thoughtfully. He knew he'd have to act fast; otherwise he'd have no option but to let Brennan go.

"Excuse me for one moment," he said rising from his

desk. "I'll just go and chase up those DNA tests. Still – if what you're telling me is true, then you've nothing to worry about – have you?"

He was about to walk out when Mick shouted, "If I come clean about McKays – what's in it for me?"

Clements turned to face him. "You're in no position to make deals with me, son. Manslaughter is a very serious offence."

"It was an accident," Mick yelled. "The old bloke tripped, I'm telling ya."

"Save your breath for the courts, Brennan," Clements said. "Plead guilty and you may - I repeat - may just get a lighter sentence."

"What about bail?"

"You'll be lucky, son."

CHAPTER NINE

Richard Deblaby sat at his deck, glancing through the recent report just handed to him. He wasn't a happy man. Sales were down by 10%. He waited for an explanation from the sales manager, who hovered in front of his deck.

The manager cleared his throat. "There seems to have been a slump in the market abroad," he began.

Richard did not appreciate excuses. "I'd say it's more due to the fact that certain people aren't pulling their weight in the company."

The manager's face reddened as he struggled for a reply.

"I think it's time we sorted out some dead wood," Richard added.

"Redundancies?" the manager said weakly.

"If it means saving the company, so be it."

Richard Deblaby was a tall man in his mid forties. His once slim physique was now a tad heavier around the waist and his dark hair sprinkled with grey. He was immaculately dressed in a crisp pale blue shirt, gold cuff links and a burgundy tie. The jacket of his charcoal suit was placed on the back of his black leather chair. From assistant marketing manager he had come a long way to managing director. He was a no-nonsense man, well aware of the fact that it was a competitive world with no room for time wasters.

The sales manager shuffled nervously. "So when are these redundancies likely to take place?"

"I have yet to sort that out with the board of directors," Richard replied.

"How many are there likely to be?" the manager asked, twitching nervously.

Richard shrugged. "I'll probably know more by the end of the year," he said.

Christmas – not a good time to hand out redundancies to his employees, but someone had to do the dirty work.

"OK, that'll be all for now," he said.

As soon as the manager left his office Richard put a call in to Donna. "Remember we have a business engagement this evening?"

How could I possibly forget?

"Did you remember to pick up my suit from the cleaners?"

"Yes. Isabella's dealing with it."

"Fine. I'll see you later."

By evening, Richard, dressed in a dinner jacket and bow tie, was pacing the floor impatiently. "How much longer are you likely to be?" he snapped, checking his watch for the umpteenth time.

Donna put the final touches to her make-up with little enthusiasm. She hated his wretched business dinners, especially having to endure long-drawn-out speeches concerning the welfare of Software International.

As always she looked sensational in a plain black dress, pearl earrings and a matching necklace, her pale golden hair wound in a sophisticated French plait.

The drive to the hotel was practically in silence, apart from Richard making a few comments on his well-rehearsed speech.

On arrival they were welcomed into the Talbot suite with a glass of champagne. Richard took her arm and guided her through the crowd, greeting various people.

"I don't think you've met my wife," he said, introducing her to a small oriental man with spectacles who politely shook her hand while staring directly down her cleavage.

Richard became drawn into conversation with the man. She left him and wandered over to a carefully laid table of savouries, helping herself to a large brandy punch.

"You must be Donna," said a blonde woman in a dated outfit.

"Yes. And you are?"

"Hilary – I'm Richard's PA."

So this was the elusive secretary Richard was always going on about. Donna wondered if he'd ever screwed her – they spent enough time abroad together.

"Richard never mentioned he had such a young pretty wife," Hilary said, helping herself to a cheese straw. "It's strange when you speak to someone over the phone – they're never quite as you imagined them."

Donna bit the cherry off the end of her cocktail stick.

Don't think for one moment you can fool me, Hilary. I'm well aware that you fancy my husband.

She made a polite exit and went in search of Richard. He was about to take his seat at the table. Printed cards had been carefully placed. To her annoyance she spotted Hilary's name on the other side of him.

"Go easy on that stuff," he said, scowling at the glass in her hand. "Remember you haven't eaten."

He made her feel like a child being scolded over a bag of sweets. "I'm quite capable of looking after myself," she replied indignantly.

The marketing director and his wife were seated opposite. Richard launched into debate about the stock market. By the time the hors-d'oeuvres had arrived Hilary was well into airing her views on shares and how to compete with the Japanese market.

"This is simply delicious," the marketing director's wife commented, tucking into a prawn cocktail.

"I love cooking," Donna replied, making light conversation. "I suppose it's something you pick up as a child. My mother was a marvellous cook. We didn't have much money but she always made sure we had food on the table."

Richard swiftly interrupted. "I don't think people are interested in your family background," he said with embarrassment.

Hilary pricked up her ears. "No wonder Richard has developed a podge– it's all that good cooking of Donna's," she said with a ring of sarcasm.

"So tell me, Donna," continued the director's wife, "do you have any tips on Yorkshire pudding? Mine always turn out flat as pancakes."

"When I helped run a business Yorkshire puddings were one of my specialities - made with vegetable oil, of course," Donna said.

"You helped run a business? How marvellous!"

"Yes. I was in charge of the meals. It was my job to see that customers had a nutritious and healthy diet. Unfortunately, he had to close the transport café due to illness."

"Did you say café?" Hilary gave a spurt of laughter.

Richard almost choked on his wine. "My wife has a wicked sense of humour," he said forcing a smile.

Silence fell upon the table, at which point the main course was about to be served. Donna played with a hard sprout, careful that it didn't shoot off the plate. She passed on dessert and polished off the rest of her drink.

"Richard, I need the loo," she whispered discreetly.

"You'll have to wait. The speeches are about to begin," he snapped.

"I need a pee," she hissed.

"I warned you about drinking on an empty stomach," he hissed back through gritted teeth. "Get yourself a black coffee – and hurry up."

She rose unsteadily and concentrated on walking in a straight line across the room. She made her way into the toilet and sat on the loo giggling to herself, picturing Richard's face.

Eventually, she left the toilets and wandered into the grounds. It was a clear evening and the moon shone on the waters of an ornamental pond. She stood in thought, watching the reflection of the fairy lights mirrored in the dark water, realising she knew very little of the man she'd married other than his mother had died when he was quite young and that his father had gone to work temporarily on an oil rig and never returned. She found it hard to confide in him. Sometimes she wanted to speak out and tell him she had killed someone. Instead, she let it bottle up inside her, this secret she would probably carry to the grave.

"Lovely evening."

She turned to inspect the owner of the voice. A man in his fifties with limp brown hair and a pullover smiled at her.

Conversation was the last thing she wanted. She caught him glancing at her wedding ring. Maybe if she ignored him he would go away?

"Such a wonderful clear night – from an astronomer's point of view, that is," he remarked, staring up at the heavens.

"It all looks so peaceful, doesn't it?" he continued.

"But you'd be quite surprised at the amount of activity going on. For instance, did you know we're on collision course with a meteorite? It's due to strike earth in thirty years' time."

Donna checked her watch.

"I'm sorry, am I boring you?"

She made a hasty retreat back to the hotel, where she bumped into a very annoyed Richard.

"For Christ's sake, where have you been?"

"Sobering up," she said, hardly glancing at him.

"Your behaviour is disgraceful," he snarled, storming ahead of her back into the room.

The speeches were still going on. Would the night ever end?

She was relieved when they finally climbed into the car. Richard was reluctant to let the matter rest.

"If you were out to embarrass me tonight, you certainly succeeded," he snapped, starting up the engine.

"Well, I'm very sorry," she replied sarcastically.

"Not only did you make a bloody fool of yourself at the table, you had to go missing for half an hour."

Knickers.

"And why bring up all that rubbish about a transport café?"

"It so happens I'm proud of the fact. I had a responsible job."

He gave a snort. "You call serving up bangers and mash to a load of truck drivers a responsible job?"

Why bother arguing – he'd never understand, anyway.

"The trouble with you, Donna, is you never take responsibility seriously," he said, taking his aggression out on his driving. "Thank God I had Hilary there to support me."

"Good old Hilary!" Donna raised her voice in mock

bravado. "I wondered how long it would be before she crept in. Why don't you just run off and marry the old frump?"

"There you go again, being childish."

Sitting glumly, Donna thought maybe he should have married Hilary – at least they had more in common.

What did she care?

CHAPTER TEN

Lenny Morgan was nervous when he entered the yard, and he had every right to be. He hadn't seen or heard from Johnny since the night of the break-in and he was usually somewhere around.

The door to the garage was slightly ajar. He paused for a moment, sensing something was wrong. Suppose Johnny was lying dead in there?

Although he was frightened, curiosity got the better of him. Gingerly he crept inside.

"Holy shite," he muttered, scanning the damage. There was rubble everywhere. Cars had been ruthlessly stripped and doors ripped off their hinges. Mick lived dangerously, had contact with various gangs. But he couldn't imagine anyone crazy enough to pull a stunt like this. At every step, he imagined finding Johnny somewhere in the debris.

Instinct told him he should turn around and get out while he still had the chance. But it was as if he had to find the truth. If Johnny was in there he couldn't just leave him.

He wandered through to a small area used as a makeshift kitchen. The sink unit was thick with grime and filth and on the worktop stood half a mug of coffee with a healthy growth of mould. A rodent scurried past him. Lenny turned, about to run, when the garage door slammed to.

A surge of fear ran through him at the sight of two sinister characters standing at the entrance. A hefty, mean-looking skinhead with an abundance of tattoos and a tall black man wearing shades and a pinstriped suit, a black leather coat draped over his shoulders.

He didn't need it spelt out – the expensive suit spoke for itself. These guys weren't from no street posse. They were well-organised racketeers, probably from some shady drugs operation of the kind which Mick so frequently indulged in.

The skinhead blocked his path.

"Going somewhere, boy?"

He shook his head. "Just lookin' for my mate," he blurted nervously.

"And who might that be?" Skinhead said.

"Johnny."

"Oh yes, Johnny. So where is this Johnny?"

"I dunno," he shrugged innocently.

"You don't know, huh?" Skinhead didn't sound too impressed.

"Maybe we need to jog your memory?" He picked up a crowbar and toyed dangerously with it.

"The last time I saw him was in here – we were all together, Mickey, me and Johnny," Lenny told them nervously. Perhaps now they'd leave him alone.

"This Johnny – where is he?" Skinhead asked, tapping the crowbar impatiently against his palm.

"I don't know, man."

"You know kid, you're beginning to piss me off, you an' your bunch of mates."

Pinstripes held up his hand as if in a gesture to hold fire for a while.

He lit up a large Havana. "Tell you what, boy," he began, placing an arm around Lenny, "you tell me where Johnny is and no one will get hurt. See, I have a problem.

I need payment for my merchandise. Now we can either work this out civilised or we can get nasty."

"I'm tellin' ya the truth, man," Lenny pleaded, trying to control the fear now leaping up inside of him. "I ain't seen 'em."

In a single swipe Skinhead grabbed the lad's hand and brought the crowbar down, smashing his fingers.

Lenny screamed out in pain.

"Where is he?"

Lenny's eyes bulged with terror. Why were they doing this? He'd told them all he knew. Why wouldn't they let him go?

"I swear man, I know nothing."

"Time's running out," Skinhead warned.

"Please, man," Lenny screamed, eyes wide with fear. The truth was simple. But the truth wasn't good enough. Whatever trouble Mick and Johnny were in he was left to face the unfortunate consequences.

Skinhead showed no mercy. As the first blows descended Lenny's baseball cap flew through the air, and as if in slow motion the ground leapt up and swallowed him.

Stunned and almost unconscious, he felt as though he was floating. Things were becoming blurred, faces distorted. He writhed in agony, unaware of his broken fingers Skinhead had crushed. He was drifting in and out of consciousness like he was dreaming. Would he wake up soon? Maybe they would leave him alone now. But Pinstripes had only delayed the boy's suffering for a more instant extermination. Somewhere in the far distance there were voices, as if from another planet and in his oblivion he heard the command; "Finish the job off."

The nozzle of the .38 was pointed directly at the boy's

head. The real world escaped him. As if suspended in space, he began his journey down a long dark tunnel. Nothing could save him now. He was barely seventeen and about to die at the hands of a maniac.

Lenny's eyes, still wide with terror, stared vacantly into space, only now there was no movement, just a trickle of blood from a single bullet hole in his forehead.

And the only recognition Lenny received was "Youth found murdered near city centre. Police are treating it as drugs related."

Exactly four weeks later the decomposed body of Maggie Thompson was discovered at her flat. The place was swarming with bluebottles, the stench unbearable.

And the cause of death was a single neat bullet hole in the forehead.

CHAPTER ELEVEN

Birmingham – six months later

Chris Ainsworth's Mini was his pride and joy – a Cooper, which he had souped up like nobody's business with enough spotlights to shame Blackpool Illuminations.

Liz Ainsworth stood with her arms folded. "It's a pity you don't spend as much time on your studies as you do on that heap of metal," she commented, addressing a slim, good-looking lad with a shock of blonde hair falling untidily over his eye.

Chris ignored his mother, head buried under the bonnet. He was fed up with her continual nagging over exams. His father was no better. Between the pair of them, they drove him crazy. His parents had big plans for him. They expected him to go to university and study law, but he didn't give a monkey's what they wanted. This was about him. It was his life.

Ever since he'd been a child, he'd always been fascinated with cars. His burning ambition was to become a racing driver. When there seemed little hope of that, he turned to the next best thing and while his parents thought he was making headway at college, he had enrolled in a night class in mechanics.

Shortly after his eighteenth birthday he passed his driving test and came across an old clapped-out Mini which was about to meet its maker. He'd rescued it from the scrapyard for twenty pounds and everyone thought he'd lost his marbles. He proved them wrong, spending the next twelve months doing the car up, building it from a shell and converting it back to its original glory. It was the best thing he'd ever achieved in his life. And now he wanted more than anything to become a successful mechanic and run his own business.

But his father had other ideas for him and since senior school the pressure had mounted. They began to disagree on most things and rows occurred often.

It hadn't always been that way. As a kid he'd got on well with his father. He remembered long, lazy summers when school holidays seemed to drag on forever and his father had taken him fishing on the canal. His brother Steve was five years older than him and his parents called him a waste of space, especially as he'd never made the grade at school.

It had all kicked off one day when Steve, at the ripe old age of sixteen, had come home and announced he had got some girl pregnant. Liz went hysterical and he thought his father was going to have a heart attack. Steve eventually left home and the next they knew he was scrimping and saving in a poky one-roomed flat with a howling baby and a sink full of nappies. Chris heard his parents go on about it for months, while at the same time piling on the pressure for him to do well at school. He guessed it was their way of making him a shining example of how his brother should have been.

School had definitely not been the best days of his life. His father had ideas of grammar school, but Liz had put her foot down and insisted there was nothing wrong with the local comprehensive.

Chris soon found out there was plenty wrong with it after two lads had threatened to beat the senses out of him unless he handed over his pocket money. Unknown to his parents, the bullying went on all through fourth year and he couldn't wait to see the back of the place.

His parents were money-orientated and his mother had gone back to part-time work shortly after he was born. She had a well-paid job in an office and his father a high position at the bank. Between them there was no shortage of cash. Status was a big thing in the Ainsworth household. They lived in a smart four-bedroomed semi in Solihull. Whatever the neighbours had, his parents always had to go one better. Last year it was an expensively-built barbecue. He couldn't make out who they were trying to impress - it wasn't as if they enjoyed entertaining.

If there was one positive thing he had inherited from his parents it was Liz's good looks. With his blonde hair and cheeky grin he had often been told he looked like Nick Hayward from Haircut 100. He was pleased with that, as they were one of his favourite groups. He often locked himself away in the garage and turned on the stereo in his car while working. It was the only way he could get to play his tapes; if he played them in the house, his old man went ballistic.

Girls? Well, he'd never really been that bothered. He much preferred tinkering with his car. And in any case most of his time was taken up on his studies. It wasn't as if he hadn't had the opportunity at college, more on a friendship basis than anything. Girls found his shyness kind of interesting. He guessed it was more of an affliction.

"Christopher! I'm speaking to you!" Liz demanded.

"What?" he yelled, popping his head up from behind the bonnet?

"What's happening with your exams?"

He carried on working while Liz waited for an explanation.

"Well?"

"I don't know," he replied irritably.

"What do you mean, you don't know?"

"I don't know," he repeated, figuring a way to tell her. He flung down the bonnet wiping a greasy hand across his face. "I'm quitting," he said without further hesitation.

There, he'd said it. But one way or another they had to know.

"What d' you mean you're quitting?"

"Quitting – as in finished."

Liz stared at him in shock. "You can't just drop out," she insisted. "Not when you've put so much hard work into it."

"I don't want to work in law, it's not me. I've decided I want to do what I want to do."

"I don't believe I'm hearing this," she said in dismay. "You've only a couple or more years to go and you'll have a good career in your hands."

"Yeah – doing something I'll hate."

"It's going to destroy your father."

Tough. For once this was about him, not his father.

"You ungrateful little so an' so!" she hurled at him. "After all we've done for you. Not to mention what it's cost."

He had wondered how long it would be before money crept into it. Liz and Jim's world revolved around money.

"I've never asked for your money," he threw back.

"And if you'd given me the chance to get a job, I could have managed anyway."

Liz was unrelenting, watching him tinker with the engine. She was forty-five, five years younger than his father. She had a decent figure and she'd recently had a shaggy perm on her blonde hair. Quite good looking for a woman of her age, he reckoned.

"Some girl's put you up to this, haven't they?" she said.

"Have they heck." His mother was laughable at times.

"Then what?"

"I've told you."

He turned on the engine and it growled like a tiger. The big bore had been a success and the tuning was spot on.

"So what are these big plans you have in mind?" she shouted sarcastically, above the roar of the engine. As if she didn't already know.

"I dunno," he shrugged, unable to resist the temptation of pulling her leg. "Maybe I'll squat with the rest of my mates and smoke pot."

"Wait until your father gets to hear about this," she warned frostily. "He'll go mental."

What did she mean by go mental? The pair of them were already mental.

CHAPTER TWELVE

On arriving back in Birmingham it didn't take long for news of Brennan's arrest to reach Johnny. Six years on three counts - manslaughter, attempted burglary and drugs.

So how long would it be before they came looking for him? Maybe he shouldn't have come back?

"Have you seen anything of Lenny?" he asked around his pals. "You know - the black kid that used to hang out with us?"

They shrugged and looked vacant.

He felt kind of bad about it. He'd never wanted Lenny on the job in the first place.

Maybe he should turn himself in. It seemed the decent thing to do. But why give Mick the satisfaction of seeing him banged up?

He wandered along, aimlessly trying to figure out where he was going. Turning out his pockets, he found enough money to play a few games on the fruit machine before deciding to look up his Aunt Rose, who he hadn't seen in years. Rose Maria was his father's sister and a devout Catholic. She had inherited the swarthy looks of the Riccis, and of all the family she was the only decent one amongst them.

When he turned up on her doorstep, she was totally shocked to see him.

"I hope everything's all right?" she said, inviting him in.

"Yeah, fine. Like I've just got back to Birmingham an' I was kinda wondering if you could put us up for a couple of days –till I get something sorted?"

"You know you're always welcome. The spare room will need a bit of tidying up. Are you sure everything's all right?"

Rose put on her glasses, which she wore on a cord around her neck. She inspected him closely as if he were a piece of prime beef in a butchers shop. "Let me have a look at you," she said. "Why, you're just as handsome as your father – he broke a few hearts in his time."

Yeah, tell him about it.

"I think the last time I saw you was at his funeral, wasn't it? How old were you?"

"Sixteen."

"Terrible thing," Rose said. "I hope the company paid dearly for their negligence."

The old lady certainly did well out of it, he thought. And he never saw a penny.

"I'll just go and put the kettle on," she said, about to disappear into the kitchen. "What have you been doing with yourself?"

"Not a lot," he replied. He glanced around the small room. Everything was still as he remembered – the furniture, the wall paper, even the rosary draped over the sideboard, everything except the recent photograph of his sister's wedding.

"When did the happy event take place?" he shouted through to her.

"Catherine's wedding? It must have been eighteen months ago. She looked absolutely beautiful – A pity you couldn't make it."

There they all were, the gathering of the clans – Rose,

the happy couple, his brothers and sisters and his mother, who couldn't even be bothered to try and find him.

"Here we are," Rose said, bringing in the tea and a plate of biscuits. "So how is your mother? Is she still over in Ireland?"

He ignored her, dunking the biscuit into his tea. It got soggy and sank to the bottom of the cup.

"Don't say you still haven't been in touch? The poor woman must be worried to death."

Like hell she was.

Somehow he managed to escape Rose's clutches and headed off to the job centre. He scanned the vacancies; a road sweeper, an assistant bookkeeper and a bricklayer at £4.25 an hour. He decided to pass on all three and pushed his luck signing on the dole. He hung around for what seemed like ages before being attended to by some obnoxious woman who gave him the third degree and asked where he was living at present.

He quickly came up with Rose's address.

"It will take a few weeks for your claim to be processed," she snorted down her nose.

Great! So what did he live on in the meantime - fresh air?

Rose was sympathetic, slipping a twenty-pound note into his hand before he set out for the club.

"I can't see you go short," she insisted stubbornly. She had even tried to palm him off with a pair of Uncle Peter's shoes. "They're real leather – hardly worn," she told him. He'd swiftly declined her offer. Wearing dead man's shoes may be a load of superstitious mumbo jumbo, but he wasn't taking any chances.

At the club he waited while the bouncer checked out the contents of two girls' handbags in front of him. Tarts, he thought critically. Far too much make up and mouths like foghorns.

When he got to the door he was refused entry. "You know the rules," the bouncer said, glancing down at his feet. "No trainers allowed."

He hung around until the bouncer became engaged with a couple of lads, and quickly sneaked through.

Once inside he glanced around for familiar faces. Middle of the week and there wasn't much going on, even the dance floor was empty apart from two dreary looking slappers gyrating around their handbags to Soft Cell.

He grabbed his bottle of lager and headed over to the fruit machine, had a couple of games, lost a fiver and then decided to quit. He spotted a blonde perched on a high stool at the bar and made his way over. She sat with her legs crossed in a leather mini skirt hitched up to her thigh, exposing a generous length of bronzed skin. Her breasts, though small, stood pert and erect through the almost transparent blouse.

Sliding onto the stool next to her, he gave her the once over.

"Is there a problem?" she asked, blowing cigarette smoke in his direction.

"Not unless you have one," he replied, stumbling for conversation. He tried to figure out how he went about chatting up the older woman, finally coming out with, "How come you're on your own?"

"Who said I was?"

"Aren't you?"

He hung around expectantly and waited for her to pick up the conversation. She didn't, so he carried on. "You've gotta lovely body," he blurted out.

Jeez! How corny was that?

He blundered on, deciding to get straight down to business. "How old are you?" he asked.

"How old are you?" she teased.

"Twenny-three," he lied.

He was still waiting for a response. "So?" he asked.

"Twenty-six," she replied.

Bullshit! More like thirty-six.

He'd always fantasized about having it off with a more mature woman. His dreams were about to come true, because ten minutes later they were heading back to her place in her black Nissan Cherry. He'd hardly got inside the door when she was ripping off his clothes.

"Has your ole man been starving ya?" he croaked, spotting the ring on her finger.

"I'm divorced," she replied, her tongue darting in and out like an avaricious lizard.

He lay mesmerized, gradually becoming aware of a second pair of hands.

"You don't mind if Natasha joins us, do you?" she whispered huskily. At that point he didn't care if Lassie the dog joined in.

Natasha –or whoever she was – had larger breasts, was blonde and quite pretty. Between them they made a desirable couple. Whatever, they certainly knew how to give a bloke a good time. By morning he had reached the conclusion that they were nothing more than a pair of nymphomaniacs.

He staggered out of bed knackered and could hardly wait to get away. The younger of the two was sitting at the dressing table wearing a pink dressing gown and fluffy mule slippers.

"Where's your friend?" he asked.

"Friend!" She broke off from applying mascara and

began to laugh, her breasts wobbling joyfully like two moulds of blancmange. "That's my mother."

"MOTHER!"

He was almost relieved when they booted him out. How the hell was he gonna explain the mass of scratches and bites to Rose?

She was busy in the kitchen chopping onions and garlic when he arrived back. She glanced up at him suspiciously, as if with secret knowledge. "You've had me up half the night worried to death," she said anxiously. "Where've you been?"

"At a mate's," he replied sheepishly, pulling his collar up and snatching a cookie biscuit.

Rose wiped her eye with the back of her hand. "It's none of my business what you get up to just as long as you let me know you're stopping out at night."

"Sure." Matter solved.

"There's some fresh tea in the pot," she offered.

She took out a handkerchief, dabbed her eyes and blew her nose and said, "You should get yourself a decent Catholic girl, my lad. Someone like your mother."

"You've got to talk to Christopher," Liz said over breakfast. "He's coming up with some rubbish about dropping out of university."

"He's what?" Jim roared.

"Ssssh! He's in his bedroom. I want you to handle it tactfully."

Chris was still her baby. She couldn't face up to the fact that her sons were now grown up. She still wanted him at home and under her supervision. It was nice having a family, even if there were only the three of them.

"He's got a bloody nerve after all we've done for him,"

Jim said, buttering his toast and heaping on a generous amount of marmalade. "They've had it too easy, the pair of them."

He was a thickset man with receding fair hair and ruddy complexion. His job at the bank had paid a decent salary. But it hadn't always been rosy. He came from a poor background and never had the opportunities that his own sons had. Everything he'd achieved was down to damned hard work. When his first son Steve was born he swore he'd give him the best education possible. Liz had always supported him in that respect. She'd always been a good wife and mother. Maybe a bit of a dizzy blonde at times, but he wouldn't have her any other way.

"Don't be too hard on him," she said, leaping to her son's defence. "He's not a bad kid. It's not as if he's on drugs or anything."

"Stop making excuses for him, Elizabeth. We've done our best for that lad over the years. He's never wanted for a penny," Jim replied sharply. "And how do we know what he's up to at college? I can see him ending up just like that half-wit brother of his."

"Steve and him are like chalk and cheese," Liz said, piling the crockery into the dishwasher. "There's no comparison between the two of them. All he needs is a bit of encouragement."

"He's had plenty of that."

"Look, I don't want any unpleasantness," Liz warned. "If you'd handled the last situation with a little more tact, Steve wouldn't have run into the arms of that scheming hussy."

"I don't want you taking his side, Elizabeth," he said. "It's time he was up, anyway. No wonder he's behind with his exams."

Liz gave a sigh. She hoped Jim wasn't going to ruin it.

Later that evening the three of them sat at the table in silence. Every so often Liz and Jim exchanged glances, while Chris jabbed his fork into a potato and wondered how long it would be before the shit hit the fan.

Jim paid a compliment to the meal with a burp. "So what's all this about you dropping out of college, son?" he said.

Kick off time, Chris thought, tossing his fringe back, a habit he practised often when under pressure. "It's just the fact... well... like I want my own space."

"Which is quite understandable, son."

There was a moment's silence before Jim continued. "Look I understand, you're coming up to twenty. Naturally you want to do your own thing. But there's no need to quit and give up all your hard work. If you need a place of your own, you've only to ask."

"I don't want your money," Chris replied shortly. Why did they think they could just buy him off? What about the pressure of exams? His freedom and independence?

"I want to go out and earn a living - do something I want to do," he said.

"So you're prepared to give up everything?" Jim said, beginning to raise his voice. "Throw the lot away, when in a couple of years' time you'll be in a decent career?"

"I've had it with studying," Chris replied with equal hostility. "I want to make some money in a job I'll enjoy."

"Will you listen to him?" Jim roared. "He's nineteen and thinks he knows the lot."

"I know a damned sight more than you," Chris hit back. "You didn't even know who Edwina Currie was - you thought she was an Indian take-away down Sparkbrook."

Liz stood up from the table. "I'll go and slip the kettle on," she suggested. "We'll all feel better after a nice cup of tea." According to Liz, a cup of tea was the cure for everything.

Chris plodded on wearily, although he knew he was wasting his breath. "I've already been offered a job," he said.

"Oh?" Jim raised a sceptical brow. "What kind of job?"

"An apprentice at this garage."

Jim almost choked on his meal. "What?" he yelled. "You're throwing your career away to work in a garage? Have you given one thought to the money and effort we've sacrificed?"

Chris jumped up. "Stuff your flaming money!" He flew to his room, packed a few things and stormed back down. Jim stood at the bottom of the stairs, blocking his path. "Where d' you think you're going?" he asked sternly.

"I've found a flat and I'm getting as far away as possible from the pair of you," he spat.

"Christopher - please don't do this," Liz begged.

Jim was adamant. "Leave this house and you don't come back," he warned.

"Fine," Chris yelled back. "So everyone's happy."

He flew out the door, slamming it behind him.

Liz broke down in tears. "Now look what you've done," she screamed at Jim. "Heaven knows where he's likely to end up."

CHAPTER THIRTEEN

Jane Pottersley stood in the queue outside the night club and smoothed down her denim mini skirt. "Are you sure I look old enough?" she whispered to her friend.

"Course, now stop panicking," Bekki murmured. Wiggling up to the bouncer she stuck out her magnificent 32DD breasts and gave him a smile.

"OK, sweetheart," he said, giving her a wink and handing her bag back, hardly looking at Jane.

"Ta," she replied with a giggle.

She gave Jane a nudge and they set off into the club.

"I told you we'd have no problem," she laughed as they headed to the ladies.

"No wonder when you gave the bouncer a right eyeful," Jane replied.

"You're so not with it, Jane," Bekki said, applying a fresh coat of lipstick.

"Why – because I don't believe in sleeping around? What's so wrong with being a virgin, anyway?"

"Nothing, I suppose," Bekki said, teasing her curls. "I guess it's something most girls want to get over and done with – like having your ears pierced - especially when they're our age."

Both girls were fifteen and still in high school.

Jane pouted her lips. "What you do think of this colour?"

"Fab," Bekki replied without even looking. "Haven't you ever wondered what it would be like? The suspense killed me. I just had to find out."

"Not particularly - they're all grotty and spotty, anyway," Jane replied staring at her reflection. "I hate these freckles."

"I lost mine when I was twelve," Bekki said, engrossed in her own little world.

"Freckles?"

"No, virginity, you pilchard."

Neither of their parents had any idea they were out clubbing. Jane's parents were on holiday and had arranged for her to stay at Bekki's, while Bekki's mother thought she was spending the night at Jane's. So far it had worked out exceptionally well.

Jane was petite and very pretty, with short blonde hair and baby blue eyes. She was sometimes shocked by her friend's behaviour. Bekki allowed men far too much privilege. Maybe that was why they flocked round her. Or maybe it was her massive boobs.

Bekki was bigger built, with dark curly hair and fully-developed breasts which she was extremely proud of. "You never told me what you think of this top," she asked, adjusting the straps of a low-cut creation she'd managed to get hold of.

"It's lovely," Jane replied, thinking what a tart she looked.

They walked out of the ladies and Bekki took control of things, as she normally did. "Now here's the plan," she began. "We'll try and find someone with a car – that way we won't have to worry about missing the last bus home."

"I don't think that's very wise," Jane said. "They could be Jack the Ripper for all we know."

Bekki threw her a disgruntled glance. "I swear you sound more like my mother every day."

"Maybe your mother has sense."

"Yeah – an' maybe you should try living with her." She suddenly froze and grabbed hold of Jane's arm. "It's him!" she squealed.

"Who?"

"The bloke who was in the queue," she said, pointing Johnny out at the bar. "Get a load of him – he's simply sex on legs."

Chris had found work behind the bar, and with his day job at the garage he just about managed. But his first night was something of a disaster.

Saturdays were not the best of nights to be thrown in at the deep end. It was 80s night and the place was jumping to Two Tribes. A large bar circled the centre of the club and there were four other bar attendants; three blokes, and a girl who looked like Cyndi Lauper with bright red spiked hair and freaky clothes. Each had their own area to cover.

"Any good for tips?" he'd asked the girl.

"You gotta be jokin," she replied blowing bubble gum. "This is the Barley Mow you're talking about!"

The place was beginning to get packed and impatient customers were piling up at the bar.

Chris was panicking. There'd been a couple of complaints regarding short change and he was ready to throw in the towel. Then he thought about his rent money.

He had managed to find some digs over in Edgbaston which took in students at special rates. The ad had been on the notice board at college. It was a single room with an old pine bed and a gas cooker which looked as if it had been rescued from the ark. A far cry from his parent's home, but at least he didn't have to put up with their continual nagging.

He could just imagine Liz and Jim's reaction if they could see him now. Liz would probably have kittens. Jim would no doubt end up with a cardiac arrest.

"Hey mate – anyone serving?" Johnny called out waiting impatiently at the bar.

Chris recognised him immediately as one of the kids who had been expelled from school and who had made his life hell, along with his toerag of a friend. Yeah, he remembered him all right.

"Hey – you were in old dickhead Thompson's class weren't you?" Johnny asked, sorting out his change. How could he forget the bookworm who jerked off with girly magazines and reckoned two O levels made him Brain of Britain?

"How's it going?" Chris replied attempting to be amiable.

"Not bad. Still pushing a pen for a living?"

"Nah. I quit college."

"Guess that went down well?"

"Yeah, like a bomb. Seen anything of that other kid you used to hang around with?"

"Mickey Brennan – Nah," he lied.

Johnny watched him rush off to serve another customer.

So that's where college got you?

Big deal!

Rose had ironed his shirt and he'd managed to buy a cheap pair of shoes and black Sta-prest trousers. He slipped her a wink before leaving and told her not to wait up as he might be late.

Taking a swig from the bottle, he was just about to head off when Bekki cornered him.

"Hiya!" she said, as if they were long-time buddies.

"Um… hi," he replied flatly. Was he supposed to know her?

"I'm Bekki an' this is my friend, Jane," she said, her boobs staring him straight in the face.

He checked the pair of them out. The busty brunette – or the pretty blonde?

In no time the pushy brunette was all over him like a rash, and although he had every intention of getting laid, he still didn't fancy having a ride on what appeared to be the town's bike. He figured the blonde was his best bet and pinned her with his eyes.

Jane flushed uncomfortably. "Come on, Bekki," she said, grabbing hold of her arm. "Let's go and dance."

"In a minute," Bekki replied, hardly taking her eyes off Johnny.

He somehow managed to catch Jane's attention and pulled her to one side. "You an' me are gonna catch up, later," he said, their conversation drowned by the music.

"We are?" she said, finding herself staring into the sexiest eyes imaginable.

Surprise! She even gave him an encouraging smile. "Yeah - Just the two of us without that pushy mate of yours," he said, keeping close tabs on Bekki who was attempting to eavesdrop on their conversation. "Meet us round the back of the car park at eleven-thirty," he added, giving her the benefit of a wink.

She watched him walk off and flushed with excitement.

Bekki was furious. "Where's he going?" she demanded. "And what was all that about?"

Jane avoided her glance, feeling her cheeks burning. "Nothing much," she said secretively.

"Some creep!" Bekki hissed, unable to control her

jealousy. "First he makes a pass at me, and then moves onto you."

"It was you who made a pass at him," Jane corrected her.

"So what?" Bekki exclaimed with humiliation. He wasn't that special, anyway," she added, her eyes already roaming the disco. "I prefer the more mature man any day."

Jane wondered what excuse she could use. Maybe she could say she wasn't feeling too well and was catching the bus, but Bekki would only insist on coming home with her?

She needn't have worried. By eleven-thirty Bekki was already occupied with her tongue down the throat of some man who looked old enough to be her father.

"Bekki," she began, giving her friend a nudge, "I'm popping outside for a while."

Bekki hardly looked up, waving her hand as if to say I'm busy.

"Fine," Jane said. "See you later."

"Stop it!"

"Hey, whatsamatta?"

"You know very well what the matter is," Jane said curtly, slapping his hand away, which he'd managed to sneak up her knickers.

"What we supposed to be playin', postman's knock?" Maybe he should have stuck with Big Tits after all.

"I'm not that type of girl," she snapped.

Jeez! He looked away in disgust. What did she think he'd invited her out there for –to admire the stars?

Jane mellowed her tone. "Besides, I hardly know you."

"So get to know me," he said, sweetening her up.

Maybe if she let him go so far? It wasn't as if they were going to have full sex.

They were up against the wall, round the back of the car park. He decided to push his luck once more, throwing in a few compliments along the way. "You like me, don't you?" he asked sweetly.

No hesitation. "Of course I do."

"So what's the problem?" he asked. "Like you're kinda special, you know?"

"I am?"

"Yeah. Don't you feel something?"

Yes, she certainly did. Something very hard and warm pressing against her thigh. All the times she had slagged Bekki off for doing these dreadful things, and she was no better.

"If I let you will you promise me you won't go all the way?"

"Course not," he mumbled.

Jane froze as she felt him slip between her thighs.

"Just relax. It ain't gonna bite."

"Y... you... promised," she stuttered weakly.

But it was too late – far too late. Her senses were drowned, caught up in something so wonderful nothing else mattered.

Bekki searched the club frantically. There was no sign of Jane and the place was now deserted, apart from a few hangers-on who were being told to drink up and go.

Thanks to Jane she had lost her lift. The man had brushed her aside. "I can't hang about for your friend," he had grumbled, eager to dump her. Why mess around with a tart when his long-suffering girlfriend was waiting back home?

She barged into the toilets. One of the cubicles was engaged. "Jane, are you in there?" she yelled. She heard rustling of paper and snorting and realised it was some crackhead.

Rushing back out she spotted Chris, busy wiping down tables. "I don't suppose you've seen my friend, have you? Remember, we were at the bar earlier on. She was the small blonde in a mini skirt?"

That narrowed it down to half the girls in the club. "Nah, sorry."

She hung around expectantly, watching him empty an over-flowing ashtray into the bin. "I guess she must have caught the bus and gone home," she said dismally. "That's mates for ya."

She caught his grin and sparkling eyes and it didn't take her long to forget about Jane. She quickly turned on the sob story. "I haven't even got enough for the taxi fare," she snivelled.

"Look… er… maybe I could give you a lift?" Chris began, feeling shy and awkward. "That's if you don't mind hanging on another ten minutes."

"Oh brill," she replied quickly perking up. "That would be really cool."

CHAPTER FOURTEEN

Richard was in one of his stroppy moods again. Tell her something new. He'd hardly spoken a word over breakfast, except to complain that his shirt had creases.

He checked his watch, gulped down his coffee and grabbed his briefcase, making a dash for the door.

"Don't bother preparing a meal this evening. I have a business lunch," he said.

"Fine," Donna replied. "I'll make other arrangements."

She called Melania and they arranged to meet at one o'clock for lunch at the Purple Room restaurant where they occasionally dined.

Jumping into the Lotus, she headed off into town. She was wearing a stunning lilac Versace all-in-one, her long blonde hair piled loosely on top in a gold braid. At the traffic lights she got stuck in a jam and bibbed impatiently on the horn. She happened to glance across in the next lane and spotted a horrid little man in a Ferrari giving her that 'I'd like to lay you' look.

God, she was uptight, what with Richard, the traffic and now this horny little creep.

She eventually arrived at the restaurant and they greeted each other in the usual fashion – a hug, a kiss, a compliment on each other's outfits and how wonderful they both looked. The place was pleasantly decorated with purple tablecloths and fresh pink flowers. Classical music played softly in the background.

The waiter, a slim, good-looking youth in a tailored waist coat and crisp white shirt, took their order. "The usual, Mrs Deblaby?" he asked.

"No. I think I'll go for the vegetable Pesto Pierre with garlic, shallots and peppers."

"Make that two," Melania said.

They ordered a bottle of Shiraz with their meal and caught up on gossip.

"So how's Richard?" Melania asked.

"As well as can be expected," Donna said glumly. "It's just I feel I'm in a three-way marriage – Richard, me and his bloody company. He's never at home. He's either at the office or away on business. We have nothing in common. We hardly speak, and when we do it always revolves around his work."

"Perhaps he's under a lot of pressure at the moment. You mentioned redundancies, maybe that's on his mind? Have you tried talking things over with him?"

"Richard isn't the sort of person you talk things over with. He can only see the situation from his point of view. To be perfectly honest I'm glad to see the back of him. When he's at home he's like a bear with a sore head. He undermines me – treats me as if I were some office junior."

"Maybe feeling responsible for you is his way of dealing with things?"

"I don't want a father, I want a lover," Donna said sharply. "Someone I can have fun with."

"Do I detect a tinge of sexual frustration here?"

Donna fiddled with her platinum and diamond ring. "I guess it's partly my fault in a way," she began. "It's just I can't bear him touching me. At one time I used to make excuses. But now he's too tired, which suits me fine."

The waiter brought the wine and poured a little into a

glass for them to sample. "Is that to your satisfaction, madam?" he asked, before filling their glasses.

Melania watched him scurry off. "A lovely firm arse. I think it's a man's main asset."

"Melania, do you think I'm frigid?"

Melania gave a chuckle. "Frigid?"

"I'm being serious."

Donna ran her perfectly manicured fingernail along the rim of her glass thoughtfully. "It's just... I've only had sex with Richard."

"You are kidding me, honey?"

Donna sighed heavily. "This may sound awful, but I don't love Richard in that way..." she began, "In fact, I've never been sexually aroused by him. Don't get me wrong – I love him– but I'm not in love with him – does that make sense?"

"I think I'm getting the drift."

"Maybe I did marry him for his money."

"You know that's not true."

"You think I'm a bitch, don't you."

"No, I don't think that at all. If anyone's to blame, it's me. I'm the one who introduced you guys."

Donna gave another sigh. "You know what it's like when you're with someone - the longer you're with them, the harder it gets. It's just – well - I feel as if I'm missing out, as if I'm letting life pass me by. Before I know it I'll be thirty. And now he's mentioned about retiring when he's fifty-five. Isn't that something old people do?"

"Honey, what can I say? At least he doesn't knock you around. You've only to look at me and Winston. He was the greatest lover possible and my soul companion, but a complete arsehole."

Donna thought maybe it was time to change the

subject. "So," she began with a smile, "How's the new man in your life?"

Melania rolled her eyes jubilantly. "Fan-friggin-tastic! He's black, handsome and horny as hell."

"What are you like!" Donna chuckled softly. "I swear if I didn't have you to turn to I'd be bored out of my skin."

CHAPTER FIFTEEN

"Where did you disappear to?" Bekki asked Jane in school on Monday.

"I was about to ask you the same question," Jane replied.

"Well, I was hardly going to hang around outside your house, was I? So I went back home."

"What did your mother say?" Jane asked anxiously.

"Evil Edna had already gone to bed when I crept in."

"I tried calling you yesterday but your mother said you'd gone out."

Bekki gave a disgruntled snort. "Edna insisted I walked the dog. Looks like I've been lumbered with the lousy job permanently."

Bekki threw her a suspicious glance. "So come on – what happened?"

May as well tell her the truth. She'll only find out sooner or later. "I was with Johnny."

"Oh great - Just take off and leave me."

"At least I didn't make you feel like a gooseberry," Jane snapped back.

"Who's Johnny, anyway?"

"The bloke with the black hair and leather jacket – remember?"

"That jerk!" Bekki shrieked, unable to control her jealously. "I thought you didn't like him – and then you run off with the creep!"

Scrambling into assembly, Bekki turned to Jane. "So are you seeing him again?"

Jane shrugged. "Who knows?" she replied, doubtful if he'd call her. All day yesterday she had waited for a phone call. Johnny hadn't even had the decency to walk her home. He'd swiftly dumped her at the first opportunity with a 'see you around' - whatever that was supposed to mean?

The head teacher took the stand. "Good morning girls."

"Good morning, Miss Smith," the school chimed in harmony.

Bekki nudged her. "I've got a date – with the barman," she whispered. "I'll tell you all about it later."

"I did it," Jane whispered back.

"You mean you had sex?" Bekki squealed, hardly able to keep her voice down. "Wow! Do you feel any different?"

Yes, as a matter of fact she did. Dirty, cheap and used.

Rose kept Johnny busy doing the odd job here and there. It was the least he could do to pay for his keep.

She was entertaining some friend who had dropped in, a thick-set, grey-haired man. He figured the bloke was probably one of the crowd from the church whose activities Rose was heavily involved with.

"This is my brother's lad," she said proudly. "You know – the one who had the unfortunate accident."

He hated being fussed over. And anyway, what had he done to feel proud about? There was nothing big in attempting to rob a company and then watch as his mate butchered an old man. Yeah. That was really something to feel proud about.

He guessed it would always come back to haunt him – the look of helplessness on the security guard's face.

He carried on fixing a shelf in the kitchen, eavesdropping on their conversation.

"Poor lad," he heard Rose say. "His parents used to argue a lot - it was just their way of letting off steam. They were really a devoted couple."

He'd heard enough. Devoted my arse! What kind of crap was that? He switched on the small portable radio and kept himself busy.

There was still no sign of work – not that Rose seemed that bothered. In fact she was only too glad of the company.

He couldn't sponge off her forever. Besides he was getting bored of hanging around.

By early afternoon her visitor finally left. "I'm doing your favourite meatballs for tea," she said. "They're from an old Italian recipe."

Already the smell of the ingredients was wafting through from the kitchen. He was beginning to smell like a clove of garlic. Even the spearmint gum wasn't having much effect. Rose was gonna have to be told. Warding off vampires was one thing. Ruining his sex life was another matter.

Rose wiped her hands down her apron and produced an envelope. "I want you to have this," she said, handing it to him.

"What is it?"

"Open it and see."

He tore open the envelope. "A hundred quid!" he exclaimed. "I can't take this."

"Yes you can. You've been a good lad and I don't know what I've have done without you."

"Hey Rose – thanks, but… "

"Take it as an early birthday present," she insisted.

"It's not till the eighth of January," he said. He always considered sharing a birthday with Elvis Presley kinda special. He glanced at the money and felt really guilty. Just as soon as he got a job he intended paying every penny back.

Later in the evening he headed for the pub and played on the fruit machine until Chris found him. "I think that bird fancies me," he said, juggling with a pile of empty glasses.

"What bird?" Johnny mumbled, stuck in the game and hardly taking notice.

"The one I told you about the other night. The one whose mate went missing – remember?"

"Oh them," Johnny replied flatly, waving a five pound note at him. "Here – go an' get us some change."

"In case you haven't noticed, I've got my hands full," Chris snorted. "Anyway, gambling's a mug's game," he added.

Johnny gave him a scouring glance. "Says who?"

Chris tossed back his fringe and quickly changed the subject. "Getting back to that bird," he began, "I'm seeing her Friday night and I thought you might be interested in a foursome with her mate?"

"No chance."

"Hey – come on, Ricci."

"Can't make it, I've already made arrangements to go down Hall Green dogs with the lads," he said, steering clear of the situation. "I'd stay well away from Big Tits if I were you. She'll eat you alive."

Chris wondered if Johnny had made out with her. Knowing his reputation he probably had. Girls swarmed around him like blue bottles round a garbage bin. Talking of which, he was getting peculiar whiffs. "Gordon Bennett!" he snorted, "Have you been eating garlic?"

CHAPTER SIXTEEN

"So what d'you fancy doing?" Chris asked bashfully. "There's a good film on in town. Or maybe if you fancy a drink?"

"I've got a better idea. Me mom's gone to Bingo," Bekki purred, squeezing his arm. "Sooo... why don't we just go back to mine?"

It was a small terraced house. A large scruffy dog jumped up and greeted them, dribbling with saliva and insisting on sniffing around his flies.

There wasn't much in the way of furniture, just a settee, chair and a television supporting some hideous vase. An old music centre stood in the opposite corner.

"What music do you like?" she asked, sorting through some tapes.

"Whatever," he replied.

"How about UB40?"

"Fine."

The next thing he knew she was diving onto the settee and clawing his zipper.

"Suppose your old lady comes back?" he croaked.

"Trust me," she muttered. Tearing off her bra, she plunged his head down towards her magnificent breasts. It occurred to him that either he was about to have a wet dream, or he'd kicked the bucket and entered the dwelling place of eternal bliss.

Helping him rip off his jeans, she obligingly supplied him with a rubber.

"Cum on, do it, Chrissy. Do it!" she screamed. They tumbled off the settee onto the floor.

"Is this your first time?" she panted.

"Nah," he replied, trying to sound cool. Well, he had kind of experimented with a girl in the science room at college but it had ended abruptly when one of the teachers had walked in and caught them in the act.

He held on tight, riding high on the wave of expectancy. Cymbals clashed, thunder boomed and the room spun around. A spurge of frenzied energy playing in tune to the music until finally reaching its peak.

"Oh Chrissy... that was out of this world!" she squealed.

If only she'd stop calling him Chrissy.

He'd hardly got his strength back when she was at it again. "Let me show you my Duran Duran posters," she suggested excitedly, leading him up the stairs.

Edna Jones's bed looked more inviting – certainly much larger and comfortable than Bekki's single divan. Together they dived on the clean white sheets in a frenzy of passion.

Downstairs, UB40 spun aimlessly around on the turntable for the third time running, much to the annoyance of the next-door neighbour, who hammered furiously on the wall with his shoe. No one heard him. No one cared.

Edna Jones headed up the path, muttering furiously to herself. It had been a completely wasted journey. What on earth were they thinking of to cancel bingo for some hideous pop group? Tomorrow she would put in an official complaint with the club secretary.

She was surprised to find the music centre blasting

away. She was even more shocked to find a pile of clothes scattered across the floor, among which were a pair of men's jeans and trainers. She grabbed a cricket bat she kept in the pantry for unwelcome intruders, crept up the stairs and poked the door open.

"Oh my god!" she screamed in horror.

"Bloomin' heck!" Chris dived off the bed wearing nothing more than a devastated expression and attempted to cup his hands over his fast deflating penis.

"You filthy animal!" she screamed at him, "And in my house – and my bed!"

It was the perfect set-up for Goldilocks and the Three Bears. But while Mrs Jones might have fitted the description of the bear, Bekki was certainly no Goldilocks.

"How could you, Bekki?" she screamed. "After all I've done to bring you up respectfully after your poor daddy passed away – God rest his soul!"

Chris attempted to dodge past her, but an almighty whack from the cricket bat knocked him almost senseless. With stars spinning in front of him, he somehow managed to stumble down the stairs and quickly went in search of his clothes only to find that the dog had carried one of his trainers off and was testing his chewing ability.

Flaming Nora – his sixty quid Reeboks in shreds!

Still dizzy, he attempted to struggle into his jeans. Unfortunately he lost his balance and went stumbling into the television, sending the vase flying.

Edna Jones came tumbling down the stairs in pursuit, screaming frantically and waving the bat at him. "I'll make sure you're prosecuted for under age sex," she shouted. "My baby's fifteen years old and you've forced her into these dreadful things."

He flew out the door and down the path. The next-door neighbour came storming past in his dressing gown and slippers and hissed a filthy word at him before banging furiously on the Jones's door.

As soon as Edna Jones left for Sunday morning service, Bekki was on the phone to Jane.

"What's going on?" Jane asked. "I tried calling you yesterday and Edna slammed down the phone."

"I've been grounded for ONE WHOLE MONTH!" Bekki screamed down the line.

"Grounded?"

"And not only that - she's forbidden me to make any phone calls," Bekki said furiously. "Why did the stupid place have to close down the bingo? They're all a load of old age pensioners - what would they know about pop music?"

"What about Chris?" Jane asked. "Are you seeing him again?"

"Are you kidding?" Bekki snorted crossly. "I doubt if he'll ever speak to me again after how evil Edna treated him."

"Maybe she'll come round."

"No chance. You don't know Edna. If there's one thing she's good at it's keeping her word," Bekki said. "I wish sometimes I could leave home. Maybe we could get a place together? How cool would that be!"

"Maybe we can once we start work," Jane suggested. But that was light years away.

"Have you heard anything from Johnny?"

"No," she said solemnly.

"What did I tell you?" Bekki replied, sounding almost pleased. "He's bad news. I've spoken to some of the girls and he's got a dreadful reputation around the school."

Thanks, friend.

Her whole world was collapsing around her and what did Bekki care? Jane refused to believe what her friend had told her, there was still a glimmer of hope – a simple explanation –maybe he'd lost her number?

Just maybe.

"I hate Edna," Bekki spat down the phone. "I really hate her."

"Me too," Jane agreed.

CHAPTER SEVENTEEN

Six weeks later

Early December dawned bright and sunny with a slight nip in the air. Johnny pulled his collar up and strode confidently along. For once he felt optimistic about the future. The work front looked promising, with an interview at a carpet warehouse coming up. Just as soon as he got paid he intended paying Rose every penny back.

Although he had known it wouldn't be long before the cops caught up, it still came as a shock when he was arrested and bungled into the back of the police car.

He sat opposite Clements, realising he had no choice other than to plead guilty to the break-in.

"I've already told you, I don't do hard drugs," he said. "Neither do I push the stuff. Anyway, what's this got to do with McKays?"

"Let's forget about McKays for the time being," Clements said. "Right now I'm investigating a very nasty homicide which took place in Brennan's yard."

Johnny gave a sigh of relief, thankful that for once he had nothing to do with it. "I ain't been near Brennan's yard in months," he replied. "I've been making an honest living down on the coast – If you don't believe me then get it checked out."

"I know you've been out of Birmingham, Ricci," Clements replied. "That doesn't mean to say you and your mob weren't involved in some drugs operation."

Johnny let out a snort. He'd heard enough of this garbage. "Are you arresting me for McKays, or what?"

Clements stroked his moustache. "Lenny Morgan was a friend of yours, wasn't he?"

Johnny shrugged. "So?"

"What kind of drugs racket were the three of you running?"

"How many more times do I have to tell you - I'm not mixed up in any drugs racket."

"What about your cannabis habit?"

Johnny shrugged. "So I occasionally do weed."

"Who supplies you?"

"This kid we know. Look, I'm telling you I've never pushed or dealt with the hard stuff."

"And apart from Brennan being involved, you had no other dealings with any such operation?"

"Hey – what is this? Twenny questions?"

Clements weighed him up cautiously. Either Johnny was a good liar or he was completely in the dark. "So you've no idea how Lenny Morgan came to end up at Brennan's yard with his brains blown out?"

Johnny gave a nervous laugh. "Lenny dead? Nah – that's a load of bollocks… " he trailed off and glanced at Clements for reassurance.

Opening his folder Clements took out some photographs of the dead boy and placed them in front of Johnny. "This is your friend, isn't it?"

Johnny stared at the photographs, unable to believe what he was seeing.

Clements continued to speak, his lips moving, but nothing was making sense.

"Well?" he prompted Johnny.

Johnny nodded, overcome with shock. "Why should anyone wanna kill Lenny?" he murmured.

"I was hoping you'd be able to answer that?" Clements replied. "Your mate – as you called him - died a very nasty death. Now either you tell me what's going on or I nick you for McKays."

Johnny sat in silence.

"Brennan must have had contact with these people at some point?" Clements continued.

"I swear I don't know who they are. All I know is he owed 'em money."

"You're an intelligent kid, Ricci – why the hell are you mixed up with a scumbag like Brennan?"

Clements lapsed into another few seconds of silence, then spoke again. "I'm going to make you a proposition. I'm prepared to drop all charges on the McKays' job in return for your cooperation."

Cooperation conjured up trouble. He didn't like Clements' propositions at the best of times.

"I want you to arrange to meet these men. Agree to hand over the money."

"Are you crazy?" Johnny replied hastily. "There's no way I'm getting involved in any of this."

"You'll have police protection," Clements assured him.

And that was supposed to make him feel safe? Stuff their protection. He'd sooner do a stretch in the nick. "No chance," he said blatantly.

"I'll give you a couple of days to think about it, Ricci," Clements said, handing him his card. "At least you owe that much to your friend, if nothing else."

Johnny sat, too dazed for words. What good would it do? It wasn't gonna bring Lenny back.

"Well – clear off then," Clements said with a wave of his hand. "Hop it, before I change my mind and nick you."

Once outside his emotions overcame him. He'd never shown his feelings, not even at his old man's funeral, but Lenny didn't deserve to be wiped out like some useless piece of trash.

He began walking, almost automatically. He didn't stop until he reached the canal where he used to go as a child when his parents embarked on one of their dogfights. His head buzzed until he felt as if he was going crazy with guilt and frustration, the words 'if only' repeating themselves over and over.

If only he hadn't gone away.

If only Lenny hadn't gone to the yard.

If only he'd never got involved with Mick.

If only he'd been more of a good mate.

If only Lenny was still alive.

If only…

It was dark when he finally made a move. He realised he could never go back to Rose's. She would know instantly something was wrong. She was good at that. She wouldn't rest until she nagged the truth out of him. It was Wednesday evening and she usually went to see friends. He waited until it was clear then crept in to collect his things. He figured it was only decent to scribble her a note. Not only that, she'd probably have the whole of the police force out looking for him.

Dear Aunt Rose

Thanks for your hospitality. I guess it's time I moved on

Take care.

Johnny.

He left the key on top of the note and crept out.

He wandered into the club and found Chris attempting to look busy, polishing glasses and grumbling about the disastrous week he'd had. "I've had the tax man on my back," he complained, "They're stinging me for sixty quid. Not only that, Bekki's old lady went berserk and attacked me with a flamin' bat..." He trailed off and glanced at Johnny.

"Are you OK mate, you look bloody awful?"

"Cheers," Johnny muttered with irony.

"Where're you going?" Chris asked, spotting his rolled up belongings.

Johnny shrugged in silence. Where was there to go?

"You can muck in at the flat if you fancy it?" Chris offered.

Johnny didn't hesitate and hung around for him to finish.

Walking out to the Mini Johnny took a brief glance. "Pretty cool," he said. "Does it perform as good as it looks?"

"Are you kidding?" Chris hit the gas and the Cooper flew into action like a bat out of hell. "Big bore, roll bars, adjusted brakes – the lot," he yelled above the scream of the engine.

Johnny lapsed into silence. One day he was determined he'd have a car - something really smooth and powerful. Yeah – one day?

They cut across town to the suburbs of Moseley. It was a large three-storey Victorian house badly in need of restoration and paint. The front door was open.

Chris led him up two flights of stairs to a dingy looking room. Again it was a free for all with no lock on the door. He'd have to remember to wear his Rolex at all times, he thought, squatting down on a beanbag.

"Sorry I've no beer," Chris said, handing him a mug of instant cocoa. "I don't usually drink this stuff. It's some freebie I had thrown in with the groceries."

There was silence, Johnny staring blankly into his drink before speaking with a slight tremor in his voice. "My mate went and got himself killed."

"Was it some kind of accident?"

"Yeah – you could say that."

Making up a bed on the floor, Johnny settled down, his hands behind his head, his mind in overdrive trying to sort things out. He couldn't sleep and lay awake for hours. Finally he reached a decision. Tomorrow he was ringing Clements. It was the only decent thing he could do for Lenny.

CHAPTER EIGHTEEN

Johnny woke early after a restless night's sleep. Taking the card out of his pocket, he glanced at it for a few seconds. Then he went down to the call box in the hall and dialled the number.

"Can I speak to Inspector Clements?" he asked a lady officer. "Tell 'im it's Johnny Ricci."

"Sorry. He's not available."

"When's he likely to be free?"

"He's on a court case today. Best if you call back tomorrow."

"What time?"

"Any time after nine," she said abruptly.

"Tell him I called. Tell 'im I'm agreeing to what he asked."

He put down the receiver, still with hesitation.

Whatever, tonight he intended getting legless. Nothing like going out with a bang, he thought.

Bekki burst through the school doors and screamed with glee. "I'm free! And in a couple of months I'll be sixteen, so there's nothing the old witch can do." She glanced at Jane. Just lately she looked down in the dumps.

"Are you sure you're OK?" she asked.

"Fine," Jane replied, hugging her books.

Bekki gabbled away excitedly. "I think I'll start by having a new hairdo – maybe a punk style – what do you think?"

Jane barely glanced up.

"Knock, knock – is anyone there," Bekki said frostily. "Oh I get it –you're still pining over that creep."

"I recall you saying he was the hottest thing since fresh baked bread," Jane snapped.

"That was until I found out what a jerk he was."

Jane rushed off to her locker in tears and Bekki ran after her. "I'm sorry Jane," she said. "I'm only trying to help you."

"I don't need your help," she snivelled, taking out a paper handkerchief and blowing her nose.

"Look, the old dragon's going out tonight so why don't we get a box of chocs an' go back to mine?" she suggested.

Jane shook her head in silence.

"Then what do you want?"

Jane gave her nose another blow. "I just want to be left alone."

"Fine. I used to think you were my friend, but now I have my doubts," Bekki said coolly. "I really can't believe you're making such a big deal over him."

"It's not just that," Jane cried back.

"Then what?"

She slammed her locker shut. "I'm pregnant. Now are you satisfied!"

"Pregnant! Are you sure?"

Jane nodded.

"How late are you?"

"Five weeks," she snivelled, using the saturated handkerchief to wipe her eyes.

"That's nothing. Sometimes I miss a period."

She glanced at Jane. "He did wear a rubber, didn't he?"

Jane shook her head. "He said he wouldn't do anything."

"And you believed him!" she screamed in horror. "Never trust a bloke, I'm telling you."

"I thought you couldn't get pregnant the first time?" Jane said.

"That's just old wives' tales," Bekki said. "Look, when we finish school tonight we'll get one of those pregnancy kits an' go back to mine."

Jane nodded and turned to her friend in distress. "Bekki, I'm so scared."

"Don't worry. We'll get it sorted Jane, I promise."

CHAPTER NINETEEN

Richard didn't believe in saying sorry. It was against his principles. Instead, he brought her expensive gifts back from his travels. This time it was a black satin kimono from Japan.

"Come here," he said, pulling her close and reaching for her breast inside the shantung gown.

Donna slapped his hand away. "It's nine-thirty. You'll be late for work," she said, turning to clear the plates away.

Since the business dinner, things had gradually taken a turn for the worst. And now he thought he could creep around her with some kimono.

"There's always some excuse," he said furiously. "If it isn't a headache it's the time of the month."

"What do you expect, Richard? You talk down to me and treat me like a child, and now you think some bloody kimono is going to change everything."

He glared at her furiously. "Fine – if that's how you want it."

He gulped down his coffee. "Don't forget I have an early flight in the morning," he said. "And can you make sure you have a word with Isabelle? My shirts are beginning to look as if I've slept in them."

"Why don't you have a word with her yourself, seeing you're the one who employed the woman?"

"No, that's your job," he replied shortly. "I'm running

a business. It's your place to see things run smoothly in the house."

With that he walked out and slammed the door behind him.

Hearing him skid down the drive, she gave a sigh of relief. He'd cut down on company cars and was now using her Lotus. No doubt one of Hilary's bright ideas. Without the car she felt even more trapped. It was a bad feeling.

She threw herself wholeheartedly into her cooking and made a casserole with some of the ingredients left over from the night before. She was just preparing a lemon soufflé with fresh raspberries when she heard Isabelle's BMW draw up.

Isabelle did not appreciate being told her job.

"I'm only following my husband's instructions," Donna said. "If there's a problem I suggest you take it up with him."

She returned to her cooking and was about to finish the sweet when Melania rang. "Hi honey – how are you fixed for a coffee later?"

"Yes, fine," she replied.

"I have a few more Christmas presents to get."

"I'm way behind. I suppose I'll have to buy Richard something?"

Melania chuckled. "You guys are crazy. You argue like mad, bore the pants off one another - and still insist on buying each other presents."

"He always gets me something. Besides, I like opening presents on Christmas morning."

"Talking of surprises you'll never believe this," Melania squawked down the line. "I had this guy come onto me yesterday claiming he is a friend of a friend of a friend of this record producer. He says he'll put a word in for me, although I doubt if I'll ever hear anything."

"You don't know. This could be your big chance. You have great potential and you know it."

"And what would you know about the music industry?" she replied. "For a start I'm too old. All they're interested in is bits of kids."

"I know a good voice when I hear one," Donna said briskly.

"Aaah - he's probably bluffing, anyway. They'll say anything to get into your pants," she replied pessimistically.

Donna couldn't argue with that.

"I'm just drying my hair, shall we say one o'clock?"

"Fine. Oh, Melania, you wouldn't happen to have the number of a taxi company would you?"

"Trouble with the car?"

"No - Richard's taken mine. I'll fill you in later."

Maybe it was a little of her fault. But there again, it didn't give him the right to treat her as he did.

★★★

Hilary stood efficiently at Richard's desk. "I've checked the flight times. The departure is eight-thirty," she said. "I've also made a temporary booking for us at the Hotel Imperial."

She was twelve months younger than Richard and quite matronly in her appearance, her size 14 figure clad in a crisp white blouse and a navy skirt. She had been widowed for two years and was extremely competent at her job. She also shared Richard's interest in golf and although she had never admitted it, secretly worshipped him.

"That's fine, Hilary," he said. "Can you ring them back to confirm the booking?"

She stood primly at his desk, her blouse open wide enough to allow a peep of cleavage. "Yes, of course."

"I'll pick you up at six – that should allow us time to check in at the airport. Oh, Hilary – make sure you bring your golf clubs."

She smiled affably. They were already packed.

Jane sat wailing on the lavatory, doing a pee in an old jug. "What am I going to tell my parents?"

"Chill out – you don't know for sure."

"But suppose I am?" she snivelled.

"We'll cross that bridge when we come to it. Just try and look on the positive side of things."

"Like what, for instance?" Jane snivelled.

"Well… we don't know for sure, do we?" She grabbed the jug back off Jane and took control. "I don't suppose you've seen anything of Johnny?"

Jane shook her head.

"Huh! Typical." Bekki snorted with disgust. "Just dunk it anywhere."

They waited anxiously for a few seconds before Bekki checked the applicator. "Oh dear," she said glumly.

"What is it? What does it say?"

"It's positive."

"Does that mean… ?"

"Yes. You're pregnant all right."

Jane let out a wail. "What am I going to do?"

"Well – first of all you need to sort this out with Johnny."

"How," Jane cried, reaching for the toilet paper and blowing her nose. "I don't even know where he is?"

"I'll think of something," Bekki said diplomatically. "He's usually at the club or failing that, Chris will know. Either way this has to be sorted. Johnny's gonna have to be told and face up to his responsibilities."

CHAPTER TWENTY

hat evening in the club the girl came onto him in a big way. He'd spotted her a few times but never quite got around to making conversation. She was the type of girl wet dreams were made of; lush body, long dark scrunched hair and green Irish eyes. Whether Aunt Rose would have approved was another matter.

They had a couple of dances, snogged to Barry White and then he dragged her over to a quiet spot in the club. He was just making headway when a pal cut in and tapped him on the shoulder.

"Johnny, there's some girl askin' for ya outside."

"Who?"

His pal shrugged.

Johnny raked his fingers through his hair and gave the girl a wink. "Catch up with you later."

Heading towards the entrance, his face dropped when he saw Jane.

"What d'you want?" he asked rudely.

"I need to speak to you," she insisted.

"What about?"

She didn't beat around the bush. "I'm pregnant," she blurted out.

"So what's it got to do with me?" he growled.

"It happens to be your baby."

"Says who?"

"How dare you!" she screamed at him. "You forced me into having sex."

"I never heard you complain," he yelled back.

They were attracting quite an audience from passers by. He pulled her to one side. "How can you be sure?"

"I've done a test."

"Weren't you takin' anything?"

"Like what?"

"Jeezus!" He looked away in disgust.

"I don't go out deliberately to do that sort of thing," she snapped. "Johnny, what am I going to do? My parents will kill me when they find out."

"Look - I know this bloke whose missus was up the stick an' he took her to this clinic," he said, quickly deciding he could always tap Rose for the money; tell her he was in some kind of financial trouble.

"What are you suggesting – that I get rid of it?" she screamed at him. "Kill our baby?"

"What else do you suggest?"

"I thought maybe we could… "

He read her face and knew exactly what she had in mind. "If you think I'm ready to play happy families, forget it," he hissed.

She began to turn on the waterworks.

"Crying ain't gonna help," he said callously.

He spent almost half an hour with her with no sign of resolving the problem. "I've offered to help," he said finally. "If you need the money, I'll get it."

With that he stormed back inside the club and found Chris. "I'm pushing off," he said.

"What about a lift?"

"I'll make my own way back. I need an early night. I've gotta take care of some business tomorrow."

He hung around for a bus, kicking an empty Coke can and sending it spinning across the road. Life was a bitch! As if he hadn't enough trouble to contend with without some dumb girl getting herself pregnant.

He jumped on the bus and stared vacantly out of the window. Maybe he should quit Birmingham for good? After all, what was keeping him here? There again, it would only make Clements suspicious.

At the next stop a drunken old bloke stumbled aboard and sat next to him, mumbling away to himself and reeking of BO, with the smell of stale beer thrown in for good measure.

"Mongrels, the dregs of society," the old codger slurred, "Smile in yer face an' stab ya in the back."

Conversation with this person Johnny did not want. "Excuse me, mate," he said, standing up and squeezing past. Scrambling onto the top deck, he had the remaining journey to himself. He lit up a nub end and attempted to chill out.

Rose's money wasn't going to last five minutes. But there again, maybe neither was he.

Arriving back at the digs he ran up the two flights of stairs to the bed-sit and flung open the door. Next thing he knew he was being hurled across the room like some rag doll and pinned against the wall.

"You know, Johnny boy, we're getting a bit pissed off," Skinhead said, shoving a .38 up his nose.

Holy Mary! He felt his legs give way beneath him. "Can't we do business in a more civilised manner?" he managed to croak.

"At least this one knows what we're on about," Skinhead jeered.

Johnny stared at the nozzle like a hypnotized rabbit. "Would you mind moving it in the other direction," he murmured.

Skinhead laughed loud and nasty. "Hey – this kid's got

balls," he guffawed. "He's also a friggin' comedian."

He heard the barrel of the gun click and almost peed himself. "What do you want?" he squawked. As if he didn't already know?

"Nice watch," Skinhead commented.

"Here – take it!" He yanked the Rolex off his wrist and hurled it at Skinhead who inspected it and tossed it over to Pinstripes. "You're the jewellery freak – take a look."

"Very nice," Pinstripes remarked. "You have good taste, Johnny boy."

Pinstripes signalled to Skinhead to lower the gun. "I like you, Johnny boy. Yeah, I like you a lot, and here's what I'm going to do. I'll take the watch as a bonus – let's say for the trouble you and your friends have caused. The money you'll bring to me by noon tomorrow."

Play along with them. Make believe he'd get the money. Admit he was skint and he'd be blown to pieces.

"Where?"

"You'll meet us at the Digbeth multi story car park on the second level with the five grand. Any sign of the police and you will be shot – do you understand?"

He was way ahead of them.

"Do as we say and you won't get hurt," Pinstripes said belligerently.

Did they think he was crazy? Either way he'd be dead.

"Oh – and just one other thing," Pinstripes warned. "In case you should get any flash ideas my men will be keeping tabs across the road."

They headed to the door and Skinhead patted him on the shoulder in a nasty fashion. "Sleep tight Johnny boy. Don't have nightmares."

Once they'd left he dived down the stairs to the pay phone in the hall to ring the station. If he could speak to

Clements – tell him that he needed the cash by noon tomorrow.

He slammed the phone down, realising the bastards had cut the line, and put plan B into action. Checking over the building, he found the ground floor had been sectioned off and made into a separate flat, so there was no back exit. He dived back up the two flights of stairs to the bathroom, which overlooked the back of the property. There was a narrow ledge running across the outside of the building leading to a lower roof. Tricky, he guessed, but it could be done. It had to be done.

"We're outta here," he told Chris the minute he returned.

"Are you crazy?" Chris snorted. It was past midnight. He figured Johnny must have taken leave of his senses.

"Listen," Johnny stated urgently, "There's a couple of blokes out there in a Merc and they're armed."

"What d'you mean – armed?"

"Like they've got fucking guns, you idiot."

The smile slowly drained from Chris's face. "Whatever you're involved in Ricci, I'm no part of it."

"You are involved 'cause you're with me," he said sombrely. "My mate Lenny thought he wasn't involved either."

Chris stared at him speechless, before releasing his anger. "Flaming great!" he spat, lashing out at the rickety old bedpost with his foot. "I knew I should never have got mixed up with you. You're bad news, Ricci. You always were, an' you always will be."

Johnny had no time for this crap. "Where's your car?" he demanded.

"Parked outside." Chris broke off and glanced at him. "Hey, now wait a minute..."

"You wanna see tomorrow, then listen. I've gotta plan," he began, leading him out to the bathroom. He opened the window. "There's a ledge along here, we can just about climb down."

"Are you crazy?" Chris said, glancing at the drop. "We're gonna break our flaming necks."

"We have no choice. If we stay here we're dead."

"We should go to the police and let them sort it out," Chris insisted.

"Will you stop going on about the coppers!" Johnny said. He climbed out of the window and called to Chris.

"You do what you like," Chris said stubbornly. "I've got a job an' I'm not leaving."

"If you stay here you won't be needin' a job," Johnny called out. "Now come on."

"No," Chris replied stubbornly, his legs turning to jelly. "I'll take my chances."

"Jeezus, Ainsworth – just get your arse out 'ere."

"What about my things?" He stood dithering with nerves, hardly daring to look, until Johnny made it across to the other roof.

"Come on - it's a piece of piss," he called.

Chris froze. "I can't."

"Yes you can. I've told you, I ain't leaving you here."

"There's no way I can do it," Chris panicked.

"I always knew you were a gutless chicken," Johnny yelled at him.

"Who's chicken?"

"You are. Cluck, cluck, cluck!"

"I'm no frigging chicken," Chris yelled back.

"Prove it?"

Gingerly Chris began to edge his way out onto the sill. "There's nothing to hold on to!" he screamed, feeling his legs had abandoned him.

"Come on. You can do it. There's a pipe sticking out of the brickwork, just above your head. Grab onto that and steady yourself."

Slowly Chris began to edge his way along the ledge.

"Don't look down," Johnny called out.

A piece of loose brick gave way, causing him to lose his footing and he froze in panic.

"Just hang on," Johnny shouted, climbing back onto the ledge. "Don't move."

"As if I'm going anywhere?" Chris muttered, clinging on petrified.

"Here – grab my hand."

Johnny somehow managed to manoeuvre him across to the flat roof and they climbed down and raced over the gardens, scaling a couple of walls and down an entry. Finally they crept up behind the Mini.

"Quick - give us the keys, Johnny whispered as they crouched beside the car.

"No way," Chris mumbled stubbornly. "No one gets to drive her, only me."

"Give us the frigging keys," Johnny demanded, keeping tabs on the two men in the Mercedes.

Reluctantly Chris handed them over. "Just take care with her," he said warily. "This car's a classic - she'll go down in history."

"Yeah, and so will we if we don't get our arses outta here." Turning on the ignition the Cooper roared into action.

"Who are these blokes?" Chris yelled above the roar of the engine.

"Drug dealers."

"Drug dealers!" he squealed. "You told me you were clean!"

"I am. It was something Brennan got involved with."

"I thought you hadn't seen Brennan in years? You're a complete arsehole, Ricci."

The Mercedes had spotted them, full beam switched on, the powerful car gunning its engine.

"God's truth," Chris screamed, "they're heading straight for us!"

"Hold on," Johnny yelled. Spinning the Mini round to face in the opposite direction Johnny slammed his foot down on the gas. He raced through the streets at full speed, blowing through Moseley and heading towards Kings Heath. Glancing back he spotted the Mercedes gaining effortlessly.

As the bullets shattered the back windscreen, Chris let out a scream. "Flaming heck, my car!" he squealed.

"Will you just shurrup!"

They were now heading up towards Wythall, the Mercedes still in hot pursuit. Coming to the brow of the hill, the Cooper flew over it and slammed back on the road, shaking every nut and bolt in its frame. The two cars were now almost neck and neck, tearing along the main stretch of road. One of the men leaned out of the window and took a shot at them.

"Jeezus Christ!" Chris screamed. "You're gonna get us killed, Ricci!"

"Keep your head down," he yelled back. "We're coming up to road works, so hold on."

"We'll never make it," Chris yelled back.

Johnny slammed the Mini into third and pointing the screaming car at the barriers, smashed through. Glancing back, the Mercedes was still on their tail.

They were approaching the traffic lights on red and with his foot flat on the accelerator Johnny roared through, bracing himself for a head-on collision with an articulated lorry. Swerving the Mini out of its path he tore down the highway. He lost the Mercedes for a moment and swung the car into a sharp left turn down a quiet road, quickly squeezing in between a row of parked cars. He turned off the lights and waited for the Mercedes to pass along the main road.

"Come on," he called to Chris.

"I'm not leaving her here," Chris complained, his priorities still with the Mini, now battered beyond recognition.

"You've no choice." He got out and tried the door to an old Ford Escort. Using his knowledge of breaking into cars, he swiftly fused the two wires together and started up the engine. "Quick – get in."

"You can't just nick it."

"Come on – hurry up."

Scrambling into the car, Chris glanced around. "Where exactly are we heading, Ricci?" he asked crisply.

"I guess south."

"South!"

"Yep."

Relieved they'd made it, Johnny let out a whoop of joy. "London here we come!"

CHAPTER TWENTY-ONE

They arrived in London in the early hours of the morning tired, exhausted and a little apprehensive. Sitting on the steps of an old building, they shared a joint.

"You've lost me my job," Chris complained, taking a deep drag. "You lost me my job, my frigging car – everything."

"At least you're still alive."

"Oh yeah – and you expect me to be thankful for that?"

"Lenny would be only too glad to swap places with ya," Johnny said, snatching the roach back.

"It was his choice - I didn't ask to get involved," Chris pointed out peevishly.

"He's dead – what choice was that?" Johnny snapped.

Chris was silent for a moment. "Ok – so I'm sorry."

Johnny inhaled deeply. "He didn't ask to get killed," he said bitterly. "It was my fault. I should have been there for him."

It was the first time Johnny had opened up and Chris felt kind of guilty. "You can't go blaming yourself," he said. "How were you to know?"

Johnny shrugged. It still didn't alter the fact that Lenny had gone.

They spent most of the day searching for accommodation and eventually came across a filthy looking apartment over a block of shops. There was a notice in the window: "Single bed-sit to rent. Apply at the laundrette."

"You go an' ask," Johnny suggested. "Make it look as if it's just for you."

He lit up a nub-end and hung around for Chris to return.

"It's sixty quid up front and the rest is by the end of the week," Chris told him glumly.

"For this doss?"

"They're all gonna be expensive. We're in London, or have you forgotten?" Chris said wearily. "I can cough up thirty. How much you got?"

"Twenny. I need a tenner for grub."

"Coming here was your idea," Chris reminded him.

"I don't see why we can't rough a couple of nights, at least we'll have food in our stomachs."

"I'm not sleeping on no benches," Chris grumbled.

"You may have to if we don't get fixed for work," Johnny said realistically.

Chris spotted the woman coming towards them. "Quick – make yourself scarce," he said. Taking the keys, he handed her the sixty pounds and waited for her to disappear. Then he gave Johnny a whistle and they both ventured into the flat.

The place was a dive. The walls were damp and most of the paper was hanging away. Johnny got that old familiar fusty smell of the camper van.

"Some filthy dump, and it's bloody freezing in here," Chris complained.

"So what were you expectin', the Ritz?" Johnny replied, fed up with his whining.

Between them they managed to find a pound coin for the meter. Glancing down in the yard, Johnny spotted two Chinese men babbling away as they unloaded a crateful of food. "At least we won't have to go far for a take-away," he said.

A couple of days later, they were desperate. "We've hardly got enough for food - never mind the rest of the rent money?" Chris said gloomily.

"We're gonna do a runner," Johnny suggested.

"Great!" Chris replied. "So we just flit from place to place and have every cop in London on our trail? I thought the whole idea was keeping a low profile?"

Maybe he was right. They decided to have another go at finding work and after sharing a kebab between them, arranged to meet up later.

Johnny headed for the Employment Agency, where a butch woman with cropped hair and a deep voice flicked through her files.

"Have you ever done building work?"

"Nah."

"Painting or decorating?"

He shook his head.

"Post Office – goods inwards –that sort of thing?"

Again he shook his head.

She glanced over the rim of her glasses at him. "There isn't a lot you have done, is there?"

She continued searching through her file. "I can't see anything suitable at the moment," she told him. "Unless…" She plucked out one of the cards. "How handy are you with your hands?"

She read out the details. He didn't care for the sound of it. A maintenance co-ordinator? What a load of crap. More like a flaming labourer.

In desperation, he went along. A weedy man in his forties with a red-pitted nose and badly-fitting dentures interviewed him. At any minute he expected them to come flying out of his mouth.

"There's a 'no smoking' policy," the man said sternly. "The hours are eight until five with half an hour lunch. And I'm a stickler for punctu... ality." He just about managed to get out the final word.

Johnny decided he'd stick it out until something better came along. Cleaning out toilets and being a general dogsbody didn't appeal to him, especially for the lousy wage they were offering.

The man took him on a walkabout. "This is the kitchen," he said. "You can make yourself a drink. Just don't make a habit of it."

It didn't get any better. Next came the First Aid room.

"The last bloke we caught snoozing in here. Needless to say he got instant dismissal."

Johnny followed him through to the machine room with a dozen or more cackling women. The moment he stepped through the door, production came to a standstill. A woman with a mouth like a foghorn glanced up.

"Hey girls, get a load of this!" she yelled, giving him a suggestive wink.

"He can fix my drawers any time," joined in another.

There was raucous laughter. And as if it wasn't bad enough having a load of sex-starved women gawking at him, the man turned on him with a threatening finger. "Don't encourage them," he warned sharply, as if it was his fault. "Any sign of trouble and you're out, son."

Jeez! Could he help it if women found him irresistible?

By three o'clock he'd had a verbal warning.

By five o'clock he had his cards.

So much for staff agencies. If that's the best they could come up with, then they could shove it.

"I might get lucky with one of those burger outlets," Chris said optimistically. "They've told me to call back in a couple of days. So what we gonna do in the mean time?"

"We have no option," Johnny told him. "We're outta here tonight."

Meanwhile, Johnny set out to look for work himself.

He walked the streets aimlessly before spotting a taxi company advertising for a driver: Please apply inside to Alf Swift.

Presumably it was Alf Swift sitting at the desk, juggling two phones. He was a small Cockney in his fifties, his brownish hair plastered back with a side parting.

Johnny waited while he took a couple of bookings. He slammed down the phone and glanced up. "Well?" he growled.

"I've come about the driver's job."

"Don't waste my time, kid. I'm looking for an experienced driver."

Johnny shot him an offended glance. "I am experienced. I've been handling cars since I was fourteen."

Alf gave a snort of laughter. "An' how old are ya now?"

"Almost twenny."

"Clear off."

"I gotta clean drivin' licence?" Johnny persisted, reaching in his pocket.

"I don't employ anyone under twenty-five. And I need a proper driver's reference."

Alf broke off to answer another call. "Am I havin' a bad day, or what?... Pause...You've gotta be jokin. My switch operator phoned in sick this morning, so I'm havin' to take the bleedin' calls. If that ain't bad enough, one of my drivers got done over by some geezer who wouldn't pay his fare."

Johnny wondered if the job came with danger money, there were certainly enough risks.

Alf glanced up at him. "Are you still 'ere?" he snarled.

"Look – just give me a break."

"I don't give anyone a break, so just clear off," he snapped, answering another call. "I can have one with you in – say – ten minutes, sweetheart." He sent a radio message to one of the drivers. "Pick up at the station – going to the Elephant and Castle – you got that?"

He slammed down the receiver and held his head.

"Is there a problem?" Johnny asked.

"Yes, you. Now get out." The phone rang again. This time it was some woman. Alf put a smile in his voice. "I'm only too happy to oblige," he said, realising he hadn't another driver spare.

He put down the receiver and glanced at Johnny. "You say you can drive?"

"No problem."

"You're on a day's trial - any trouble an' yer out," Alf warned, glancing over his glasses. "Know your way around London?"

He hadn't a clue, but he wasn't about to bottle his chance. "Yeah," he said. "I heard you mention one of your drivers getting beat up." He might as well make his stand now rather than later.

"So what's it got to do with you?" Alf snorted.

"It's just – well, shouldn't I be getting some kind of danger money?"

"Would you Adam an' Eve it?" Alf snorted. "You've only just walked in the bleedin' place and you're demanding danger money."

Obviously Alf didn't consider his drivers' safety that important. "D'you want the job, or not?" he asked.

Johnny didn't argue.

"Good. You know your way to the Hilton?"

Alf filled him in with the directions. "This is a valid customer," he said. "Her husband's big news, she's only been on our books a couple of weeks and she's already reported one of our drivers – so watch your P's and Q's. Her name's Mrs Deblaby."

When he arrived at the Hilton there was no sign of the woman.

"I've gotta pick up for a Mrs Debaby," he called to the doorman.

"Hold on sir, I'll go and check for you."

Sir? He'd been called a few names in his life but never that. He hung on impatiently. Maybe she'd got tired of hanging around? After all, he was five minutes late due to traffic. He could just imagine some old bag with loads of money and a bad attitude. Whatever the case he'd have to stick it out, he couldn't afford to lose another job. He lay back in his seat, tapping his fingers to the radio, hardly prepared for the classy blonde heading his way. She wore tight blue jeans and an expensive-looking sweater, and she was loaded with parcels.

Jeez! He felt as horny as hell.

"Sorry darlin'," he said, glancing into her large baby blue eyes. "This cab's taken."

Donna regarded him as if he was a turd the sea had washed up. "I'm not your darling," she said curtly. "And I happen to be the one who booked it."

He shot up to attention. "Mrs Debaby?"

"It's Deblaby, with an L."

She stood with her bags and he realised she was

waiting for him to help her. He walked round the cab and took the parcels off her.

"Do be careful. I have some valuable items in there," she said, staring back at him. He was quite rough looking in a leather jacket and scruffy jeans, very lean and his jet-black curly hair fell in a strand over his forehead. He reminded her of Tony, except his eyes were more deep and intense. For some obscure reason a tingle of excitement ran through her.

She obviously wasn't up for conversation, so he fiddled with the radio and got the Quo. He left the radio playing as they drove along, every so often stealing a sly glance through the rear view mirror.

"You'll have to direct me," he shouted. "I'm new around these parts… " Screech! Out of the blue another cabbie cut him up. He slammed on the brakes and the carrier bag flew off the back seat with a thud.

"Fuck you, arsehole!" he yelled, sticking his fingers up at the cabbie.

"You idiot!" she screamed at him. "If you've broken the vase, I'll see the company pays for the damage."

"If it makes you feel happy, go ahead," he replied without so much as an apology. "Like I said, I'm just passing through."

He waited until he was out of the main stream of traffic before pulling the cab over to one side. He'd got the sack, so what had he to lose?

"What are you doing?" she cried.

"Get yourself another cab," he said rudely.

"You can't do this."

"Try me."

"And suppose I don't want to get another cab?" Never had she been so humiliated.

They both glared at one another, two very angry people. She found his eyes intimidating and looked away. "I'm not moving," she said stubbornly.

"Just so long as you know it's your bill you're running up," he said, leaving the meter ticking over.

"I shall make sure Swifts are held responsible for every penny," she replied bluntly.

"Looks like we're in for a long night then," he said smugly, leaning back in his seat and taking out a cigarette.

"OK," she said. "Here's the deal. Run me home and I promise I won't mention this."

Yeah right – like hell she wouldn't. There was more chance of the Pope not praying. "It so happens I don't do deals," he said.

They stared at each other long and hard, before he dubbed out his cigarette and started up the engine.

The rest of the journey was spent in silence. She directed him up a long drive with a wealth of conifers and perfect landscaped gardens. The property itself was massive and stank of money. So this was how the other half lived?

He helped her out with her bags and carried them up to the front door.

"Well?" she said, staring back at him.

"I need payin'."

"I have an account with Swifts," she replied curtly.

Bitch.

He headed back to the cab and spun the wheels on the gravel as he screeched off the drive.

He figured that maybe driving cabs wasn't for him after all.

CHAPTER TWENTY-TWO

Johnny entered the office gingerly the following morning, expecting to have his cards thrown at him. Instead he found Alf in one of his more placid moods, maybe because the switchboard operator had turned up. She was a plump woman in her forties, with short blonde hair and massive bosoms.

"So how did yesterday go, son?" Alf asked him.

"Umm… fine." Obviously the woman hadn't reported him.

"That's the way I like it. Keep the punters happy an' we're happy - especially when it comes to customers like the Deblabys."

Evelyn glanced up from eating a bacon and mayonnaise roll. "Even so, money don't give you the right to think you're better than the rest of us," she commented.

Alf didn't appreciate her comment. "Like I said – they're the ones keeping us in business."

"I kinda expected someone different," Johnny said.

"Oh? In what way?" Alf asked testily.

"I dunno. Maybe someone a lot older."

"Blimey! Ain't you got enough bits of crumpet to keep you satisfied, son, without sniffin' around the likes of Mrs Deblaby?"

"Hey, who said anything about fancying her?"

"Stop taunting the kid, Alf," Evelyn said, with a subtle wink in Johnny's direction.

"Who's taunting? I'm warning him. See a classy bit of

skirt and they think they can push their luck. At the end of the day it's my reputation at stake."

Evelyn threw him another wink. "If you want my advice, luv, you're wasting your talents here. They're crying out for good-looking male strippers and escorts."

"No one asked for your advice, Evelyn," Alf cut in sharply. "And how many times have I told you about using this office as a café? You're supposed to set an example. Before I know it, the cabs will be stinking of vindaloo."

She stuck out her tongue to Alf before answering a call, using her sleeve to wipe the remains of mayonnaise from her mouth.

Was it usual for an employee to speak to their boss like that? He figured maybe something was going on between the pair of them. A picture conjured up in his mind of the big buxom blonde and scrawny Alf sprawled across the desk. It didn't bear thinking about.

She slapped the details into his hand. "Pick up from that address, going to the station. You'll have to put your foot down – train departs in half an hour."

"Well - what are you waiting for?" Alf snapped, hardly giving him chance to get out of the door. "And remember – the customer's always right!" he yelled after him.

Donna met Melania and some friends for drinks at an exclusive wine bar. Among their crowd was a businessman who bred racehorses, a retired golfer, a beauty therapist who owned a string of salons, and Edison, a tall, wispy man with a pony tail who, when he wasn't busy bragging about his wealth, occupied himself by being a nuisance.

"So darling, how are you fixed for waxing?" the businessman teased the therapist.

"Why? Are you interested in a back, crack and sack?"

she replied, extracting a powder compact from her Gucci bag. "I'm sure if you're desperate I can fit you in."

"As long as you haven't got cold fingers," he replied with a lusty smile. She wasn't exactly in the flush of youth. Now Donna was a different matter. Beckoning the young waiter over, he ordered more champagne.

Donna sipped her drink and wondered if men usually had their bits shaven. Richard had a hairy chest. She hated it, found it quite a turn off. She racked her brain to think of something she did find attractive about him.

"How's that little filly of yours?" the golfer asked the business tycoon.

"It depends which one you're talking about?" he said with an impertinent expression.

Eddie gave a loud horse-laugh. "The one he greets like a proud cat with its tail in the air... " He stopped short and glanced at Donna. "Oops! I do apologise. I forgot we have a lady in our midst."

Donna shot him a frosty glance.

"Where's this ruddy champagne? Christmas will have come and gone by the time we get it," the businessman shouted haughtily.

Eddie continued to stare at Donna. She cut him dead. He reminded her of some dog on heat. Why did she always attract the creeps?

The young waiter brought a bucket of chilled champagne to their table and after making some snide remark, the businessman attempted to fill their glasses.

"Not for me, thank you," Donna said, checking her watch "I really have to be going."

Edison jumped in quickly. "Can I offer you girls a lift?"

"No thanks," Donna swiftly replied. We've already booked a cab."

"You mean I couldn't tempt you with a bit of rough and tickle?" the businessman slurred. "Oh well – I'll just have to settle for golf," he said, rising unsteadily from the table. "Anyone care to join me?"

The therapist stuck out her freshly-tanned boobs. "Are you sure you'll manage to find the hole, darling?"

"My dear lady, I can assure you that when it comes to finding holes I never miss a shot."

Finishing the remainder of her champagne, Donna wondered why she bothered to mix with them. Apart from Melania they were just a bunch of phoneys.

"It's pouring with rain," Melania said, making their way to the door. "I hope the cab isn't going to be long?"

"Mrs Ainsworth?"

Liz peered around the door, took one look at the two police officers and screamed hysterically. "It's my son, isn't it? Something's happened to him!"

"May we come in?" the lady officer asked.

The male officer followed them through. "Did your son own a red Mini Cooper, Mrs Ainsworth?" he asked.

"What's happened to him?" Liz screamed.

"We found his car abandoned near Wythall," the lady officer said.

"So where's my son? Where's Christopher?" she demanded.

"There are a few details we need from you before we can carry out any investigations."

"Is your son living at home?" asked the male officer.

"No," Liz sobbed. "He left a few weeks ago."

"And you haven't heard from him since?"

Liz shook her head. "I knew there'd be trouble the minute he walked out. He was upset over his exams. It was getting on top of him."

"Would you like to sit down, Mrs Ainsworth?" the lady officer suggested, guiding her to a chair.

"You know something, don't you?"

"The fact is there were bullet holes in the car."

"Bullet holes? Oh my God!" she screamed, her world collapsing. "My son's dead, isn't he?"

"We don't know that for sure," the male officer replied. "The car could have been stolen. That's why we need your help. Can you think of anywhere your son may have gone? Friends? Relatives?"

"He hasn't many friends. He hardly went out," she sobbed. "He either worked on his car or studied up in his room."

"No girlfriend?"

"No - at least not that I'm aware of," she snivelled.

The lady officer put a comforting hand on her shoulder. "We're going to do everything we can to trace him. I'm sure he's still alive."

The male officer wasn't so tactful. "Did your son make a regular habit of not taxing his car?"

Liz looked up at him through tear filled eyes. "How dare you!" she screamed. "My boy is missing – he could even be dead and all you're concerned about is whether or not his car was taxed."

Johnny had worked through a straight shift and put in two extra hours of overtime. Maybe if he stuck it out for the next couple of weeks, by Christmas he'd have enough cash to see him through comfortably.

They'd managed to find another bedsit, this time a little more comfortable. At least it didn't have moth holes in the curtains.

It had rained most of the day, adding to the build-up

of traffic around the city. All Johnny wanted now was to get back to the office. He dropped off his passenger and was handed a miserly twenty pence.

Just as he was heading back Evelyn's voice came over the intercom, crackling and distorted. "Mrs Deblaby - pick-up from La Sensa wine bar... just off... " There was bad interference and Evelyn's voice faded out.

Why the hell couldn't Alf get some decent equipment?

He pulled up and asked someone for directions. Considering the traffic was bad, he made it in record time. Spotting Donna making a dash out of the doorway into the pouring rain he made no attempt to slow down, ploughing through a large puddle of water in the gutter. He held back the urge to snigger as she glanced down at her jeans and sodden feet.

Her eyes blazed furiously. "Exactly what is your problem?" she screamed at him.

"What's my problem?" he yelled back.

Melania was impatient. "I'm getting soaked," she complained. "Can you guys just stop arguing and let's get in the cab?"

Alf's cars had no partition, so it was easy to listen in to their conversation. The coloured woman was making a song and dance of it. "He really needs reporting," he heard her say.

Stuff the bitch. What business is it of hers?

He carried on listening. Now they were running down some old fart that owned racehorses. Is that what these people did all day – hang around bars, flash their money and slag each other off?

"What are you doing about Christmas Eve?" he overheard the coloured girl ask. "Are you still up for Saks?"

"Why not."

"I'm going there tonight. I'll get the tickets."

The coloured girl poked him rudely in the back. "Drop us off anywhere here."

He stared at Donna as she got out, giving her the benefit of his intense dark eyes and watched her walk off. He wondered how long it would take to screw the bitch.

Yeah - in his dreams!

CHAPTER TWENTY-THREE

"So how did your exam go today?" Sylvia asked.

"OK," Jane replied, throwing her school books down and helping herself to a chocolate biscuit. She didn't give a hoot about exams. She was more concerned with how she would explain to her parents that she was pregnant and thinking how she could have been so foolish to have allowed Johnny into her life in the first place

"I wish you wouldn't eat biscuits before your dinner," Sylvia complained.

Jane turned on the television and sat down watching a Danger Mouse cartoon.

"I bumped into Edna Jones this morning," Sylvia began.

How nice for you, mother. What did the old bat have to say?

"You never mentioned Bekki had been grounded."

"Umm... I guess I forgot," Jane said, grabbing the remote and changing channels.

Sylvia was anything but impressed. "She also said that Bekki stayed here while your father and I were away."

Trust old Edna to open her trap.

"Well?" Sylvia waited for an explanation.

"It's no big deal, mother."

"I distinctly said you were to stay at Edna Jones's," Sylvia said harshly.

Jane took another biscuit and Sylvia snatched the packet. "As it is I don't like the girl. I wish you'd get a decent friend."

"Why are you so hung up about her?"

"She's common. And she's a bad influence on you." The girl wore make up and skirts far too short. Sylvia wasn't impressed by Edna Jones neither. The woman was a hypocrite who went to church while her daughter run riot. Admittedly she'd done her best to bring up a teenage daughter, which wasn't all that easy when you were a single parent.

"Edna mentioned something about catching a boy in her bedroom. Do you know anything about it?"

"No," Jane lied. "Why should I?"

Sylvia weighed her up suspiciously. "I hope you didn't bring boys into this house while we were away?"

"No, mother – I didn't."

Sylvia glanced at her daughter. She was growing up far too quickly. It was time to have a heart to heart chat with her.

"You know you're always welcome to bring a boy home. I'd rather you did that than hide things from me."

Jane felt the flush rising to her cheeks and avoided her mother's wary glance. Soon the bump would begin to show. Soon her parents were going to find out. In the meantime she decided to keep quiet.

"Evelyn, you gorgeous creature," Johnny began, perching himself on the edge of her desk.

"What are you after?" she replied.

"A favour."

"Well I am surprised."

"You couldn't ring up Saks an' ask them if they've any tickets left for Christmas Eve, could ya?" he said, giving her one of his intense smiles. He knew he could twist her round his little finger. She often helped him out by giving him the airport runs – normally business people who tipped well.

Picking up the phone she rang the number and spoke to someone.

"They're thirty pounds a ticket?" she said, holding her hand over the mouthpiece.

"Tell 'em I just want the tickets, I don't want shares in the joint."

"It's going be that price wherever you go on Christmas Eve," she hissed.

"Ask 'em if it's OK to wear jeans?"

"You are joking!" she muttered. "This is Saks we're talking about?"

She went back on the phone. "Yes that's fine. By the way, what's the dress code for that evening… suit or smart jacket and tie? Thank you." She hung up. "They're putting two tickets aside for you to collect."

"Where am I supposed to get a jacket and tie from?" he asked.

Evelyn shrugged and in her dry sense of humour said, "Have you ever thought of trying a clothes shop?"

He gave her a wilting smile.

"I'm not promising," she said, "But I may be able to sort out a jacket. My son's about the same build as you."

"I don't suppose you could throw in a couple of ties an' all, could you?"

"What d' you think I am, a flaming charity shop?"

He gave her a wink. "Come on, Evelyn. Christmas only comes once a year."

"Good job an' all," she said.

The next day Evelyn was as good as her word and brought in the stuff. "I've sorted out two jackets in case the one doesn't fit," she said. "They're only hanging around the house, so you may as well make use of them."

He blew her a kiss. "Evelyn, you're a star."

"More like a flaming fairy godmother," she said. "I only hope this girl's worth it, whoever she is."

"I thought we were looking for trousers?" Chris complained. "So what are we doing in Ladies' Underwear?"

"I figured on a bit of light entertainment," Johnny replied leading him over to the lingerie counter.

"Knock it off, Ricci. I've gotta be back at work in half an hour."

The girl was more than obliging. "Can I help you?" she said politely to Johnny.

"Yeah, you sure can," he replied, giving her a moody stare. "Say – has anyone ever told you you've got gorgeous eyes?"

She flushed uncomfortably. "Are you buying for your mother or girlfriend?" she asked.

"Neither," he smirked.

Chris was embarrassed. "Come on, Ricci. You'll get us thrown out."

Johnny ignored him. "How about taking us out one night?" he asked, flirting dangerously.

"Please, you'll get me into trouble," she replied, glancing suspiciously around.

"I'd love to."

The manageress looked over. "Is everything all right, Miss Porter?" she called across.

"Fine." She glanced at Johnny with a lingering smile. "Please go," she asked politely.

"Come on, Ricci," Chris urged.

He spread the charm, giving her the benefit of a wink.

"Maybe catch up with you later?"

They headed back up the escalator to the Men's Department.

"Hey – look at this," Johnny said, picking up a shirt.

"Have you seen the price tag?" Chris hinted.

"It's pure silk an' it's got twenny percent knocked off."

"It's still seventy quid."

"So what?"

This was his big chance and he couldn't afford to blow it. If it impressed Donna, then it was worth every penny.

CHAPTER TWENTY-FOUR

On the night of the Christmas Eve dance, Donna tried on four different outfits. First, a little black figure-hugging dress with spaghetti straps. Maybe black was a bit drab for a festive occasion. Next she tried on a Versace creation with a large shoulder bow. Again she decided it wasn't suitable – much too fussy. Thirdly, she tried on a glittery all-in-one cat suit. Definitely not. It made her look dated and the midnight blue taffeta dress was much too formal.

She finally changed back into the black dress and brightened it up with a thin diamante necklace and matching bracket – simple yet effective.

What was all the fuss about, she asked herself? It was only another night out with the same old crowd.

It's Christmas Eve – at least make an effort.

So Eddie can drool all over me?

Richard was watching some tournament on television and nursing a scotch and although pleased he had the box to himself, he was not altogether happy about his wife going to a dance on her own.

"How do I look?"

"Fine," he said, hardly glancing up.

Thanks. A compliment would have been nice.

"Are you sure you don't want to make the effort?" she asked, feeling a little guilty.

"Quite," he replied. "Discos are certainly not my idea of a night out. Just make sure you don't leave late - and watch what you drink."

"Don't say the offer wasn't there," she said, giving him a kiss on the forehead.

Donna was disappointed to find Melania had gone with another taxi firm. "Swifts' are getting a little too expensive," Melania said. "This company's a lot cheaper – and more courteous."

Their table had been reserved. It was tucked out of view in the corner and of all the people there, it was Donna's unfortunate luck to be seated next to Edison.

"May I just say how beautiful you look tonight?" he said. Under the table she felt his leg a little too close for comfort.

"Thanks," she replied with a weak smile. She had tried on numerous occasions being polite, which had failed miserably. And now it seemed the only way was to spell it out clearly – she was not interested.

The doorman didn't quite know what to make of them; Chris in an oversized jacket and Johnny with his tie knotted any old fashion. He ripped their tickets in half. "This entitles you to a free drink," he told them. "I don't want any trouble lads. And make sure you do your tie up properly."

Yeah, right. Like he'd spent seventy quid on a shirt to ruin it with some poxy tie.

"I feel a right prat in this get up," Chris complained. "Just look at the sleeves. I thought it was only monkeys who had long arms."

"So now we dump it," Johnny said, making their way into the gents. It was like walking into Buckingham Palace. The carpet was thick and cushioned and the basins had gold taps set in black marble with small bouquets of flowers placed decoratively on top. Soft music played in the background.

"No wonder the tickets were thirty quid," Chris complained.

Johnny dumped the jacket and tie in the paper towel bin and checked himself out in the carved gold mirror.

"You only need your cavalier boots and you'll look as if you're auditioning for the Three Musketeers," Chris sniggered.

"Jealousy'll get you nowhere," Johnny sneered back, running a comb through his glossy hair.

They ordered lagers and handed over their tickets.

"I'm sorry, this doesn't include beer," the barman told them. "Only wine and spirits."

"So make it a whiskey chaser," Johnny replied.

"Make that two," Chris piped up.

Johnny scanned the room. He couldn't see Donna anywhere. Maybe she'd changed her mind.

★ ★ ★

"So," Eddie began, turning towards Donna, "How's married life treating you these days?"

"Absolutely fine," she replied, taking a large gulp of champagne and wishing he'd just disappear.

"Good. I'm glad to hear that," he said, not believing a word of it. "How about a dance?"

"No, thank you."

"Maybe later?"

Maybe not.

She was relieved when Melania suggested they danced.

The moment she stepped onto the dance floor Johnny spotted her. In fact he couldn't take his eyes off her. She looked incredibly beautiful, moulded into a little black dress, her blonde hair cascading down her back.

"She's one of our regulars," he said, pointing her out. "Her husband owns some company. They're loaded."

He wasted little time. "Come on," he said, nudging Chris and leading him over to the edge of the dance floor.

"Jeezus Ricci, don't even think about it. Her old man's bound to be here," Chris said warily.

Johnny continued to stare at her across the smoky room. One way or another, he intended to catch her attention.

Across the crowded dance floor their eyes finally met.

Oh God what's he doing here. Why isn't he working? Donna's heart began to flutter erratically.

"Isn't that the cab driver?" Melania said, suddenly spotting him.

"Hmmm?" She acted as if she hadn't seen him.

"Over there by the edge of the dance floor."

"Don't let him see we're talking about him. Why let him think he's that important?"

"She's well out of your league," Chris jeered.

"An' what would you know about class?" Johnny sneered back. "You wouldn't know it if it jumped up an' bit you on the arse."

He clocked up the situation, taking a swig of beer while continuing to stare across at her.

"I'm gonna nail her," he said with a smug expression.

"You're gonna what?"

"You heard - I'm gonna give the bitch one."

"Oh really?" Chris jeered.

"Oh really," he sneered back. He shoved his glass onto Chris. "Just watch me."

He bounced onto the dance floor and joined Donna and Melania. An old Billy Ocean classic was belting out and he gave it his best shot, staring directly at Donna.

"Baby, love really hurts without you
Love really hurts through and through
- an it's breakin' my heart but what can I do... "

153

Melania walked off in disgust and Donna glared back at him. "What are you doing here?" she said crossly, as if he had no right to be there.

"Me? I guess I'm here to have fun. How about you?"

The slimy creep had an answer for everything. She tried to avoid his glance. He looked kind of different. She noticed he had nice teeth when he smiled. He wore an expensive white shirt which dazzled under the ultra violet light and his glossy black hair had been cut. She wasn't sure she could handle it any more.

"Why don't you just chill out," he said, fed up with her arsy attitude.

She stared back at him. "Excuse me?"

"Relax. Have fun."

She was about to walk off when he pulled her back, sweetening his tone. "Hey, come on," he said, laying on his charm. "Isn't this supposed to be the season of goodwill? So how about a dance?"

Whether she would have accepted he never got to find out, because at that moment Eddie, who had witnessed the whole incident and didn't appreciate the competition, stepped in between them.

"The lady doesn't want to dance," he said, placing his arm around Donna as if he had some marital right. "So stop harassing her."

This freak with the ponytail is her husband?

"Hey – no offence," said Johnny, quickly backing out of the situation.

Donna was fuming. She pushed Eddie's arm away. How dare he dictate who she could and couldn't dance with?

She turned to Johnny. "Yes, I'd love to dance," she said.

He didn't know what to make of the situation. Taking

her loosely in his arms, they shuffled around the dance floor. "Is that your husband?" he asked, wondering what the hell he was doing getting involved.

"No he isn't," she replied curtly. "And don't flatter yourself. The only reason I'm dancing with you is to get rid of him."

"Thanks for the compliment," he sneered, pulling her close. "So how come your husband isn't here?"

She got the faint smell of aftershave and felt herself responding to his touch. This was ridiculous. Why was her body reacting in this way and with him, of all people? As soon as the dance finished, she intended making a hasty retreat.

"Well?" he insisted.

She tried to avoid his glance. "Well what?" she replied, acting as if she hadn't heard.

"Why does he let you out on your own on Christmas Eve? Isn't it supposed to be a family thing?"

"What business is it of yours?"

"None, I guess."

He pressed his cheek against hers. "He must be crazy. If it was me I wouldn't let you outta my sight."

She felt the warmth and hardness of him pressing against her, but somehow she hadn't the strength to push him away.

"Suppose you divorce him an' marry me?" he said, the flippant words of a nineteen year old.

"Cut the crap," she snapped. "You're not chatting up one of your seventeen-year-olds now."

"Hey, I mean it," he said. "You're gorgeous. You're really gorgeous." He attempted to kiss her.

"No!" she objected strongly.

"Why not?"

"I'm married – remember?"

"I thought you had this mutual understanding?" he mocked.

She was relieved when the slow number finished and the music changed up-tempo. Before she had time to escape he lifted her up and spun her around. Was it the atmosphere, too much wine or the fact that she was having fun? But she found herself giggling. She hadn't felt this alive in years.

He caught her in his arms and they were suddenly staring at one another. She could hardly resist when he brought his lips down on hers; a soft warm kiss which sent shivers of excitement down her spine. Somehow she mustered the strength to push him away.

"That was a mistake," she said, flushed with embarrassment.

"Yeah? Well it sure didn't feel like a mistake to me."

She rushed off the dance floor into the ladies', her cheeks burning.

Melania was standing at the mirror, applying highlighter to her already immaculate cheekbones. "A rough diamond – really?" she mocked.

"It was just a dance, nothing more," Donna said, trying to act casual. She checked her appearance. Her hair was messed, her cheeks were flushed and her pupils dilated.

"Just a dance, huh?" Melania raised a sceptical eyebrow. "I should hate to think what happens when you really let your hair down."

"For crissake, Melania, he's nineteen if he's a day."

"Horny little devil, though. Incidentally, did you know that men are at their peak between the age of twenty and twenty-five?"

"I can't believe we're having this conversation."

"I'm teasing you, honey," she said, snapping her compact shut. "Just be careful, that's all."

"Of what?"

"Don't get too familiar with him."

"Thanks. Next time I need an agony aunt I know who to come to," Donna replied derisively.

As if she'd be stupid enough to get involved with some creep like that.

Up at the bar, Edison challenged him. "Just leave the lady alone. All right?"

Johnny swung around to face him. "Sorry mate. Are you talking to me?"

"You know very well who I'm talking to. And I'm not your mate."

"Sorry mate."

Chris fidgeted uncomfortably.

Eddie stamped his foot. "Look, I don't want any trouble. All I'm asking is that you leave the lady alone."

"And suppose I don't?" Johnny retaliated. "What you gonna do about it?"

"I'm asking you nicely."

"And I'm tellin' you nicely to get lost."

"Jeez, Ricci, just leave it out," Chris intervened. "She's not worth it, mate."

Johnny ignored him, his eyes pinned firmly on Eddie. "If you wanna make something' of it, then step outside."

"I wouldn't lower myself to your standards," Eddie threw back.

Johnny sneered in his face. "Piss off."

He was about to turn when Eddie brought up his fist, catching him with an unexpected right hook. He stumbled back, dazed for a second. Wiping his hand across his nose he noticed blood spurting down his white shirt – his new white shirt, for crissake. He quickly regained his balance and lunged for Eddie, sending him sprawling into the crowd.

The spectators quickly scattered with horrified screams. Within seconds the
bouncers were over.

* * *

"There's been a fight," Melania said, walking back to their table. "You always get some idiot ready to spoil things."

It didn't take Donna long to discover Eddie nursing a bloody nose. "What happened?" she asked anxiously.

"I'm surprised at you, Donna," he hissed at her. "Encouraging gutter trash like that. I thought you had class, but I was obviously wrong."

"Where is he?" she demanded, realising she didn't even know his name.

"If you're referring to lover boy, he's been thrown out."

She didn't waste any time and rushed out of the club. She found him and his friend waiting for a cab.

"I'm sorry," she said, attempting to dab his nose with a handkerchief.

He slapped her hand away. "It's no big deal," he said standoffishly. "Just tell that friend of yours he's dead if I ever catch 'im."

Eddie's no friend - nor has he ever been.

They stared at one another intensely for a second before his taxi arrived. She watched him walk off, and just like the festive balloons, her spirits deflated.

CHAPTER TWENTY-FIVE

Donna spent New Year's Eve with Richard at the golf club. She wasn't particularly enthusiastic about the coming year. What was there to look forward to? She didn't need a clairvoyant to tell her they'd still be arguing and she'd still be thoroughly miserable.

In the flickering candle glow, she glanced at Richard. He looked tired and strained. He really had to start slowing down. She felt guilty about Christmas Eve. Maybe she should have stayed in with him? Perhaps tonight was an ideal time to mention a holiday. Spend some time together.

"Richard… " she began.

"I made a mistake," he said, leaning back on his seat, hands clasped together.

"About what?"

"Getting rid of Bob. I could have got at least another eighteen months out of him."

Oh Lord. She didn't want this conversation. The last thing she wanted was redundancies shoved down her throat on New Year's Eve.

"Richard, please… " she began, reaching across the table and taking his hand. "I'm sure you made the right choice."

"You think so?"

"Yes, of course," she said. "Has this Colin got a family?"

"Yes. He's married with two children," Richard replied

earnestly. "That's partly what I took into account. It's just that I've known Bob since I first joined the company. It was the hardest thing I've had to do – how do you tell a fifty-five-year-old man he no longer has a job?"

Richard with a conscience?

"Well I don't see the point of keeping someone on when they're due to retire," she said. "He's going to get a good redundancy package as well as his pension."

"So you think it was the right choice to make?"

"Definitely."

He gave a weary sigh. "Sometimes I get fed up with this whole bloody lot," he said. "Why do I always have to be the one who makes the decisions?"

"Let's not talk about this tonight, Richard," she said dolefully. "Let's just try and enjoy ourselves."

"Yes – you're quite right," he said with a smile.

The band struck up, bursting into 'The Lady is a Tramp'.

She hoped he wasn't going to ask her to dance. When it came to dancing he hadn't an ounce of rhythm in his body. In fact he reminded her of uncle somebody-or-other, who always got up and made a fool of himself at family get-togethers.

For a few moments Richard put his problems behind him and tapped his fingers to the beat. "She hates California, it's cold and it's damp, that's why the lady is a tramp… Come on," he said, grabbing her arm. "We'll show them how it's done."

Having to work the New Year's Eve shift was a bum. No booze, no fun, no sex; while everyone else was out there enjoying themselves, here he was stuck in some lousy cab.

Chris had managed to tag along with some of the staff

from the take-away which, as he was quick to point out, wasn't such a bad idea after the way Christmas Eve had turned out. In fact he'd done nothing but whinge about it.

Johnny thought briefly of Donna. Bad move. Best forgotten.

After eight o'clock things had quietened down. He tuned into the radio and lit a cigarette. A few minutes later the evening operator's voice came crackling over the transmitter. "Pick up from Bermondsey Street, going to the hospital."

He flicked his cigarette out of the window and stepped on the gas.

Ten minutes later a small man in glasses was flagging him down. It was obvious the man was in some kind of distress, leaping hysterically on the pavement in his slippers.

"My wife's having a baby," he panicked, relieved to see the taxi. "She needs to get to hospital."

"Shouldn't you be calling an ambulance?" Johnny suggested.

The man totally blanked him. "Come on, sweetheart," he called. A woman came waddling down the path towards him, carrying a small suitcase. It looked as if she was going to drop the sprog at any moment.

"Have you got everything, sweetheart?" the man asked anxiously, taking the case off her. "You haven't forgotten your medication or haemorrhoid cream?"

She nodded her head and let out an agonising wail, clutching her stomach and holding onto the cab door. "I think it's coming!"

Oh Jeezus! "Look - maybe you should call an ambulance," Johnny repeated.

Again his words went unheard.

"Hang on in there, sweetheart. We won't be long." He manoeuvred her into the cab and Johnny looked on anxiously.

The woman gave another prolonged scream.

"Can you put your foot down?" the man yelled.

"Yeah if you wanna get us killed," Johnny screamed back. This really was a bad situation. Suppose she had the kid right here in the cab?

"Ooooooooh!"

"Just try and stay calm, sweetheart. Remember the exercises they taught us at the clinic? We'll do them together, OK?"

"This is all your fault," she screamed at him. You're never coming anywhere near me again… ooooooooh… my waters are breaking!"

Jeez! Alf was gonna go apeshit. He'd just had the cab valeted.

"We're nearly there, sweetheart, we're nearly there - Just a few blocks away."

He was more than relieved when he dropped the pair off. The man threw a twenty pound note at him.

"Hey – wait for your change," he called out. But they were already disappearing into the hospital.

Turning on the radio he picked up some Hogmanay party with Jimmy Shand. He closed his eyes and drifted off.

The next thing he remembered was the chimes of Big Ben.

"Happy New Year," Richard whispered, reaching towards her with an affectionate kiss.

"Happy New Year," she whispered back. She wished things could be different between them. Maybe if she tried

– really tried?

Richard slipped an envelope into her hand. "I know it's a bit late. It was meant to be a Christmas present, but there was a slight hiccup," he said.

"What is it?" she asked curiously.

"Why don't you open it and see?"

She tore open the envelope and the bubble wrap. Inside was a set of keys. "A Porsche!" she exclaimed in excitement, reading the tag.

"It's waiting in the garage," he said. "I know how you hate catching taxis."

The midnight sky lit up with fireworks and the street was a mass of revellers, singing, shouting, dancing and scrambling for cabs. Some were diving into the fountain fully dressed, while others were out to make trouble. A gang of youths pushed their way forward from the back of the queue, foul mouthed and exceptionally drunk. Yelling and shouting abuse they made their way over to Johnny's cab. A row broke out amongst the crowd and a girl began to spout off. "You bunch of wankers," she yelled, "what d' ya think I'm standing 'ere for – the bleedin' fresh air?"

"Get to the back of the bloody queue!" screamed another.

Someone smashed a bottle and things began to turn nasty. There was more abuse from the lads as they all attempted to pile into his cab.

"Out, the lot of ya," Johnny yelled to them.

"Says who?"

"Says me."

"Fuck you an' your cab."

Next thing a hefty boot kicked the side of the cab in. There was laughter and another spurt of bad language.

Screw it! He decided he wasn't hanging around to get beaten up for Alf and his lousy company. Putting his foot on the gas, he sped off. Some New Year's Eve this had been.

Welcome to 1992

CHAPTER TWENTY-SIX

"You owe me ten quid," Chris said, busily squeezing a spot on his chin.

"For what?" Johnny said, about to leave for work.

"That bet we had with the posh bird – remember?"

"There's no bet," Johnny replied. "She happens to be a nice respectable lady."

"Are you sickening for something?" Chris said, breaking into a giggle. "Ricci has the loooove bug."

"Shut your mouth," Johnny shouted, picking up a pillow and hurling it at him.

"Hey Ricci, come back! I need to ask you something," Chris called out. "There's this bird I fancy at the take-away. You've had... well... more experience in these things... how do you suggest I go about it?"

"Why not slip her a message in her hot dog bun?" he sneered.

"Hey, I never thought of that."

"It was meant as a joke, Ainsworth."

"No – it's really a great idea. Cheers mate."

Johnny shook his head in disbelief and set off for work. Arriving at the cab firm, he found Alf checking his watch. "What bleedin' time you call this?" he growled.

Before Johnny had time to answer Alf strode off into his office and slammed the door shut. He hadn't even had the decency to ask how he'd got on, his only concern being for his cab. He accused Johnny of negligence and vowed to take a slice of his wages for repairs.

Jeez! Some way to spend his twentieth birthday!

"I wouldn't get upset over it," Evelyn said, glancing up from reading the morning newspaper. "His bark's worse than his bite, luv."

Yeah – he wouldn't fancy putting it to the test. He could just imagine if Alf got wind of Christmas Eve.

"What's this about a fight, son?"

"Ah nothing – just some jerk who didn't appreciate me giving Mrs Deblaby one."

"Never mind. Next time you see her give her one for me."

"Cheers Alf."

Yeah – that would really go down well.

***

"For crissake – what's all this?" Richard snapped, glancing over the bank
statements. A few days into New Year and already the arguments had begun.

Donna carried on preparing breakfast. "Christmas shopping," she said placidly.

"Christmas shopping!" he snorted. "I should think you've bought up the whole of Oxford Street."

She bit her tongue. "Toast?"

He gave a grunt. "I'm trying to uphold a business and you go and throw money down the drain," he protested.

"How would you like your egg – scrambled or plain?"

"Are you listening to me?" he raged.

"Yes – I heard you."

"Then don't ignore me when I'm speaking to you."

Donna tuned out. So much for turning over a new leaf, she thought. She'd tried, God knows she'd tried. Things would never change – not with Richard. He was a pompous arsehole and always would be.

She could hardly wait for him to leave for work.

Melania dropped by to announce she was jetting off to Barbados at Easter.

"Remember me telling you about that guy who knew this record producer? Well, he's offered to take me on holiday," she squawked. "A whole month in the glorious sun. I can't wait."

"He's certainly got into your pants, I see," Donna said making fresh coffee.

Melania gabbled on excitedly. "Oh honey he's simply a dish. I can't wait to introduce you to him." She took a bite of one of Donna's freshly baked cakes. "Hmmm – these are delicious," she mumbled through a mouthful. "I don't know why you never invested in a little tea room."

"I've often thought I'd like to."

"Then what's stopping you?"

Richard – that's who. The very mention of her going to work and he'd hit the roof.

"Oh I almost forgot," Melania said, reaching into her bag. "I've got these tickets. I'd already booked when Dexter sprung the holiday on me. So if you can make use of them you're welcome."

"A rock concert!" Donna exclaimed, glancing at them. "And who am I supposed to take with me?"

Melania shrugged. "Richard, maybe?"

"Richard!" Donna broke off with a snort of laughter. "You've got to be joking. An old time music hall would be more up his street."

"Well they're no good to me, so if you do know anyone they may as well have them."

Johnny flashed through her mind. But the idea was too ridiculous for words. She hadn't seen anything of him since the dance. She didn't expect to. And why was she suddenly thinking about him again?

Later that night she decided to tackle Richard. "I think we should have a serious talk," she began.

Richard responded as if nothing had happened between them. "What about?" he said casually, checking out the details for the following day's conference meeting.

"Oh come on, Richard – stop pretending. We've never hit it off from the beginning."

"And whose fault is that?" he snapped. "You're the one who's never put any effort into this marriage."

"Me!" she screamed at him. "And how do you make that out? You're never here. We have no shared interests. The only time we're out together is at those wretched business lunches."

"You're lucky to think I'm here at all," he cut in.

Her eyes flashed angrily at him. "What's that supposed to mean?"

Richard checked over the documents, not even looking at her. "I think you know very well what I mean."

She could hardly bear to look at him. She hated him and his insults, and the way he belittled her. "If that's the case, why don't we just get a divorce and have it over and done with?" she said with indignation.

He ignored her outburst. He was angry – in fact he was bloody furious with her. "I suggest you start behaving yourself and act like a proper wife," he answered in a tone of authority.

She stormed up to the bedroom and locked the door, tears stinging her eyes. She couldn't go on much longer like this. Fumbling in her bag for a handkerchief she found the tickets.

Don't even think about it.

Why not?

Because he's too young.

So what? At least he's fun.

He's a rogue and you know it.

She lay there for an hour or so before Richard came charging up to the bedroom.

"Open the door," he demanded.

"Go away."

"I have to be at the airport for six in the morning. Now open this ruddy door."

"Use one of the other bedrooms."

She heard him storm off muttering to himself and gathered her thoughts.

What am I going to do?

What can I do? Walk out? Leave him?

She'd managed it before. She could do it again.

CHAPTER TWENTY-SEVEN

Sylvia had had her suspicions for a while. The sickness in the mornings and the lack of interest in her schoolwork were just two of the reasons. She was waiting as Jane came out of the bathroom.

"You're pregnant, aren't you?" she asked.

No use denying it. Sooner or later her parents would find out.

"Yes," Jane replied sedately.

"Oh my God! I knew it!" Sylvia screamed. Jane was sure her mother was going to have a seizure.

Flying down the stairs, her mother screamed at her father, "Have you heard this? Our dear daughter has only gone and got herself pregnant."

She heard her father rage from the living room, "Who's the father?"

"I've no idea," Sylvia screamed back. "But she'll have to get rid of it."

They spoke as if she wasn't there.

"I'm ringing the school," Sylvia said. "I'll make sure the boy is expelled."

"I think it best if we handle this discreetly, Sylvia," replied her father. "We don't want anyone knowing of this."

"The whole school probably knows by now!" Sylvia shrieked.

Jane came down to the living room slowly and calmly. "It's no one from school," she murmured.

They both turned to face Jane and waited for an explanation.

"Then who is it?" her father demanded.

Jane shrugged helplessly. "Someone I met."

"Met where?" her father snapped.

"In the pub," she muttered.

"The pub!" Her parents exchanged horrified expressions.

Kevin raised his voice. "What were you doing in a bloody pub, for god's sake?"

Sylvia snivelled. "I knew that girl would lead her into trouble. I should never have allowed her into my house."

Her father glanced at her in outrage. "So are you going to tell us who this man is?" he demanded.

Jane shook her head. "I don't know."

"What do you mean you don't know?" Sylvia screeched. "You do these dreadful things with someone - you must know! Did he force you? Did he rape you?" she asked anxiously.

Jane lowered her head in shame. How do you explain to your parents that you've had unprotected sex with a total stranger?

"I can't believe I'm hearing this," Sylvia cried, distraught.

"You're a disgrace and a bloody slut," her father yelled about to raise his hand.

Sylvia intervened. "Violence won't help, Kevin. I'll get her to the doctor's first thing in the morning – let's hope it's not too late."

Jane's eyes began to fill with tears. Why did everyone want to kill her baby? First Johnny and now her parents.

"How far are you?"

Jane shrugged. "I don't know… maybe five months."

"Oh my goodness – twenty weeks," Sylvia gasped. "It's far too dangerous to have it aborted. She'll just have to go somewhere private and then have it immediately adopted."

"I'm keeping this baby," Jane shouted adamantly.

Even though Johnny had hurt her so much she couldn't deny the fact that she still loved him.

"It's out of the question," Sylvia snapped. "Do you understand the seriousness of this? Not only will your schooling be affected – your whole life will."

"I don't care!" she screamed back. "I'm keeping this baby and no one's going to stop me."

Evelyn was busy painting her nails when Johnny arrived at the office. "Where's Alf?" he asked.

"He's popped out to get an MOT on one of the cars," she said, blowing her nails dry. "By the way - you've had a call."

"Who?"

"Mrs Deblaby."

"Did she say what it was about?"

"No, only to call her back."

"Are you sure it was for me?"

"That's who she asked for."

"Got the number?"

Evelyn passed it to him and waited suspiciously as he dialled out.

"Hi Johnny, it's Donna," she began. "I know you're busy. It's just I've been given two tickets for a rock concert. I thought maybe you'd like to come along with me? It's all absolutely free."

He remained silent, doodling on Evelyn's note pad. Did he really want to get involved with a married woman?

So his first intentions had been to get her in the sack. But now it was kind of different.

"Johnny –are you still there?"

"Yeah."

"Is it awkward to speak?"

"You could say that," he replied, spotting Evelyn sizing him up.

"I won't keep you. It's just… well, it's the least I can do after the way Eddie behaved."

"What's wrong with your husband taking you?" he cut in brusquely.

She filled with humiliation. "Forget I asked," she snapped, about to hang up.

"Hang on – when is it?"

"Next Saturday."

He checked his shifts. As it happened he had next Saturday off. They arranged a time and meeting place, where she promised to pick him up.

He came off the phone and Evelyn was ready to quiz him. "What was all that about?" she asked nosily.

"Nothin," he shrugged. "She wanted me to drop her off at some pop concert."

Evelyn raised a sceptic brow. "Mrs Deblaby at a rock concert?" she snorted. "We are talking about the same woman?"

He managed a smug smile.

There's a lot you don't know about Mrs Deblaby.

Evelyn carried on painting her nails. "So that's what Christmas Eve was all about," she said presumptuously. "You must have a death wish. Either Alf will kill you or her husband will."

CHAPTER TWENTY-EIGHT

"How much do I owe you, dear?" the sweet old lady asked. She was one of his regulars. Every Thursday he picked her up and dropped her at the bingo hall.

He checked out the meter. "Six-fifty, darling," he replied, raising his voice for her benefit.

"I'm not deaf, you know," she said crisply. She sorted through her purse and handed him a note. "I can't see without my glasses - is that five or ten pound?"

"Ten," he replied honestly.

She told him to keep the change and he helped her out of the cab.

"My legs aren't as good as they used to be, young man. Would you mind helping me up the steps?"

He'd never given much thought to all that Good Samaritan stuff, but now it seemed only right to do it.

"You're a good lad," she said. "The Lord looks after those who are good to others and you'll be rewarded one day."

Yeah – well I wish it would hurry up and happen.

He got back in the cab and was about to pull away when he felt the barrel of the gun in the back of his head. He glanced in the rear view mirror.

Holy Mary!

"Just... take it easy?" he said, trying to disguise the tremor in his voice. If it was money the bloke was after, he could take the lot.

"Drive," the man snarled.

Johnny trembled with fear. If the bloke wasn't interested in money it could only be one other thing. He started up the engine, his leg shaking on the controls. Maybe as soon he reached a quiet spot the man would bump him off.

"Um… where am I supposed to be goin'?" he croaked.

"Don't ask questions, just drive," the man said, jabbing the barrel further into his neck.

He was told to pull up at a deserted warehouse, where the man ordered him to get out of the cab. He spotted a pile of black rubbish bags and wondered if it was where he'd end up.

"Get out," the man snarled waving the gun at him. "Come on – get out!"

Gingerly he edged his way out of the cab, his heart beating so fast he thought it would explode.

"Hands up where I can see 'em," the man ordered, marching him over to the entrance.

"Where you takin' me?" Johnny asked, raising his hands and shaking uncontrollably.

The man ignored his question and began to push open the large steel sliding doors.

Johnny knew only too well what would happen once he was inside. The truth was he was gonna die, so he might as well risk it. Taking his chance, he grabbed one of the black bags, slung it at the man and ran for his life. He felt the bullet rip through the shoulder of his leather jacket, but thought nothing of it – his adrenalin was pumping so fast he didn't feel a thing. He fled into a doorway as the bullets kept coming. Then he made a dash up an alley and out into an open market, ploughing into stalls.

There were screams of hysteria as the gun went off and someone yelled, "Call the Bill!"

In panic he dived into a picture house and rushed past the astonished cashier.

Entering the cinema, he fumbled his way through the darkness. He reached the front circle. The row stood up to let him through and he settled down next to a fat lady stuffing popcorn into her mouth.

Trying to figure out his best move, he realised he couldn't keep running forever. In the end they were going to catch up with him. They were probably in there right now. He remembered Clements's card, which he still had in his pocket. If he could just get to make a call…

His shoulder began throbbing violently and he felt kind of faint. He didn't realise how serious it was until he slipped his hand inside his jacket to retrieve the card and found his T-shirt saturated in blood.

Oh Jeezus! I've got to do something.

He glanced at the woman, who was laughing loud and spitting popcorn. He was losing his concentration and his mind was beginning to wander. The figures on the screen were becoming blurred, their voices slurred and distorted. Slipping his hand back inside his jacket, he felt the blood gushing from the wound and began to slip into unconsciousness.

"Is this the man?" The manager stood over him with the cashier, shining a torch into his face.

"Yes – that's him."

He slumped sideways on the seat and collapsed across the fat woman. The last thing he remembered was a piercing scream. And then there was blackness.

CHAPTER TWENTY-NINE

On his break at the take-away, Chris confided in Angela over a carton of chips and a coke.

"Johnny never came home last night. Something's definitely wrong. I've checked with the taxi company this morning and he never showed up for work either."

"From what I've heard about Johnny, he's quite capable of taking care of himself," Angie smiled reassuringly.

"You think so?"

"Yes. Now stop worrying."

He wasn't so sure.

Angie was nineteen, with soft pretty features, bobbed auburn hair and large hazel eyes. "If you're that worried, you should go to the police," she suggested.

"There's something I never told you," he began, staring solemnly at her. "The reason why we came to London wasn't by choice. The fact is Johnny got involved with drugs – he wasn't taking the stuff or anything, he just happened to get in with this bad crowd."

"Oh Chris, don't say you're mixed up in all this?"

"Nah, course not," he said, trying to sound convincing. "But that's why I get kind of worried."

"Oh my God!" she said suddenly. "You don't think... "

"Think what?"

"Nothing."

"Come on, Angie. You were going to say something?"

"It's really very silly," she said, wishing she'd never mentioned it. "You know – the shooting in the market."

"What shooting?"

"Some man got shot."

"What happened, is he dead?" Chris panicked.

"I don't know, I wasn't really taking that much notice. I think they're waiting to question someone."

He was in a complete panic. Johnny had specifically told him never to go to the police. But if he'd been shot how long would it be before they came looking for him?

"Angie -there's something else," he said. "These drug dealers were chasing us. They somehow got the idea we had the stuff."

She stared at him wide eyed with anguish. "Chris, you really must go to the police."

"Look Angie, I think it best if we don't see each other for a while. Promise me?"

"But Chris… "

"Promise me. I don't want you getting involved in all this - not until it's sorted?"

His life would never be the same. From now on he'd always be looking over his shoulder.

***

"Inspector Ross and Inspector O'Brien, we're from the drugs squad," one of the plain-clothed men said, flashing his identity badge to Evelyn. "We'd like to have a word with whoever owns the business. It's concerning one of your drivers."

Evelyn took off her headphones and scurried to Alf, who sat in the back office wading through a pile of invoices. She swiftly filled him in, intrigued to find out what had happened.

"What bleedin' driver?" he said, snatching off his glasses.

Evelyn shrugged. "They didn't say."

She ushered them into his office and strained her ears, attempting to listen in at the door. All she could hear was Alf's voice ranting.

By the time the men left he was red-faced with rage. "I knew it. I bleedin' well knew it."

"Knew what?" Evelyn asked anxiously.

"The minute I clapped eyes on him I knew he was trouble."

"Who?"

"He's probably dumped the cab somewhere with a load of heroin stuffed in it."

"Alf, are you going to tell me what's happened?"

"The kid you thought the sun shone outta his arse."

"Johnny? He can't be involved in drugs – he's such a nice lad."

"Nice my arse," Alf spat. "Scum like that should be off the street. He deserved all he got."

"I really can't believe this," Evelyn said, thinking aloud. "I heard it on the news but never gave it a second thought."

"Listen, Evelyn, you don't breathe a word of this to anyone. So far nothing was mentioned about who he works for, and I don't want it getting out, otherwise this business could be finished. And we'd be finished."

"Don't you think you're taking this a bit too seriously?"

"What planet are you on, Evelyn?" Alf burst out. "In case it may have escaped your attention those geezers were from the drugs squad. It doesn't get any more serious than that."

CHAPTER THIRTY

Slowly, very slowly, Johnny came round. Was he dead? Maybe this was heaven? He pinched himself to make sure.

Thank God, I'm still alive!

"Hey," he called to a staff nurse in a crisp white uniform, taking notes. "What happened? How long have I been here?"

"You were admitted yesterday, Mr Ricci," she replied in an Irish brogue. "You lost a considerable amount of blood and you've been given a blood transfusion."

He attempted to sit up. "I have to get outta here – I need to speak to the police," he said anxiously.

"Just stay where you are," she said firmly, tucking him back down. "The police are already waiting to question you."

Good. Maybe now he could get this whole thing sorted once and for all.

Things didn't go quite as he'd planned. Once he had sufficiently recovered, he was arrested and taken to the station where he sat with the chief inspector and his sidekick, a slimy man with a crooked grin.

"Let's get this straight. What you're saying is you lived with this kid Brennan, and you had no idea he was dealing in drugs?"

"I didn't say that," Johnny said, tired of the whole business. "I said I had nothing to do with it."

The inspector's colleague sat grinning like a Cheshire Cat. "So these geezers who you reckon you don't know from Adam just happened to come along and take a pot shot at you?" he sneered.

"Well, yeah."

"Do you take us for idiots, sunshine?"

"Look – if you don't believe me just call this bloke Clements at CID in Birmingham," Johnny said, fumbling in his jacket for Clements's card, only to find it stained beyond recognition.

Why weren't they out there looking for these blokes instead of giving him a hard time? He was the one who'd been frigging shot.

Before he knew what was happening, a fat sour-faced officer was bungling him into a cell.

"I'm innocent!" he yelled.

"That's what they all say," the officer said scathingly.

As if they cared.

The cell door slammed shut and the officer peered at him with bloodshot eyes through the vent before sliding it to.

Johnny slumped down on the hard bed and collected his thoughts. Wasn't today some kind of special day? Wasn't he supposed to be meeting Donna? Still, there was nothing he could do about it now. And anyway, why would she want to get mixed up with some loser?

★★★

Donna changed into her scruffed jeans and T-shirt. She hadn't felt this excited since schooldays when she had sneaked off to meet Tony. It was almost as if she was a teenager all over again. And the thrill of it came flooding back to her.

She decided to keep her make-up simple; just a touch of blusher and lip gloss and her hair in a pony-tail.

She stood back and glanced at her reflection. Not bad – she looked about the same age as him.

Richard was due back later that afternoon. She felt slightly guilty, but if he hadn't been such an arsehole she wouldn't be going in the first place.

She counted the minutes and eventually set out driving to the spot where she waited anxiously.

She sat checking her watch at regular intervals. By one o'clock she realised Johnny wasn't going to turn up.

That'll teach you to be unfaithful.

I don't call spending an afternoon at a pop show being unfaithful?

But you ran after him.

Oh, just shut the hell up.

She returned home in a state of depression and opened a bottle of red wine.

Men were all the same, and they all had one thing in mind. Her father -Frank -Eddie - Richard... so why did she expect him to be any different?

She was blotto when Richard returned home from work.

"I thought you were going out?" he asked in a stand-offish tone.

"Melania couldn't make it," she lied.

A Bryan Ferry CD spun loudly on the music system. Richard stormed across the room and switched it off. "What the hell is wrong with you?"

She stuck out her tongue.

"You're paralytic," he spat. "I was going to suggest we ate out. But that's definitely out of the question."

"There's some cold meat in the fridge, I'll do some fresh vegetables," she said attempting to stand up. She almost fell over and began to giggle insanely.

"You're bloody disgraceful," he snarled at her.

"Go to hell Richard," she slurred. "Go to hell and take that bloody… hiccup… business with you."

***

Johnny sat biting his nails nervously. Almost a week now and there was still no sign of him being released. If he spent another night in this dive he'd go crazy.

A prison nurse had seen to his injury. She tore off the old dressing without mercy and replaced it with a fresh one.

"I'm innocent," he told her. "There's no way I should be locked up in this place."

"You should have thought of that before you committed the crime," she said belligerently.

What crime? Were they all crazy? Maybe he was gonna get banged up permanently. And even if he was released the dealers were likely to catch up with him again, so what chance had he got?

He heard the cell door open and jumped up anxiously.

"You're free to go," the warden snarled in a nasty begrudging tone, "an' don't let me catch your skinny arse in here again."

"Hey – did they find out I was innocent?"

The warden ignored him. But what did he care? He was free.

Out on the front desk he collected his belongings. "What's happening?" he asked a stern faced lady officer.

"There's no charge brought against you," she said abruptly. "Sign here."

Outside, he hung around with apprehension. Suppose they were waiting for him? At every step he imagined being dragged up some alleyway and having a bullet pumped through his head. If only he could get hold of Clements.

He decided to call in at Swifts and see if he still had a job.

Evelyn wasn't her usual cheerful self. She was quiet and subdued.

"Is Alf in?" he asked.

He had a feeling there was going to be some repercussion, but not quite as bad as the greeting he got. He'd hardly stepped in the door when Alf threw his P45 at him.

"Hey – it was a misunderstanding," Johnny said, doing his best to explain.

Alf was having none of it. "I don't give a toss about your misunderstandings," he snapped. "Now get out."

Screw his lousy job. Who the fuck did Alf think he was?

He headed to the flat and made a mug of coffee and a sandwich from a withered tomato and scrawny bit of cheese he found in the fridge, and waited for Chris. He decided he was going back to Birmingham. What was to keep him here now? And at least he could get to see Clements.

When Chris eventually arrived, he was overwhelmed to find Johnny. "Jeezus, Ricci, I never thought the day would come when I'd be glad to see you."

"I got done for the drugs," Johnny mumbled. "I tried explainin' but they were havin' none of it."

"It's over - they caught 'em. Ricci, they finally got the dealers," Chris said excitedly. "Here – take a look." He produced a newspaper and handed it to Johnny and the headlines hit him: Cop offered £1 million in cocaine. Johnny scanned the article.

An undercover cop led police to their biggest-ever

drugs bust after being offered cocaine worth £1 million. It followed the shooting of a twenty-year-old man last Thursday. As the police officer posing as a prospective buyer was about to wrap up the deal, police swooped in and arrested two men. The case is due to be heard in court later in the year. Chief Inspector Clements from the West Midlands police – who was the brains behind the operation and who is due to retire later this year, said he couldn't have wished for a better way to end his 35 years in the police force.

"Holy Mother!" Johnny exclaimed. "Hey – you think old Clements had me bailed out?"

Chris shrugged. "Who knows? The main thing is we can finally get on with our lives."

"I'm outta here," Johnny said

"When?" Chris asked

"Tonight – you comin?"

Chris thought about Angie. She was special and he didn't want to lose her. "I dunno," he said

"You'd better make up your mind," Johnny said, collecting up his stuff. "I'm on the next train to Birmingham."

CHAPTER THIRTY-ONE

Liz Ainsworth, although elated to see Chris alive and well, wasn't quite so sure about the young man in a leather jacket and battered trainers accompanying him. Wasn't he the reason their son had got into this mess to begin with?

She waited her opportunity before tackling Chris. "He can't stop here," she whispered.

"He's got nowhere else to go."

"What about parents?"

"He has none."

"He almost got you killed, Christopher."

"I've told you, it wasn't his fault," Chris muttered back.

Liz wasn't sure about any of it, but taking a closer look at Johnny she changed her mind.

"He's a nice-looking boy," she mentioned to Jim later on in the evening.

Jim remained pessimistic. "Hasn't he got a home to go to?" he said, begrudgingly.

"According to Christopher, he hasn't got any parents. Apparently his father was killed in some kind of accident and his mother's in Ireland."

"So now we take in waifs and strays," he complained. "Heaven knows, Elizabeth, our son decides to pack in what could have been a decent career, puts us through months of hell and then has the cheek to turn up with some rough diamond for us to support."

"It's only until they get something sorted," she reassured him. "Although Christopher would be better staying here for a while. At least we know where he is."

Five weeks down the line and she wasn't so sure about Johnny.

"You'll have to have a word with your friend," she told Chris. "He's taking us for mugs. He hasn't even had the decency to offer anything for his keep."

"He's waiting for his money," Chris said.

"What's wrong with him getting a job? From what I can gather he's quite capable of working."

Meanwhile, Johnny wasn't exactly happy with the way things were developing. He'd caught Liz on a number of occasions giving him come-on looks at the table.

He was in the bathroom having a pee when she burst in, wearing some flimsy see-through creation. "Oooh!" she gasped with a half amused, half shocked expression.

She was drenched in perfume, which almost choked him. "Um… I guess I forgot to lock the door," he said.

She made no attempt to leave. "I don't know whether Chris mentioned… " she began, panting over him like a bitch on heat as he shook himself dry. "It's just with the cost of meals I thought maybe you could put a little towards your keep?" she smiled. "Of course, if there's a problem you could always pay me back… well… in other ways." She deliberately let her negligee fall open and her sagging breasts dangled in front him.

"I think you know what I'm getting at," she murmured.

He sure did – and he wasn't particularly thrilled by the offer, but if it meant he had a meal and a bed it seemed he had little choice in the matter. He slipped the catch on the bathroom door.

And then he proceeded to make her a very happy lady.

***

A very annoyed Chris confronted his mother at the kitchen sink. "Have you been at it with my mate?"

"I beg your pardon?" Liz replied sharply.

"You know very well what I'm getting at," Chris said with equal hostility.

"What a dreadful accusation to make," Liz snapped, attempting to straighten an invisible crease in her mini skirt.

Did she take him for stupid? He knew exactly what was going on. "So who's responsible for the groaning noises in the lavatory – the phantom fucker?"

She glared at him angrily. "Christopher! I will not tolerate that kind of language in my house. I love your father dearly. He means the world to me."

"Really? You could have fooled me."

"You must try and understand. The fact is, he's developed trouble retaining an erection. I can assure you this is purely medicinal."

"Medicinal – is that what you call it?" he spat with disgust. "Well I've got another name for it – it's called being a filthy old woman."

"How dare you!" she snapped, deeply offended. "And I'm certainly not old."

"You are old, mother, whether you like it or not."

"Your friend doesn't seem to think so."

That's what you think.

He moved to go. "Christopher, you must not mention a word of this to your father – do you understand?" she said incisively.

"Don't worry, I don't intend to, but don't kid yourself – I'm not doing it on your account."

Chris was humiliated and embarrassed. How could his mother have done this, and with his mate of all people? It wasn't as if she was some young vulnerable girl Johnny had taken advantage of. It was his bloody mother, for crissake.

★ ★ ★

There were several reasons why Johnny decided it was time to move on. Firstly, Liz was requiring his services on a regular basis. Secondly, Jim Ainsworth was beginning to give him suspicious looks. And thirdly, although Chris was a good mate, he was getting pissed off with having Angie rammed down his throat every five seconds.

Chris caught him slinging his things into a bag. As far as he was concerned it was for the best. He didn't blame Johnny. There was only one person he blamed – his mother.

They had little to say to one another on the subject. Johnny kept silent and Chris thought best not to mention anything.

"Got anywhere to go?" he asked.

Johnny shrugged. "Hey – I'm cool, I'll manage."

Things didn't get any easier.

Over the weeks Johnny was fast realising he'd become dependent on cannabis. It was no longer a pleasant relaxing drug he could take or leave as he pleased. But just lately he'd hit an all-time low and he couldn't get his hands on the stuff quick enough.

Chris found him in some squalid bed sit. He looked rougher and skinnier. There was a tin full of nub ends and a couple of empty beer cans on the threadbare mat. The curtains were filthy and discoloured against a grimy window.

"Where d' you get this dump from?" Chris asked.

"Hey – it's not that bad," he sneered in a half stoned manner. "It's berra than nothing."

"Have you eaten?"

"Nah – it's no big deal," he said vacantly, dragging on a joint.

"Any sign of work?"

"Work?" he sniggered. "Who needs a frigging job? I got my dole. I'm doin' just great."

"You don't look great to me."

"Well I feel it," he replied sharply to Chris. "Just need to get some sleep, that's all."

"They're… um… offering a job at the supermarket stacking shelves. I know it's not much… "

"Piss off."

"It's money at the end of the day," Chris suggested. "At least it'll get you out of this doss hole."

"You think I'm working my balls off for peanuts?"

Chris swiftly changed the subject. "Angie's coming down the weekend," he said excitedly.

Johnny gave a sneer. "Watch it, she'll have you round her little finger. If you thought livin' with your old man and lady was bad enough, just wait till a girl's on your case."

Chris shrugged. "She's kinda special, you know."

"She's kinda special!" Johnny mimicked in an ironic tone. "So what happened to the big plans of becoming a self-employed mechanic?"

"Watch this space."

"Yeah right."

"Hey – guess who I bumped into yesterday," Chris said. "Remember that blonde bird who used to knock around with Big Tits?"

"Now let me see – which one would that be?" he sneered.

"She's up the stick," Chris said bluntly. "She's about to drop it at any moment."

"You're kiddin?" Johnny said, trying not to look involved.

He thought maybe her parents would have persuaded her to get rid of it. And now there was a kid on the way – his kid.

Holy cow! He was gonna be a father.

He wasn't quite sure how he felt.

Happy?

Angry?

Proud?

Responsible?

Maybe a little of them all?

CHAPTER THIRTY-TWO

Ronnie 'the Weasel' Gillespie was without a doubt one of the smartest conmen in Birmingham, a kind of Arthur Daley of the Midlands. He was in his fifties with greyish wavy hair and wore a mohair coat. A cigar was permanently wedged in his right hand.

In the pub he approached Johnny. "I hear you may be interested in making a bob or two?"

Interested was an understatement. More like desperate.

The plan was that Gillespie had some merchandise he needed transporting down to London ready for shipping abroad, the contents of which Johnny had no idea.

"So what exactly am I handling?" he asked. Much as he needed the cash, if it was anything to do with hard drugs he could forget it.

Gillespie lit up a large fat Havana. "Videos," he muttered.

"Videos!" Johnny repeated. "Is that it?"

"These, my son, are the censored type – hard porn an' all that stuff," he winked slyly. "The quicker we get them shifted, the better."

Nothing he couldn't handle. "What's in it for me?"

"Hundred an' fifty nicker."

"Hundred an' fifty quid!" Johnny snorted, "I ain't riskin' my neck for that."

"Two hundred."

"Make it three hundred," Johnny bartered.

"Two-fifty, take it or leave it."

He took it. Gillespie produced a large wad of notes and peeled off tens and twenties.

"There's only a hundred quid here," Johnny complained.

"The rest is cash on delivery," Gillespie told him.

"How do I know I can trust you?"

"You don't."

Great. What kind of business deal was this?

***

Jane was more than surprised to find Johnny leaning against the railings outside the school, waiting for her.

"Hi," he said. "How ya doin?"

"Fine," she replied, attempting to sound cool.

She was very pregnant and struggling with her books. "Here – let me take them," he offered, falling into step. "You look... um... great."

"Thanks," she replied. "I feel like Humpty Dumpty."

"I've been kinda thinkin," he began. "Like with the kid on the way, maybe we should move in together?"

It was the words she'd always wanted to hear. "What's brought all this on?" she asked.

He shrugged. "Maybe it's the right thing to do."

"It isn't about doing the right thing, Johnny," she said. She'd done a lot of growing up and his pity was the last thing she wanted. "Is this what you really want?"

He gave a shrug. "Why else would I be here?" he replied shortly.

She stopped in her tracks. "Do you love me?"

He avoided her question. "Hey – what is this?"

"Look at me, Johnny. Tell me you love me."

"I can't do that, Jane. I don't know how I feel," he said.

Jane snatched her books back off him. "Just get lost!" she hissed.

"I was only tryin' to help out."

"I don't need your help. You're lucky I didn't tell my parents," she said bitterly. "I don't want to see you ever again – so just stay away from me and my baby."

What kind of gratitude was that? Here he was trying to help her out of a bad situation and this was what he got. Maybe there was a kid on the way but who needed this crap? He was free. He was single. What more could he want?

CHAPTER THIRTY-THREE

The evening of the run down to London brought back bad memories. But he was here to make money, not dwell on past experiences. He'd eventually got his life back on track and he decided not to let the bad things get him down.

He found the place deserted. It was an old factory secured by a high wire fence. He tried the gates but they were locked, and no one appeared to be around. He checked out the name and found he definitely had the right place. Around the back he could just about make out a light.

He scaled the fence. Half way down he realised he was not alone. A ferocious growl and large ugly fangs made him freeze.

Jeez!

"Hey, down boy," he murmured.

Not that it made much difference. The Alsatian leapt up against the fence, missing his trainer by a fraction. He was relieved when a man appeared out of the shadows and called the dog off.

"Gotcha!" snarled the man, pointing a rifle at him.

"Hang on – I'm Johnny," he said, still frozen to the fence.

"Johnny who?"

"Ricci."

"Never heard of ya – Now getcha arse outta 'ere before I blow ya brains out."

Great. What kind of set up was this?

"I've come with the videos. Gillespie sent me."

"Why didn't ya say?" the man said, lowering the gun. "This way."

He slid open some large doors and let him into a warehouse. It seemed a big operation hidden away at the back of the factory.

"Tell Gillespie if he keeps his side of the bargain, we'll be doin' business on a regular basis," he said.

Once the videos were safely delivered, he was too shattered to drive back to Birmingham and slept in the van overnight.

Next morning he woke with pins and needles in his arm. He got up, stretched his legs and hung around for a while. Donna crossed his mind - maybe he owed her an explanation?

After giving it some serious thought he started up the engine, then drove across to her property.

"Hey kid," he called out to a young boy delivering papers. "Do us a favour. See that house? Go and tell the lady she's wanted."

"What's it worth?" the boy said, businesslike.

He fumbled in his pocket and came up with fifty pence. "If a bloke answers, just say you've got the wrong address."

"Watcha doin', knockin' her off?" the boy said, glancing miserably at the tip.

What were they teaching kids in school these days?

The kid ran up the drive and Johnny got out and lit a cigarette. He figured at least she'd be pleased to see him, but then he wasn't so sure.

"Hi," he said, flicking his nub end into the gutter.

Donna met him with a cool reception, in spite of her heart doing a double somersault. He looked kind of rough and wild and his black curly hair had grown.

"I'm down here on business so I thought I'd drop by," he said, expecting some kind of welcoming acknowledgement.

"How very thoughtful of you," she replied curtly, "Never mind standing me up like a fool."

"What d' you want – a written apology?" he said, staring at her with those incredible eyes.

"An explanation would be nice."

He figured she wouldn't appreciate the true facts. But he decided to give them to her straight. "I got shot," he said. "And then the coppers arrested me." He never expected for one minute that she would believe him.

"Oh my God – it was you?" she gasped.

"You heard about it, huh? I guess bad news travels fast."

She realised there was very little she did know about him other than he was from the wrong side of town. But it was as if he were some kind of addictive drug. She knew he was bad for her, yet when he was near she was on a constant high.

"Hey, do I get invited in for a coffee?" he asked.

Following her into the house he looked around, taken in by the luxurious surroundings.

"How do you like your coffee - with sugar, black or white?" she asked.

"Two teaspoons - white's fine."

She caught him glancing at the large landscaped painting on the wall. "It's from the school of Constable," she said. "Richard got it from an auction at Christies."

"Mind if I use your toilet?" he asked.

"It's the first on the right at the top of the stairs. If you want to freshen up there's a bathroom further along the landing."

He'd never seen a bathroom like it. There was a large corner bath, which you stepped up to. The whole room was done in black glossy tiles and there was a large Roman type statue of some naked woman. For a second he thought of the filthy stained lavatory back at the yard, with its leaking roof and newspaper used as a bog roll.

Jeezus! How had he lived in such a flea pit?

They sat and chatted over coffee, getting to know one another.

"How long you been married?" he asked.

"Almost six years."

"You don't look that old – I mean you look pretty good for your age," he said, quickly rephrasing the statement.

She smiled. "You're so full of bullshit."

"Hey what's bull? You look great and you know it." He stared intensely into her eyes. "Age doesn't bother me, anyway. I went with this woman almost forty. Found out she had a daughter a year younger than me."

She smiled, amused by his attempt to impress her. "How long are you planning on staying in London?"

"I'm not," he replied, checking his watch. "I've gotta get the van back to Birmingham."

They stared long and hard at one another and she pecked him twice chastely on the lips.

"What we supposed to be, a couple of penguins?" he murmured, pulling her to him.

Before she had chance to answer he kissed her, soft and gentle at first, until they both wanted more. Taking his hand she led him up to the bedroom. But as much as he wanted her he felt this was wrong. "Um… like maybe we shouldn't?" he said, trying to hold back how he felt.

"Yes. I want to," she whispered, helping him out of his T-shirt.

She undressed down to her cream camisole and panties and he could hardly take his eyes off her.

"You're gorgeous," he whispered. "Jeezus! You're gorgeous."

He was leaner than she'd imagined, his arms and stomach finely muscled, his black hair and dark eyes even more intense against his pale skin. She kissed the wound on his shoulder, her lips soft and gentle against his skin. He helped her unhook her bra and brought his head down towards her erect nipples, gently teasing her with his tongue until she groaned softly.

This was different from anything he'd ever experienced; her soft perfume, her silky smooth skin. Taking her hand he pulled her down on the bed beside him. Gently he entered her with an urgency her body accepted only too willingly. Together they rocked the earth, riding high on the waves of expectation as if their lives depended on it. Something wonderful was happening to her. Something she had never experienced before. She wanted to hold on to the feeling for as long as possible.

They finally crashed to earth and snuggled in each other's arms.

"How did you learn to make love like that?" she whispered.

"Remember I told you about that older woman? I guess she taught me a lot."

"What happened, Johnny? Why did you get shot?"

He shrugged. "I knew this kid way back at school. He got mixed up with these guys. Before you know it you're involved."

"How about your family – parents?"

"My parents?" he gave a brittle laugh. "What is there to tell? My ole man got killed in a scaffolding accident.

The ole lady couldn't wait to leg it back to Ireland with my brothers and sister."

"I'm sorry."

"Hey –There's no need to be. I'm well rid of 'em."

Taking a drag from his joint, he passed it to her.

She took a puff and almost choked.

He gave a chuckle. "So how about you?"

"Me? I guess I've lived a quiet life compared to you," she said.

If only you knew I'd killed a man.

"How come you've never had kids?" he asked.

"I'm really not the maternal type," she said, thinking it best not to mention personal issues.

"Nah, me neither."

She leaned on her elbow and studied him minutely. A wisp of black hair fell over his forehead and he looked so boyish. "You bite your nails," she said.

"Yeah – I guess I had to pass the time somehow while I was in the nick."

He never gave a thought to Gillespie. Out of sight, out of mind.

They spent most of the morning together. He went with her to the supermarket, helping her put the groceries into her car. Then, holding hands, they ran giggling to a photo booth and took shots of themselves sticking out their tongues and pulling faces.

"How about we take a serious one – for a keepsake?" Johnny said.

"OK."

"Ready?"

"Ready."

He was about to press the button when she burst into giggles. "I can't help it – you're making me laugh."

"Great! I guess I missed my post as a comedian."

"OK, OK. I'm serious."

"Are you sure about that?"

"Yes."

They waited for a second for the shot to come through and both laughed. "Hey – we look kinda good together," Johnny said.

"Ummm," Donna agreed squeezing his arm.

"We're now inseparable," he said. "Our souls are entwined forever in the picture."

They headed over to the record section where some type of music was beating out.

"What's that playing?" she asked.

"Hip Hop," he said. "You never heard it?" He explained what Hip Hop was and bought a tape.

"Here – keep it safe an' don't say I never buy you anything."

It was two o'clock before he set off. "I'll give you a call," he said.

"Promise?"

He pulled her close to him. "We're soulmates – remember?"

CHAPTER THIRTY-FOUR

"Where the hell have you been?" Gillespie demanded.

"Hey Ronnie, don't get your knickers in a twist."

"Get my knickers in a twist? I was beginning to think the old bill had picked you up! I've practically got through a box of best Havanas."

Johnny followed him into his office. "How about the rest of my money? Balance with goods on delivery - remember?"

"Be patient, my son."

He was beginning to wonder if he'd done the right thing by accepting Gillespie's offer.

"I took the risk and now I want my money."

"I'm not about to skip the country," Gillespie quibbled, producing a wad of notes. "There's another favour I need. I want you to pay off a debt for me. I've got two hundred nicker. Tell Charlie I'll have the rest in a couple of weeks."

"Who's this Charlie?" Johnny asked.

Gillespie sniffed evasively. "Me an' Charlie are bosom pals. We go back a long time."

"So what's wrong with you takin' it?"

"That's what I'm paying you for, son. I'm trying to help you out of a bad situation. Course, if you don't need my help..?"

He grabbed the packet and headed off for town.

Charlie owned a club up Broad Street. It was early evening and the place was empty. He managed to find a croupier wearing black fishnet tights and a basque, her cute arse squeezed into black satin hot pants.

"D' you know where I can find Charlie?" he asked, trying to resist the temptation to stare down her cleavage.

She eyed him over approvingly. "Who wants 'im?" she asked in a distinctive Brummie twang.

"Tell him I've got some money off Ronnie Gillespie."

She gave a bang with her chewing gum and wiggled off in her high heel stilettos disappearing through a door by the bar and leaving a trail of perfume behind.

He thought of Donna and the fresh, delicate scent about her. Ah – Donna. It was crazy but he couldn't stop thinking about her.

Within seconds a hefty looking man with muscles like Rambo appeared. "Yeah –watcha got?" he growled.

"I've been told to give you this," Johnny said, handing him the packet and hoping there'd be no repercussion.

He hung around while the man checked the notes.

"Is this supposed to be a joke?" the man snarled, already flexing his muscles.

Did he look as if he was laughing? "Umm… like… Gillespie said to tell you… he'll have the rest in a couple of weeks."

The man grabbed hold of him by the scruff of the neck, almost strangling him. "I don't appreciate being messed around."

He was well aware of that. "Hey – I'm just the messenger," he croaked.

"Tell your boss if he doesn't cough up by tomorrow I'm coming round there to personally beat him and his business to pulp – you got that?"

He nodded in silence and the man released his grip. He fled through the door like a frightened rabbit.

So much for bosom pals, he thought. If Gillespie ever suggested any more favours he could go screw himself.

"This is Angie," Chris said, introducing her to his parents.

"Angie – we've heard so much about you," Liz said, fussing over her. "Chris never stops talking about you."

He tossed his fringe back with annoyance. Yet again his mother was out to embarrass him.

"I've heard you're studying physics?" Liz said, taking a bunch of flowers from her.

"Yes," Angie smiled. "I'm just waiting for my results – fingers crossed."

"How wonderful." Liz threw Jim a glance of approval. "Of course, Christopher had a brilliant career in his hands and he threw it away. He could have become a lawyer you know - isn't that right, Christopher?"

He could hardly look at his mother. When he did, he had this vision of her and Johnny humping away. In fact he would never look at his mother in the same way again.

"You're a dark horse," Angie smiled. "You never mentioned any of this to me."

"It's nothing," Chris managed with a smile.

"I'd better put these flowers in water – they're simply beautiful," Liz said.

"Come on, Angie!" Chris grabbed hold of her hand, eager to drag her away from his parents. "There's something I want to show you."

Liz watched them walk off. "She seems a nice girl," she said, arranging the flowers.

"Hmm," Jim replied, buried behind the newspaper.

"I'm glad he's found someone respectable," she said. "I should hate him to end up like our Steve. I thought at least he'd have brought the children to see me on my birthday."

"What do you expect from Steve?" Jim grunted. "He's always been bloody selfish."

"I hope things work out for them both."

"Why shouldn't they?"

"Well - men are so elusive," Liz said. "They flit from woman to woman."

"I never did," Jim quibbled.

"Oh yes you did. Remember Molly Fisher? We'd only been seeing each other for a couple of weeks when I caught you."

"Ah, Molly Fisher," he said with a twinkle in his eye. "She certainly was a frisky little thing."

"Maybe I should have let you run off with her?" Liz criticised.

Jim wagged a threatening finger at her. "Don't think I don't know what was going on with you and that friend of Chris's."

Liz turned the colour of beetroot. Oh God, he knew. "Whatever do you mean?" she asked flippantly.

"Well… it was obvious you had a roaming eye for him. I caught you glancing at him a few times."

"Oh that!" she smiled, relief flooding through her. "It was nothing."

"Come here, you sexy minx," he said, giving her bottom a squeeze. "You've still got the best arse in town."
★★★

"Close your eyes – no peeping," Chris said, leading Angie into the garage. "Watch the step."

He guided her over to the Mini – what was left of it – a solitary shell covered in grey primer. "OK – you can open your eyes."

Angie stared. "What am I supposed to be looking at?" she asked negatively.

"The Cooper," he said. "They wrote her off so I bought her back. What do you think?"

"It's… um… "

She paused, trying to show enthusiasm. "It's great."

"She's a star – can you believe she took on a Mercedes?" he said, beaming from ear to ear.

"I know one thing," Angie cut in sharply, "You're lucky to be alive. I could have been looking at a corpse, not just the remains of some Mini."

CHAPTER THIRTY-FIVE

Gillespie was throwing a lot of work his way. They had struck up a successful partnership making a killing out of blockbuster videos. Before long thousands of illegal copies were exchanging hands before they were released on the UK market. Gillespie even had the packaging done professionally. Johnny made the deliveries, mostly to London, where he was paid four hundred up front for each batch. Pirating was a dangerous game, but it was paying off nicely.

Meanwhile, the trips to London were a bonus.

Over the last few weeks he and Donna had worked it carefully between them. He'd given her Gillespie's number so if there were any problems she'd only to ring him. On days when her husband was out of the country he stayed the night and always made himself scarce when the daily help was around. The five-bedroomed house was becoming a second home to him.

And he couldn't think of a better way to spend his time.

***

"You're sleeping with this guy and allowing him into your home?" Melania exclaimed, making no attempt to lower her voice.

They were in a restaurant and a few of the diners were throwing them wary glances.

"Get real, honey – he's twenty and fickle."

And Richard's forty-six and boring, Donna felt like saying.

Melania rolled her eyes in disbelief. "Honey he's gonna drop you like a hot cake as soon as the next pretty girl comes along – he won't think twice about dropping his pants."

The waiter intervened with a polite cough. "Is everything to your satisfaction, madam?" he asked.

"Fine, thank you," Donna replied.

Melania continued, "And how do you know he's not just hanging around for your money?"

Donna prodded at a pickled gherkin. "He's not like that," she replied crossly.

"Huh!" Melania snorted. "I thought I knew Winston, until I found out what an arsehole he was." She broke off with a sigh. "Look honey – I just don't want to see you get hurt."

"I'm a big girl. I can take care of myself."

"Anyway, changing the subject," Melania began. "Me and Dexter have booked into a health spa for the weekend. There's a sauna, tennis courts, the lot. How about if you and Richard come along?"

"I doubt if Richard will be interested. And anyway, he plays golf on Sundays."

"Why not ask him?"

"Whatever," Donna replied.

When she got back to the house there was a letter from Isabelle explaining that she was starting up her own business and would no longer be doing their cleaning.

Over the evening meal she tackled Richard. "By the way," she began. "Melania's asked if we'd like to go to a health spa this weekend."

Richard hardly glanced up. "You know Sunday's my golf day," he replied shortly.

There was a moment's silence before Donna spoke. "Isabelle's leaving," she said. "She left a note to say she's starting her own business."

"Really?" he said. "In that case you'd better get onto the agencies."

"Why bother with a cleaner? I can do the job efficiently myself," she replied. "You're the one complaining about cutting back."

Richard glanced up from his meal. "You've always insisted your mother worked her fingers to the bone and how worn she looked. I'm sure you don't want to end up looking an old hag like her, do you?"

"How dare you speak about my mother like that!" she screamed at him. "You've never even met my mother."

She threw down her napkin and stormed up to the bedroom, deciding to ring Melania from the bedside phone. "I've changed my mind," she said. "Can you make two extra bookings?"

"So you persuaded Richard to come?"

"No – I'm bringing Johnny."

"Johnny!"

Melania wasn't particularly happy about the situation but Donna didn't really care what she thought.

Later that evening she rang Johnny to tell him the plans. "Pack your toothbrush. We're going away for the weekend," she said excitedly.

"Hang on… what if I can't get the van?"

"I'm sure you can work your magic on Gillespie."

"How come he's allowing you out?"

"Don't be facetious."

"Don't be what?" he teased.

"Be serious and listen – Melania is picking me up. She's calling me back with the arrangements so I'll let you know."

"Jeez! That crazy bitch! If looks could kill I'd be six foot under."

"Melania's OK. You'll be fine once she gets to know you."

He wouldn't like to bet on that.

CHAPTER THIRTY-SIX

"Where are you going?" Richard asked as she slipped past in white shorts and pumps carrying an Adidas sports bag.

"I'm going to the health complex I told you about – remember?"

Richard tapped his foot with annoyance. "You mean to say you're flitting off for the weekend?"

"I gave you the offer."

"And what am I supposed to do for lunch?"

"Surely you can get something at the golf club?"

Or maybe Hilary can conjure up a meal for you?

"This has to stop, Donna," he said, talking down to her as if she was a rebellious teenager. "In future you consult me before making any arrangements."

She didn't even feel guilty any more.

They had planned it carefully between them. As arranged, Melania picked her up and they drove back to Dexter's place, where Johnny had been told to leave the van.

Donna had never met Dexter before. He was a good-looking Jamaican, tall and muscular with a great personality and a dazzling white smile.

The four of them drove down in Dexter's swanky BMW convertible. Johnny sat in the front seat and they hit it off immediately, talking about anything from football to the latest fast cars.

"I must have been mad to have gone along with this," Melania murmured. "I still say you're making a big mistake."

Donna hoped Melania wasn't going to give her a hard time. It was bad enough having to put up with Richard.

On arriving they were ushered into a space by the parking attendant, a smartly dressed man in a red coat and hat. The place was massive and had every facility imaginable.

Johnny glanced casually around. It seemed everyone drove a Mercedes and looked as if they were loaded – and that was just the staff.

"I'll take the bags up to our room," Dexter said.

Melania pulled him back. "That's what the porter is paid for," she said disdainfully.

Johnny took Donna to one side. "How much is this little lot gonna cost?" he asked, realising he only had fifty pounds on him.

Donna smiled. "Don't worry – the treat's on me," she said. "If you need the gym or sauna you'll need a ticket, and that allows you anything."

"Anything?" he teased.

"Behave," she said.

He gave her a cocky half smile. She looked kinda fresh and girlish in skimpy shorts and a Nike T-shirt, her hair tied up in a ponytail. He almost got carried away. "Hey – Donna," he said, pulling her close.

"Yes?" she replied, holding his glance.

"Ah nothing - just that you look great."

Later, he and Dexter watched football on a large screen in the sports room, while Donna and Melania used the gym and afterwards took a sauna.

"Men!" Melania complained, lying back and enjoying the sensation of the warm water cascading over her body. "If their mind isn't on their dick it's watching some football game."

Donna relaxed with a glass of bubbly and thought of Richard. It wasn't as if he couldn't cope on his own? Maybe he'd eat down the golf club? Or perhaps Hilary would jump at the chance of cooking for him.

I'm being unfaithful.

Relax and stop worrying.

But I can't help thinking something will happen to spoil things.

"So what are your plans?" Melania asked.

"In what way?"

"Well... what exactly are your intentions with this guy?"

"If you mean are we planning to run off together – the answer's no. We just like each other's company and having a laugh together."

"At Richard's expense?"

"Whose side are you on?"

It seemed Melania's only interest was in defending Richard.

"I'm on nobody's side. I just hope you realise what you might lose if he gets to hear about this." She broke off with a sigh. "Honey - you're ready to risk all you have for some... "

"Some what?" Donna cut in harshly.

"Some guy you hardly know anything about."

"How's your singing career going?" Donna asked briskly.

Melania looked at her with a blank expression. "What's that got to do with it?"

"Exactly what any of this has to do with you?" she replied bluntly.

They lapsed into silence for a moment. Maybe Melania was right. Johnny had come into her life –

whether it was a good thing or bad she wasn't sure. All she did know was she'd never felt this happy.

The evening meal was five courses with a choice of menu. A far cry from burgers and chips, Johnny thought.

The waiter brought the wine list and handed it to him. "Would you like to choose, sir?"

"Um... maybe you should let the ladies choose," he said, quickly escaping the situation.

When the first course arrived he was still trying to figure out which fork to use.

"Hey – what is this stuff?" he asked, glancing down at what appeared to be a plateful of frogspawn.

"It's caviar."

"Fish eggs," he mumbled.

"It's really nice – try some."

"No thanks," he said, pushing his plate to one side.

Donna nudged him. "You're using the wrong fork. Always start from the outside and work your way inwards," she whispered.

What was she trying to do – re-educate him?

No chance.

After the meal they piled into the lounge for drinks. Dexter insisted on paying for most of it.

"I wish he'd let me pay," Donna offered when he went up to the bar.

"He'll only be offended," Melania whispered.

Johnny offered her a cigarette and she cut him dead. He was beginning to feel uncomfortable.

"Did I mention Dexter has offered to pay for me to make a recording?" Melania said suddenly.

"Great - I can see you making it yet," Donna said reassuringly.

"Don't bank on it, honey."

"Do you think you'll marry him?"

"Who knows?"

"What's the big deal about marriage?" Johnny cut in. "It's just a piece of paper."

"You don't agree with it then?" Melania commented, giving Donna a glance that said, "I told you so."

Donna ignored her. Johnny was probably right, anyway, especially if her marriage to Richard was anything to go by.

Later that evening they shuffled around the dance floor to the strains of Hot Chocolate. Johnny held her close and murmured the lyrics in her ear.

"It started with a kiss, in the back row of the classroom How could I resist the aroma of your perfume..."

They clung on tightly to one another, lost in the magic of that moment, neither of them thinking of tomorrow. Neither of them caring.

CHAPTER THIRTY-SEVEN

"How did your weekend go?" Richard asked in a threatening tone.

He knows something.

Stop feeling guilty and act normal.

"Would you like some cheese on toast? I'm just going to make some," she asked.

"No thank you. I've already eaten," he said, scowling into his brandy glass.

"So you managed to get something at the golf club?"

"Yes – no thanks to you."

She suddenly felt extremely guilty.

"Are you sure you don't want any?" she asked sitting down at the table.

He never replied. and she caught him throwing her an evil glance.

If he knows something, why doesn't he just come out with it?

Just lately, she couldn't make him out. But that was Richard.

She got up from the table and went for a shower. She was about to get some fresh underwear from the bedroom when she froze in horror – pinned to the dressing table was the photo clip of her and Johnny. Scrawled across the mirror in bright red lipstick were the words, "Liar and cheat."

Oh my God! How on earth could she explain this?

Did she just deny it? Or did she face up to him and tell him the truth – but where would that get her?

She jumped, realising he was standing right behind her.

"That's what all this trash is about, isn't it?" he shouted, waving the tape in her face. "Well – there's only one place for rubbish."

She watched him throw it on the floor and then trample on it.

Now her guilt swiftly transcended to anger. "You had no right to go mooching in my dressing table!" she screamed at him.

"I had every right when my wife's being unfaithful," he spat, hatred blazing in his eyes.

"What's all the fuss about?" she screamed. "It's only a photograph."

"Don't dare insult my intelligence," he snarled, grabbing the photo strip and tearing it up. "Do you think I don't know what's been going on in this house – behind my back?"

"I don't know what you're talking about."

He grabbed her firmly by the wrist. "You're not only a bad liar – you're a cheat and a slut."

"Please Richard – you're hurting my arm." For one moment she thought he was going to hit her.

Just try it – one man did and he died.

His eyes pinned her dangerously. "If I ever catch him in this house, or find you're still seeing him, so help me God – I'll make you suffer."

★★★

They hardly spoke at breakfast next morning. Even the thought of sharing a bed with him made her feel physically ill. Why did he insist on clinging to this dead marriage?

She tried calling Johnny, but Gillespie said he wasn't around. She needed desperately to speak to him. And now she hadn't even got the photograph or tape to cheer her up.

Later that morning a girl from the cleaning agency turned up on her doorstep.

"I come to do you work," she said, speaking in broken English.

"You'd better come in."

The girl handed Donna her letter from the agency and continued to eye the property up. "You have nice home," she said, picking up one of the Japanese vases. "Nice too."

"Be careful," Donna said, taking the vase off her.

"They are very expensive – yes?"

Donna pointed out the lounge. "I'd like you to vacuum," she said, showing her where the vacuum was kept and thinking it would be quicker to do it herself.

Again she tried calling Johnny but she still couldn't get hold of him. She hadn't heard anything from him since the weekend, which was unusual.

By the end of the week the girl from the agency had shown little improvement, in fact she had developed quite a slapdash attitude. "Please don't slam the plates in the dish washer," Donna told her. It had little effect.

After giving the house a quick lick over she was about to leave. "I go," she said, putting on her coat.

Donna glanced briefly around. There was still dust on the hall table and from what she could see little had been done. She decided to tell the girl there and then. "There's no need to come back Monday. Thank you."

The girl shrugged, not unduly bothered.

Why couldn't Richard listen for once, instead of being so bloody pig-headed?

Later that evening they continued their meal in silence.

"How long are we going to keep this stupidity up?" she asked coolly. If they were living together they may as well make an effort and speak to one another, at least.

"I didn't start this – remember? It was you who decided to cheat."

"Fine – so what are you going to do?" she said curtly. "Lock me up? Make sure I never look at another man again?"

There was no point in arguing. Johnny would be thrown in her face at every opportunity.

Richard rose from the table and screwed up a receipt from his pocket. Flicking it into the waste bin he spotted a cigarette packet. "Who smokes Camel cigarettes?" he asked suspiciously.

"It must have been the girl from the cleaning agency."

She could tell by the look on his face that he didn't believe her. "I'm not arguing, Richard. Think what you darn well like."

She got up to clear the plates away. "Incidently – I sacked her."

"You did what?"

"I said I... "

"Yes, I heard what you said. You had no right. You should have gone through the appropriate channels and spoken to the agency."

"I've spoken to the agency and told them in so many words not to bother sending anyone else."

"That was a stupid thing to do," he said furiously. "The girl will no doubt take us to a bloody tribunal for unfair dismissal."

CHAPTER THIRTY-EIGHT

The strain on their relationship was beginning to take its toll on both of them. Donna was full of guilt and fed up having to lie. While Johnny's mind was beginning to buzz with second thoughts, he couldn't get his head around things any more. The whole weekend had been nothing but a disaster, with Melania glaring at him as if he was some psychopathic maniac. Why couldn't Donna have settled for a normal weekend with just the two of them? Instead she had to drag him off to some frigging top star hotel with a load of hypocrites flashing their money as if there were no tomorrow. He was fast realising she was well out of his league. Donna in her world of champagne and caviar, and him – just a kid from the back streets.

Meanwhile Gillespie sat at his desk, counting up his money like an old miser. As soon as he spotted the girl, he pounced on her like a spider after its prey.

"Nice little car," he said, indicating to the one and only motor car standing outside his business. "She only came in yesterday."

"It's got a few scratches," she said cautiously.

"Look – why don't you step into my office and we'll discuss it? I can work you out a good deal."

Jeez! Gillespie sure had the banter. He could talk his way into selling mouldy cheese.

"Umm – I don't know," the girl said. "I'll have to sleep on it."

"Of course, my sweet, but don't leave it too long. I've already got two other people interested."

Johnny waited for her to leave the office and approached Gillespie. "Two other people - oh really?" he sneered.

"Business, my son, business," Gillespie replied furtively. "She's a valid customer and she may be back tomorrow. We might just get it off our hands."

"You can't sell her that clapped out piece of crap. It's clocked up over a hundred an' twenny miles."

"She's not to know. It's all been reinstalled," Gillespie said wagging his cigar at Johnny. "I can see I'll have to teach you a thing or two about salesmanship. Incidentally, I need you to sort out some rubbish round the back."

What did his last servant die of? "I thought I was supposed to be dealin' with the videos?"

"I forgot to mention – I may be changing my tactics. I'm getting bad vibes about this porno stuff."

He was getting bad vibes? "You wanna try driving around with the stuff," Johnny quibbled.

Gillespie gave another evasive sniff. "Exactly, my son, so the quicker we get rid of it, the better."

★★★

On the 28th of July, after a long and exhausting labour, Jane gave birth to a healthy baby girl weighing six pounds eight ounces. Both mother and baby were fine.

Sylvia was secretly over the moon. She'd always looked forward to becoming a grandparent; naturally, she would have preferred different circumstances.

"What are you going to call her?" she asked excitedly.

"Kylie – I'm calling her Kylie."

"I thought maybe Victoria, after the Queen of England," her mother said patriotically.

"No mother. I see no point, it would only be abbreviated to Vicky," she said, sticking to her guns.

Jane could hardly believe the tiny miracle in her arms. She had large brown eyes and a crop of fine dark hair. There was no mistaking the resemblance. She wanted to forget Johnny ever existed. He'd hurt her so bad, but looking at Kylie she wondered if that would ever be possible?

"Oh mother, she's so beautiful. She's perfect. Look at her tiny fingers and her cute little nose."

"Jane, this is going to be hard work," Sylvia stressed. "This baby is a person, not just some passing fantasy."

"I know, mother."

Dashing up to her room the first thing she did was to change into her jeans. It was so good to have her figure back once more. She stood gazing at herself for a few minutes. Maybe a little fat around the waist but nothing a diet wouldn't cure.

"Jane the baby's crying," Sylvia called out. "She probably needs her feed."

"I'm coming, mother."

Kevin glanced up from his newspaper. "I hope she isn't going to keep us up all night," he grumbled.

"Course not, are you sweetie pie?" Sylvia said, picking the infant up and rocking her two and fro, making silly cooing noises.

Whose baby was this?

Over the next few days, Sylvia's interference began to annoy Jane. "She'll expect to be picked up every time she cries," Jane snapped.

Her mother ignored her and took over the feed.

Great! First her mother wanted her to get rid of it, now she couldn't keep the child away from her.

"Breastfeeding would have been so much nicer, Jane," Sylvia said, interfering once more. "I don't believe in all this artificial milk."

"Thank you, mother, but I'll bring the baby up the way I want," she said firmly.

She decided the only way to have the baby to herself was to take her out.

"Where are you going?" Sylvia cried in a mother superior voice.

"To see friends," Jane said, slipping Kylie into a pink matinee coat and bonnet her grandmother had kindly knitted. "I haven't had a chance to show her to Bekki yet."

"Bekki? You're seeing that dreadful girl?"

Oh just shut up, mother.

"You know what I think of her," Sylvia snapped. "And the baby's not a doll to be passed around," she added. "She could catch a chill."

Jane sighed wearily. Bouncing the pram out of the house she wheeled it proudly down the street.

"Alone at last, away from silly old grandma," she said, smiling down at Kylie. The baby looked up at her with a chuckle as if she understood every word.

"Thanks Johnny," she murmured. "Thanks for giving me the most precious gift imaginable."

CHAPTER THIRTY-NINE

"Try and look a little more enthusiastic," Richard said, as they approached the Banks's house for dinner that night.

Donna shot him a cool expression. Get the hell off my case, Richard.

She had only agreed to this meal to keep the peace. She knew if she hadn't she would never have heard the end of it.

Flinging the door open, Stella greeted them with a hug and a kiss. "I'm so glad you could make it," she said, greeting them with her usual show of extravagance in a blue chiffon dress and matching Roland Cartier shoes. From the kitchen the aroma of cooking wafted through the air.

"May I say you look absolutely stunning," she said to Donna, leading them through to the dining room.

"Thank you. What a lovely dress, Stella."

Her face lit up. "You think it's me?"

"Definitely," she replied, thinking it was more for a girl of twenty.

"I shouldn't tell you this," she whispered discretely as if people were listening. "But I bought it in the sale last week – a hundred and eighty pounds reduced to just fifty. I simply couldn't resist it."

Bustling off into the kitchen, Stella returned with the meal and placed it on the table.

"Smells good," Richard replied, rubbing his hands together.

Donna gave a faint smile, not in the least bit hungry. "How's golf, Richard?"

She tuned out and picked at her food, thinking about Johnny. She hadn't heard a thing from him for over a week – was he cooling off? Didn't their relationship mean anything to him? Suppose he had used her? Maybe she was a big joke between him and his friends – the rich lady he'd finally managed to get in the sack?

The thought was soul destroying.

"Is there something wrong with the food?" Stella asked her.

"Um no. It's lovely, thank you," she replied politely.

"Don't tell me you're dieting?"

Donna forced a weak smile.

After dinner, Stella offered them chocolate mints and coffee. "I believe you're off to the Greek islands," she said.

"Greece?" Donna looked at Richard. "I wasn't aware," she said, confused.

"Hasn't the naughty man mentioned it to you?" Stella said briskly.

Richard gave her hand a squeeze as if nothing had happened between them. "It was meant as a surprise. We both need the break."

"Greece is such a beautiful place," Stella said. "I'm sure you'll have a wonderful time."

I sure we won't. Anywhere with Richard was hell on earth.

David poured out brandies and took Richard into the other room to discuss business.

"I suppose he's had a lot on his mind," Stella began, "What with the redundancies and all that."

It was late when they left and Richard insisted on hailing a cab after consuming too much brandy.

"So when are we supposed to be taking this holiday?" Donna asked when they finally reached home.

He paid the taxi fare and walked ahead of her up the drive. "I hadn't got round to telling you... " he began.

She wondered if the holiday was meant for him and Hilary, and Stella had misunderstood.

"You don't deserve it after the way you've behaved," he snapped.

Here we go again, she thought. It was almost midnight, she was tired and the last thing she wanted was a confrontation with him.

"Whatever," she said wearily, following him into the house.

"Did you forget to set the alarm?" he asked.

"No, of course I didn't."

"You must have," he insisted, reaching for the light switch.

The first thing they noticed was that the Constable painting was missing.

Richard stared aghast at the large discoloured patch on the wall. "Christ almighty, we've been burgled!"

Donna let out a gasp. Glancing around she noticed the Japanese vases had also been taken.

Richard immediately picked up the phone. "There's no forced entry, so whoever it was had access to the house," he said.

He tapped his foot impatiently, waiting to be connected. "This is your ruddy fault," he said.

Wasn't it always?

"I hope you're satisfied with yourself," he snapped. "You will encourage scum into the house."

"He didn't do it!" Donna shouted, leaping to Johnny's defence.

"Why must you insist on protecting him?" he hissed back.

"I'm not protecting anyone – I just know he wouldn't have done it."

"You're so bloody vulnerable, Donna. This scumbag has screwed you in every sense of the word."

Within half an hour a starchy inspector with bad breath, spectacles and a wilting moustache arrived at the house.

"Who else has access to the building?" he asked.

"The cleaner always had a key," Donna said. "But she left some weeks ago and handed it back."

"Is there anyone else who's likely to have had a key?"

She racked her brains. It couldn't have been the girl from the agency, she never was given a key.

All the same, Donna had her suspicions that she had something to do with it. "I think it may have been the girl from the cleaning agency."

"Don't you think you should tell him the truth?" Richard cut in abruptly.

The inspector scratched his head. "Tell me what?"

"It's really nothing – my husband's jumping to conclusions."

Richard paced the floor uncomfortably. "My wife... she had this... this young thug in the house."

"Hmm, I see," the inspector said, jotting down the details on his pad. "And what was your relationship with this man?"

"I really don't think that is relevant, inspector," Richard said bluntly. "The fact was he had the key to the property."

"I see. And this person's name?"

"This is ridiculous!" Donna snapped. "I've already told you who's responsible."

"You know very well who did it," Richard cut in sharply.

The inspector gave his head another scratch. Flakes of dandruff settled on his black jacket. "Unless you co-operate, I can't continue with this investigation."

Reluctantly she gave the inspector the details. "Look – will you check with the agency? I'm almost certain it's that girl."

"We shall certainly investigate all suspects," the inspector said. "You'll be hearing from me in a few days' time. Don't worry; we'll soon have this matter settled."

Donna spent an uneasy night. She tossed and turned and counted the hours before daybreak.

Johnny couldn't possibly have done it. She trusted him.

But just suppose he had?

Next morning she rang his garage and managed to get hold of him. "I thought I might have heard from you," she asked. He didn't reply, so she continued. "Richard knows about us, he found the photo we had taken… Johnny, are you still there?"

"Yeah, I heard," he muttered, toying with Gillespie's cigar box.

"Why are you acting like this - is it because of Richard?"

Did she think he gave a toss about Richard?

"You just don't get it, do ya?" he said bluntly. "This isn't about him – it's about us. We're on totally different planets."

"What are you saying?" she cut in agitatedly.

Did he need to spell it out?

She gave a brittle laugh. "Oh – I get it. You think because I live in a posh house and have expensive things I'm different to you?"

Who was she trying to kid?

"Well let me tell you something," she continued, "I was raised in poverty. My mother struggled to put a decent meal on the table. I left home when I was sixteen because… " she had to stop herself before she blurted out the whole story. "Maybe you should try sleeping in doorways with all your possessions in a carrier bag and wondering where your next meal was coming from? Oh believe me, Johnny… I know all about having nothing."

He slammed down the lid of the cigar box and the spring flew off.

"Bollocks!" he spat.

"Excuse me?"

"Not you," he said, scrambling on his hands and knees to find it.

He guessed it made sense. Desperate girl meets older man with bags of money. But that still didn't change the fact of what she had now become accustomed to. There were a few seconds of silence before she spoke. "We had the Constable painting stolen," she began. "Whoever did it must have had access to the building."

It suddenly struck him what she was getting at. "You think I had something to do with it?" he said abruptly.

"No, of course not," she said, pausing for a second. "You would be honest with me wouldn't you, Johnny?" she asked, waiting to be reassured.

Is that what she thinks of me – some lousy tea leaf?

He never answered and put down the phone. He was annoyed and hurt – in fact he couldn't have felt more hurt if she'd have kicked him in the balls.

CHAPTER FORTY

"Pornographic material!" Gillespie gasped at the two plain clothed policemen standing in front of him. "I should coco."

"We're investigating an illegal transaction reportedly carried out from these premises," said the one.

"Goodness gracious, Inspector I hope you're not suggesting I had anything to do with it?"

"How is business these days, Mr Gillespie?" the inspector asked, glancing at his box full of quality cigars. "Looks as if you're in a pretty comfortable position, I'd say."

Gillespie gave a cagey grin. "I'm struggling to run a respectable business, I'll have you know."

Just then his phone rang. "Excuse me," he said.

"Mind if we take a look around?" the officer cut in.

"Be my guest. Everything is above board and legit I can assure you," Gillespie replied. Taking his hand off the receiver he answered the call. "I'm sorry I didn't catch your name, sweetheart?"

"Donna. I'd like to speak to Johnny," she said, thinking that she owed him an apology.

"I'm afraid he's not here, sweetheart. I'm the proprietor, how may I help?"

"It's a private call," she stressed.

"I can always pass a message on."

"If you wouldn't mind," she began, "Could you tell him I know he wasn't responsible for the painting. He'll know what I mean, and that I apologise."

"Of course, my love," Gillespie said, keeping a watchful eye on the two officers.

He came off the phone and shook his head with a toot. "Porn videos – a dreadful business, I hope you catch whoever's responsible."

The inspector gave him a wilting smile. "I'm sure we will. Good day Mr Gillespie."

He sat sweating, hoping Johnny wasn't going to be too long. Suppose they pulled him up in the van?

Oh good lord. He grabbed a cigar.

The minute Johnny walked through the door he pounced on him. "I've had the Old Bill around," he said. "Get shut of that stuff ASAP - I want no trace of it left."

"Hang on," Johnny said. "We're talking about four grands' worth of videos."

"I know, and my heart bleeds, but there's no other choice. Just get rid of it. Burn it – anything."

"So what happens to my share of the money?"

"You'll get it – just as soon as business resumes."

"And when's that likely to be, Ronnie?" Johnny said sharply.

"Now don't let's rush things – time is the essence."

"When Ronnie?" Johnny demanded.

"In case it's escaped your attention, I've hit rocky times," he replied, sitting regally at his desk and puffing on a large Havana. "Think yourself lucky, my son, that I didn't deduct the cigar box out of your earnings. That was a family heirloom – it had sentimental value."

"Suppose you dump the stuff yourself," Johnny said, throwing the van keys on his desk.

"Goodness me! There's no need to get nasty."

"I want paying – now."

Gillespie lifted his hand, "All right, all right," he said. "I may have something up my sleeve."

Reaching for the phone Gillespie dialled out. "Charlie, my old pal, about that deal...Pause...Well, of course you'll get paid. Just as soon as the stuff's up and running we'll reach a negotiable price – say a grand for the first lot?" Gillespie cringed and held the receiver away from his ear as Charlie yelled down the phone. "Ok – eight hundred then?"

Johnny had no idea what Gillespie was up to, but he knew he didn't like the sound of it.

"All done, my son," Gillespie said coming off the phone with a delighted expression. "From now on we're in the antiques business. I've got a nice little earner coming our way. There's this bloke from the auctions and I've agreed to take a few things off his hands."

"Antiques? You've gotta be jokin!" Johnny snorted. The thought of Gillespie being involved in antiques was beyond belief.

Gillespie looked offended. "I've done my research and I know a good bargain when I come across one."

"So where does Charlie fit into all of this?"

"Charlie's going to be doing a bit of titivating up, so to speak. Making sure everything runs smoothly."

"You mean you're gonna buy in a load of dodgy stuff?"

"Goodness me, my son, I never touch anything dodgy."

Yeah right. Was Gillespie crazy, or what?

CHAPTER FORTY-ONE

"I'm leaving Richard," Donna announced over the phone to Melania. "I can't take it any longer. He's making my life hell."

"This wouldn't have anything to do with that young stud, would it?" Melania probed.

"Johnny?" Donna gave a brittle laugh. "You know very well I haven't heard or seen anything of him, and before you say anything, I already know."

He hadn't even had the decency to return her call. So what was all that rubbish about their souls being entwined? Melania was right; he was fickle, although she wasn't prepared to give her the satisfaction of saying 'I told you so.'

"Did the police ever come back to you about the painting?" Melania asked prudently.

"We had a letter last week saying it had been traced to an art dealer's in Watford along with the vases - and I was right all along. It was that girl from the agency. Her boyfriend stole the blessed thing. He must have taken the key and had it cut."

"Well – at least you've got it back. I thought maybe… "

"I never thought it was him to begin with," Donna cut in sharply.

Melania quickly changed the subject. "So will you go back to your parents?"

"No – that's impossible."

"Look, honey, whatever happened between you and your folks, I'm sure they'd be pleased to see you."

"Melania you don't understand. I had a real bad falling out with my father."

"So where will you go?"

"I'll find somewhere." She'd managed under worse circumstances. "I'll get a job – at least I'll have my own independence."

"You're always welcome to stay with us."

"Thanks, Melania, but I don't want to impose on you and Dexter, besides it's the first place Richard will look for me."

"When are you thinking of going?"

"Today. I've just got a few more things to pack."

"Are you sure you're doing the right thing?"

"Melania, will you stop saying that? You're beginning to cramp my confidence."

"Style, honey."

"What?"

Oh never mind. She was too concerned with planning her future to care what Melania was babbling on about.

"I think Richard is still very much in love with you," Melania said. "Otherwise he would have given you a divorce."

"Don't Melania, you're making me feel guilty."

"I'm sure if you'd have sat down together you could have at least tried to sort your differences out."

"Richard is beyond reasoning. He'll never forgive me. He's made that perfectly clear. Every time we argue it's thrown in my face."

"I did warn you, honey."

Donna checked her watch and gave a sigh. "Look – as soon as I'm settled I'll give you a call."

"Remember I'm here whenever you need someone to talk to."

"Thanks. I'll catch up with you later."

She hung up and began the task of writing Richard a letter. How did you tell someone it was over?

Johnny managed it quite well.

Why do you have to keep bringing him into it?

She started off with, "Richard,"

That sounded a bit too formal. She doodled with the pen thoughtfully but just couldn't find the right words to put to paper. Finally she lost patience.

Just give it to him straight.

Dear Richard,

As you won't give me a divorce, I've decided to leave you. I think it best in both our interests. Don't think I'm not grateful for all you've given me, but sometimes these things just aren't enough.

I'll be in touch over legal proceedings.

Donna.

She put the letter in an envelope and left it on the kitchen table then carried on with the rest of her packing.

She was about to leave when the phone rang. She ignored it. Probably a sales call.

It continued to ring. She hesitated before putting down her case to answer it.

"Donna, it's Hilary – Richard's secretary. He's had some kind of breakdown."

"Breakdown? He was perfectly all right when he left this morning."

"He hasn't been well for sometime - you of all people should know that," Hilary said in an acid tone. "It's all the business of the redundancies; it's just got on top of him."

Donna was fuming. "Where is he now?" she asked, annoyed that he'd confided in Hilary rather than talk to her.

"He's with the company doctor. He'll obviously be referred to his GP. I think it's only fair to say he will need your support."

How dare this woman tell her how she should look after her husband?

She slammed down the phone and tore up the letter. There was no way she could leave him. Not now.

PART 2

CHAPTER FORTY-TWO

Birmingham 1994

The girl roaming around his bedsit, wearing nothing more than a pair of large loop earrings, had no intention of leaving. Humming to herself she wandered over to Johnny lying on the bed, hands clasped behind his head. "Why don't I come along with you and keep you company?" she suggested, her pert dark nipples staring him in the face.

"Because it's strictly business," he replied.

"You won't get bored, I promise," she purred.

Of that he had no doubt. What had started out as a one-night-stand had somehow developed into a two-day sex marathon.

Chandelle – black father, white mother, tall with an exquisite body and a great personality. What more could he want?

He wasn't sure any more.

It was stupid, he knew, but he couldn't help thinking that one day he might have a call from Donna. But what was the point? She was very much married and she obviously didn't want to know, otherwise she would have called him back to apologise. So why did he keep thinking about her? Why couldn't he just forget? Chandelle never played hard to get, she was easy – maybe too easy.

He made an attempt to get up and she pulled him back down. "You can't escape that easily," she complained.

Laughing they rolled across the bed and she straddled him with her long coffee coloured legs. Chandelle liked to be on top and he let her have her way. He always aimed to please.

They began to make passionate love and Chandelle's screams rang out. There was banging from the flat above. By now he was used to complaints from the neighbours.

When they'd finished he rolled away. "Hey – I've really gotta go," he said, checking his watch and jumping off the bed.

"Maybe I'll hang around and cook you something?"

"No," he insisted.

"Well maybe I'll tidy the place – make it comfy for when you get back?" she suggested affably.

"If I needed a cleaner I'd advertise for one," he said, gathering her clothes and dumping them onto her. "I'll call you when I get back."

"Like you promised last time," she said moodily.

"So I forgot."

He managed to bundle her out of the door and set off to the garage. Gillespie was waiting when he arrived.

"Get this stuff shifted," he said, waving his cigar to a load of junk. "I need the room."

"What now dare I ask?"

"Bubbly, my son. I've got fifty crates being delivered. Charlie's taking care of the labels. We'll knock em' out as vintage champagne at thirty nicker a bottle."

"Are you crazy?"

"No one's going to know the difference."

Geez! He sure didn't know how Gillespie got away with it. The antiques were bad enough. Now he was scheming up another bright idea.

He wasn't sure why he was still working for Gillespie. Maybe he liked living dangerously?

The delivery eventually arrived and cheap wasn't the word.

"Someone's gonna sus this little lot out," he said.

"You worry too much, my son," Gillespie told him.

"Yeah – well I'm bound to, ain't I, considering I'm the mug whose gonna be dropping the stuff off."

Gillespie ignored his comment. "I've got a nice little order set up with those blokes from the restaurant down the road. They're having fifty bottles. I've told them they can have it at a reasonable price."

"How much?"

"A grand for the lot."

"Are you off your flaming rocker?"

"It's a bargain price for best bubbly."

"This ain't bubbly, it's piss water, Ronnie."

"How dare you cast judgement on me? Just you wait – the orders will be flocking in."

"Yeah – together with a warrant for our arrest no doubt?"

Heading back to his bedsit he called in at the off licence and bought a couple of cans of lager. He needed to relax after the day he'd had. He couldn't help but think about what Gillespie was up to. The videos had been dodgy enough and now it seemed he had another dilemma to contend with. He wished he could find some other way he could make a fast buck or two.

As he turned into the road who should be sitting on his door step but Chandelle, surrounded by luggage.

"What the hell are you doing here?" he said coolly, realising there'd be no getting rid of her once she moved in.

She stood up and greeted him in a pair of black ankle boots and a skirt that resembled a belt. "Babe, I got behind with the rent," she purred, giving him an affectionate squeeze. "You wouldn't see little old me out on the street, would you?"

CHAPTER FORTY-THREE

Alex Spencer had the most piercing blue eyes imaginable, canopied by luxurious long lashes and pale flaxen hair. Donna was mesmerised as he spoke. Much too pretty for a man, she thought, but there again, didn't she find fault in every man she met? It was as if she couldn't help but compare everyone with Johnny. It was a hard habit to break.

"So, Donna," Alex asked. "What are your typing skills like?"

She sat poised at his desk, wearing a navy blue Yves St Laurent suit, her make up simple and her hair worn neatly in a French plait. "To be perfectly honest I'm not a typist as such, although I have managed the odd letter for my husband."

"So you're quite familiar with a computer?" he asked.

"Yes."

The position had specifically stated a Receptionist/Typist and she was certain that she hadn't got the job.

Helping Richard back to recovery had been a tedious job and had taken a lot of patience on her part. He'd only been back at work a month when the doctor had diagnosed angina, which left him with severe depression. His mood swings were intolerable but somehow she had learned to cope. This was her life and she now had to accept it.

She was thirty and doomed to spend the rest of her miserable existence with him. All she knew was she had to get herself back on track; get away from the house, meet people and escape from the formality and boredom of her marriage. She saw the job advertised in the newspaper. What had she to lose? If it meant getting herself out of the rut, then so be it. Unknown to Richard, she applied.

"I don't see the typing presenting a problem," Alex said. "My secretary, Bea, does most of it. He glanced over the details he'd written down. "So, Donna, are there any more questions you'd like to ask?"

"I don't think so," she replied. She'd been offered an exceptionally good salary. It was part time hours between eleven and three o'clock, which suited her fine, as there was no need to let Richard know a thing.

"Well – the position's yours if you're still interested," Alex said.

Bea extended her hand across the desk. "Welcome to the company, Donna."

It was a small publishing company and she was in charge of reception. She quickly got the hang of her duties and enjoyed meeting people. It gave her a sense of wellbeing. At last she was beginning to get her life back in order.

She headed to the bank and opened up her own account. Independence at last.

In the meantime, she began to think more of her family, her mother in particular. There were so many things she missed; little things like helping her in the kitchen, or her mother's insistency on giving thanks for the meal on the table, the wonderful Christmases as a child, or the smell of lavender her mother kept in small bunches around the house.

Oh dear God, would she ever see then again?

Had her mother given birth to a boy or a girl? Would

Kitty Baker still own the post office? So many questions spun in her head.

Still time didn't heal the fact that she had killed someone. It was a living nightmare that never went away. No matter how many times she tried to convince herself that it wasn't her fault, she always ended up taking the blame. The older she got, the more difficult it became to accept. Maybe if her mother had listened to her when she first complained about Frank, things may have been different.

The only way she could escape the situation was by throwing herself wholeheartedly into her work. Sometimes she would think of Johnny – she couldn't deny the fact that she still had feelings for him, despite everything.

Alex fussed over her whenever he had the opportunity, which was frequent, and she had to admit she found him physically attractive.

"Donna?"

"Yes, Mr Spencer?"

"Please call me Alex."

"Yes, Alex?"

"I know you're about to leave but Bea's took the afternoon off and I need this letter typed – it has to go first class tonight," he said. "Obviously I'll see that the extra time is made up to you."

He was the boss, who was she to argue?

She found out from Bea that he was thirty-eight and divorced with no children. He led a reasonably quiet life on his own.

"Would you care to have dinner with me this evening?" he asked.

"Thank you, Alex, but I really do have to get home."

He smiled politely, "Of course."

He's got ideas.

Haven't all men?

She tried to avoid him whenever possible, but it wasn't always easy when he fluttered in and out of reception.

It wasn't until the firm's Christmas party that a pleasantly inebriated Alex made a pass at her. It was nice to have the attention of a man again. She couldn't remember the last time Richard had shown any real affection towards her. He would only become fussy when he got the urge for sex, which she was relieved wasn't often. Once more it would be lie back and think of England. Luckily, it was all over in seconds.

Under the influence of champagne she found Alex's charm hard to resist and when he invited her to his room, she accepted.

She was riddled with guilt again.

What exactly do you think you're doing? You were unfaithful once before and look where it got you.

Do I care?

He arranged for a bottle of champagne to be sent up to their room and they sat on the edge of the bed and talked for a while. "I think you know how I feel about you, Donna," he said.

"You know I'm married, Alex," she replied.

"Yes. And I won't force you into anything you don't want to do, you know that."

At that moment she wasn't sure what she wanted. She didn't argue when he began to fumble with the zip on her dress. She stood up and let it fall to the ground. And then she lay back on the bed and waited in anticipation. She watched as he threw off his jacket and stumbled out of his trousers down to his striped boxer shorts, socks and shoes. She didn't know whether to burst out laughing or run.

"I'll wear a condom," he said. "It's always best to be on the safe side."

She waited as he took one out of the packet and carefully peeled it onto his erect penis, and before she had time to argue he dived onto the bed.

Get the hell out of there. You know what you're doing is wrong.

He was about to slip inside her when she flew off the bed. "I'm sorry, Alex, I can't go through with this," she said modestly.

Flushed with embarrassment, she gathered her bag and dress and rushed out of the room. Struggling into her clothes in the ladies, she quickly left the building in a state of confusion.

When she arrived home she was still hot and flushed. Richard hadn't yet come home so she decided to write out her notice. First thing tomorrow she would hand it in.

Bea was sorting through the morning post when she arrived next morning. "Are you OK?" she asked.

"Yes I'm fine. Is Alex in his office?"

"Yes," Bea replied. "And where did you two disappear to?"

"I left early," she lied.

She walked through to his office, her cheeks burning with embarrassment. "May I come in, Alex?"

She handed him her resignation.

"Is this what I think it is?" he asked.

She nodded. "I'm sorry but under the circumstances I think it's for the best."

"Are you happy in the work you do here?"

"Yes, of course I am."

He tore up the letter. "Then let's just forget the incident happened. I already have."

She wasn't sure about it. But she agreed to stay on.

A few weeks later she was having breakfast when the phone rang. Richard picked it up.

"Is Donna there?" a voice asked.

"It's for you," he said handing her the phone. "Someone called Theresa."

Hesitating she took the phone from him.

"Hi, Donna. Alex has asked me if you can come in this morning? Bea has rung in sick and he needs an extra pair of hands."

"I'll... um... do my best to get in for nine thirty," she replied in a whisper. "I'm afraid I can't make it any earlier."

"Fine. I'll see you later."

She put down the phone and waited for the fireworks.

"What exactly is going on?" Richard demanded.

She couldn't deny it. In any case it was her business if she wanted to go out to work.

"I have a job," she said.

"That's bloody obvious."

"Don't get yourself worked up, Richard, you'll only make yourself ill."

"How many more little secrets have you got that I should know about?" he stormed.

"I'm not arguing with you."

"For crissake, it isn't as if you need the money."

"This isn't about money, it's about gaining my confidence. About doing something with my life," she threw back.

"There's plenty of things you could do," he said heatedly. "Take up painting or write a book."

"What are you suggesting – that I stay at home and vegetate?"

"This job is taking up far too much of your time," he replied sharply. "I've noticed the house is starting to look a tip. It was your idea to get rid of the daily help."

Is that what he thought, after all the hard work she'd put in? He was becoming obsessed not only with his work but with the home – she couldn't even allow a cushion to be out of place. If it weren't for her job, she thought she would lose her mind.

He said no more on the subject, but she could see that he was far from pleased with the situation.

A week later she decided to call at the doctor's on the way home. "It's Richard," she began. "I can't put up with his mood swings any longer. One minute he's fine, the next he turns on me – he's like a Jekyll and Hyde."

"He's always been an active man as far as I can gather and this has been a shock to his system. I'm sure he doesn't mean to take it out on you intentionally."

He checked Richard's files. "He's fifty, isn't he? Has he given any thought to taking early retirement?"

Retirement. There was that word again? The thought of growing old with Richard was unbearable, especially having to put up with him 24/7.

"No – he's far too busy with his work at the moment," she said. She paused for a moment. "There's something else," she began. "He's begun to act strangely."

"In what way?"

"Well… he's become obsessed with little things around the house, things like an empty tea cup."

"It could be a form of compulsive disorder. It's quite common with stress-related illnesses. I could always have a word with him."

"You won't mention that I came to see you, will you?"

"I'm afraid he'll have to know, Donna. Your husband

is also my patient as well and I cannot break confidentiality rules. Besides, he'll want to know why I'm concerned. Look – what I suggest is that you both come in and see me together."

"Richard would never agree to that," she said, thinking what a waste of time it had been.

"Can I prescribe some tablets for you? It may help you to cope."

She shook her head and left his office. She didn't have a single person to turn to and she didn't know what to do any more. She'd tried to leave him once before and now it was impossible.

When she arrived home, Richard was pacing the floor anxiously. "You're late," he said, checking his watch.

Memories of her father's manner sprung to mind. "I had to stop by and get some groceries," she said.

"I've just made some tea. Want some?"

"Yes. Thanks."

He handed her a cup. "I've had a meeting with the board this morning," he began. "We're about to expand the company. There's a new IT department opening up in the Midlands. I'll be in charge of training up there – so I shall be putting the house on the market."

"The Midlands?" she repeated.

"Yes – I'll get things moving tomorrow with the estate agents. I'm sure you'll soon have plenty to keep you occupied."

CHAPTER FORTY-FOUR

Chandelle stayed for nine months. What had been a temporary arrangement had somehow snowballed into her being stuck permanently at his bedsit.

Would he ever get rid of her?

Did he want to get rid of her?

The sex between them was electric. It was the one thing he could give her credit for, although he still wished he had his own space.

"Look, babe. That ring is definitely me," she said, glancing thoughtfully in the jeweller's shop window. "After all, we're practically married," she added with a giggle.

Marriage – he shrank at the thought. Women seemed to have this mad idea that just because they were living with someone they had some marital right over them. He quickly dragged her away from the shop and they headed back down the high street. Who should he bump into but Jane? She had a kid with her; a small bundle with dark brown eyes and a mass of dark curly hair protruding from beneath a white fur hat. Was this his kid? He suddenly felt kinda proud.

Jane glared at him and the tall, slim half-cast girl clinging onto his arm. He would never change. There would always be some pretty girl tagging along.

"Hi gorgeous, how about a smile?" he said buoyantly, bending down to touch the child.

Kylie clung onto her mother's skirt and puckered her lips, her eyes wide with fright.

Great! Even his own kid didn't want to know him.

"She's only four and my daughter already has you weighed up," Jane spat.

"Our daughter," he corrected. "You're forgetting she's my kid as well."

"Your child!" Jane said with a snort of disgust. "You were the one who told me to get rid of her."

"So mistakes happen."

"Yes – and apart from Kylie, you're the biggest mistake I ever made."

"Are you saying I can't see her?"

"Read my lips – NEVER."

Chandelle fidgeted awkwardly. "Look – if you guys want to sort things out, I'll catch up with you later, babe."

"There's nothing to sort out," Jane cut in. "I could have demanded child support off you. Know why I didn't? Because I don't want you anywhere near me, or my kid."

"You bitch, Jane."

"Yes – and I wonder who made me that way?" She grabbed hold of Kylie and led her away.

Could she do this, he wondered?

He didn't know. But he was sure gonna find out.

Getting back to the garage there was a note waiting for him from Gillespie: 'Had to slip out, be back in half an hour'.

Take your time, Gillespie – old muggins here will do the work.

He answered a call. Some grizzly old man came on the phone. "You got any more of that champagne stuff, whatever you call it?"

"You liked it, yeah?"

"Crap," he hissed. "It's the only thing that shuts the missus up. Couple of them an' she's out like a light."

"How many are you looking for?"

"Can you do me six bottles at a fiver a piece?"

This man was asking him to drop the price by fifteen quid? He could see Ronnie agreeing to that.

Johnny decided he could take the order and face the consequences or let Gillespie deal with it himself.

He took the chance.

"I'll have it with you later this afternoon," he told the man.

He put down the phone, deciding Gillespie would just have to be thankful for small mercies.

"Hi, Johnny, I thought I'd drop in and surprise you." So spoke the blonde who had just wandered in, turned the sign on the door to 'closed' and was now peeling off her sweater.

"Jeezus! Chelsea," he said glancing up. She was tall with fair skin,a contrast to Chandelle's more exotic features. Both of them kept him happy beneath the sheets.

Both of them were wearing him out.

Chelsea never wore a bra and her magnificent breasts sprang out in front of him.

"Gillespie's gonna be back any minute," he mumbled.

"Maybe he'd like to join in the fun," she purred.

Within seconds she was clawing at his jeans and they stumbled through to the back room. "Hang on," he said, attempting to remove some boxes from a filthy, threadbare chaise longue that Gillespie had deemed unfit for auction. She hardly gave him a chance.

"You're something else," he mumbled.

"Tell me about it," she rasped, hoisting up her skirt and straddling him. She was the only woman he knew who carried on a conversation while she was having sex, the dirtier the better.

"Ummmmm," she purred sweetly, jigging up and

down on top of him. "You know Johnny, you are incredible," she panted. "Maybe we should get together more often. Purely for sex, naturally."

"Naturally."

Grabbing hold of her arse he thrust deeply into her until her screams filled the office.

He came a few seconds later, just as Gillespie returned.

"Johnny... Johnny, my son - are you there?"

Chelsea burst into giggles."

"Ssssh!" Johnny said, swiftly zipping up his jeans.

"Is bossy man going to be cross?" she whispered.

"I'm glad you find it amusing," he hissed back, raking his hand through his hair. "Make out you're interested in some booze, OK?" he suggested.

"If you think I'm crazy enough to get involved in any of Gillespie's illegal transactions, think again," she hissed.

Straightening her skirt, she walked through to Gillespie, who was momentarily stunned into silence. "I hope you don't mind but I borrowed Johnny for five minutes," she smiled.

Sticking her magnificent breasts in his face she bent to pick up her sweater and then walked to the door and paused. "Oh... I almost forgot," she said, turning the sign around and blowing him a kiss. "Chow."

Gillespie, still speechless, watched her leave before gathering his senses to speak. "Have you been using my office as a knocking shop?" he grunted. "They should have nick named you Ricci the Ram - you certainly have the constitution of one. How you do it, I'll never know."

Quite frankly, neither did he.

"By the way, I sold six bottles of that crap you call champagne," he said.

"I told you we were on to a winner," Gillespie beamed.

Johnny braced himself. "I sold it for five quid a bottle, you'll be happy to know."

"You sold my best champagne for five nicker?" Gillespie exploded.

"Come off it, Ronnie. It ain't fit for cleaning the lavatory with and you know it."

"Are you telling me how to run my business?" he grumbled. "I'll have you know I was in this game when you were still wet behind the ears."

"I'm just suggesting you get rid of this stuff and work your way upmarket – speculate to accumulate as you're always tellin' me."

Gillespie sucked on his cigar. "I didn't tell you to give the stuff away. When I'm bankrupt I've only you to blame!"

Johnny gave up. Why did he bother? It wasn't as if he was going to make anything out of it.

Chandelle was waiting when he got back to his apartment. He hoped she hadn't got any ideas. He couldn't take much more; he'd end up a physical wreck.

"I hope you don't mind, babe," she began. "But I'm going to Jamaica for six weeks – my father's folks are paying my fare and I'm really looking forward to it."

"That's OK," he shrugged, trying to sound disappointed.

"I promise I'll make it up to you when I get back."

"I dare say you will."

He couldn't believe his luck – the place to himself again. He'd even help her pack.

As soon as Chandelle had sailed off to Jamaica he wasted little time getting it together with Chelsea. She kept him busy and with Chandelle safely out of the country it was sex all the way. The one good thing about Chelsea was she didn't hang around or give him the third degree. Their relationship was purely casual, although he had to admit there was some kind of spark between them.

"When's your girlfriend back?" she asked, lying naked across his bed.

"I keep tellin' you, she's not my girlfriend," he said. "We just happen to share this place together."

"Have you slept with her?"

"Nah, course not."

"How many times?"

"OK – maybe a couple."

"You're so full of bullshit, Johnny," she said as they shared a joint. "What's she like? Come on – marks out of ten?"

He shrugged. "I dunno – maybe seven."

"I think the three of us should get together and have a bed-warming party when she arrives back," she said suggestively.

"You're unbelievable."

"Isn't that what you adore about me?" she teased, grabbing the joint off him and taking a hefty drag.

"Sure. I guess that's why we're so compatible together."

Five weeks later he realised Chandelle would soon be home. He decided to give it to her straight – tell her he needed the space, besides which he was getting along fine with Chelsea.

He was ready to face her when he received a postcard.

Hi babe.

I 'm lovin it ere, so I've

decided to stay a while – my roots I guess.

Hope you won't be too disappointed
Lots of luv. Chan. XXX
Disappointed? He was over the moon.

★★★

"I'm getting married," Chris announced, busy doing an oil change on a car. "The thing is, I'd like you to be best man."

"Married?" Johnny let out a snort of laughter. "An' you want me as best man?" He was not exactly thrilled by the idea.

"I think it kind of appropriate, since we're best mates."

"How about this brother of yours – shouldn't you be askin' him?" Johnny suggested.

"Steve? Nah - he's somewhere up north. We haven't seen him in months."

"Look... I'm kinda crap at speeches," Johnny said trying to wriggle out of it.

"It's simple. You just make it up as you go along – like how we're close mates... and things we've done together... " he trailed off. "On second thoughts maybe not. You could always mention the bridesmaids – and before you say anything they're Angie's sisters. One's eight and the other is spoken for."

"I'm hardly gonna get involved with the sister of my mates wife, am I?"

He could just imagine if Angie caught him cheating with her beloved sisters.

"When is this big day?" he asked.

"The eighteenth of September."

"I'll make a note in my diary," he jibed.

"Maybe I'll do the same for you one day?" Chris said half jokingly.

"Yeah – like when I'm seventy."

"Do you ever see anything of that classy bird from London?" Chris asked.

"Nah - she went arsy on me. Accused me of nicking her painting."

Even now he still thought about Donna. Would he ever forget her?

He hung around while Chris finished tinkering with the engine. "You were keen on law, weren't you?" he asked.

"Once. Why?"

"Remember that bird – Jane?"

"The one who got pregnant?"

"Yeah – well… I'm the father."

"Surprise, surprise! And there was me thinking the tooth fairy was responsible."

Johnny ignored his witty remark. She's tellin' me I can't see my kid."

"Are you paying her child support?"

"Nah -she refuses it."

Chris slammed down the bonnet. "Then she's got you over a barrel, mate. She could decide to take you to court, and it's your word against hers who the kid's father is. Unless you go for a blood test."

He couldn't see Jane allowing that.

"Maybe you should start being nice to her?" Chris suggested, grabbing a rag and wiping his greasy hands.

"Be nice to that bitch – are you kidding? I'd sooner stick pins in my eyes."

CHAPTER FORTY-FIVE

Within six months they had moved to Warwickshire. The rolling countryside was the most beautiful she had ever seen. It brought back memories of Norfolk. She tried to put the bad things out of her mind. But all she could remember were Frank and her father.

Her lifestyle changed dramatically from the one she was used to in London, and although she enjoyed the tranquillity she still missed the hustle and bustle of the big city.

Keeping herself busy, she began to unpack some boxes and attempted to get the place in reasonable living order. It was a detached house in need of renovating, which she and Richard had fallen in love with the moment they had set eyes on it. There was a study and living room with a large patio window, which overlooked fields and three large bedrooms on the first floor. She enjoyed the task of choosing curtains and carpets and arranging pictures and furniture.

In the meantime, Richard had hired builders and they were busy drawing up plans for an extension to include a games room and a shower unit on the ground floor.

Things had looked up between them since they had moved. They actually sat down and discussed things together without the arguments.

New house, new start.

"Richard, can I have a puppy?" she asked. "It would be ideal in the fields and it would be company while you're at work."

"No," he objected. "A dog will tie us down. And I don't want animals in the house."

So that was the end of that bright idea.

Things got boisterous when the builders arrived. One had muscles and brown curly hair and a contagious smile. "You're certainly gonna find it quiet around these parts after the Smoke, sweetheart," he said, eyeing her up.

The other builder sipped his tea and said, "Is that really your husband, darlin? He looks more like your father."

They continued their work and carried on hammering away, whistling cheerfully to a transistor radio they'd brought with them. She had to admit she enjoyed their company, especially the one called Rob.

"Know where your gas mains are, sweetheart?" he asked.

She pointed it out and watched him bend down, revealing a builder's bum. She didn't know why but she suddenly felt extremely horny.

"You should have been a model," he said. She found out he was married with three children and lived a few miles out of Stratford. He put down his tools for a moment and offered her a cigarette. "So how come you moved here?" he asked.

"My husband's work," she replied, refusing the cigarette. "He's director of an IT company."

"It must get lonely for you, here on your own."

Watch yourself – Remember you're married.

"I cope," she said. "I have plenty of things to keep me busy." She felt herself blush and turned away, walking back to the kitchen.

At lunchtime she made them tea and brought out some chocolate brownies she'd made.

"Ever played pontoon?" Rob asked, busy shuffling a pack of cards. "Here- I'll teach you."

He was flirting with her and she knew it. But she enjoyed the attention.

They were laughing and joking when Richard walked in. She could tell by his face that he wasn't happy. He called them to one side and inspected their work. A few minutes later he stormed into the kitchen. "What in hell's name are you playing at?" he snapped.

"What now, Richard?" she said wearily.

"You know very well what!" he spat.

"It was nothing – I just made them tea and… "

"They're working for me. You're my wife. At least try to show some self-respect."

Here we go again. And I was foolish to think things would be different.

"I was being sociable. Is there a crime in that?"

"This is your trouble, Donna, you're too friendly and men get the wrong idea."

"Oh for God's sake Richard, I've heard enough of this nonsense."

The arguments had resumed and once more things were back to normal. She tried her best to stay out of their way. Anything to keep the peace.

Once they had finished the job and left, she found the silence unbearable. She went into Stratford, browsed around the shops and bought new bed linen and towels. On her way home she decided to drop in Richard's office and surprise him with a meal out.

The receptionist glanced up at her with a flustered expression. "Richard left about half an hour ago with Hilary," she told her. "She had her car in for service, so he gave her a lift."

How very convenient. She stormed back to her car and drove home in outrage. Good old Richard, she thought. He could do exactly what he pleased but if she tried it there'd be hell to pay.

He eventually arrived home later that evening. "Had a good day?" she asked.

"I had some unfinished business to attend to," he said, throwing down his briefcase and taking off his jacket.

I bet you did.

"Is dinner going to be long?" he asked. "I've got some paperwork to deal with. I need to get started."

"I didn't get anything. I thought maybe… "

"For crissake I've been at work all day!" he exploded, "And now I come home and find there's nothing to eat."

"Did Hilary get home all right?" she cut in casually.

"What?"

"I called in your office – I was going to suggest we ate out."

"Oh Christ!" he muttered.

She wasn't sure if he said it because he was sorry or because he'd been caught out.

He turned to her. "Look – if you want to eat out then we'll grab something at the White Swan."

"What about your work?"

"It can wait."

She didn't know what was happening in their relationship any more and worst of all, she didn't really care.

In the weeks that followed she found herself thinking more of her family. She wanted desperately to contact them but she just didn't know how. She began to compose a letter:

Dear Mother,

This is Donna, your prodigal daughter. I hope all the family are keeping well...

She tore it up. Why bother? Her mother had reading difficulties. And if it got into her father's hands who knows what might happen? There was always the possibility of paying them a visit. That would surprise the village, rolling up and telling them exactly what she thought.

Remember me? I'm the woman your wonderful Frank tried to rape. Yes I did kill him in self-defence and the bastard deserved all he got.

She gave a deep sign. The family probably weren't even in the village any more. The cold reality was, she'd probably never see them again.

PART 3

CHAPTER FORTY-SIX

Birmingham– 28 July 2003

At last things were beginning to look up. Johnny had quit his bedsit and moved into an apartment. Gillespie was about to open up new premises he'd bought with some money he'd come into. Johnny didn't bother to ask how or why, but he figured he was now entitled to a share in the business– at least a sixty/forty arrangement.

He'd been meaning to look Rose up and now he was settled he decided he'd pay her a visit. It was the least he could do after all she'd done for him. But first he was taking his daughter out for her birthday. Eleven years old today. Jeez! Where had the time gone?

Jane had eventually agreed for him to see her on birthdays and Christmas, but only just.

As he pulled up outside her house, he was wary of what to expect. She opened the door to him with her usual sour face, greeting him with as much enthusiasm as you would a dose of the clap.

"Is she ready?" he asked.

"Don't think for one moment you're making a habit of this," she said frostily.

An excited Kylie came running towards him. She wore jeans and a Spice Girls T-shirt, her dark curly hair tied in a ponytail.

"Uncle Johnny," she squealed.

"Hi angel. How's my birthday girl?" he said, giving her a generous hug.

Jane didn't appreciate how well they got on. "I want her back by five," she said firmly. "And please don't give her sweets and ice cream."

She was pregnant again. She'd put on a considerable amount of weight and looked a lot older than her twenty-seven years. It had taken him a lot of patience and hard work to persuade her to let him see his daughter. And now he was going to make up for all those lost years.

"So what d' you fancy doing?" he asked as she climbed into the car.

She shrugged and rolled her large brown eyes. "Could we go and see some animals?" she asked.

"Animals?" he said, racking his brain. He could only think of the Safari Park and that was miles away.

"Can we, Uncle Johnny? Please?"

He started up the car, a flash BMW that Gillespie had put up for sale at fourteen grand and which he had made believe needed to go into the garage to have the brakes adjusted.

"So how's school?"

"OK, I guess."

"Got any boyfriends?" he teased.

She shook her ponytail. "Boys are pretty stupid."

"Is that so?" he said with an amused smile.

They breezed through Kidderminster and reached the park. He paid the attendant. All seemed to be going well until they got to the monkeys.

"Oh look, Uncle Johnny!" Kylie screamed excitedly, "they're jumping on the car and one's pulling the wiper."

"Scram!" he yelled, trying to frighten them off. "Don't these people know how to control their animals?"

"Look – there's another one doing a pee."

"Filthy bastard!" he spat. The words were out before he realised.

Kylie let out a squeal of laughter. "Oh, Uncle Johnny, you're so funny. I wish my dad was cool like you."

The word cut like a knife. How long did he have to put up with this uncle crap?

Coming out of the park there was a traffic jam trailing a least a mile long.

"Uncle Johnny, I'm hungry."

"Your mom will have tea ready when we get back," he said, glancing at the time.

"Today has been really cool, can we do it again? Next time I can bring some bananas for the monkeys."

"You'll have to try an' persuade your mom," he said with a wink.

She was silent for a moment. "Uncle Johnny," she began. "I know you're not really my uncle."

"Yeah?" he quizzed. "So who d' you think I am?"

She shrugged. "Maybe an old friend of mom's, I guess?"

"I'm your dad, sweetheart – your real dad."

She sat puzzled for a moment. "So how come you never married Jane, then?"

Johnny shrugged. "I guess sometimes people find they're not really suited for one another."

"But they still make babies?"

Time to change the subject. "So, what other groups d' you like besides the Spice Girls?"

"Take That – they're really cool."

It was almost six when they arrived back.

"She gave him a kiss on the cheek, whispering, "Thanks for my birthday treat, dad."

Dad! She called him dad.

"Bye angel," he said with a wink.

An anxious Jane was waiting. "I thought I told you five o'clock," she crowed.

"So we got held up in traffic," he yelled from the car. He may as well have been talking to himself for all the notice she took.

She bungled the child into the house and slammed the door.

"Love you too," he mumbled.

On his way back he called to see Rose.

"Well, this is a surprise," she said, elated to see him.

"I was passing so I thought I'd slip in," he said, walking into the living room.

Rose gave him the third degree. "Why did you suddenly disappear, leaving just a note?" she asked crossly.

"I figured you've done enough for me," he replied, settling into an armchair. He took the money from his pocket and handed it to her. "And I guess I owe you."

She glanced at the money. "What on earth is this for?"

He shrugged. "It's just to say thanks."

She handed the money back. "I don't expect any money from you," she said aggressively. "And I gave you that money for your birthday."

"How are you managing here on your own?" he asked, glancing around the place and thinking it was time she treated herself to some new stuff.

"I've my state pension and my widow's pension. I don't need charity, Johnny, if that's what this is about?"

"It's not about charity, Rose. It's about paying you back for what you did for me."

"What are family for if they can't help one another?" She glanced at him critically. "I don't suppose you've got in touch with your mother?"

He didn't believe he was hearing this and went to stand up.

"Sit down," she said sternly. "I'll go and put the kettle on." She came back with a plateful of custard creams and poured the tea. "By the way, your sister Catherine's been asking about you."

"Catherine? What did she want?"

"She asked if I knew were you were. I told her it was some while back since I'd last seen you and that you didn't leave a forwarding address."

"She's in England?"

"She moved back here two years ago. Her marriage broke up – a terrible shock. They were such a lovely couple. Your mother's remarried, you know?"

"Really?" he replied flatly. He couldn't care less what she'd done. Had she ever thought once about him - where he was, or what trouble he may be in?

"Yes. He's a nice man, from Dublin I believe. Just shows you're never too old."

Johnny bit into his biscuit. He felt sorry for the bloke. What a dumb prick, whoever he was.

"Would you like to stay for dinner – I've made some of your favourite ravioli?"

He quickly declined the offer.

"Did Catherine leave an address?" he asked.

"Yes. But it was only temporary until she found something more suitable. I haven't heard from her since."

Before he left he gave her his address. "In case you

should see Catherine again," he said. He tried once more to talk her into having the money but she flatly refused.

"And don't leave it so long next time you decide to drop in," she cried.

★ ★ ★

"Well – what do you think?" Gillespie stood back proudly, cigar in hand, admiring his new premises – the business bought lock, stock and barrel for an attractive price, an offer he could hardly refuse. Red, white and blue flags were flying high around the forecourt, along with a bevy of expensive cars.

"Yeah - very nice," Johnny replied without enthusiasm. Maybe now was a good time to ask him for an equal share in the company? After all, he didn't intend being Gillespie's lackey all his life.

"So... how about considering me as a partner?" he suggested.

"Now, my son, there's no need to get over-ambitious," Gillespie said evasively. "We've got to make sure it's a profitable business first."

"Over ambitious? Some hopes of that." He was the skivvy, while Gillespie was raking in all the profit.

"Don't forget who picked you up when you hadn't got two pennies to rub together," Gillespie prompted.

"Yeah – so you keep reminding me," Johnny retorted.

Gillespie had insisted on keeping the old telephone number. "Changing numbers only makes people suspect you're running a dodgy business," he stressed.

Some joke - the whole business was corrupt. Although keeping the old number wasn't such a bad idea. He still had this crazy idea that maybe one day Donna might pick up the phone and ring him? As if she gave a toss about him. She probably wouldn't even remember his name.

Gillespie checked over the cars. "Where's the BMW?" he asked.

"It's still in for repair."

"Repair? I thought it was only the brakes that needed adjusting?"

"They found an oil leak," Johnny lied, thinking Gillespie wouldn't appreciate the fact that it had been vandalised by a load of monkeys. And now he'd ended up having to fork out for new wipers and the scratches to be removed.

"Get on to them and chase it up," Gillespie ordered with a wave of his cigar. "They're pulling a fast one – you can't trust anyone these days, there's crooks everywhere you turn."

He wasn't kiddin.

"And while you're at it, give these cars a hose down," he instructed. "We want them sparkling clean if we're going to attract custom."

"What's wrong with you doin' it?" Johnny said, pissed off with being ordered about.

"I've got a busy schedule ahead of me, son," Gillespie said. "Oh, and when you've got a minute, chase up that security firm. I'm still waiting for a quote."

"Anything else you'd like me to do?" Johnny said sarcastically. "Maybe stick a broom up my arse and sweep the floor as I go along?"

"I'll ignore that remark," Gillespie said, eager to dash off. "I'm just slipping out for five minutes. I'm sure you can take care of things?"

"Don't I always?"

Johnny was half way through hosing down when a girl

in a bright pink leotard and leggings came dashing up to him.

"My car's broken down – can you help?" she said. He found her vaguely attractive with her dark curly cropped hair, an elfin face and hazel eyes. She was five foot three, superbly toned with a flat chest.

"We don't deal with repairs here, darlin," he said. "There's a garage just up the road."

"I have to take a class in fifteen minutes," she said, checking her Armani watch.

"What's the problem?" he asked.

"It just cut out on me."

"Where is it?"

She led him down to the road, where the car was parked and he jumped in and had a quick look. "You flooded the engine," he said.

"It wouldn't start so I used the choke."

"It wouldn't start because your spark plugs need changing."

"I really do appreciate this," she said. She glanced at his finger. "Are you married?"

"Nah. I don't believe in self affliction."

She smiled, thinking he was joking. "How much do I owe you?" she asked.

"Ah – forget it."

Jumping into her car she leaned out the window. "Maybe I could treat you to a meal sometime?"

"Sure," he said. "What's your name?"

"Michelle – Michelle Phelan."

CHAPTER FORTY-SEVEN

For Donna, time had neither healed nor eased the memories of what she had done. More and more she began to think of her family. Suppose they were ill – or worse, suppose they were dead?

Day after day, week after week, she went over the situation in her head. She hadn't stabbed Frank. If he hadn't taken a lunge at her he might still have been alive. And who was to say that he hadn't left the house and died before anyone had had the chance to speak to him? After all, Tony had never mentioned her name.

She would never know – unless she took a trip over there.

She thought long and hard about it. Next morning her mind was made up.

"Richard," she began over breakfast, "I'm going out and I may not be back until late. I've prepared your dinner you only have to warm it up."

"Out where?" he demanded.

"I thought I'd try and find..."

"You haven't time to go out gallivanting," he cut in heatedly. "There's things that need to be done in the house."

"I've spent my life looking after you and the bloody home," she snapped, jumping up from the table.

"And I've done my upmost to provide you with all of this – you ungrateful swine."

"Bastard!" she hissed under her breath.

As soon as he left for work, she got herself ready. Collecting a few things she threw them into the car along with a map. She only hoped she was doing the right thing. God knows why she wanted to see her father. Maybe just to tell him what an arsehole he was.

It suddenly occurred to her that they could reopen the case. If so, she would get the best solicitor there was. One way or another she was determined to clear her name.

By eleven o'clock she had reached Bury St Edmunds. After checking the map she drove steadily on. Her plan was to go to the post office and see Kitty Baker, if anyone knew anything she would.

As she reached the village, she hardly recognised it. The stores and post office had disappeared, replaced by a supermarket. Even the family butchers had gone. There was now a take-away with a bunch of teenagers on skateboards hanging around outside. Further down the lane a row of cottages had been demolished, and in their place stood a block of modern flats. So much for making a grand entrance, she thought.

Her heart leapt in her mouth as she spotted the small council house standing back off the road. Pulling up, she turned off the engine.

Maybe her parents weren't there anymore? Maybe she'd made a mistake coming back?

After sitting there for a while she finally plucked up courage and got out of the car. Walking up the path, she paused with apprehension and took a deep breath before knocking on the door. A few seconds later a woman with grey hair and strained expression peered at her.

"Mother?" Donna said softly.

Doris Layton stared at her daughter as if she'd seen a ghost. At the best, she imagined her daughter roped into prostitution and drugs. At the worst, she imagined her dead.

"Mother, it's me – Donna," she said, shocked to see how old Doris looked.

"Dolly?" Doris muttered through thin purple lips.

Half laughing, half crying, Donna flung her arms around Doris. "It's so good to see you, mother. So many times I've wished I could've picked up the phone and rung you."

Doris wiped the tears and after the initial shock of seeing her daughter quickly regained her composure. "If only you knew the worry you've caused me an' your farther."

"I'm so sorry, mother."

Following Doris through to the small kitchen, Donna's heart sank the minute she entered. This was where the nightmare had begun – right here in this kitchen.

"We'd given you up for dead we had. Prayed to the Lord that you'd cum home... I've never stopped prayin'."

The logs were piled at the side of the fireplace and everything looked clean and tidy, just as it always had. "Where's father?" Donna asked.

"He ain't bin well, he's bin bedridden for some time," Doris said, filling the kettle. "You should make your peace with 'im Dolly. If anythin' were to happen you'd never forgive yourself."

Donna suddenly felt guilty; after all, he was still her father. "How are you coping without him?" she asked, glancing at her mother's wrinkled hands.

"Tom's bin good. He's still at home you know. Thought maybe he'd meet a nice girl an' marry," Doris said handing her a cup of tea. She sat down and glanced at her daughter. "Why did you do it, Dolly?"

"I was frightened, mother."

Donna paused, taking a sip of tea and braced herself

for her mother's reaction. As Doris never mentioned anything regarding Frank, Donna smiled and said, "So – do I have a new brother or sister?"

"I lost it. It just weren't to be. Still – less of me," Doris said, forcing a brittle smile. "So whart you bin doin' with yourself – are yer married?"

"Yes."

"An' how many grandchildren have I got?"

Donna shook her head. "I have no children."

"No children!" Doris said in disbelief. "Children keep a marriage together."

Try telling Richard that.

Donna smiled and changed the subject. "So much has changed around here mother. I didn't recognise a soul."

"The youngsters have all moved on – nothin' much for 'em 'ere."

"What about Kitty Baker? I noticed her shop had gone."

"She's still around, so is Betty."

The local gossipmongers, Donna thought. Pity they hadn't seen her drive through the village. That would have given them plenty to talk about.

"So how's Sarah?"

"She's got a job in Birmingham. Bin there some time. Had the phone put in for me before she left."

"I must have her number before I leave," Donna said.

As Doris hadn't mentioned anything, Donna decided to do her own investigating.

"What happened about Frank?"

"Frank? He died you know – poor soul."

"Yes, so I heard."

"Have a scone," her mother said pushing the plate under her nose. "I only made 'em this mornin."

For the moment Donna let it rest and went up to see her father. She heard him coughing. The door was ajar so she went in. She hardly recognised the frail old man as he lay in bed ashen and wasted looking.

"Sarah?" he murmured weakly through glazed eyes.

"It's Dolly, father."

"Dolly?"

She sat at his bedside and held his frail hand.

"I'm so sorry father," she said trying to control the tremor in her voice. "Can you forgive me?"

His thin bony hand clasped hers. "I'm not long for this life, lass."

"Don't talk like that," she said her vision blurred with tears.

"Don't think I haven't blamed myself for what happened," he murmured. "I only did what I thought best for you."

"Father, you mustn't blame yourself."

He gave her hand a squeeze, fighting to catch his breath. "I prayed you'd come home, that I could see you well and happy – now I can go to my grave in peace."

She left him to rest and went back down stairs. Tom had come back from shopping and was putting the groceries away. Doris turned to him excitedly. "You know who this is?"

He glanced up briefly. "Should I?"

"It's your sister, Dolly."

"I don't know any Dolly."

"Of course you do."

"Hello Tom," Donna said extending her hand towards him.

He ignored it and carried on putting the shopping

away. There was no sign of brotherly love or 'nice to see you, sis'.

"You've got a nerve to show your face," he muttered belligerently.

"Now Tom, I won't have any of this unpleasantness," Doris cut in sharply. "She's your sister no matter whart."

He gave a snort turning towards Donna. "Don't kid yourself for one moment that all the worry of what you did hasn't contributed towards father's illness," he hissed.

"What a spiteful and malicious accusation to make," Donna snapped back. "Unless you know the full circumstances of what happened, then keep your snide remarks to yourself."

"Oh I know the circumstances full well."

Doris flew to her daughter's defence. "Stop this at once, Tom," she said sharply.

Donna jumped to her feet. "I think it best if I go, mother," she said, beginning to wish she'd never made the effort.

"You'll do no such thing, Dolly. You'll have somethin' to eat before you rush off."

Somehow Donna managed dinner. Tom remained silent, every so often giving her an impenitent glance. Shortly afterwards she made an excuse that Richard would be expecting her home. Tom's harsh words had hit hard. Maybe she had made a mistake by going.

"Next time you cum bring your husband," Doris said, exchanging phone numbers.

As soon as Donna left, her mother picked up the phone and called Sarah. "You won't believe this," she began elatedly. "Your sister Dolly's alive an' well. She's just bin an' seen us."

CHAPTER FORTY-EIGHT

"So, Michelle, besides pumping iron, what else d' you do?" Johnny asked.

"I'm a nanny – I work as a kindergarten teacher."

"You sure keep in good shape," he said.

"Thanks," she smiled, sipping her iced tea.

They were sitting in a Chinese restaurant, tucking into chicken chow mein, which Michelle had kindly offered to pay for.

She beckoned to the waiter, an Oriental man in a white apron. "Can we have another cold beer and tea with ice please?"

"You use this place often?" Johnny asked.

"Yes – well rather daddy does. They do business together."

"Daddy?" he mocked. "So what business is daddy involved in?"

"He runs a wholesale food chain. They supply to most of the restaurants and outlets."

Just then his mobile went off and Jane's number came up. He swiftly deleted it, but a few minutes later it rang again.

"Hadn't you better answer it?" she said.

"Yeah - excuse me, it's a business call," he said. Walking out to the foyer he hissed down the line, "What d'you want?"

"What have you been telling Kylie?"

"I told her nothing," he answered with equal hostility. "She's a smart kid, she worked it out for herself."

"I forbid you to see her again."

"You can't do that," he snarled back.

"I can do what I damn well like."

"Why don't you get real? I'm her father," he hissed. "I have every right to see my kid."

"Phil's her father. He's brought that child up as if it were his own," she snapped. "You're not fit to be a parent."

"And you are?"

"I don't sleep around."

"You think I'd do it deliberately in front of my daughter?"

"I'm not surprised at anything you're capable of," she snapped sourly.

"You ain't heard the last of this, Jane," he snarled.

"We'll see about that," she replied.

She hung up.

"Damn!" he spat.

He marched back into the restaurant and Michelle glanced at him with suspicion. "Is everything OK?" she asked.

"Yeah, fine," he replied bluntly.

She paid for the meal and they left the restaurant. He drove her home and parked outside her flat. They kissed. And then his hand wandered to her breasts, what little there was of them.

"I… I have to go," she said, jumping out of the car as if she had a ferret up her arse. "I'll give you a call."

"Whatever," he shrugged. He wasn't particularly bothered. She did little to arouse his sexual desires and Jane had put him in the wrong frame of mind.

Next morning he reached the garage and found Gillespie on the phone. "Are you quite certain about this, Charlie?" he said, holding on for a reply. "In that case stick me four hundred nicker down."

"What was all that about?" Johnny asked when he came off the phone.

"Nothing – just some boxing match," he said. "Did you manage to chase up that security company?"

"Yeah, I rang them and left a message on the answering machine but they haven't got back to me."

"I thought companies were desperate for work," Gillespie grumbled. "I can't be messed about with. Get hold of another firm."

"From where?"

"I don't know, maybe Yellow Pages? You're in charge of the miscellaneous side of things."

That was news to him.

"In fact, look up a couple while you're at it, so I can pick the best quote."

Johnny glanced at him suspiciously. "So what's this about a boxing match?"

"One of Charlie's boys is up for it, so I've put some money on him to win."

"What, four hundred quid?"

"It's a certainty. Black Panther has it practically in the bag."

"Is it fixed?"

Gillespie took a deep drag on his cigar. "Let's just say the other bloke's been temporarily dealt with."

"You mean he's been paid off to lose?"

"No – what I mean is Charlie's slipping a couple of tranquillisers in his drink. It's harmless enough."

"An' suppose it backfires?"

"Why should it? They'll just assume he's not up to scratch."

"Suppose they get a doctor to check him over?"

"No, no. You worry too much, my son."

"OK," Johnny said. "In that case stick me fifty quid on this Black Panther."

"That's my boy," Gillespie grinned with a pat on the back. "You won't regret it – I promise you."

Somehow he'd got talked into a second date with Michelle. He didn't feel that much enthusiasm, but she'd shown up at the garage. They drove back to her flat and again he tried his luck.

"I'd rather you didn't," she said, pushing his hand away. Yet again she had rejected him. Either she was a lemon, or she'd never had sex. He chose the latter.

"Are you a virgin?" he asked her outright.

She nodded in silence.

"Hang on - you're twenty-six an' you're telling me you've never had sex?" he said with disbelief.

"I'm sorry, Johnny, but I don't believe in sex before marriage," she said primly.

"You've gotta be kidding!"

"I'm sorry Johnny – it's just that I gave daddy my word."

"Just stop sayin' sorry!" he snapped.

Jeez! He'd heard of close relationships with parents but this was ridiculous.

"There'll be plenty of other times," she smiled, snuggling up to him.

That's what you think, darling. He stood up to leave.

"Where are you going?"

"Look… maybe this was a mistake," he said, trying to let her down lightly.

"Can't we just talk about this?"

"There's nothing to talk about. It's late an' I've gotta go," he said hastily.

"If this is about not having sex, Johnny?"

"It's nothing personal. Look - you're a nice kid. But that's as far as it goes."

He grabbed his chance and rushed for the door. "No hard feelings. Thanks for the meal," he said, making a quick escape.

A few days later, on the evening of the match, Gillespie was in top spirits. "Just wait, my son," he said, rubbing his hands together. "Tomorrow we'll be laughing all the way to the bank."

"I wouldn't count on it," Johnny replied pessimistically.

He followed Gillespie into the club where they were greeted by a voluptuous blonde in a plunging tight fitting dress.

"We're guests of Charlie's," Gillespie said.

She gave them a smile, her eyes lingering on Johnny. He knew a come on when it smacked him in the face. "Cheers darling," he said, giving her the benefit of a wink.

Things were about to warm up when Gillespie whisked him away. "What are you playing at?" he hissed. "We're here for the sport."

"Exactly," Johnny said, following him into the hall. "So why d' you have to go and spoil it, Ronnie?"

The place was packed with supporters and they managed to grab hold of a ringside seat.

"I've got good vibes, I can feel it in my water," Gillespie grinned, rubbing his hands together.

"Yeah, well don't get too excited, Ronnie, we don't want an accident."

The crowd let rip – a mixture of cheers and boos as the Black Panther made his way into the ring draped in a black satin dressing gown and a smug expression on his face. His opponent, a mean looking man built like a brick shithouse, was taken to one side by his coach and given a few tips.

"He doesn't look sedated to me," Johnny muttered.

"Just you wait," Gillespie said confidently.

The bell went for round one and Gillespie cheered on excitedly.

By round two he didn't look so happy. "What's happening, Johnny? What's going on?" he panicked.

"I reckon Charlie got his Valium mixed up with his Purple Hearts," Johnny shouted back.

Gillespie winced as Black Panther hit the ropes and almost came flying out of the ring. "Oh my God – I can't look."

Johnny gave a snort. "He's been taken care of all right."

"It's rigged," Gillespie yelled, his words drowned by the up roar from the crowd.

In a matter of seconds it was all over.

Johnny got up and followed him out. "You've just lost me fifty quid," he complained, "so much for laughing all the way to the bank?"

"Come on, I'm sorting this out with Charlie," Gillespie said, rushing off.

"D' you think that's a wise idea?" Johnny said, rushing hastily after him.

"How else do I get my money back?" Gillespie complained.

Following him down a long narrow corridor they eventually came to a dingy looking changing room where they found a very disgruntled Charlie giving a bruised and battered Black Panther a lecture.

"Charlie – what happened? What about my four hundred nicker?" Gillespie blurted.

"What about your four hundred nicker?" Charlie growled with a crack of his knuckles.

"Well, under the circumstances surely I'm entitled to a refund?"

Charlie got up. He didn't look too pleased.

Johnny grabbed hold of Gillespie. "Maybe we should go?" he suggested, glancing at the pair of them.

Gillespie shook him off. "Now look, Charlie," he said coaxingly. "I know you're upset, which is quite understandable. You've had a nasty shock. But I'm in a rather bad financial predicament."

Charlie smashed his bare fist through a chair with a grunt and Gillespie flew to the door. "Perhaps we can discuss this when you're in a more placid frame of mind," he said. "Come on, Johnny, I think we'd better leave."

That was the first sensible statement Gillespie had come out with. For once Johnny couldn't agree more. He followed Gillespie back along the passage. "I could have gone out tonight an' got pleasantly pissed with that money," he complained.

"Think yourself lucky it's only fifty nicker you've lost."

"Yeah – I feel lucky all right."

One of the attendants came past with a bucket and towel and Johnny grabbed hold of him. "Hey – maybe you can tell me where I can find that blonde? The one in the red dress?"

"Oh – Natalie? She's probably with her husband."

"Husband?"

"Yeah, the big bloke who's just won the fight. Come on, I'll take you to them."

"Umm… it's no problem… I'll catch up with her later," he croaked, making a fast retreat. Maybe she was the lay of the month, but there was no way he intended getting slaughtered just yet.

CHAPTER FORTY-NINE

A squeal of excitement rang down the phone. "I can't believe it Dee… I'd given up the idea of ever seeing you again. I thought maybe… Oh never mind what I thought, this is so exciting."

"Mother says you're working in Birmingham?"

"Yes. I work for an alarm company. I've been there five years now. Where are you?"

"At present I'm living just outside Stratford."

"What happened, Dee? Why didn't you come back?"

"I'll explain when I see you," Donna said, realising Sarah was just a kid when she left home.

"Maybe we could meet up some time?"

"How about lunch tomorrow - I could catch the train into Birmingham?"

"Sounds great. I'll have to check my appointments and call you back. Oh Dee, I can't wait to see you."

"Me neither."

Richard hadn't said much. She'd tried explaining to him about meeting her parents but he pushed it to one side, more concerned with her neglecting her duties.

Driving to the station next day she parked the car and bought a return ticket into Birmingham. It was the first time she'd seen the city. It reminded her of London and she couldn't say she was overjoyed by the experience. Walking up from the station she passed a busker in the underground strumming Lennon and McCartney and threw a fifty pence piece into his case, then heading towards the Odeon she stood and waited. She was ten minutes early and every so often she checked her watch. Excited, she tried to visualise what her sister would look like. All she could remember was a pretty child with golden hair and large blue eyes.But that was almost twenty years ago.

A few minutes later a young woman in a smart navy suit and cravat came towards her. She wasn't quite as tall as Donna. She had blonde hair worn in a French pleat.

"Sarah?"

"Dee?"

They both squealed with delight and hugged one another with tears of joy.

"Wow! You look fabulous," Sarah said.

"You too."

"I wish," Sarah chuckled. "I've only to look at a chip and I gain weight. Talking of which they do a fabulous burger with green peppers, just across the road at the Palisades."

They walked across to the restaurant, settling at a table. "I'll have whatever you're having," Donna said, glancing at the menu.

Sarah rushed off to order. While Donna was waiting she glanced at the couple at the next table. They were laughing and joking and seemed blissfully happy together. Briefly she thought of Johnny. He was probably married with children by now.

You're thinking about him again.

I can't help it.

"Excuse me, is this seat taken?"

She glanced up. A man with a tray hovered at her table.

"Yes. Afraid so," she smiled.

After five minutes Sarah returned. "It took me ages to get served," she complained settling back in her seat. "It usually isn't this packed."

"You use this place often?"

"Yes. I work just around the corner," she said, squeezing a generous amount of relish on her burger. "So you went to see mother and father?" she asked.

"Yes. I was surprised to see how ill father looked."

"He's deteriorated in the last few months – I suppose it's something we all have to face one day. Anyway – let's talk about something cheerful," Sarah smiled. "Come on – what have you been doing with yourself?"

Donna shrugged. "I went to London. Then met a man and got married. How about you? Are you with anyone?"

Sarah took a bite of the burger and shook her head. "Afraid not," she joked, "No one will have me."

She hesitated for a moment before she continued solemnly, "Dee... I waited, thinking that one day you'd come home."

"Sarah. It wasn't that simple, believe me."

Sarah gave a smile. "The main thing is you've come back."

Donna took a sip of coffee. "Did our parents or anyone mention the reason I left?" she asked curiously.

Sarah shook her head. "It was always a taboo subject. I understand something
bad happened because mother and father did a lot of shouting and every time we walked into the village people would stare. I knew they were talking about my family... you know what the villagers are like?"

Yes, she most certainly did.

"Did you ever remember seeing the police at the house?" Donna asked in a casual manner.

"Police?" Sarah laughed. "Good heavens Dee, you were sixteen when you left home – it's hardly a crime." She paused for a second before saying, "It really doesn't concern me, Dee. Whatever happened between you and father is your business."

Donna was in two minds whether to question what the outcome of Frank's death had been, but thought better of it. "What happened to Tony Phillips?" she asked curiously.

"Tony? He married a local girl from the village – Carol somebody or other? I believe they emigrated to New Zealand. Didn't you have a crush on him?"

Donna chuckled softly. "It was more than a crush. We planned to get married. I used to sneak off and meet him at the old barn. Father went berserk when he found out. The rest is history."

Sarah gave her a smile. "Things could have been so much different if you'd married Tony. You could have been some dreary old farmer's wife. Now look at you – happily married and living in style."

Donna forced a smile. "Sarah, you must come and visit me. Maybe next time Richard's away. We can make a day of it."

"Yes. I'd like that."

It was turned three o'clock when she finally arrived home. She made a coffee and began to tidy up and get tea ready.

Richard walked in at five o'clock, threw down his brief case along with some magazines and poured himself a scotch.

"Had a good day?" Donna asked, attempting to be sociable.

"As well as can be expected," he mumbled back.

She hesitated for a moment in two minds whether to

mention she'd had lunch with her sister. He looked as if he had things on his mind so she let it rest. Walking off into the kitchen she spotted one of the magazines with properties in the Algarve and Greece. "Are these holiday brochures?" she shouted through.

"No. I'm thinking more in terms of living there," he shouted back. "It will be our future home."

She walked through to the lounge and stared at him. "Our future home?" she repeated.

"Yes. I've decided to retire at the end of the year and we need to plan our future, Donna."

Retire! That word rears its ugly head again.

"Suppose I don't want to live abroad," she snapped.

"You'll love it once we're out there."

"I doubt that very much. What's wrong with England?"

"The weather for a start," he said bluntly. "I've been advised by my GP that angina is more tolerable in a warmer climate."

"How can you be so darned selfish?" she said, raising her voice. "Have you given any thought to how I might feel?"

Richard stood his ground. "We'll go and have a look at the properties and then you can decide."

There was nothing to decide. She hated the idea. She would never live abroad – never.

CHAPTER FIFTY

Kefalonia was every bit as breathtaking as the brochure had promised. A jewel in the ocean, set against hazy purple mountains and white sand.

"We'll unpack, and then we can take a look around town," Richard said, hanging his clothes neatly in the wardrobe.

"Fine," Donna said, gazing at the view from the balcony.

"Tomorrow we can look at the properties and then we'll take it from there."

Donna remained silent, her thoughts on the home she had left behind.

"I understand how you feel," he said. "It's a big step. But once everything is settled, you won't look back."

Is that what he thought? Her whole life was being turned upside down, but he could only see the situation from his point of view.

"Richard, this is all very well. The place is stunning as a holiday retreat, but I don't particularly want to spend my entire life here."

"When we have our own home, you will feel completely different."

She totally disagreed. She would never settle here.

Later that evening they dined under candlelight at a small taverna. It was a romantic setting with Greek music playing.

A young Greek waiter took their order, his eyes lingering on her. She let her sarong slip from her thigh deliberately. If Richard thought the local men were ogling her, maybe he'd change his mind.

"You would like to try the moussaka?" the waiter said, his eyes engrossed on her thigh. "It is very good." It appeared that either he was oblivious to Richard's presence, or it simply didn't bother him.

Richard was showing signs of annoyance. "Cover your legs up," he hissed, as the waiter walked off. "Remember you're in a foreign country. At least show some morals."

"You'll just have to accept the fact, Richard," she replied, taking a sip of red wine. "Greek men are all hot blooded."

A few minutes later the waiter returned. "Compliments to the beautiful lady," he said, handing her a red rose.

"Shoo! Go away!" Richard hissed, as if to ward off some annoying insect.

Donna waited for the waiter to leave their table. "That was very rude of you," she said. "He was only trying to be polite."

"Must you insist on encouraging them?" he murmured.

She smiled to herself. Two weeks of this and Richard would be only too glad to return to England.

When they got back to the hotel he suggested an early night. For once he had forgotten about work. She knew only too well he was in one of his horny moods. It would be the first time they had made love in weeks and she could only console herself with the fact that it would all be over within seconds.

Next morning they went to view the properties. The first one had panoramic views across the bay, and a swimming pool. The inside was bland and clinically white throughout.

"Well... what do you think?" Richard asked.

"It feels cold and unwelcoming," she said, unimpressed.

They drove to the next property. It was further in land, an old farmhouse in need of restoration. It had a large open fireplace with an attached oven and a flagstone floor and stood in three and a half acres of land with apple and olive trees. Some chickens were pecking at the dried parched grass and a goat grazed nearby.

"It has potential," Richard said.

Donna sighed. Was this to be her future?

Back at the hotel, Richard discussed business over his mobile with Hilary of all people.

"I'm just walking down to the beach," she said.

He continued speaking on the phone, engrossed in conversation, so she slipped out. Strolling along the shore she found a quiet spot and sat on the sand. She thought long and hard about everything. Her life would never be the same again.

Deep in thought, she suddenly realised she was not alone. She glanced up at a swarthy, good-looking man in shorts and sandals. He was bronzed, with raven-black hair and smouldering dark eyes.

"I am Carlos," he said, in broken English. "What is your name?"

"Donna."

"Ah... Madonna," he said, squatting down beside her. "You are very beautiful. You are on holiday?"

"Yes – well not exactly," she said, scrolling in the sand. "I may be living here permanently."

"You are married?" he asked, glancing at her wedding ring.

"Yes."

"Happily?"

"Very. Thank you."

"Your husband – he is not with you?"

"He's back at the hotel."

"I have a motorbike – I would like to show you the island."

Yes. I bet you would.

She checked her watch. "I really must be getting back."

"I will walk you to the hotel," he said. Before they parted he took her hand and kissed it. "Bye, my sweet Madonna," he said.

Richard was pacing the hotel room when she returned. "Where have you been? I thought you'd got lost."

"I've been thinking, Richard."

"And?"

"And I really don't want to rush into anything," she said adamantly.

"Why? Is it the properties? The place? What?"

"Everything," she said, hoping he'd change his mind.

"I need an answer, Donna," he said bluntly. "We need to get this settled."

Richard... Pleaaase get off my case.

Later that evening they had dinner at the hotel. Then they went into the bar. It was heaving with holidaymakers, and music was blasting out. She spotted Carlos busy serving cocktails and flirting with every pretty girl in sight.

"Richard, I've come to a decision," she began with hesitation. "If you're so determined to live here then I think you should consider the farmhouse." She realised that no amount of persuasion would make him change his mind.

"I will ring the agent up first thing in the morning," he said keenly. "If we delay any longer we may lose it."

"As you wish," she said with little enthusiasm.

Most of the following morning he spent making calls. She grabbed her bikini, sun creams and personal headset and went down to the hotel swimming pool.

Richard turned up a while later with his binoculars and camcorder. "You're not sitting here all day?" he complained.

She hadn't heard him. She had her headphones plugged in and her eyes closed.

He gave her a sharp prod. "I thought we'd go and explore the island," he said sharply.

"Umm?"

She turned off her headphones and glanced up. "I prefer to stay here. If this is to be our future home, then there's plenty of time to go sight-seeing," she replied.

"You know the sun is ageing."

"Yes. That's why I have my factors."

Richard huffed. "A fine lot of company you are. If you're not cooking yourself in the sun, you're running off to the beach on your own. Maybe it's time I looked for another woman, one who's willing to share my interests," he said, throwing it in her face yet again.

Who's stopping you?

She lay back and adjusted her headphones. Richard stormed off.

She was just enjoying the peace and quiet when Carlos turned up with a rose. It reminded her of Shirley Valentine, and she stifled a giggle.

"I bring you rose because you are my true English rose," he said.

"You are so full of bullshit, Carlos."

"Bullshit? I don't understand?"

"You are an outrageous flirt."

"Ah – flirt!" he laughed, finding it highly amusing.

"It is true the way I feel," he said, patting his chest. "You are married – you break my heart."

They laughed and joked and he taught her some Greek words. "Kalimera. It means good morning. Kalispera – good evening. Yeah?"

They sat and talked for a while and then he took her hand. "Come on," he said, leading her to the pool.

"I can't swim, Carlos."

"I will teach you." He stripped down to his red briefs. She noticed he was extremely well blessed. Grabbing hold of her hand he pulled her in.

"Ooooh Carlos – I'm drowning," she screamed.

"You will be fine. Here, I will help you." He held her round the waist and let her float. "Now –move your legs."

"Like this?"

"Yes, that is good."

They laughed and splashed around in the water. "You are mine," he said, grabbing hold of her and squeezing her playfully. "I want to make mad passionate love to you under the stars."

"Carlos," she giggled. "Pleeease… behave."

But when he brought his lips down on hers, she didn't object.

CHAPTER FIFTY-ONE

"Mr Gillespie?"

Johnny glanced up at the blonde standing by his desk. "He's had to slip out," he replied. "Can I help?"

She appeared very businesslike, carrying a leather folder with paperwork, her hair scraped neatly back. "Mr Gillespie was interested in having a security system installed," she said. "So I'm here with a quote."

"I'm Mr Ricci and it was me who rung your company, Sarah," he said, noting the name on her security badge. "So if you'd care to take a look around the place and give me some idea of the cost."

"Yes, fine," she replied, giving him a lingering smile.

He followed her through, wondering if they were stockings she was wearing.

"Do I know you from somewhere?" he asked.

Sarah shook her head. "I don't think so," she said. No way would she have failed to recognise someone so intensely good looking.

"It's just you remind me of someone," he said. It was probably the blonde hair and piecing blue eyes. Not that she was as beautiful as Donna; nor did she have the same shapely legs. Donna? It was crazy, but he still had the photo they'd had taken together. Would he ever forget her?

While they were checking around the building a message came through on his mobile from Michelle. He quickly glanced at it.

Johnny I need 2 C U. We need 2 talk. Mitch X

He deleted it. Best to ignore her, she'd get the message eventually.

"Have you worked here long?" Sarah asked, making notes.

"Long enough," he replied.

By the time she'd finished, he figured he had her pretty well in the sack. Before she left she slipped him the quote along with her business card and private number. "In case you might be interested?" she said, flirting with her eyes.

He was very interested.

Two days later he gave her a call and they arranged to meet up later that evening. He picked her up and they drove back to his place with a take-away.

"You don't look much of a country bumpkin to me," he smiled, as they tucked into a KFC.

"I can assure you, I am."

"How many of you were there?"

"Me and my three brothers and three sisters."

"Quite a big family."

"Yes," she smiled.

Later, they were in bed when his doorbell rang.

"Just ignore it," she insisted, pulling him back.

"Whoever it is, I'll get shut of 'em," he mumbled.

He slipped out of bed, threw on his jeans, and raked his fingers through his hair.

Who should turn up but Michelle. "I've changed my mind," she said.

"What?" he barked, peering cautiously around the door?

"About having sex with you," she said, "Seeing we're going out together."

Was she missing the point? He'd made it perfectly clear he wanted nothing more to do with her.

"Fine. But can we talk about this some other time?" he said, attempting to close the door on her.

She glanced suspiciously through the gap. "Have you got someone in there?"

"Nah, Course not."

"Then why are you half naked with your flies undone?"

"Because I'm just about to take a shower," he said tiresomely.

"I'll come in and wait."

"No, Michelle. Believe it or not but I'm knackered and I wanna chill out an' get an early night," he said abruptly.

"I'll see you tomorrow, then."

He closed the door with a sigh, figuring out his best way to deal with it.

"Who was that?" Sarah asked casually.

"Ah, just someone trying to sell stuff."

They spent the night together. Next morning Sarah got up, made coffee and scribbled a note:

Bye lover boy. Catch up with you later. X

He read the message and smiled to himself. He was about to leave for work when Kylie rang him.

"Hi dad."

"Hi angel – where are you?"

"I'm just going into assembly," she said. Unknown to Jane, they kept in touch with one another by mobile.

"I've been speaking to this boy – well, I suppose he's a man. He's sixteen and really cool. He hangs around outside the school."

"What d' you mean – he hangs around?" Johnny asked suspiciously.

"Like he sells stuff to the other kids."

Jeezus! "Kylie, listen to me. Keep away from him – d' you understand?"

"Dad!" she said wearily. "I know all about wacky backy. The older kids in fifth year take it, not me."

"Does your mother know about this?"

"No, I don't discuss things like that with her. You're not angry with me, are you?"

"Course not, angel. Look – I'm gonna have to mention this to your mother," he said.

"She won't be there. She's got a hospital appointment."

"So how're you getting in the house?"

"I've been given a key."

Come the evening, he couldn't wait to ring Jane.

"What do you mean... drugs?" she snapped.

"There's this kid outside the school," Johnny told her anxiously.

"How do you know?"

He realised he'd put his foot in it, but she had to be told. "I found out from Kylie."

"I thought I told you to keep away!" she snapped.

"Are you gonna do something about it or not?" he said sharply down the line.

His doorbell began ringing like crazy. "And do you always let her come home to an empty house?" he said angrily, rushing off to answer the door.

"It so happened I had an appointment with the gynaecologist. Not that it's any of your business," Jane said furiously.

Michelle stood at the door, giving him a challenging look. "Are you going to invite me in?" she demanded.

He waved her through and continued his conversation with Jane. "My kid's my business," he snarled.

"I wish you'd stop interfering," Jane said. "I don't need you to tell me how to bring up my daughter."

"Our daughter," he corrected yet again. "So how come you haven't noticed what's going on at the school?"

"How do I know what to believe from you?"

"You can believe what the hell you like," he spat. "But I'm warning you – if I find she's taking any of this crap I'm holding you responsible."

He hung up and Michelle was ready to quiz him. "I thought you weren't married?"

"What?"

"You told me you weren't married – and you have a child."

"So?" he said abruptly. "You don't have to be married to have a kid."

"Are you still seeing the mother?"

"What business is it of yours?" he said bluntly.

"Are you?" she insisted.

"No, does that answer your question?"

"I'm sorry, Johnny – but if we're to have any kind of relationship, then I won't be used or made a fool of."

"What relationship for crissake?" he hissed. "And what the hell are you doin' here anyway?"

"I didn't come to argue."

The next thing, she was ripping off her clothes.

"Wattaya doing?" he yelled.

"You want me, don't you?" she whispered. "So here I am." She lay back expectantly on the bed, raring to go.

CHAPTER FIFTY-TWO

Back in England, Donna was more than pleased to be in familiar surroundings. The holiday had been magical. They had taken a ferry across to mainland Greece and visited Athens. She had been blown away. But all she wanted now was to get back home.

She finished unpacking and gave Sarah a call. Taking a deep sigh, she gave her sister the news.

"Richard's decided he wants to live there permanently," she said flatly.

"Greece!" Sarah exclaimed.

"Yes. He sprung it on me. Sarah, I don't want to go."

"You must be mad. I wouldn't turn an opportunity like that down. When are you thinking of leaving?"

"Richard's put an offer in and it's been accepted."

"Oh Dee – that's wonderful. Surely you're excited now?"

"Nope."

"I bet you won't be saying that once you're settled over there."

"I bet you I will."

"You mean all those red-blooded Greek men couldn't persuade you to stay?" Sarah giggled.

"Especially those Greek men," Donna joked back.

She thought of Carlos with a tinge of guilt. She had kissed him – but it wasn't as if she'd jumped into bed with him. When they had parted he had taken her hand and pledged his undying love for her. Of course, she hadn't believed a word of it. He was charming and romantic but it was no more than a holiday flirtation. "You will divorce your husband and marry me," he had insisted. Hadn't Johnny once said that to her all those years ago on the dance floor?

Oh God, Why did he always have to crop up?

"Dee, I really think you should make arrangements to see mother and father before you leave."

"Yes. I've already thought about it."

"Is the offer of coming to see you still open?"

"Of course. I'll let you know when Richard's next in Greece."

"Oh – by the way, Dee, I've met this man. He's drop dead gorgeous. It's nothing too serious at the moment, but fingers and everything crossed."

In the days that followed, Richard kept things strictly under surveillance. She did her best to fall in with his plans, until he mentioned that they were going to Greece that weekend.

"Do I have to go?" she began.

He shot her a hostile glance. "Of course you do."

"But I told my sister she could come and stay," she said heatedly.

"Your sister?" he raised a sceptical eyebrow, "I thought you'd lost ties with your family?"

"I mentioned it the other day but you were too busy talking about Greece."

"You'll have to cancel it," he said sharply.

"Richard please… It's not as if I'll see her again and I've promised."

"What's more important - me or your sister?"

"Don't be ridiculous. I can't very well put her off."

"You mean you won't," he snarled, straightening his cuffs.

"If you get back early enough the three of us can go

out for lunch?" she suggested doing her best to persuade him.

"Do what the hell you like – you normally do."

She heard him slam the door. Watching a fly caught in a spider's web, she released the insect and let it fly off. She knew only too well the feeling of being trapped. But there'd be no one to come to her rescue. A chill of despair ran through her.

She carried on wrapping a few things placing them in a large container ready for shipping.

At two o'clock she called her mother.

"Sarah tells me you've found a place in Greece," Dolly said.

"Yes. But you know very well I don't want to leave England, mother."

"The good lord works in mysterious ways," Doris said. "Everything happens for a reason."

If that was the case, what was the purpose of her killing Frank? What good had it achieved? Except make her life a misery.

"You, my girl, should have had a family. Children keep a marriage together."

Donna gave a sigh. Already she felt ancient, without her mother rubbing it in. A child would have been nice but it just wasn't to be.

"Are you sure everythin's all right?" Doris asked.

"Yes, fine, mother. I'll call you as soon as something is arranged."

She hung up and carried on packing a few more things. Closing her eyes she prayed that somehow, someway there might just be an answer.

It was early evening when Hilary called. "Has Richard arrived home?" she asked.

"No. Not yet."

"I missed him at the office. It's only to let him know the times of flights to Greece. I suppose you're quite excited, aren't you?"

"Yes - quite," she lied.

"Oh you're such a lucky girl. I'd give my right hand to live there."

How about if you go in my place, Hilary?

But of course - the gods wouldn't be that kind to her.

CHAPTER FIFTY-THREE

Once Michelle got the taste for sex, there was no stopping her. She was eagerly waiting outside Johnny's apartment when he got back from work. In fact she couldn't wait to get him inside.

Afterwards, she lay back with a contented purr. "Daddy wants to meet you," she said.

Too bad, cos I sure don't want to meet daddy.

"I think it's the least you can do, seeing as we're an item."

She was off again with this relationship crap. "Who says we're an item?" he said curtly.

"Please, Johnny. He wants to discuss things with you."

"Like what?"

"I've told him about you and me... and... well, you know, that we've had sex and naturally he wants to meet you."

"Hang on," he began, not liking the sound of things. "Are you tellin' me you told your father?"

"I mentioned it casually. We don't have any secrets, not since mummy died." She smiled demurely at him. "How about if we make it this weekend?" she prompted.

Warning bells were ringing in his head. What the hell had she been telling him? He decided he had to get rid of her - fast.

"I can't make it," he said, swiftly inventing an excuse. "I'm running a car down to London. In fact," he began, checking his watch, "I've gotta make an early start in the morning."

Bungling her out of the door, he gave a sigh of relief. He couldn't fathom her out. She was like some annoying pain that wouldn't go away. He treated her with as much affection as he would a bog brush, yet she still insisted on coming back for more.

Next morning on walking into the office he found there was no sign of Gillespie. Instead, he was greeted by some girl perched on the corner of his deck. She was quite attractive, with red highlighted hair and slender, pale thighs.

"Who are you?" she asked, busy filing her nails.

He looked her over. "I just happen to work here, sweetheart," he said.

"You must be Johnny." She put down the file and slithered off the desk, towards him. "I've heard a lot about you."

"Really?" he said, checking her over.

"Are you really a naughty boy?"

"It depends what you call naughty," he said, playing along.

"A little bird tells me you like to have fun," she whispered, breathing down his neck.

"Maybe," he whispered back in her ear.

He wondered who the hell she was – maybe a customer. But this wasn't exactly how customers behaved. "So what brings you here?" he asked.

"I need some money."

"Whattaya got planned – robbing the safe?" he joked.

"Not quite," she said with an alluring smile. "I'm hoping to tap Uncle Ronnie for a few bob."

"Uncle Ronnie?" he sneered.

"I'm his niece."

His niece! Quickly he changed tactics. Maybe he did

fancy shagging the pants off her, but there was no way he intended getting involved with any of Gillespie's relatives.

"Well?" she whispered, sliding her tongue seductively across her lips.

"Well what?" he murmured back.

"Do you live up to your reputation?"

"Suzie – Jenny – whatever your name is, sweetheart, you'd better find someone else to cream your knickers with."

He thought that would be the end of it. But the next day she was back again, unwilling to take no for an answer. He had no choice but to mention it to Gillespie. "You're gonna have to have a word with your niece, she's got ideas," he said.

"And I suppose you had no part in it?" Gillespie replied in an ironic tone.

"Come on, you know I'm already shacked up with someone."

Gillespie had seen Sarah at the office a couple of times. He'd also caught Michelle there.

"So who's the flavour of the month this time, the blonde or the brunette?" he jibed.

Johnny broke off from polishing one of the cars. "Look, just have a word with her, OK?"

"Yes, yes, all right. Look, I've been thinking," Gillespie began.

"Don't, it's dangerous," Johnny replied. "Last time you came up with something I lost fifty quid."

Gillespie puffed on his cigar. "What if we put on a bit of a spread? You know – wine, cheese and biscuits. Have one of those late opening nights, whatever they call them? I can get Charlie to organise a few bottles of cheap plonk."

"I thought you an' him had fallen out?"

"Charlie – nah – we're thick as thieves."

He wasn't kidding.

"It'd certainly get the punters in," Gillespie said, blowing a cloud of smoke in his direction. "And maybe we could throw in a few sidelines."

Johnny didn't bother to ask what the sidelines were.

Later that evening, Sarah turned up with a pizza and a bottle of red wine. "I thought maybe you could do with some company," she smiled.

"I guess you thought right," he said. He followed her through to the tiny kitchen where she attempted to open the wine. "Have you got a corkscrew?" she asked.

"A what?" he teased.

"Are you ever serious?"

"Not if I can help it. And the answer is no. I don't possess one."

"What about glasses?"

"What d' you think this is – a five star hotel?"

She shook her head with disbelief. "There're only two mugs here, and one of them is chipped," she complained. "You really do need to get yourself sorted, Johnny."

"Hey – I am sorted. I gotta job, a flat and now I've got a sexy girlfriend," he said, coming up behind her and giving her arse a squeeze.

She swung round to face him with a kiss on the lips and then watched him hack away at the cork with a penknife. "I can see you've done this before."

"Comes with practice – so who needs mod cons?"

Michelle tried to call him twice. Each time he ignored it.

They tucked into cheese and tomato pizza, laughed, joked and talked about the latest films on release. He was actually beginning to enjoy her company, and when they climbed into bed she was more than ready to please him. She had a knack with her mouth. In fact it was more than a knack - it was mind-blowing.

And then her mobile rang.

"Hey, leave it," he rasped, pulling her back down towards him.

"I can't – it's my sister."

"So... just call her back later," he insisted.

She pushed him away. "Hi Dee."

Jeez! What was it with women?

Johnny decided to leave them to it. Once they began to rabbit there was no telling when they'd finish. He jumped out of bed and grabbed a cigarette.

Sarah gave a giggle. "He's right here, wandering around the room... and he looks as horny as a rhino."

She beckoned him over. "Say hello to Dee."

Was she kidding? Her sister had just ruined the best blowjob he'd had in years. He walked into the next room and checked his texts.

Johnny must speak 2 U –it's urgent

Call me. Mitch X

He deleted it. Best forgotten.

It was almost twenty minutes later when Sarah finally hung up. "Come here," she said, patting the bed. "I've got a proposition to make... and I think you'll be pleasantly surprised."

He didn't like surprises. They usually turned out to be frigging disasters.

Her eyes lit up with excitement. "How do you fancy a dirty weekend in the country?"

"I thought we were doing just that right here?"

"Yes, but this is special. My sister has invited us over."

"Nah, forget it," he said bluntly.

"Pleasssse."

"Hey, I don't even know your sister," he said. "An' if she's as randy as you, there's no way I can cope with two of you," he joked.

"Dee is married and she'll be deeply offended if you don't come."

He shook his head adamantly. "Then she'll just have to be offended."

"Come on, Johnny, I haven't seen her for years, and this is special."

So what? Neither had he seen his family in years.

"You won't be disappointed," she cooed, tracing her tongue down his chest towards his groin. "I promise."

★ ★ ★

"I'm... er... knockin' a couple of days off this weekend?" Johnny began.

Gillespie was anything but pleased. "The weekends are our busiest day for sales, you know that."

"Believe it or not, Ronnie, I could do with a break," Johnny said firmly. "Is that too much to ask?"

"I suppose some girl's involved?" Gillespie snorted. Not that it was any of his business.

"Not just some girl– it happens to be Sarah."

"What - that classy piece from the alarm company?"

"Right on."

"Oh, very nice," Gillespie replied with a hint of sarcasm. "So while you're out gallivanting I'm up to my neck here."

"Don't stew, Ronnie – it's bad for you."

Half way through the day he had another call from Michelle. This time he answered it. "What's so urgent?" he asked, losing his rag.

"Daddy needs to see you."

"I thought we'd already discussed this?" he said abrasively.

"He needs to talk to you, Johnny. So do I."

"Aren't we doing just that?"

"I can't discuss this over the phone."

"Where are you?" he asked, deciding to get this finished once and for all.

"I'm in Spain at Daddy's villa."

"Spain! So what d' ya want me to do – jump in my jet and fly over there?" he said sarcastically.

"I need to see you as soon as I get back," she stressed.

"I can't make it. I'm going away myself for a few days."

"Who with?"

"Does it matter?"

"Are you being unfaithful, Johnny?"

"What if I am?" he snapped back. She was becoming a constant annoyance.

He slammed the phone down.

She tried calling him back, but he ignored it.

CHAPTER FIFTY-FOUR

"I can't wait to introduce you to Dee," Sarah said excitedly. "You're just going to love her."

"Is that a fact?" he said flatly.

They drove along in an old Ford Fiesta, which Gillespie had bought for a hundred quid from the auctions and kindly offered to lend him. It drove as well as it looked – an old knackerbox. After the BMW incident he'd been lucky to get even this.

"So, this sister of yours – you say she's married?" he asked, making light conversation.

"Dee? Oh yes. Her husband won't be there, though. From what I can gather he's away quite a lot."

"Is she as pretty as you?" he teased.

Sarah blushed. "Actually, she's a lot prettier."

"Then you'd better keep tabs on me," he joked.

Half way through the journey the car seized up. "I knew we should have used mine," Sarah complained.

He opened up the bonnet and checked it out. "We're gonna have to let it cool down for ten minutes," he said, climbing back in.

"So what are we going to do for ten minutes?"

"You mean you've really got no idea?" he said. He reached for the lever and the seat sprung back.

"We really shouldn't – not here," she gasped.

"Is that a complaint?" he muttered, sliding his pants down.

"Only if you stop," she whispered back.

A few minutes later there was a tap on the window and a stony-faced policeman peered through the steamed glass. "Would you mind moving on, sir? This is a public highway and you're committing an offence."

"The car got overheated, so we're kinda waiting for it to cool off," Johnny said, struggling to pull up his trousers.

"From what I can see it's not the only thing that needs to cool down."

As soon as he drove away, they exchanged a burst of giggles. "Young man, you're committing an offence," Johnny mimicked, turning on the ignition. The old Fiesta gave a few splutters and finally fired into action.

Donna put the finishing touches to the meal she had prepared, checking carefully to see if she had missed anything. The table was laid, complete with a bottle of chardonnay, and she'd placed a candle for decoration.

Richard had left for Greece earlier on in the week and was due back sometime Monday. He hadn't been particularly pleased about things when she'd told him that she would probably have left for Norfolk by the time he arrived back.

"Sarah's bringing someone with her, and in any case the train leaves at nine am," she had explained. He probably thought she was making the whole thing up.

Hilary had somehow managed to wangle her way into going with him – not that he needed that much encouragement. She couldn't help but notice there was a spark between them.

The doorbell rang and she quickly ripped off her apron and checked herself in the large hall mirror. Rushing excitedly to answer the door she flung it open.

And there stood Johnny.

Donna couldn't speak. She was in a state of shock.

"Dee – this is Johnny - and Johnny this is Dee," Sarah

announced excitedly. She hardly stopped talking, while they stared at one another in silence.

He had hardly changed, maybe slightly more mature, still with those intense dark eyes and jet-black hair.

If only she could disappear into thin air.

"I'm sorry we're a bit late," Sarah continued, "but we had trouble with the car. I knew we should have come in mine... are you OK, Dee?"

"Um... fine," she managed with a weak smile. "I'll just check the meal." She dashed into the kitchen and pulled the door to, her heart pounding, her hands trembling. What the hell was he doing here, and with her sister of all people? Oh God! How was she going to deal with this?

"Do you need any help?" Sarah said, bursting in on her.

"No, everything is under control."

Donna tried to compose herself. Just get the damned meal served up – make an excuse that you're not well –that you have a headache - just say anything.

She carried the food into the dining room, almost certain they could see her hands trembling.

"Aren't you having any?" Sarah asked.

"No, I have this dreadful migraine suddenly come on."

"Oh, Dee, we can't eat without you... please?"

She put a small portion on her plate and picked at it - all the time aware of his glance.

"Hmmm, this is ready delicious," Sarah remarked, giving Johnny a nudge. "What do you think?"

"Yeah, fine," he managed solemnly.

Donna served up dessert and couldn't wait to escape, disappearing back into the kitchen.

Sarah turned to Johnny. "You're quiet," she said. "You've hardly said two words since we arrived. Dee must think you're very rude."

"Why d' you insist on calling her Dee?" he snapped.

Sarah glanced at him with a confused expression. "I've always called her Dee – what difference does it make?"

She got up and walked into the kitchen and found Donna very quiet and subdued. "Have you taken anything for it?" she asked.

"No, it'll pass."

"I've got some aspirin in my bag. I'll get you one."

"Please Sarah – it doesn't matter."

Sarah gave her a little smile. "Well, what do you think of him?" she asked, brimming with happiness.

"I don't like him," Donna said, trying to put her sister off.

"How can you say that – you don't even know him?"

"I know a bad apple when I see one."

She glanced suspiciously at Donna. "I do believe you're jealous!"

Maybe she was. But she couldn't just stand by and see her sister hurt the way she had been.

Later that evening Sarah tried every trick in the book to get him to bed but he wouldn't budge. How could he when her sister was in the next bedroom? He made an excuse and hung around, checking out videos and making believe he was watching some movie in the hope that by the time he went up she'd have fallen asleep.

No such luck. She was wideawake and waiting expectantly. Reaching immediately for him, she was disappointed to find he was completely deflated. "What's the matter?" she asked.

He slapped her hand away. "I'm tired."

"Tired?" she snorted. "Doing what?"

"Driving, I guess."

She gave a brittle laugh. "We've only done twenty miles, if that."

"Just leave it out, Sarah," he snapped with frustration.

"Fine," she said, equally as hostile. She turned her back and buffed up her pillow. "Good night. I hope you're in a better mood in the morning."

He lay awake, his mind in overdrive. He just had to see Donna. It seemed like hours before she finally dropped off.

Quietly and carefully he edged his way out of bed and tiptoed out of the bedroom.

Donna couldn't sleep no matter how hard she tried. In the next room her sister was in bed with Johnny – her Johnny – which was stupid, because he didn't belong to anyone, least of all her. She was married and he was a free agent; he could do what he liked, but not with her sister – please dear lord – not with her sister.

"We have to talk, Donna," Johnny said, bursting into her bedroom and taking her by surprise.

"Please leave my room," she said sharply.

"Fine. But not before you tell me what's going on."

"It's no concern of yours," she said harshly, although inside she was a dithering wreck. "And you had no right to come here."

"D'you think I planned this?" He came over towards her and sat on the bed. "How was I supposed to know who this Dee from Stratford was?" he said.

She glanced at him, her heart beating erratically. "Please, just leave me alone."

"Is that what you want? We're special together, and you know it."

"We were once, but that was a long time ago," she murmured, trying to sound as if she meant it.

She looked into his dark intense eyes; they still had the same effect on her, and that jet black curly hair that fell in tiny wisps over his forehead.

"Look – If anyone should feel sore it's me," he said. "I'm the one you branded a thief."

"And I rang to apologise. But you never even returned my call."

"What call?"

"I left a message with Gillespie, or whatever his name was?"

That certainly figured.

"I never got any message, otherwise I would have called you back," he said.

"Does it matter now?"

"It matters a lot to me."

"Aren't you forgetting my sister?"

"Donna… " he began, looking intimately into her eyes. "You're the only one I have those feelings for, and I always will."

She felt herself melting under his glance. But how could she ever trust him? He'd used her – and now he was using her sister.

"I've missed you, Donna," he whispered.

Oh God! She was losing control. She tried to push him away. "Johnny… this is wrong… "

He silenced her with a kiss and they fell back onto the bed, her long soft hair fanning the pillow. He'd forgotten just how beautiful she was, how good she felt; the sweet delicate scent of her hair, the smoothness of her skin. "I've missed you, Jeez! I've missed you," he kept repeating, caressing her breasts and sending little shock waves through her body.

She lost all sense of right or wrong. What difference

did it make? In three months' time she would be miles away across the sea and out of his life for good. But right now she needed him as much as he needed her. She groaned with pleasure as he entered her, pulling him deep into her, until it felt as if their souls were on fire. She had only dreamt of this moment, and now she wanted to feel part of him for as long as possible.

Finally they lay in each other's arms. He kissed her sweetly and ran his fingers through her hair. "You're gonna get a divorce," he whispered earnestly.

"Yes," she whispered back, with no intention of doing so. How could she leave Richard? He had a heart condition and it would probably kill him.

She was utterly and hopelessly trapped.

"Richard had a breakdown," she began. "So I did the decent thing and supported him."

"You can't put your life on hold forever, Donna."

"Yes – I know."

She thought of her past and needed someone to share this nightmare with. Who better that Johnny? "I didn't just leave home on account of my father," she began hesitantly. "I had no choice – I killed a man."

He thought she was joking. "Whatcha do? Clobber him with your hockey stick?" he laughed.

"This is no laughing matter, Johnny," she said, desperate for his support. Before she knew it she was blurting out the whole story.

"Jeeez... us!" he said, long and slowly. "Who else knows about this?"

"Most of the villagers have their suspicions. Richard doesn't know. Neither does Sarah. Johnny, promise me you won't mention this to her?"

"Hey, come here," he said, cradling her in his arms.

"You're with me an' nothing's gonna happen, I promise."

She lay in his arms. How could anything that felt so right be so wrong?

"Pack your bags and come back to Birmingham with me," he urged.

"It's not that simple."

The door opened and they both glanced up. There stood Sarah, solemn faced. "What's going on?" she asked, placidly at first, then raising her voice. "I turn my back for five minutes and you've jumped into bed with my sister."

"Sarah, please wait." Donna jumped out of bed and grabbed her dressing gown. "I can explain!"

"You bloody cow!" Sarah hurled at her, storming off down the stairs. "Tom was right. He warned me you were bad and I didn't believe him." She gave a brittle laugh. "How wrong can you be?"

"Sarah – where are you going?" Donna cried, chasing after her.

"Away from both of you," she yelled. "And I never want to hear or see either of you again."

"Please wait until morning. I'll run you back first thing."

Sarah turned on her. "I don't want any favours from you, you heartless bitch!"

"Sarah – please listen – I need to explain."

"Explain what? That you couldn't wait to get him into bed? You're disgusting!"

Johnny slipped on his trousers and came down to the kitchen. "Sarah, we need to talk," he said urgently. "And I should have been honest with you when we first got here."

"Honest – don't make me laugh!" she screamed at him. "You don't know what the word means. You're both as bad as one another."

"Sarah, just listen!" he yelled at her. "Me an' Donna...
we kinda go back sometime."

"Why didn't you tell me you knew her?" she cut in
abruptly.

"Because I didn't know myself until I got here."

She stared at Donna. "Are you telling me you had an
affair with him while you were married?"

"Yes, but... "

"You had some sneaky affair behind your husband's
back?" she screamed. "You don't give a toss about anyone,
do you?"

Donna exchanged glances with Johnny. "We never
intended anyone to get hurt."

Sarah snorted with disgust. "I've never met your
husband, but I feel extremely sorry for him."

"Sometimes these things just happen," Donna said,
trying to ease the situation.

The three of them sat arguing over cups of coffee until
dawn.

"You deserve one another," Sarah snapped jumping up
from the table to call a cab.

"Sarah, please wait," Donna said hastily. "I'll go and
get dressed and I'll run you to the station."

Waiting her opportunity to catch him alone, Sarah
turned on him spitefully. "You fool – do you think for one
moment she'll give all this up for you?"

"Just shut up," he hissed.

She could see she'd touched a raw nerve. "I've known
my sister for just three weeks and already I know what a
scheming little gold digger she is. And what have you got
to offer her? Sweet FA."

"I said shut up," he said, raising his voice.

"Has she told you about Greece?"

"What about Greece?"

"Obviously not," she said, milking the situation. "My dear sister and her husband have bought a properly over there and are moving shortly."

"You're lying."

"If you don't believe me, ask her yourself."

"Ask me what?" Donna said, walking back into the room.

He stood up and confronted her. "Is this true about Greece?"

"Yes."

Why deny it? The odds were against her and Johnny ever being together.

"You can't do this."

"I have no choice."

"Yes you do. Come with me now!"

"I... I can't."

"It's your last chance," he pleaded.

Donna froze into silence as a car drew up outside.

"Oh God! It's my husband," she gasped.

Johnny grabbed hold of her arm. "You're gonna tell him," he insisted. "We'll tell him together."

Sarah stood with her bag. "Well, this should be interesting," she said belligerently.

Richard's expression was that of malice when he walked through the door. "I hate to break up the party," he said, glancing directly at Johnny. Maybe it had only been a photograph, but he never forgot a face.

Donna rushed over to him. "Richard! Sarah and Johnny were just about to leave."

"He's certainly not with me," Sarah said crossly. "And I think my taxi's just arrived." On her way out she extended her hand towards Richard, and said, "Sarah

Layton. I'm sorry we couldn't have met under more preasant circumstances."

A grim silence fell between Donna and the two men. With equal hostility they stared at one another - the scorned lover and the estranged husband. "Get the hell off my property," Richard snarled at him.

One last glance at Donna, "With pleasure," Johnny snarled back.

CHAPTER FIFTY-FIVE

It was dark when he finally woke, with one hell of a hangover. His head was throbbing and he felt he'd gone two rounds with Mike Tyson. On the floor was an empty whisky bottle. He didn't even remember leaving the television on.

It was almost eight o'clock in the evening. He must have freaked out for eight hours. Driving the Fiesta back to his apartment like a maniac, he'd stopped on the way to pick up a bottle of Jack Daniel's, intending to get drunk – very drunk.

He couldn't believe it. Donna had done the dirty on him yet again. She'd had the ideal opportunity to tell her husband, he would have stood by her. But instead, she had to grovel and lie her way out of the situation. He may as well have not been there for all the notice she'd taken of him. He must have been crazy to ever believe she'd leave her husband. She'd be with the old fart until he dropped dead.

For the first time in his life he felt lonely. That was crazy because he could have his pick of any girl he chose; any girl except Donna.

What did it take to forget her?

He was beginning to slip back into a depression again but this time he intended to steer clear of drugs.

He lay back and tried to get a grip on things. Then his mobile rang. He ignored it. He wasn't in the mood to speak to anyone.

A few minutes later it ran again. Switching the

television off he answered it and was about to yell down the line when Kylie came on sobbing.

"Angel... whatsamatta?" he asked, making an attempt to collect his senses and not slur his words.

"Dad, it's Jane and Phil. They've sent me to m-my room," she snivelled.

"Hey, just calm down," he said. "So what's happened?"

"They're so mean. They're refusing to let me go to France with the school. So I swore back, and Phil gave me a slamming." She gave a few more sobs. "All my class are going. It's just not fair."

"How much is this trip?"

"Two hundred pounds. Dad... can you lend it me? I'll pay it all back out of my pocket money."

"Don't worry, sweetheart."

He remembered his own lousy childhood and how he'd been deprived of things. Somehow he had to get her the money. "Leave it with me angel."

"You mean you'll get it for me?"

"I promise. Just be a good kid an' I'll catch up with you later, OK?"

He hung up and closed his eyes for a second. Then the doorbell rang.

Why the hell can't people just leave me alone?

It carried on ringing. He got up and staggered to the door and was greeted by an outraged Michelle.

"I thought you'd give me a ring when you got back," she said haughtily, barging her way into his apartment.

"Michelle, just give it a rest," he said, nursing his head.

She glanced at the empty whiskey bottle on the floor. "This place is disgusting," she said. "Do you get off living in a pig sty?"

He held his head and blanked her.

"I can see you're in no fit state to discuss anything."

"Let's get one thing straight," he told her. "There's no me an' you – you got that?"

"Oh, you may think it's over, but believe me we're not finished by a long way," she yelled.

She sounded like a bossy wife. He wasn't taking it a minute longer. "Just get the hell out," he yelled.

"Don't think you can get out of your responsibility that easy," she threw back at him.

"What friggin' responsibility?"

"I'm pregnant!" she yelled back.

"You can't be. You told me you were taking the pill?"

"I lied."

He stared at her in horror. The bitch had done this deliberately, he was sure of it.

"Have you checked it out at the doctor's?"

"No. I don't have to," she replied stubbornly.

He was more than pissed off.

"Daddy needs to sort things out with you – urgently," she said.

It was time to face her father. One way or another daddy was gonna have to be told that this was one big freaking mistake.

"I'll tell him you'll be round tomorrow evening?"

"You won't, because tomorrow night I've got some serious business to take care of."

"What business?" she demanded.

"Private business," he snapped back.

And this took priority over everything.

CHAPTER FIFTY-SIX

"You whore! You filthy cheating whore!"

Riddled with guilt, Donna now had to pay the price of sleeping with Johnny. Desperately she tried to explain.

"Richard, I swear Sarah and Johnny were going out together – and I had no idea he was coming here until they arrived."

"You lying bitch," he spat, smacking her across the face. "You couldn't wait to jump into bed with him."

Donna's hand flew to her cut lip. She shivered in fear. This wasn't the man she had known all those years. This was a man on the brink of insanity.

"I warned you. I told you that if ever I caught you with him again I'd make you suffer – and so help me God I will."

She knew she was wasting her time. No amount of explaining would make him change his mind. He was beyond all reasoning.

"I'll see you in hell before you get a penny of my money. You've made your bed, now you can bloody well lie on it," he said, tensing the muscles in his face. "Let's see if that piece of trash is still interested in you once he finds out you've no money."

She ran up to her bedroom and sat on the bed trying to sort things out in her mind. Wasn't this what she'd always wanted? Hadn't she prayed for an escape – dreamed that one day she could be free from him?

Only now she felt ashamed and at a loss.

It wasn't as if they'd planned it. Johnny just happened to turn up out of the blue. It all seemed to happen so quickly – one minute she was in his arms, the next he was gone, and this time she knew he wouldn't be back. She gave a sigh, torn between her duty as a wife and the love she had for a man she knew she could never trust. And now it had lost her everything.

"Pack your bags and get out," Richard ordered standing at the bedroom door.

"Richard, please don't do this," she pleaded.

"You heard me. I want you out of this house."

Collecting her things together, she began placing them into a case. "Can't we at least talk this through?"

"There's nothing to talk through," he said bluntly. "You're a whore and always will be. I should have known when I picked you up from that sleazy club what type of woman you were."

Collecting her suitcase and coat, she struggled downstairs with no help from him.

"You're making a mistake," she said.

"The only mistake I ever made was getting involved with a slut like you."

"Richard, please," she begged.

"Just get out! I can't bear the sight of you," he spat.

She could see she was wasting her time. Slowly she began walking to the door.

"Just a moment," he called after her. "Aren't you forgetting something?"

She turned to face him with a glimmer of hope.

"The keys to the car," he shouted.

Sorting through her bag, she flung them at him. Then she walked out of his house and out of his life.

She had just enough money to catch a cab to the station. Then, drawing two hundred pounds out of her savings account, she bought a ticket to Norwich. No trains were running until next day, so she spent a cold and miserable night on a bench in the waiting room.

Early the following morning, she called Doris.

"Mother," she sobbed, "Can I come home?"

"What were you thinking of?" Tom exploded.

"She's your sister, Tom. She has nowhere else to go."

"Don't give me that rubbish. Only the other day you were saying how well off she was," he said harshly. "Did you see her expensive clothes or the car she was driving?"

"All I know is somethin's wrong an' she needs her family. We should be grateful she's turned to us."

"Has she given one thought to her family over the years?" he said bitterly. "She's using you, mother. What has she done expect bring you misery? When are you going to realise Donna has no interest in you, father or any of us?"

"I know Dolly did some bad things," Doris began objectively. "But you can't keep blamin' her."

Tom shook his head. "Twenty years, mother. Twenty years without so much as a letter. She almost killed you with worry and you think she's changed?" he spat with disgust.

"The good Lord made us all the same – it's just some folk are weaker than others when it comes to temptation," Doris said. "Let he who's without sin cast the first stone."

"I've heard enough of this nonsense," Tom said getting up from the table. "Donna brought shame on this family. And if she does arrive she'll bring trouble – mark my words."

CHAPTER FIFTY-SEVEN

Johnny sat with the customer and went over the sale. "It comes with a twelve-month warranty," he said, filling in the paperwork, "And it's just had two new tyres."

"Blue is my wife's favourite colour," the man said, beaming with joy. "She'll be thrilled with it."

Johnny returned his smile. "I'm gonna need a deposit," he said.

"Is two hundred OK?"

"Yeah, that's just fine."

"When can I pick her up?"

"I'll get the log book sorted and you can pick her up tomorrow."

"Thanks, Mr Ricci," he said with a handshake.

"Don't mention it."

The man walked off with a delighted smile and Johnny pocketed the money. Two hundred pounds should just about cover it, he though. Gillespie would never know, and he intended putting every penny back.

"Grandma, Grandma! Trick or treat!" The twins, in scary masks, rushed to Liz with excitement.

"Oh my goodness!" Liz said, pretending to be scared.

"We're witches, grandma!" screamed one.

Angie watched them proudly. "The girls wanted to show grandma their outfits," she said. "You know how excited children can get."

"Aren't they a bit young for this Halloween stuff?" Liz asked.

"Don't worry, I'm going to be with them when we call at the houses."

Jim looked up. "Another stupid idea from America," he grunted. "Calling on elderly folk and scaring the life out of them. It should be banned."

"Don't be starchy," Liz said, "it's just a bit of harmless fun."

"You won't say that when there's paint thrown over the car," Jim complained.

Liz gave a toot. "Come on, grandma's got something for you," she said, ignoring him and leading the girls off. "Let's go and see what treat we can find."

There was a scream of excitement as they ran off with Liz and Angie.

Chris turned to Jim. "I need a favour, dad," he said.

"Oh yes?" Jim replied sceptically. "And what might that be?"

"I need a loan."

"A loan – is that all?" Jim replied peevishly.

"You'll get it all back."

"What's wrong with the bank?"

"I'll be paying interest for years, before I even begin to pay back what I've borrowed."

"So I'm an interest free bank, am I?"

"I'm desperate - otherwise I wouldn't come to you."

"Daddy! Daddy! Look what grandma's given us!" The twins rushed up with books and crayons.

"Have you thanked her?" Chris asked.

They shook their heads.

"Well, go and thank her."

Turning back to his father, he said, "There's this lock up garage in Olton. It's ideal. I don't want to be doing mobile all my life."

"How much money are you talking about?"

"With what me and Angie have saved, I reckon about twenty grand."

"How much!" Jim snorted. "Christ, son, you expect me to come up with that kind of money? Me and your mother need every penny for our retirement."

"I've said you'll get it back. It's just things are going well at the moment and I need to set up a proper business. I've never asked for money, you know that."

"How soon do you call soon?"

"Like now. I've already put an offer in – five grand below the askin' price and it's been accepted."

"You'd better make a go of this, Christopher," Jim warned. "You've already thrown one good career down the drain."

"I will. And I won't let you down, I promise."

"What do you want?" Jane snapped, flinging open the door.

"I brought the money for Kylie's trip to France," Johnny said, holding out the packet.

"What gives you the right to come round here interfering? And what makes you think we can't afford it?"

"Look, just because you hate me doesn't mean you should take it out on the kid."

"I told you never to see her again – and I certainly don't want your money," Jane said, about the slam the door.

Kylie sat crouched on the stairs as they argued.

"I'm not asking to see her," he said belligerently. "I know how much this trip means to her."

"She's not going on any trip."

Kylie stood up. "I want to go!" she screamed at Jane.

"Now look what you've done because of your interfering," Jane yelled at him.

Kylie ran between them. "Stop it," she screamed. "Stop arguing!"

"Can't you see what you're doin' to the kid?" he said sharply.

"Dad – I want to go home with you."

"That's not possible, Kylie," he said. "Just be a good kid for your mom and we'll sort this out."

They stared at one another with hostility. "I'll do this – but only for her sake," Jane said, snatching the money. "And on the condition that you stay away from her."

"I love my dad!" Kylie screamed.

"Kylie – go to your room. Now!" she ordered.

Johnny gave her a withering glance.

"Just leave!" she yelled at him.

He turned to walk away.

"Dad!" Kylie screamed. "Dad, come back!"

Jane slammed the door in his face without so much as a thank you and Kylie's screams rang in his ears.

He tried to put it out of his head, but he couldn't.

CHAPTER FIFTY-EIGHT

Struggling with her case, Donna handed in her ticket to a thin, ferret-faced man with limp greasy hair and pitted skin.

"Cheers lovely," he grinned, giving her the benefit of his bad teeth.

Outside the station the sun appeared briefly from behind the cloudy winter sky. She shivered, pulling her coat around her, and waved down a taxi.

"You don't look as if you're from these parts," the cab driver said.

"No," she said bluntly, not particularly in the mood for conversation.

She was free at last from a loveless marriage, but at what price? Two thousand pounds of her savings account was hardly going to last five minutes once she paid solicitors' fees.

"So where you from – London?" the cab driver asked. "I can tell a cockney
accent. I spent five years in the smoke myself."

Spotting the house, she told him to pull up and after paying her fare he helped her with her suit case.

Doris greeted her with a hug. "You look exhausted, me girl. Come on in an' sit yourself down."

Donna realised what a mess she must look. She hadn't washed since yesterday and her lip was bruised and swollen.

"So what's all this about?" Doris asked.

Donna settled into the chair with a sigh. "I'm getting a divorce, mother."

"Divorce!"

"It's finished, mother – over."

"You can't just run off when it suits you," Doris said sanctimoniously.

"I didn't come here to be criticized," Donna said, jumping to her feet.

There was no point in bringing up the subject of Frank again, not while her mother was so intent on throwing the divorce in her face.

She unpacked and slipped out to buy a copy of the Norwich Times. Spotting a couple of job vacancies, she rang up after them. The first had already been filled. The second firm arranged for an interview the following morning. Then she rang a solicitor. Her interview was for 12.30 and the solicitor was for 2.30, which allowed her plenty of time.

After taking a bath, she dressed for dinner. Tom was already seated at the table when she came down. He hardly glanced up. She sensed there was going to be a repeat performance.

"Mother I'm not very hungry, do you mind if I skip tea?" she said, eager to escape to the privacy of her room. Rushing up stairs she popped in to see her father before going to her bedroom. Again memories came flooding back. Sitting on the bed she composed herself and taking out a sheet of paper she began to prepare a neatly-written curriculum vitae for tomorrow's interview.

Surprisingly, she slept well.

The next day she was up early. It was another dull, miserable December morning. Taking the navy suit she had worn for her last interview, she ironed the creases out. Maybe it would bring her luck this time. Scraping her long blonde hair into a French pleat, she then applied just a touch of make up; better to be natural, she thought. Finally, she slipped on her trench coat and set out for the bus.

She reached her destination and checked the piece of paper she'd written the directions on. Harper, Smith and Edgar were a small chartered accountant based in Norwich. There were three partners. The senior partner interviewed her. He was a tall, thin elderly man and wore glasses with grey wavy hair and he had quite a starchy attitude. He asked her for a reference, which she didn't have. She told him there would be no problem getting one. Alex Spencer would be only too happy to oblige.

"You haven't mentioned in your CV your marital status, Ms Layton?" he asked.

"I'm in the process of going through a divorce," she replied.

"I see," he said in a tone that suggested he didn't approve. "Any children or other obligations we should take into account?"

"No."

"And have you ever been in trouble with the law?" he asked. "Trivial questions, I know, but they have to be asked for security purposes."

"No," she replied. Only the fact that she'd killed a man.

After covering holidays and wages he told her that the job was hers if she was still interested.

She paused for a second, considering the possibilities. The job was boring without a doubt, but if she turned it down she may not get another opportunity and she was now desperate for money. What other choice was there?

At 2.30 she made her way to the solicitor. A man in his forties with thick set features and glasses extended his hand. "Dennis Thornton. How may I help you?"

She began giving him her side of the story. "And now my husband says I won't get a penny," she concluded.

"By law you are entitled, even though you have violated the marriage," he said. "Providing you have no further contact with the third party I can't see a problem. Leave it with me and I'll speak to your husband's solicitors."

She didn't know exactly what it entailed, but she was happy to leave it in his hands.

CHAPTER FIFTY-NINE

Louis Phelan was a large stocky man with a belly which hung over his trousers. He walked with a limp, due to gout.

"Whiskey?" he offered Johnny, pouring himself a straight scotch on the rocks.

"No thanks," he said, remembering his last encounter with the stuff.

"Johnny prefers lager," Michelle cut in, giving him an encouraging smile.

"Then go and get him a beer out of the fridge." Turning to Johnny, Louis said, "So Mr... ?"

Obviously Louis wasn't on first name terms. "Ricci," he replied.

"Mr Ricci, what are you intentions with my daughter?" he asked, waving a box of cigars in front of him.

Again, he passed. It was bad enough having to put up with the stink from Gillespie all day.

"I'm... er... quite prepared to settle for some kind of agreement. That is to support the kid?"

Louis Phelen bit off the end of the cigar and spat it out. "You'll do a lot more than that, young man," he retorted. "You'll make an honest woman of my daughter."

Marry the bitch? No chance.

He was ready with his trump card as Michelle handed him the beer, a demure smile on her face. "Don't get me wrong," Johnny began. "I think a lot of your daughter an' she deserves the best, but there's no way I could support her. Not on my wages."

He felt confident the way he'd handled it. Any minute now Louis Phelen was gonna kick his arse out the door.

"In fact," he added, piling on the agony. "I'm pretty well skint."

Louis blew a cloud of cigar smoke in his direction, almost choking him. "I've already discussed this with my daughter," he said. "And for some reason which is beyond me, she is besotted with you. So it is for that reason, and that reason alone, that I have agreed to set you up in my business."

"Excuse me?" Johnny said, thinking maybe he'd heard wrong.

"I'm offering you a directorship within the company. It is an extremely flourishing business as I'm sure my daughter has already pointed out."

For once, Johnny was speechless.

"I can't say I'm particularly keen on my daughter's choice of husband, Mr Ricci, but under the circumstances I appear to have little say in the matter."

Louis produced a form. "So if you'd care to sign on the dotted line?"

"What am I supposed to be signing?" he asked, still numb with shock.

"It's a contract of employment with my company. I don't think we need go over the rules and conditions, they won't apply to you." Louis held out a gold pen to him.

Johnny hesitated for a second to consider the possibilities. A director – Jeez! Gillespie had never made him a real partner in the business. He was just some underdog to run and fetch his errands. He'd be set up for life. Big house, car - all the things he'd ever dreamed of.

He'd have everything except love. Still, what difference did that make? Donna was the only woman he'd ever had those feelings for and she'd made it perfectly clear who she preferred to be with.

He grabbed the pen and signed.

Michelle had finally caught her man, and she couldn't wait to get an engagement ring on her finger.

"It's a beautiful piece of jewellery," said the weedy little sales assistant in spectacles.

"It should be for three hundred quid," Johnny said. "For that price I'd expect the crown jewels."

He pulled Michelle to one side. "Where d' you think I've got that kind of money from?" he hissed.

She threw him a frosty glance. "It's only once you get engaged."

"And it's only once you get thrown on the street," he hissed back.

The assistant coughed politely. "I can offer you something not quite so expensive?" he suggested. He presented another tray of rings and Johnny glanced briefly at them. "Got anything cheaper?" he asked.

The assistant came out with another tray. "This is the cheapest we do," he said derisively, placing it on the counter.

Michelle ended up with a fifty-pound rose chip on her finger. She wasn't happy by any means. "It'll do for now," she complained as they walked out of the shop. "But I want a proper diamond, Johnny, not some glass chipping."

"Michelle, you can have what the hell you like once I get this job," he said.

When they arrived back at his apartment, there was a note shoved under the door. Michelle was quick to grab it. "Who's Catherine?" she demanded to know.

"It's my sister," he said sharply, snatching the piece of

paper off her. There was no address or phone number, just a brief message – Called but you were out, Catherine.

"Sister!" Michelle spat. "I don't believe you."

"I don't care what you believe," he snarled back. But it happens to be the truth."

"You never mentioned you had a sister."

"There's a lot of things I've never mentioned," he said.

"So I've gathered. What else is there you haven't told me?" she said demandingly.

They'd hardly been engaged an hour and already he was losing his patience.

"Michelle, if we're gonna make a go of this you'd better start trusting me."

CHAPTER SIXTY

"Have you ever operated a switchboard?" Trudy asked Donna, as if she was incompetent.

"It's written on my CV."

"That's not what I asked," Trudy replied crisply.

Stay calm – remember you need the money.

"Yes. I've operated a four-line Panasonic."

"What about your typing skills?"

She felt like telling the woman exactly what she could do with her job, but she smiled sweetly.

"I'm a copy typist, as I've already explained to Mr Harper, and he seems quite satisfied."

Trudy didn't appear impressed. She was in her forties, with short blonde hair and stubby legs, and wore far too much make up. Donna sensed immediately that they weren't going to hit it off.

"I will need your reference," Trudy said, determined to show her authority.

"Yes – it's already being dealt with."

Trudy threw her a withering glance and led her through to the small reception area.

"You'll be announcing the partners' calls. Some of our clients can be persistent when asking for one of the partners, so I'm afraid you'll have to use your discretion."

"Fine," Donna said, smiling faintly.

"I'll leave you to it then," she said.

As soon as Trudy had disappeared, she called Alex at his publishing business.

"I desperately need a favour," she asked him. "I've

started a job in Norwich and they've asked for my reference. Is there any chance you could send me one?"

"Of course," he replied. "How are things?"

"Fine," she replied. She decided not to mention the fact that she was getting a divorce. It would only complicate matters.

"I thought you were moving to Warwickshire?"

"There was a change of plan."

"I'll get one in the post tonight for you," Alex said.

She was about to hang up.

"Oh… Donna? If ever you return to London and need a job there's always one here for you."

"Thanks, Alex," she smiled.

If only the circumstances were different, she would have jumped at the chance.

Trudy was standing by her desk when she came off the phone. "I forgot to mention private calls are not allowed," she said sternly.

"I was just enquiring about my reference…" Donna began.

"Then I suggest you do it in your own time," Trudy snapped.

Bitch!

She was forced to apologise.

A few days before Christmas an official-looking brown envelope arrived addressed to her. She tore it open. It was a copy of the divorce petition from the County Court, requesting that she returned the document acknowledging that she had received the petition and that she agreed to the charges brought against her.

She gave a heavy sigh. Seventeen years, and now it was all about to end with a piece of paper.

Christmas was a quiet time spent with her family. There were no festive parties at Harper Smith and Edgar. All she was given was a box of chocolates and a miserly bonus of twenty pounds.

On Christmas day her family arrived – her brothers and sisters along with their spouses. Not one of them bothered to ask how she was.

"So what made you decide to come back after all this time?" spouted her sister Helena.

"I guess I missed having such a caring family," she replied with equal sarcasm.

Helena spotted the large diamond ring she still wore on her finger. "You obviously did well for yourself."

"Yes, as a matter of fact I did."

Doris interrupted. "I'm surprised Sarah never came this Christmas. She comes every year."

Donna was suddenly overcome by the heat in the small, crowded kitchen and stood up to get some fresh air. She'd been feeling queasy for the last couple of days and she'd missed a period. She was always on time. She couldn't possibly be pregnant.

Or could she?

It had been exactly five weeks since she'd slept with Johnny. As much as she wanted a baby this just didn't seem right.

She put it at the back of her mind. She was probably late due to all the stress of the divorce as well as her father's illness.

In the next few days his condition weakened. She kept vigil at his bedside every night, holding his hand, talking to him and praying silently that he would pull through.

"Mother, we have to talk about what happened..." Donna began, helping to tidy away.

"What's done's done an' there's no puttin' it right," Doris said in an obstinate tone.

Just then Tom burst into the room. Why were there always interruptions just as she was trying to get some sense out of Doris?

She took an early night. Next day on arriving at work the first thing she

noticed when she walked into reception was the national newspaper on the table. She stared at the photograph of Melania under the heading:

MELANIE MOON HITS THE STATES

She read on:

"Melanie Moon, tipped to become the next Ella Fitzgerald, is currently working on her first album, 'Only Time Will Tell.' It's shortly to be released on Capital records. Melanie, who recently split from her husband, is almost certainly set to become a big star on both sides of the Atlantic."

Before she had finished reading, Trudy burst into the reception with a pile of letters for typing. "She certainly likes to get it about," she said with a hint of irony. "Three husbands, would you believe. One's enough for me."

Donna kept her silence. The less Trudy knew about their relationship the better, she thought.

"Can you get these letters typed first?" Trudy asked, placing them on top of the pile. "And if you could bring them to me for signing?"

"Yes, Trudy."

Anything you wish Trudy.

Smile. Don't forget you need the money.

Trudy was beginning to push more and more typing on to her, with little thanks. It wasn't as if she was an experienced typist. By the time it was five she couldn't wait to escape.

As soon as she got home she put a call in to the international operator. "Capital Records in the United States, please," she said. She was given the number. A well-spoken American woman answered the phone.

"May I speak to Melanie Moon?"

"She's over at our recording studio."

"May I have the number?"

"I can connect you if you'd care to hold the line."

Donna propped the receiver under her chin and checked her watch. It was 5.30 pm in the UK. She reckoned it would be somewhere around noon in the States. She held the line and hoped they wouldn't take too long connecting her, as she only had £10 credit on her phone. There was music in the background and then a lot of commotion. She distinctly heard Melania screaming and throwing one of her tantrums.

Nothing had changed.

"Who is this?" Melania barked down the line.

"It's Donna."

"Donna? Oh... my... god!" she screamed. "Where are you?"

"England. I happened to see your picture in the newspaper."

"A lot's happened, honey."

"So I see."

"So how are things with you?"

"I'm finally divorcing Richard."

"Well, now there's a surprise. So - who are you with at the moment?"

"There's no one."

"No one!" Melania exclaimed with disbelief.

Donna heard Melania's name called out. "Be with you in five minutes," she yelled. Then, turning her attention back to Donna, she went on to say, "They're waiting to record. It's like a freaking madhouse in here."

"What happened to you and Dex?" she asked.

"Oh, honey, I guess he couldn't stand being my shadow. He was fine until I started making a name for myself. I guess that's fame for you. Anyway – things turned out for the best and I married my producer."

"And the name change, is that part of this new image?"

"I was advised by my manager. He told me to drop the A for an E and chose Moon - said Melanie had a better ring to it."

"Melania, I've hardly any credit left on my mobile."

"I'll let you know when I'm next in London."

"I've moved out of London. I'm in Norwich working for an accountant."

"Accountant!" Melania chuckled. "I thought you wanted to do catering?"

"I do, but I had to accept what came along."

She gave her mobile number and they promised to keep in touch.

"I knew you could make it – what did I tell you," Donna added before hanging up.

She thought gloomily of her own life. Melania was made. She had a brilliant career, a man - everything she could possibly want.

And she was left with nothing.

CHAPTER SIXTY-ONE

Chris had eventually achieved his ambition and had now opened his own business. It was a lock-up garage in Olton, above which were the letters:

C A Ainsworth

Auto repairs, bodywork and MOT's

Johnny glanced briefly at the sign before stepping inside. He found Chris busy, working underneath a car.

"I need an MOT," he shouted, disguising his voice. "ASAP?"

"No chance today," Chris shouted back. "Leave your details with the kid in the office and I'll get back to you as soon as I can."

"Don't bother. I'll take my business elsewhere," Johnny replied, controlling the urge to snigger.

Chris immediately slid from beneath the car and glanced up. "Ricci – you bastard!" he spat.

Johnny burst out laughing. "How ya doing, arsehole?"

"Busy, I tell you."

"I see you got yourself an apprentice?"

Chris stood up and grabbed a rag. "Yeah – he's only sixteen. Seems quite keen."

"I need a favour."

"If this is about your car, there's no chance. I'm up to my neck here."

"Nah. Remember you offered to be my best man?"

"You're not...?"

"Yeah."

"You crafty old sod," Chris sniggered.

"Not so much the old."

"So who's the lucky – or should I say- unlucky lady?"

"Michelle."

"Michelle?"

"Yeah, remember? Short, dark hair – works at the nursery."

"You're marrying her?"

"Why? Is there a problem?"

"It's just… well… she don't seem your type."

"So what is my type?" he replied bluntly.

Chris shrugged. "I mean don't get me wrong – she's pretty enough," he added, quickly covering his tracks. "It's just… "

"She's having my kid," Johnny cut in briskly. "I figured I should do the right thing."

"Bloody Hell, Ricci, have you never heard of wearing a rubber?"

"Yeah, I tried it once, it was like having a bath with my socks on," he said remembering his last experience. He'd only ever worn a condom on one particular occasion when Brennan had dragged him to a brothel. He was sixteen at the time and the old tale had insisted he put one on. He'd never worn one since.

"What about your other kid?"

"Kylie? - I got to take her out for her eleventh birthday a few months back, but the bitch is still insisting I don't see her."

"She may see things differently once she knows you're married?"

"Yeah – maybe?"

On his way back home he called into Rose's.

"Well… this is getting regular. Two visits in the space of a few weeks," she said.

Johnny followed her into the kitchen and helped

himself to a cookie. "Catherine called and I was out," he said. "She left no number, or address I could contact her."

"Oh. She mentioned she was going to see you."

"You've seen her then?"

"Yes. She was here a week ago and brought my birthday card."

"Your birthday?"

"I don't make a fuss of them these days. Much rather forget."

He took a twenty-pound note out of his wallet and handed it to her. "Get yourself something," he said.

"No," she said firmly, pushing it back into his hand. "You can't afford it."

"Take it, Rose. I'm fine – honest."

He took down Catherine's address. "By the way, I'm getting married," he said.

"Married? You never mentioned you were seeing anyone."

"Yeah, well I guessed maybe it's time I settled down. I'd like you to come, if you can make it?"

"Of course. I wouldn't miss my nephew's wedding for anything. Have you let your mother know?"

"Jeezus, Rose, you know how I feel about things. I was fifteen when I left home. You wanna know why? Because I couldn't put up with their stinking arguments a minute longer. It was like being in a war zone when she started throwing plates around."

"Your mother did her best to bring you up, under the circumstances," Rose replied. "She didn't have an easy life, not with your father, may he rest in peace. My brother came across from Italy and worked for our father for a time. He met your mother. She was seventeen when she fell pregnant with your older brother. She came from a strict Catholic family and your dad had no other alternative but to marry her. He had women, lots of women, but your mother stuck by him religiously."

The truth was coming out at last. History was about to repeat itself. He was following his old man's footsteps – like father, like son.

God forbid.

It was gone two o'clock when he finally got back to the garage. Gillespie was waiting for him. "I've had a bloke round here. You sold him a blue Fiesta –remember?" he said disgruntled. "Well – he's come back demanding two hundred nicker off his bill. He says he gave you the money as a deposit."

Oh Christ! He'd forgotten all about it.

"Ronnie, I was gonna tell you... "

"You mean you helped yourself to two hundred nicker of my money?"

"I was desperate. It was for Kylie. I'll pay it back."

"Too right, my son. I'll deduct it out of your earnings along with the interest."

Gillespie never missed a trick. He was always hot on the trigger when it came to money.

Maybe quitting the job was for the best, he thought. Soon he'd have all the money and things he'd ever dreamed of.

Almost.

CHAPTER SIXTY-TWO

Over the next couple of weeks, Donna knew there was something wrong. She'd taken regular hot baths, drank a bottle of gin and tried every old wives' remedy imaginable. There was still no sign of her period. Before going into work she rung the doctors' and made an appointment for later that evening.

At ten o'clock her solicitor called her. "I would like you to come into the office," he said. "Can you make it today?"

"I could slip in on my lunch break," she murmured, making sure Trudy wasn't lurking around.

"It should only take a few minutes. Shall we say one o'clock?"

"Fine."

By lunchtime she had braced herself for the worst.

"I have some good news for you," he began, shuffling through his paperwork. "Your husband's not an easy man to negotiate with. However I have spoken to his solicitor and we have finally reached an agreement – which I think you'll be pleased with."

She felt as if a weight had been lifted from her shoulders. At last she was free to do what she wanted.

Calling in at the doctor's that night, she found the waiting room full. As she sat, she began to have a more optimistic outlook. Soon she'd be able to put all this behind her. For the first time in twenty years she was actually looking forward to her future.

Her name was finally called and she wandered in. A grey-haired man with glasses sat transfixed to the computer screen. "And what can I do for you?" he asked, glancing at her over his spectacles.

"I think I may be pregnant," she began solemnly.

"Were you and your husband planning a child?"

"Umm… no."

"Loosen your skirt and jump on the bed for me," he said. After doing the necessary tests he sat back down at his desk. "Well, Mrs Deblaby, you are definitely pregnant."

"Pregnant?" she repeated in shock.

"Yes," he smiled. "So I suggest you go home and give your husband the good news."

She stood up and left the surgery in a daze. As she sat on the bus she gathered her senses. The idea began to grow on her. She suddenly felt elated, a warm feeling spreading through her. She was having a baby, Johnny's baby – the child she thought she'd never have. All she had to do was tell her family it was Richard's and no one would be any the wiser.

Lies and more lies. But who cared? She'd never felt this happy for years.

She reached her parents' house on a high, ready to break the news.

"Mother," she cried. "Mother, I have some… " she broke off and glanced at Tom and her mother. Both had solemn faces. "Is something wrong?" she asked.

"Thank heavens you're here, Dolly," her mother said in a shaky voice. "He's gone, Dolly. Your farther's passed away."

CHAPTER SIXTY-THREE

"I want to see my dad," Kylie demanded.

"And I've said you can't," Jane replied, standing at the ironing board and looking as if she was about to give birth at any moment.

"Why not?" Kylie scowled.

Phil glanced up. "Listen to your mother for once."

"This is all about her, isn't it?" Kylie shouted, pulling a face at Jane. "She wouldn't even let me see him at Christmas."

"She happens to be your mother," Phil said, raising his voice. "And if I have any more of your cheek you'll be sent up to bed without your tea."

"I hate you – I hate you both!" she screamed, storming up to her bedroom.

Phil and Jane exchanged horrified expressions.

"You spoil her," Phil said briskly. "She has her own way far too much."

"If anyone's to blame, it's Johnny," she replied scornfully. "Goodness knows what he's been filling her head with."

"It may be a good idea to let him have her for a week," Phil said, shuffling his newspaper. "Let him put up with her tantrums. He'll soon be glad to bring her back."

Jane slammed down the iron. "Are you mad? You don't know the half of it. What effect would it have on Kylie seeing what he gets up to with all those women he brings home?"

A loud burst of Westlife made them jump out of their skin.

"Do something, Phil," Jane snapped.

Charging to the foot of the stairs, he yelled out, "Kylie! Turn that row down now! Do you hear me?"

"I knew it," Jane said furiously. "I knew the minute I allowed him to see her there'd be trouble."

* * *

Catherine's apartment was on the Warwick Road in Olton. The newly developed site stood in a large courtyard secured by black and gold gates. Johnny drove up and found he needed a code to get in.

He was about to back off when a woman in her fifties in a smart MG pulled up behind him. She leaned out of the window and shot him an impatient glance.

"I'm here to see my sister, Catherine Ricci," he shouted across, not sure if she was still using her married name. "She's at 5A. I don't suppose you could give me the code?"

"No. I certainly couldn't," was the woman's snobby reply. "That's the whole point of having security."

"Thanks for nothing," he replied in an equally nasty tone. He waited as she tapped out the code and then swiftly followed her through. He drove in, found the apartment and rang the bell. There was no reply, so he decided to sit and wait in the car.

It was twenty minutes later when Catherine arrived. She hadn't spotted him and walked up to the front door. She was juggling with her groceries and keys when he crept up and grabbed her from behind. She let out a scream, almost dropping the bag.

"Hi sis."

"You bastard!" she squealed, half jokingly. "You gave me the fright of my life."

He followed her through. "It's like trying to break into Buckingham Palace," he said. "I had some old bat in a MG refusing to give me the code. Anyone would have thought I was gonna break into her flaming pad."

"Oh that'll be Mrs Reynolds," Catherine said with a smile. "She can be a funny old stick at times."

Placing the bags down, she began unloading the groceries. "Have you eaten?"

"Nah. Don't bother. I can grab something when I get back."

"I'll fix us some risotto. It won't take long."

"Nice place," he said, glancing round. It was ultra modern. The walls were light cream and the room quite spacious, with pine wooden floorboards and a large bay window overlooking the grounds.

"If you think this place is nice you should have seen the house back in Ireland. Liam had it specially built."

"What happened to you two?"

Catherine stirred the mince in the saucepan. "He drank," she said. "I mean he couldn't control it. Morning, afternoon, evening – it never stopped. I managed to get him into rehab. He was doing quite well. And then suddenly he started again. I just couldn't handle it. I couldn't stand by and see him ruining himself and our marriage."

She was two years younger than Johnny, exceptionally beautiful with long dark, glossy hair and the same intense eyes. "So how are things with you?" she asked.

He gave a shrug.

"Let's see – the last time I saw you was at… "

"Father's funeral," they chorused together.

"You haven't changed - still as good-looking as ever," she smiled. "I can remember back home when you were just twelve and all the girls lining up at the door asking for you."

"Jeez! That brings back memories. Seems ages ago, an' here I am knocking thirty-two!"

He grinned. "Remember that time you and Robbo kicked that ball through the window? I was eight at the time and I got the frigging blame. I had the hiding of my life."

Catherine laughed. "So what about when you stole my sweets from under the Christmas tree?"

"Revenge, I guess."

"You were always the rebel, Johnny. I've thought a lot about you over the years," she said, handing him a bottle of spring water.

"Yeah – me too."

"If you prefer tea I can make some."

"Nah, this is fine." It made a change from carrot juice and all the weird concoctions Michelle dished up.

"So -what have you been doing with yourself?" she asked, busy at the cooker.

What had he been doing?

Where did he begin - the attempted robbery, the old man, or the drug dealers? He thought it best not to mention any of it. "Not a lot," he said. "I'm getting hitched, by the way."

"Well – congratulations," Catherine said. "Have you let mother know?"

Why the concern about his old lady? "Nah," he said. "She couldn't give a toss about me, so why should I care?"

"She's getting married again, did you know?"

"Yeah, Rose mentioned it. If he's got any sense he'll do a runner."

"Well, they seem happy enough together," she said, settling down at the table. "She sent a photograph in her last letter. Next time I write I'll give her your address."

"Don't bother."

"I think she should know."

Who cares if she rang him or not?

But still... she was his mother.

"So do I get an invite?" Catherine smiled.

"Yeah, course. Michelle's sent out invitations for all her side. But well... what family have I got apart from you an' Rose?"

"So what's she like, this girl?"

"You may as well know, I got her pregnant," he said.

Catherine shook her head. "Trust me to have a brother who can't keep it in his pants. So how do you feel about things?"

He shrugged. "I don't know, Cath. I honestly don't know."

Catherine could tell by a glance that he wasn't happy. "Is there no way you could suggest paying for the baby's keep?"

"I've already been down that road. Her old man's got me over a barrel. He got me to sign this contract."

"What contract?"

"Ah – something about setting me up in his business," he said flatly.

"You're not marrying her for money, surely?"

"Nah, course not."

"Perhaps it's just pre-wedding nerves," Catherine said, attempting to sound cheerful. "Maybe once you're married you'll feel different about things."

Who was she kidding? He knew exactly how he'd feel.

As far as his feelings towards Michelle were concerned, nothing would change. There was just nothing there. He thought of Donna often. After almost twelve years he still had the photo they'd had taken together. Why he still kept it in his wallet he didn't know.

Maybe he just hadn't bothered to throw it away.

Maybe?

It was Monday, his day off. When he got back to the flat, who should call him but Jane. "Johnny..." she began sharply. "I need to speak to you about Kylie, she's becoming totally out of control."

"So why you telling me," he said, equally as curt. "You're her sole parent – or so you keep reminding me."

"I should never have allowed you to see her," she snapped.

"Oh, so it's my fault?" he said. "And how d'you make that out?"

"You're teaching her bad habits."

He gave a snort of laughter. "Bad habits? I guess she's told you I pick my nose then?"

"I didn't ask for your sarcasm," she said crisply. "Kylie's begun to use four-letter words. We've never used that kind of language in front of her and I won't tolerate it."

"And you think it's me?" he spat. "I suggest you check out the kids she's hanging round with at school before you come accusing me."

"Don't tell me what I should and shouldn't do concerning my daughter."

"Our daughter," he corrected. Did she think she'd had some kind of miraculous conception and that he'd had no part in it?

"I'm warning you, Johnny. If I find you've been seeing her again I'll put it in the hands of my solicitor."

"Just try it."

"I intend to."

Bitch.

CHAPTER SIXTY-FOUR

"We commit our dear brother Jack's body to the ground. Earth to earth, ashes to ashes, dust to dust, in hope of the resurrection… "

Donna, dressed in black, stood with her family at the graveside, trembling with both emotion and the bitterly cold wind.

There was a small turnout of villagers. She was aware of their condemnatory glances. She was the bad girl who had run off and left her parents to face the consequences. She could almost hear their whispers. They were all hypocrites, the lot of them. As if they gave a fig about her father; her dear father, who she had seen so little of. And now it was too late to make up for all those years. She was only thankful that she'd seen him, thankful that she'd spent the last few months with him.

Sarah had arrived two days before the funeral and had hardly spoken to her, only to rub in the fact that Richard had done the right thing by divorcing her. At that moment she was too upset about her father to care what her sister thought.

Doris threw a single red rose onto the coffin and was helped by Tom as the cortege made its way out of the cemetery and back to the car.

As they drove along, Donna glanced out of the window in silence.

"Lovely service," said Kitty Baker, who had somehow managed to squeeze herself into their car. "Is this Donna?" she asked with a surprised glance.

You know very well who I am, Donna thought, throwing her a withering smile.

"Let's see – how long has it been – twenty years? I can remember when you were just a little girl."

"Donna went to work in London," Doris cut in, as if she couldn't speak up for herself. "She's done very well for herself."

"London? Oh my word!"

Donna let their conversation slip by. She was beginning to feel queasy again and hoped they wouldn't be long getting home.

By the time they reached the house she knew something was wrong. She'd begun to experience bad stomach cramps and she'd had a show of blood. How could she possibly call the doctor with the house full of people? She hadn't even told her mother she was pregnant. After the shock of losing Jack and the funeral arrangements, she thought it best to save the news until things had settled down.

Betty Parsons grabbed a ham sandwich and gave Kitty a nudge, glancing in Donna's direction. "She's a brazen floozy. Can you believe she's just turned up like that?"

"Apparently she's been living in London," Kitty replied, filling her in with the gossip. "No doubt she's been running some den of iniquity down there, judging by her expensive clothes."

Donna went in search of her mother and found her spreading more sandwiches. "I can't believe they've eaten all that plateful," Doris complained.

"Mother, have you any aspirin or pain killers?"

"Are you all right, Dolly? You look dreadful."

"I'll be fine. I just need to lie down a while," she said,

watching Kitty Baker stuff a large chicken leg in her mouth.

She took a couple of tablets, went up to the bedroom and lay on the bed. "Please don't let me lose this baby," she prayed. "It means so much to me."

She thought of Johnny and the baby she was carrying and fell asleep with a smile on her face.

It was late evening when she woke, and she was feeling wet and sticky. She touched her clothes and found herself saturated in blood.

Oh dear God!

She got off the bed and panicked. "Mother!" she cried from the top of the stairs. "Mother, I need your help."

Doris was mortified to find her daughter trembling uncontrollably and covered in blood.

"I've lost it. I've lost my baby," she screamed.

"Oh Lord, Dolly, does Richard know you were pregnant?" Doris demanded.

Dear mother, what difference does it make?

"He has a right to know you were carryin' his child, Dolly. He might even consider changin' his mind about the divorce."

"Will you just listen, mother!" she shouted. "I don't love Richard. It's over and finished between us – do you understand?"

Sarah heard the commotion and came rushing to see what had happened. "Is everything all right?"

"Your sister's had a miscarriage. Can you get some clean sheets," Doris said, collecting the soiled bed linen.

"Shouldn't we call a doctor?" Sarah suggested.

"No – I don't want a doctor. I want my baby," Donna screamed. She filled up with tears. "This is all a punishment for what I did, isn't it?"

"The Lord giveth an' the Lord taketh," Doris said piously. "You can only pray for forgiveness, my girl."

"But I never meant to kill anyone," Donna shouted, becoming hysterical. "He... he tried to rape me. I had no other choice."

"Rape? Doris stared at her in shock. "Why didn't you mention this to me or your farther? We could have sorted it out without you runnin' off like thart."

"And who would you have believed – me or Frank?"

Her mother glanced at her in confusion. "Frank? What has Frank got to do with it?"

Sarah returned with the fresh linen as they continued to argue.

"Your sister's running a fever."

"I killed him. I killed him!" Donna repeated hysterically.

"Stop this nonsense," Doris said sternly. "I won't have any more of this, Dolly."

"I killed Frank, because he tried to rape me. Don't you understand?"

"Frank died of natural causes," Doris said harshly.

"What do you mean – natural causes?"

"He had a heart attack a few weeks after you left. Poor soul, it happened so sudden."

Donna stared at her mother, trying to take in what she had just been told. All those years she'd blamed herself for a crime she'd never committed.

Suddenly she was confused.

"What about the knife wound?" she asked.

"What knife wound?" Doris questioned.

"I stabbed him right here, down in the kitchen."

"Get some rest – you'll feel better after a good night's sleep," Doris said, attempting to calm her down.

"I want to know what happened, mother," she screamed.

"I've told you all there is to know."

"So why am I being persecuted? Why are people talking about me as if I've done something terrible?"

"You know very well whart you did – carryin' on with that Phillips lad, leavin' your poor farther to face the village an' Don Phillips."

It suddenly struck Donna what she was getting at. "You thought I was pregnant? You thought I'd run off and killed our baby, didn't you?"

"Just try an' get some rest," Doris said, avoiding the question.

"Didn't you?" she demanded. Almost twenty years she had lived a nightmare on account of Frank while those small-minded people had jumped to their own petty conclusions.

"Do you want to know the real reason I ran away?" she began with bravado. "Because while you were both out that Saturday morning, dear old Frank, the village pervert, turned up and guess what? He tried to rape me. So I picked up the kitchen knife and I stabbed him."

Even now her mother stood defiant over Frank's innocence. "What a vicious and wicked story to make up. May the Lord forgive you," Doris said, about to walk out of the room.

"That's right, mother, defend your precious Frank as you always have. It's the truth and I don't care if you believe me or not," she shouted after Doris.

"I believe you."

She glanced up at Sarah.

"I believe you because... because he touched me – on several occasions."

Donna choked back the tears. "Oh God, Sarah, if only you'd have said something!"

"How could I when you ran off and left me? I was five, frightened, and too ashamed to tell anyone."

"I'm so sorry, Sarah."

They sat hugging one another with the knowledge and understanding of what they had both endured. "It's going to be all right, Sarah," Donna whispered. "Everything is going to be all right."

The following day Sarah began packing ready to return to Birmingham. She sat on the bed with Donna.

"Dee... can we put things behind us?" she asked.

"Yes. Of course," Donna smiled, giving her sister a hug.

Sarah hesitated for a moment before she spoke. "It was Johnny's baby, wasn't it?"

"Yes," Donna replied solemnly, picking at a strand of cotton on the bed linen. "Richard never wanted children. He had an operation shortly after we married."

"Does Johnny know about the baby?"

"No, and I want it to stay that way," Donna replied firmly. She knew exactly how he would react, and his pity was the last thing she wanted.

"I thought you loved him? You were willing to throw your marriage away for him."

"You don't understand. He's not the type to settle down. I remember him saying – and this would only make him despise me."

"Dee, I have a confession to make," Sarah began guiltily. "I told him you'd never leave your husband and you were a gold digger. I was so jealous and angry at the time. I'm so sorry."

Donna tried to keep the bitterness out of her voice.

"Just forget it, Sarah. It's over and done with."

"You don't mean that, because you still love him."

"Love?" she laughed bitterly.

What was that - the feeling of wanting to be with someone? Having their children and growing old with them?

Hadn't she known from that very first Christmas, when he had taken her in his arms on the dance floor, exactly how she had felt about him?

"Oh come on, Dee. You may be fooling yourself but you can't fool me."

"Anyway – it's too late," Donna said. "I've no idea where he is."

"I can give you his number."

"I don't want his number," she said stubbornly. "What would I say to him?"

"Tell him the truth," Sarah said. She jotted down the number and handed it to her. "Promise?"

"I promise," Donna said taking the piece of paper. Not that she had any intention of calling him.

CHAPTER SIXTY-FIVE

"This will be your office," Louis said. They had taken the lift up to the eighth floor of the building and Johnny followed Louis into a room with a large window which had panoramic views over the city centre. If you were contemplating suicide you wouldn't have to look much further.

"Naturally, the name on the door will be changed," Louis said.

Johnny could hardly take things in. His feet sank into the thick beige carpet and the light oak desk had two cream telephones; one for external use, the other for internal calls. There was a picture on the wall of the factory taken from the air. It was a massive complex.

Holy Cow! He was gonna be partly in charge of all this?

"Excuse me for one moment," Louis said, turning to answer his mobile.

Johnny ran his hand over the cream chair, taking in the smell of genuine leather. He felt power sweep through him as he sat engrossed by his surroundings. Was this really happening? Or maybe he was dreaming?

"The men are ready to meet you," Louis said, waving him out of the chair.

They took the lift back down to the basement and went to the factory floor, where Louis insisted he put on a white coat and mesh cap.

"They're processing food orders. Everything has to be checked and re-checked before it's sent to the consumer," he explained. He smiled at one of the white-coat workers.

"This is my future son-in-law," he said, introducing Johnny to a man old enough to be his father. "Mr Ricci will be the new marketing director and in charge of this department."

Johnny shook the man's hand with a faint smile. He hadn't a clue what he was supposed to be doing, but obviously Louis would put him in the picture nearer the time.

"What's going on over there?" he asked.

"They're processing orders. Throwing out consumables that don't meet the required standards."

"It seems perfectly OK to me."

"Once you're trained, you'll know exactly what to look for."

Louis caught hold of an attractive blonde with a figure that sent him into overdrive. "This is Penny and she'll be your secretary. Anything you want you've only to ask."

You bet he would.

She threw him a generous smile and their eyes lingered on one another. Already he was figuring how to get a quick shag without Louis knowing. It would be the ultimate icing on the cake.

Michelle was in one of her frequent bad moods. He was watching a football match on TV when she stormed over and switched it off.

"I want to talk," she said sternly.

"You're always talking – you never stop," he said, grabbing the remote and switching it back on.

"You're putting no effort into this wedding, Johnny!" she screamed at him.

"I'm marrying you – what else d' you want?" he yelled back.

"Sometimes you're really annoying," she snapped.

He was annoying! Had she ever considered her own behaviour? She was nothing but one big annoyance. Already he was beginning to regret his decision.

"Where are you going?"

"Down the boozer, where I can watch the match in peace," he replied.

"What about your dinner?"

He didn't reply. Knowing the crap she dished up, it wasn't worth bothering with.

Next morning he climbed out of bed bleary-eyed and staggered into the kitchen in nothing more than his birthday suit. Michelle had gone to the nursery and left him a bowl of muesli on the table.

"Bloody crap," he spat, slipping it down the toilet. He stuck two rounds of bread in the toaster and opened up a can of baked beans. Checking the post, he came across a postcard with a leprechaun sitting on a toadstool with the slogan, 'Good luck from Ireland.' He flicked it over and scanned the message.

Dear John,

I heard you are getting married. I hope all goes well

Mother.

Was that it?

After almost sixteen years, she couldn't even be bothered to pick up the phone and call him. Well stuff you, mother.

He was on his way to the garage when he received a call from Sarah. "It's Donna," she began. "I take it she hasn't spoken to you then?"

"Nah – why what's up?"

"She's divorcing Richard."

He was suddenly elated by the news.

"Johnny… I want to apologise. I said some dreadful

things about her. It isn't true..."

"Forget it," he cut in anxiously. "Sarah, where is she?"

"She's back home in Norfolk with my mother. I think you should know she had a miscarriage at ten weeks – it was your child."

"Jeezus!" he said sharply. "Why didn't someone let me know?"

"I'm sorry, Johnny."

"Sarah, I have to speak to her."

She gave him the number and he hung up.

Somehow, some way, he had to call off the wedding.

CHAPTER SIXTY-SIX

"Richard wants the divorce settled as quickly as possible," Dennis Thornton said. "Your decree absolute should take about six weeks to come through."

"And this will finalise things?" she asked.

"Yes. It'll mean that both parties are free to remarry if they so wish." Dennis glanced at her over the rim of his glasses. "I don't know whether you're aware, but your husband is remarrying."

"No, I wasn't. But it doesn't surprise me."

She didn't need three guesses to know who it was. There'd always been a spark between him and Hilary. But at least she'd no cause to feel guilty any more.

A black cloud had suddenly been lifted. Richard, thank heavens, was finally out of her life. She could now begin to plan a new future. Soon she'd be able to buy that little tea room she'd always wanted.

Harper Smith and Edgar had been anything but sympathetic towards her when she had taken time off after losing the baby. She couldn't wait to hand her notice in. She intended to go back to London. Apart from her mother, there was nothing to keep her in that godforsaken village. Alex had already told her there would be a job waiting.

There wasn't a single day that passed when she didn't think about the baby. What sex would it have been? If it had been a girl she could have dressed it up, told her how handsome her father had been. And if it had been a boy, would it have looked like Johnny?

She would never know.

She'd so wanted a child and now her only chance of having a baby seemed hopeless. Nature had not intended for her to become a mother. She was going into her thirty-eighth year and would probably never get the opportunity again.

She checked her mobile and found she had two missed calls. Whoever it was would probably call back.

Doris was busy sorting through some of her father's clothes and belongings when she returned home. "They need to go to jumble," she said.

Coming across some old photographs, Doris smiled, "Just look at you. You were two years old there. Your farther took it on an old camera he had."

Donna studied the photograph - a little girl with blonde hair and a cheeky smile, playing happily with not a care in the world.

"It was your farther's favourite picture – called you his doll."

"So that's where Dolly came from?" Donna said with amusement.

"Oh – he loved you, me girl. There's no mistakin' thart."

"And this is you and father?" Donna asked, picking up an old wedding photograph.

"Ah, would you believe it? I was quite handsome in them days," Doris said reminiscently.

The picture showed a beautiful young woman with pale golden hair and large grey doleful eyes. Her once soft peach skin was now weathered and wrinkled with tiny red veins.

Donna sighed. Frank had ruined her life. Everything could have been so different. She thought about Doris claiming his innocence.

"Mother," she began, "do you really believe I'd make up such a beastly story about Frank? And what would I gain from it?"

"I don't waunt to talk about it," Doris said stubbornly, shoving the matter under the carpet.

"He tried to rape me – have you any idea what that felt like?"

"Oh – here we are," Doris said coming across the life insurance policies. "An' look whart else I've found."

Donna glanced at the small dress ring sealed in a polythene bag.

"Yer farther insisted on keepin' it. He always said you'd come home one day."

Donna took it and tried it on, but it was too small and only went half way down her finger. Memories of that day came flooding back as clear as if it were yesterday. She visualised her father, his face tense with anger and the terrifying ordeal of having the ring ripped off her finger.

How she had hated him.

She glanced at Doris, who seemed to have accepted her father's death as a normal part of life and was carrying on with her day-to-day duties. But to Donna the house had an eerie quietness about it.

From the time she had first arrived, Tom had hardly given her the time of day apart from abusing her. So it came as a surprise that shortly after dinner that night he spoke.

"Why didn't you tell father?" he asked.

She looked at him blankly. "About what?"

"I heard everything," he said.

"It wouldn't have made any difference. Mother still doesn't believe me."

"I'm sure father would have."

"Tom, you were here that day it happened. When you and mother came back to the house, did you see anything of Frank?"

"I didn't come home with mother, I went straight to the farm. Have you asked her?"

"She refuses to talk about it."

She broke off and glanced at Tom. "Do you think she's covering up something?"

"Surely you're not suggesting mother had anything to do with it?"

"I don't know, I honestly don't know. None of it makes sense."

Tom glanced solemnly at her. "If it's as bad as what you say he couldn't have got far?"

"Then how could he simply disappear without any knowledge of it?"

"I don't know why you're worrying, Donna. The bloody maniac deserved all he got. The main thing is you didn't kill him."

"I'd just like to know what happened, that's all."

"You'll probably never know." He broke off. "I'm sorry Donna –I guess I owe you an apology."

"There's no need, Tom. The whole village thought badly of me."

"It must have been bloody awful for you."

"It was. You don't know what all those years were like, thinking you've killed someone. I can't begin to explain what it felt like."

He paused, searching for words. "I'm glad you came back."

"Thanks." She smiled.

She intended to sort her own belongings out, discard everything that Richard had given her including her engagement ring. She knew of a shop in Norwich that bought in second-hand jewellery. Maybe tomorrow she could try there.

She was about to leave the table when she received a call.

"Donna."

Oh my God! She froze. "Who is this?" she asked, pretending not to know.

"It's Johnny. Why didn't you tell me you were havin' my kid?"

She got up and walked outside. "I didn't know how to contact you – besides, after what happened I didn't think you'd want to know."

"Jeezus, Donna, what kind of bastard do you take me for?"

"Does it matter? I lost it – end of story," she said despondently.

"Did he know about the kid?"

"No. I didn't know myself until we separated."

"I have to see you," he insisted.

"You can't. I'm in Norfolk."

"Then I'll book a couple of days off and come over."

"No," she said bluntly. "I... I don't want to see you." She hung up, her hand trembling. He tried calling back, but she ignored it. There was no way she could face him. He'd hurt her once and she couldn't bear to go through it again.

CHAPTER SIXTY-SEVEN

"I got a postcard from the old lady," he told Catherine.

"What did she have to say?"

"Not a lot – fourteen words to be exact."

"It's better than nothing, Johnny. You know mother – she never was the world's greatest writer."

"So what was wrong with her calling me?"

"It works both ways, you know."

Like hell he'd ring her. If she couldn't be bothered to pick up the phone –why should he?

"How's the wedding coming along?" Catherine asked.

He shrugged. "I've got problems," he said.

"What kind of problems?"

"I was kinda seeing this woman," he began. "I just heard she's getting a divorce."

"Oh God! Johnny, don't go down that road," she said hastily.

"We go back some time, Cath," he said.

He couldn't believe it. Yet again Donna had rejected him. Why did he persist on running after her? Hadn't she made it perfectly clear she wanted nothing more to do with him?

Catherine glanced at him. "I think you'd better take a good look at things and get yourself sorted. No one can help you in this. It's all up to you, Johnny."

"Yeah – you don't have to tell me."

A few days later he decided to call Sarah.

"What gives with your sister?" he asked. "I try ringing her an' she ignores my calls."

"Johnny, you have to realise her emotions are all over the place at the moment. She's just lost a baby and she's going through a difficult divorce. She just needs time."

"How much time does she want?" he said derisively. "Does she expect me to hang around for another twelve years? Just tell her I called and that she has my number if she needs me."

* * *

"What were you thinking of, Sarah?" Donna said sharply down the phone. "You had no right to give him my number."

"He needs to speak to you, Dee. At least give him a call."

"He's unreliable – he can't be trusted."

"Why are you doing this, Dee?" You love him and I can't see what the problem is?"

"You made him call me – how does that make me feel?" she threw back.

"I didn't make him do anything. Believe it or not he genuinely cares about you."

"He used both of us. You of all people should know that."

"If it were me I'd jump at the chance," Sarah said wistfully.

"Go ahead, don't let me stop you," she blurted out.

"It's you he loves!" Sarah screamed back. "When are you going to realise that?"

"Just leave it," Donna said stubbornly.

"I suggest you do something about it," Sarah said heatedly. "Because one of these days you'll realise it's too late."

Over the following weeks Donna glanced hesitantly at the number several times.

Well… what are you waiting for?

Suppose he rejects me?

Ah rubbish. Just pick up the phone and call him.

She tapped out the number and waited as it rang.

"I'm sorry but the person you're calling is not available. Please leave a message after the tone."

That settled the matter. It wasn't meant to be. She screwed up the piece of paper and tossed it in the bin.

He's gone, so just get on with your life and forget him.

He waited six weeks for Donna to call. He heard nothing. Finally he gave up, accepting that she didn't want to know.

They were married in a registry office. Louis had insisted on a formal affair, but Michelle wanted to tie the knot as soon as possible before the baby bump showed.

They spent three weeks on honeymoon in the South of France on her father's yacht and came back to a £500,000 house that Louis had bought them as a wedding gift. It had five bedrooms, two with en-suites, a large conservatory, a double garage and a massive kitchen. In the meantime Johnny started his job as a director and had his own company car, a smart pale blue Jaguar.

He should have been the happiest man on earth – but all he could think of was Donna. The truth was, he'd be willing to give up the whole lot if it meant he could be with her.

CHAPTER SIXTY-EIGHT

"Hi honey."

"Melania!" Donna squealed down the line.

"I'm in London next week. I thought maybe we could meet up at some point?"

"Great. I'll come down on Friday night after work and make a weekend of it," Donna suggested.

"I'm staying at the Embassy. If you can make it, there's a hotel just down from there."

By the end of the week Donna was growing increasingly excited. London had always been her favourite place. And now she was returning.

There were no trains running on Friday evening, so she caught the next available one early on the Saturday morning, arriving in London at nine forty. She went straight to the hotel and checked in.

A man in a worn dark grey suit handed her the key and she struggled with her luggage up to her room. Glancing round at an old rickety dressing table covered in dust and a cracked basin in the corner of the room, she was thankful she was only there for the weekend. She was hungry, but decided not to eat. If this was anything to go by, what would the kitchens be like?

Just down the road she found the Embassy, where a crowd had gathered. She pushed her way through. "Excuse me," she cried to the door attendant, "I'm looking for Melanie Moon."

"Isn't everyone?" he replied rudely.

Struggling to keep her balance from the surge of fans,

she pushed forward and cried out, "I happen to be a personal friend."

"They all are," he said bluntly.

A white limo suddenly drew up and the crowd went berserk, charging forward. "Take her round the back," a man yelled through the deluge of photographers.

Fighting through the barricade of people, Donna scrambled after the car to the back of the building where the paparazzi had already gathered. "I need to see Miss Moon," she told a man on the door. "I have some personal documents for her." She was ushered through to where Melania, along with her six boxes of luggage and entourage, had already made their way.

"Honey, I'm glad you could make it." Melania greeted her with a hug and a kiss. Then she called for a bottle of champagne to be sent to her room.

"Oh Miss Moon, could I please have your autograph?" a maid asked excitedly, rushing forward.

Melania grabbed the pen and scribbled her signature. "I really need to rest," she told one of her entourage. Donna followed her up to her room, along with her PA, make-up assistant and dresser.

The room was massive - a spacious eighth-floor apartment with chandeliers and thick wall-to-wall carpeting. A cream brocade chaise longue stood directly beneath a large window draped in ivory satin curtains.

"It's quite a place," Donna said, glancing around and taking it all in.

"The air conditioning in here is crap compared to the States," Melania said, taking one of her dresses out of the case. "Maybe I should have the Yves St Laurent one," she mused thoughtfully, holding it against her.

Meanwhile, her harassed assistant was running in all directions trying to please her.

At that point Donna was beginning to wonder what she had let herself in for. Melania had star quality, there was no mistaking that. But sometimes she let it go to her head. Her long black hair was now cut into a short bob with subtle highlights. It suited her face. And her figure was even more toned and supple.

"I have a nice little venue arranged for this evening," she told Donna. "I think you're going to be pleasantly surprised."

"Remember Sacs?" Donna said, thinking back. It all seemed such a long time ago, but it still held sentimental values.

"Sacs!" Melania screeched. "Now you are showing your age, honey."

"It's called the Rio Club now," said her dresser.

"I've only been in there once – can't say I liked it," her PA added.

Donna managed a weak smile.

They left via the back door and were escorted into the waiting white stretch limo.

"Don't you ever get fed up with all this?" Donna asked her.

"It comes with the package," Melania said. "Once you get a taste for it there's no stopping you."

They arrived at the club and ordered their meal. Donna recognised a few celebrities but decided to keep it low key.

"So – how's life been treating you?" Melania asked, taking a sip of wine.

Donna shrugged. "OK, I guess." She paused. "I lost a… "

"Excuse me," interrupted her press secretary. "I have Mr Bandeau on the line calling from the States?"

Melania grabbed the phone. "Hi there, handsome. And to what exactly do I owe the pleasure of this call?"

Donna tuned out. Was there no way they could have a normal conversation without interruptions?

"Have you known Melanie long?" asked one of her colleagues.

"Yes. We met working at a club in London." She was about to say the name but thought better of it.

"She's done quite well for herself," he said in an American accent. He was tall and skinny with a mane of shaggy blonde hair, probably in his early twenties – much too young, she thought.

"Are you joining Melanie on tour?"

"No," she forced a smile. She wasn't exactly in the mood for conversation, at least, not with this guy.

Melania came off the phone. "So, honey, you were saying?"

Donna paused, not sure if she should mention the baby or not. "I... um... had a miscarriage eleven weeks ago."

"Jesus honey, you never told me! Richard must have been devastated."

She gave a faint smile. "Remember Johnny?" she said. "Johnny?"

"We all went to the health complex together?"

"Oh him," Melania replied in a flat tone. "So what racket is he involved in these days?"

Just then a camera flashed, almost blinding them, and Melania went berserk. "I told you distinctly I didn't want any paparazzi in here," she screamed at her press secretary. "Get them out – all of them!"

Donna had already decided that this had been a bad idea. She was contemplating her escape when Melania turned her attention back to her. "I really must get you fixed up with a real nice guy," she said. "Come along and met some of the crowd."

"No thanks," Donna replied. "I've just got rid of the last one you found me - remember?"

She got up to go to the loo and was cornered by a young journalist. "Excuse me, Madam?" he called.

What now?

"Are you Melanie Moon's PA?"

"No. I'm just an old acquaintance... Thank God," she added in a murmur.

"Pardon?"

"Never mind."

She dashed into the toilet and gave a sigh. If only she was back at home in the comfort of the small house. Never again would she envy Melania. If that was what stardom did for you then she'd rather be without it.

The night seemed to drag on and what had once seemed an exciting chapter in her life had now become boring. She made an excuse and turned in at eleven thirty.

She had a restless night and woke early next morning. It was six thirty and already there was noise coming from the next room. She heard a bed hammering against the wall and then a woman screaming in the throes of ecstasy.

She collected her thoughts and got out of bed, deciding to call it a day. As soon as she could, she intended calling Melania. She got washed and dressed and called the station and was told the next train to Norwich wasn't until 8.45 that evening. The thought of having to put up with Melania and her party for another day was mind destroying, to say the least.

At 8.30 she went down to see what was on offer for breakfast. She decided the safest thing would be a croissant and a pot of tea.

"There are no croissants," she was told, "Only toast."

"Fine," she agreed wearily. The man came back a few seconds later and said they would have to slip out and get a loaf. She settled for just the tea and thought of ringing Alex. She had his home number, although he probably had other arrangements made.

After hanging around for a while, she called Melania and spoke to her PA.

"Would you mind telling Miss Moon that I'm not too well and I'm going straight back home," she said.

"Of course. Who may I say is calling?"

"Donna."

"Donna?"

Apparently, the PA had already forgotten her - either that, or she'd failed to make an impression.

She packed her few belongings ready to check out of the hotel and then paused for a moment before picking up her mobile to call Alex.

"Hi Donna," he said briskly. "How are you?"

"Fine. I'm in London."

"London?"

"I came to see an old friend last night – you may have heard of her – Melanie Moon."

"The Melanie Moon?"

"Yes – didn't I mention we go back a long time?"

"Nope."

"She was once a good friend. A lot's happened, Alex. I'll tell you sometime."

"So where's hubby?"

She decided now was the time to put the cards straight. "I'm here on my own. Richard and I had a divorce."

"I'm sorry to hear that," he replied, unable to keep the zest out of his voice. "So what are you doing at the moment?"

"Nothing in particular. My train isn't until this evening."

"How do you fancy lunch?"

"Sounds great."

"Good. I'll pick you up in, say, twenty minutes?"

They spent a wonderful day together. He took her to lunch and then they went on a boat trip down the Thames. Come the evening he asked her to stay the night with him.

"I can't, Alex. I have to be in work tomorrow."

"Ring them. Tell them you have a migraine," he said persuasively.

It sounded very tempting. "I don't know, Alex…" she said.

"Come on," he said. "Be a little bit naughty for once."

He began to kiss her, softly at first, then becoming more demanding.

What are you doing?

I can do what the hell I like – remember I've no husband to feel guilty about any more.

They rolled into the bedroom and this time she gave him her whole being. What had she to lose? She'd been lonely far too long.

CHAPTER SIXTY-NINE

"Who's responsible for seeing this is checked properly?" Johnny said, examining the pre-packed food rolling off the production line. "By the time it reaches the consumer it won't be fit for the dogs."

"I'll make sure it's sorted, Mr Ricci," the man said wearily.

"And I want the order ready by five tonight," he demanded.

"Yes, Mr Ricci."

He marched back up to his office and sorted through some paperwork. Reaching into his top drawer, he grabbed a bottle of Jack Daniel's and took a couple of swigs. Marriage to Michelle was no picnic, and apart from the fact that he was looking forward to becoming a father again he could have willingly walked out. Putting the bottle back in his desk he summoned his secretary, Penny, to his office.

"What are you doing in your lunch hour?" he asked her.

"I have nothing planned, Mr Ricci."

"Johnny," he said. "And be ready for one o'clock."

"Fine, Johnny," she said with a broad smile.

He took her to an elite restaurant, where they ordered a bottle of wine with their meal. She was twenty-two and lived with her boyfriend, who she was quite prepared to forget.

"So you've worked for the company two years?" he asked her.

"Yes. And I've also met your wife a couple of times." She paused. "You know you're treading on thin ice," she added, taking a sip of wine.

"Do I look bothered?"

"You're obviously immune to danger."

"I guess I get off on the buzz," he said.

They stared at one another across the table, both feeling the same desire to rip off each other's clothes.

"I know what you're thinking," she said.

"Are my dirty thoughts that obvious?"

"You're playing dangerous games with Louis. You could get us both fired."

"I'm willing to take the risk if you are."

"So what are we waiting for?" she smiled.

He quickly settled the bill and they drove to a quiet country lane, where he parked the Jag. He reached for the seat recliner and they lay back. Within seconds his hand was exploring her body. It seemed ages since he'd had a real woman – someone with curves – and Penny had curves in all the right places.

He slid his hands up between her legs to the skin above her stocking tops. Jeez! Suspenders! He felt the urge to come right there and then. Tearing open her blouse, he brought his lips down to her rock-hard nipples, taunting and teasing her with his tongue until she began to moan with pleasure.

"Don't stop Johnny... pleeeease don't stop!"

He had no intention of stopping. Maybe he was playing a dangerous game, but it was worth the risk. It compensated for every miserable fucking moment he spent with Michelle.

When he returned to the office, he put in a call to Jane.

"I want to see my daughter," he demanded, using the phone on his desk.

"Oh do you?" Jane said equally as sharp. "I think you know perfectly well I won't allow it. Not the way you conduct yourself. I suggest if you want to see your daughter again you start acting responsibly."

"And you call giving an eleven-year-old kid the key to the house responsible?"

"You know perfectly well it was a one off."

"That's not the impression I got."

"Well, whatever impression you've got, you're still not seeing her."

"I'm sorry it's come to this, Jane," he said, stamping his authority. "But you leave me with no choice. You'll be hearing from my solicitor." He slammed down the phone.

Jane was more than curious about the sudden change in his attitude, so she rang the number back. She was greeted by a chirpy voice. "Good morning, Phelan Products."

"Have you a Johnny Ricci working there?" she asked.

"We have a Mr Ricci, the marketing director, if that's who you mean?"

"Did you say the marketing director?" Jane repeated, taken back.

"Yes – would you like me to connect you?"

She hung on and when he answered she was still mortified. "What exactly have you been up to?" she asked suspiciously.

He ignored her question. "What d' you want? I'm busy."

"I need to talk to you about Kylie," she began.

"I'm listening."

"I'm agreeing for you to see her on a monthly basis."

She paused before adding, "Any signs of fooling around with other women and you can forget it."

"I'm hardly going to fool around with my wife present."

"Your wife?" She let out a howl of laughter. "I can hardly see one woman satisfying you."

Again he ignored her comment, not intending to rock the boat at this stage.

"I thought maybe the last weekend in every month," Jane suggested. "I'll get back to you at some point."

"Fine."

He put the phone down and smiled to himself. The bitch was finally thawing out.

"You're eating far too many bad things," Michelle quibbled as he pushed the plate of pulses and kidney beans to one side.

"I want proper food, not this crap," he grumbled.

"It's time you started re-educating yourself and ate properly."

"If you wanna starve yourself that's up to you, but don't think for one moment you can push this rubbish onto me."

Bouncing up from the table he stormed into the bathroom. When he came out of the shower she was busy on the phone.

Something wasn't quite right. He'd had his suspicions for a few weeks. It had been over three months since she had broken the news that she was pregnant. There was no baby bump, nor were there any normal signs of pregnancy.

He checked she was still on the phone, then glanced in her bedside cabinet. He found half a packet of contraceptive pills and her diary. He flicked briefly through the pages, and began to spot things – right from the first time they'd made love. Then he came to the last entry, dated a week ago.

"Still no sign of a baby. Have to try harder."

Jeezus! The bitch had stitched him up.

She put down the phone and turned to him. "I've composed a list which hardly contains any saturated fat..." she began.

Fury was boiling up inside him. He could hardly look at her. "How's the baby?" he cut in.

"Fine," she smiled, without the faintness sign of suspicion. She broke off and glanced at him. "What's wrong with you tonight?"

"This," he shouted, holding up the diary. "Do you take me for an idiot?"

She began to cower. "I really don't know what you're going on about."

"There's no baby – never has been. What were you hoping – that you'd suddenly get pregnant and that I wouldn't have the brains to work it out?"

She turned on the waterworks. "Please, Johnny, I did it because I didn't want to lose you. I knew if we were having a baby you'd marry me."

He glanced at her with disgust. "You'd got it all worked out – you an' your old man."

He turned to leave the room. He desperately needed a drink.

"Where are you going?" she screamed after him. She ran across to the door and attempted to block his path. "We have to talk!"

"Get outta my way."

"No!" she screamed at him.

"Get outta my way – or else." He went to bring his

hand up. Jeez! What was happening to him? He'd never hit a woman in his life. His old man was beginning to take over.

"Johnny... pleaaase... " she screamed.

He pushed her aside and slammed the door behind him. Making his way to the local he took his aggression out on the fruit machine. He got through ten pounds and decided to quit while he still had some change on him. He had a couple of lagers, counted his money and then headed off to the club.

It was full of kids. He felt ancient in there. Were clubbers getting younger, or had he just got older? What the hell – he was thirty two. He didn't feel any different – maybe a little more ragged around the edges.

At one o'clock he rolled back into the house, only to find Michelle sitting up in bed, waiting anxiously. He reached for his case and she jumped off the bed.

"What are you doing?" she screamed.

"It's finished, Michelle," he said. "There's no baby and there's no us."

"But we can still be happy without the baby... just me and you. We'll be fine." She was babbling so fast he could hardly get a word in. "In fact, we can try for lots of babies. I love children, and I'll be a good mother."

"Michelle..."

"We can go to places... do what we like together."

"Michelle – will you just listen!" he yelled, trying to break it to her as gently as possible. "You an' me – it's not gonna work. I don't love you."

"But you will in time – I know you will. Please, Johnny don't go... " She began to go hysterical. "I... I'll kill myself if you do." She ran into the bathroom and grabbed a razor blade. "I'll slit my wrists!"

"Jeezus, Michelle – just put it down," he panicked.

"No I won't," she sobbed, taking the razor to her wrists. He watched the thin steel blade cut into her flesh. The blood began to pour.

Oh sweet Mary – how had he got into this mess? More to the point, how would he get out of it?

"OK, sweetheart – just put it down." Gradually he eased the razor out of her hand.

"Promise you won't leave me– promise?" she sobbed.

Wrapping a cloth round her wrists he held her loosely in his arms. "It's OK," he whispered. "It's OK."

CHAPTER SEVENTY

It had been the most wonderful weekend Donna could remember. They'd wined and dined at an exclusive restaurant and then he'd taken her to the theatre. She'd told him all about the tough times with Richard and he'd listened sympathetically.

Trudy had been a complete bitch over the phone and told her she must take in a doctor's note.

"I'm not in the habit of running to the surgery with every little ailment," Donna said coolly over the phone.

"Then you can't be that ill!" was her stern reply.

"Hand in your notice," Alex prompted. "You know your job's safe here."

The offer was tempting and gave her a sense of security. Maybe she'd do just that.

Just as she was about to leave, Alex came up with a surprise. "I know this is a bit sudden... " he began, "But the thing is... I mean... damn it Donna, will you marry me?"

She was completely taken back. "I don't know what to say," she said.

"Will you think about it?"

"Yes. Of course," she said in a state of bemusement.

"I don't expect an answer straight away," he murmured. He kissed her. It was
nothing like she'd experienced with Johnny, but it was soft and gentle, and it warmed her deflated ego.

"You'll call me?" he asked her.

"Yes. As soon as I get back," she told him.

He drove her to the station and waved her off. When she got home, Doris was waiting. "Did you have a nice time, dear?"

"Lovely, mother, thank you."

She unpacked a few things and then gave Alex a call to tell him she had arrived safely. It was almost six when she went down to the supermarket. On the way she bumped into Kitty Baker and Thelma, Frank's widow.

Greeting them with a chirpy hello she glanced at Thelma, who was clutching a bunch of chrysanthemums and humming away to herself, oblivious to the rest of the world.

"She suffers with dementia," Kitty muttered. "She hardly goes out, so I offered to help her get some flowers for the cemetery in the morning. She's never been the same since Frank died," she said discreetly. "It must have hit her hard – he had a heart attack, you know."

"Yes. So I heard," Donna replied trying not to stare at Kitty's blue rinsed hairdo. "I'm glad I caught you, Kitty. I'd like to clear a few things up," she began. "I believe people thought I ran away because I was pregnant with Tony's child. Well I wasn't, and even if I had been there's no way I would have run off and left him."

"No one's blaming you, dear," Kitty replied. "In any case, what you do is your business."

"Is that so?" Donna replied with an edge of irony in her voice. "Well it's not that easy when people are talking behind your back."

"No one's talking about you, luv," Kitty replied, with one of her false smiles.

"Don't act the innocent with me, Kitty."

Thelma was still humming away to herself, so Donna continued, "Which brings me to the real reason I ran away," she muttered. "I was alone in the house that Saturday when Frank turned up. He tied to rape me – yes rape," she repeated to a horrified Kitty.

"I can't believe Frank would do such a thing," Kitty gasped.

"I want to go home," Thelma demanded tugging at Kitty's arm.

"Yes – in a minute dear," Kitty said eager to hear the rest of the story. "You should have gone to the police an' let them have sorted it out."

Donna thought it in her best interests not to mention the fact that she had stabbed Frank - she'd only be accused of GBH.

"I believe Frank had an accident a few weeks before he died. Do you know anything about it?" she asked.

Kitty shook her head. "No dear. Can't say I do... unless," she paused for a moment. "Wait a minute, now you come to mention it I remember Betty saying something about an accident he had at the farm. Betty found him crouched on the pavement and rushed him to hospital. Why do you ask?"

"It doesn't matter."

Noting the sudden distress on Thelma's face, Donna wished she'd never have mentioned anything.

"I want to go home," Thelma demanded, terrified and confused. "I want to go home – now!" Throwing the flowers at Kitty, she made a lunge for her, thumping her in the face.

Quickly grabbing hold of Thelma, Donna attempted to pull her away.

"Who are you? Why are you interfering? " Thelma screamed at Donna, about to strike out.

A dazed Kitty stood nursing an angry bruise on her cheek, too traumatised to speak.

"Come on, Thelma, stop this at once," Donna said firmly, struggling to cope with the woman's sudden burst of strength.

"He deserved all he got," Thelma spat. "That's why I killed him."

"You didn't kill anyone, Thelma," Donna said, doing her best to calm her down.

"Yes, I did," she said, eyes staring wildly at Donna. "He just kept shouting at me, going on and on. He wouldn't stop shouting. Then he complained of chest pains. I stood there watching him suffer, the way he'd made me suffer all those years. 'Get me my tablets, you stupid woman,' he kept shouting. 'Get me my tablets!' And then it went quiet and the shouting stopped."

"Who else have you told, Thelma?" she asked, imagining what it must have been like living with Frank all those years.

Thelma's lips remained sealed, reluctant to talk about the matter any further. She began to hum away to herself again.

"Thelma, you can tell me?" Donna urged.

"Ah – you're wasting your breath," Kitty said, suddenly finding her tongue. "The authorities are bound to know. They're treating it as a mental disorder."

"You look shaken up, Kitty. Are you sure you'll be OK?" Donna asked.

"I'll be fine," she said, putting on a brave face, "Nothing a nice cuppa tea won't cure."

"Can we go home now?" Thelma asked, acting as if nothing had happened. "Frank will be angry – he'll be waiting for his tea."

CHAPTER SEVENTY-ONE

"Dad!" Kylie squealed excitedly down the phone. "Mom's gone into hospital to have the baby. I'm going to have a brother or sister. How cool is that!"

"Hey, sweetheart, that's good news."

"Phil's here. He wants to ask you something."

"Hi Johnny," he said, grabbing the receiver. "I wondered if you wouldn't mind having Kylie while Jane's in hospital?"

"You know you don't have to ask."

There was a scream of delight from Kylie.

"It may be a few days. There are a few complications. It seems it's a breech birth and they're considering a caesarean. They're carrying out some tests. I guess it's just routine stuff."

"Sorry to hear that," Johnny said. "I'll pick Kylie up on my way home."

He needed something to cheer him up and bring him out of this morbid depression and what better than having his daughter.

Michelle was hostile towards Kylie as soon as they arrived. She didn't even attempt to make the child feel at ease.

"I don't like her, dad," Kylie said as soon as they were alone.

"Kylie – listen, there's no way I'm gonna get back with your mother, if that's what this is about. And if we're going to make this work, you've gotta accept Michelle."

"But she's just horrid."

He put 'Grease' on and they sat and watched it. He'd seen the film loads of times, but if it made Kylie happy, so be it.

"Danny's really nice," she said. "He's cool like you, dad."

"Yeah – you reckon?"

Michelle sat crossed legged wagging her foot in a strop. "Are you going to spend all evening glued to the television?" she complained.

He ignored her comment. "If you're going in the kitchen, bring some chocolate chip ice cream out," he called.

"Get off your skinny butt and do it yourself," she snapped.

A few minutes later she returned with the ice cream and slammed it down in front of him.

"Thanks," he said coolly. He gave Kylie a wink. "Enjoy, sweetheart."

He made an attempt to be sociable to Michelle. "Hey – come an' sit down," he said, patting the couch.

"You know I have to be at the gym for seven," she replied moodily.

"Yeah – well try an' work off some of that aggression," he called after her.

Next day he took Kylie to school and at three thirty he collected her and brought her back to his office, giving her a puzzle book to keep her occupied.

"I like her," she said as Penny dropped in with some paperwork. "Have you slept with her?"

"Jeez! Kylie, what kind of question's that?"

"I know what goes on, dad," she said in a grown up voice. "And if you have, I don't blame you."

He got the feeling that even if he'd said he hadn't she still wouldn't believe him.

In the evening he took her to ballet classes and even made an attempt to help her with her French homework. In the meantime, he spoilt her rotten. She had ice cream and cookies whenever she fancied them.

"How long is she staying?" Michelle asked in a tone that suggested she wanted the girl out of the house.

"For as long as it takes," he replied abruptly.

"It's hardly right to have a child hanging around. Our sex life has become non-existent since she arrived."

It's not the kid, sweetheart. The fact is, you simply don't turn me on any more.

"That happens to be my daughter you're talking about," he said coolly. "If there's a problem, I suggest we go our separate ways."

She didn't bother to answer.

★ ★ ★

"Phil, how are you coping, you poor soul?" Sylvia said over the phone.

"As well as can be expected," he said, not particularly overjoyed to hear his mother-in-law.

"Have you heard any more news?" Sylvia asked anxiously. "I called the hospital and all they'd tell me is she's comfortable. Phil, I just don't like the sound of this."

"I'm sure she's in the best hands, Sylvia."

"Why are they doing all these tests?"

"It's just safety precautions, I imagine. As soon as I hear something, I'll let you know."

"I'm coming over to do some washing and cleaning for you."

"There's really no need, Sylvia. I can cope," he said briskly, managing sufficiently without her interference.

"Well I'll come and take Kylie off your hands. I'll be only too happy to have my granddaughter."

"She's away at the moment."

"Where?"

He braced himself to tell her. "She's with her father."

"Father!"

"He came and picked her up a couple of nights ago."

"Are you telling me that despicable creature who got my little girl pregnant has taken my grandchild?"

"He seems a genuinely nice bloke," Phil said. "And all he wants is to see his daughter."

"Over my dead body!" she spat. "I don't know how you could have allowed this to happen, Phil."

"Sylvia, if you're not happy, I suggest you take it up with him," he replied.

"I intend to."

She demanded Johnny's address and hung up.

"You're never going to believe this," she screamed at Kevin. "That monster has only gone and taken Kylie."

"Monster?"

"That creature - who else!"

"You have to let go," he said. "By rights he's the father and unfortunately there's nothing you can do about it."

"We'll see about that."

"In any case, if the child's happy with him I don't see a problem."

Sylvia glared at him. "You don't see a problem?" she shrieked. "You never see a problem until it's too late."

CHAPTER SEVENTY-TWO

"How did your London trip go?" Sarah asked over the phone.

"Don't mention it."

"You mean she never introduced you to any of the celebs?"

"I met plenty of those. It was a complete nightmare, Sarah. I only stayed one night."

"So what were you doing the rest of the time?"

"I met Alex, my old manager."

"Oh yes. Now things are getting interesting. So what happened then?"

"Sarah, please," she replied, putting his proposal to the back of her mind. "We're just good friends, nothing more."

She thought of Alex. What was stopping her from remarrying? She was now a free agent.

"Has mother said anything more about Frank?" Sarah asked.

"No, but you'll never guess who I bumped into the other day. Remember Thelma Brooks – Frank's widow? She reckons she helped to kill Frank."

"I thought he died of a heart attack?"

"He did, but she held back his medication."

"You're kidding," Sarah giggled. "Thelma deserves a bloody medal... Did you mention anything about...?"

"Frank trying to rape me?" Donna cut in. "Yes, but I never mentioned stabbing him. Apparently it was Betty who found him. He told her he'd had an accident at the farm and she rushed him to hospital."

Donna gave a deep sigh. "I can't understand why

mother is so reluctant to discuss it. Why doesn't she believe me?"

"I think she believes you, Dee. It's just her way of trying to accept what's happened – maybe she's trying to shut it out because she feels that in some way she should have protected you."

"I'm just relieved it's finally all over," Donna sighed. "For all our sakes."

The next day Alex got in touch. "Have you given any more thought to what I asked you?"

"Yes."

"And?"

"I'd love to be Mrs Spencer."

She was blindly plunging into her second marriage, despite the apprehension and doubt. He had charisma and style. He always wore expensive suits and she knew he'd offer her security – but?

I don't love him.

So what? You're too fussy. Take what's given. Nothing better is going to come along.

"I'm getting married," Donna announced to her mother.

"Married?" Doris gasped. Why, you've only bin divorced a few months. Shouldn't you wait for things to settle?"

"Wait for what, mother? I'm coming up to thirty-eight and I would like to try for another baby before I'm too old."

"You should've thought of thart before you rushed off an' left your husband!"

Donna felt like screaming out to her mother that it was Richard who never wanted children and that he'd gone ahead and had the snip without even consulting her. But it would only complicate matters, and it still didn't explain the fact that she'd conceived another man's child. Instead she kept things to herself.

"Mother, please… at least try and be happy for me."

Over the coming weeks, Donna was kept busy. She had a wedding to arrange. Her weekends were taken up with travelling to and from London. It was happening so fast that she didn't give it much thought.

Alex's apartment was small yet clinically clean, and he always insisted on cooking. It was a way of life he had become accustomed to.

On that particular night they sat over a candlelit dinner with soft background music. She had a glass of wine – and then two or three more. Was she making a mistake? Somehow this just didn't induce the thrill and excitement she expected – as if she were embarking on a future she might regret.

She picked at her food and gulped down the wine. "I don't usually drink this much," she laughed nervously.

He smiled and took the glass out of her hand, then led her over to the settee. He began to kiss her and run his fingers softly through her hair.

"Are you sure you're OK, my sweet?" he asked.

"Yes. Of course," she replied, trying to sound in control of the situation. He repeatedly kissed her, moving his hand slowly towards the dip in her cleavage. "Shall we go into the bedroom?" he whispered.

Why did he always ask questions? Why didn't he just do it, for crissake?

She had now slept with three men; her husband, Johnny, who had got her pregnant, and now Alex. Her marriage had broken up almost nine months ago, and yet there was no immediate urge to jump into bed with this man.

Oh God! What was it with her? She could only focus on one man.

You must let go.

I can't.

You have to. He's gone – it's too late.

He lifted her up and carried her into the bedroom. "My dearest Donna," he whispered, "You're so very beautiful."

They kissed and he began caressing her body, teasing her with his tongue. Lifting her dress, he removed her panties and began to probe with his fingers until she became aroused and felt herself longing for more.

"Congratulations," Sarah said. "So when are you choosing the ring?"

"There's no rush," Donna replied.

"Seriously Dee, I'm so happy for you."

"Thanks."

"What are you doing about work?"

"I'm giving my notice in this week. I've been offered a job at Alex's company. I suppose I'll stick it for a time until… " she trailed off.

"Until baby Spencer comes along?" Sarah said excitedly.

"Something like that."

She thought of Johnny and the child she might have had, and gave a sigh. It wasn't to be. Their lives had gone separate ways. And now she intended to make a fresh start.

CHAPTER SEVENTY-THREE

"Look at the mess your dear daughter's made in the kitchen," Michelle complained.

"Dad!" Kylie screamed. "I was only trying to surprise you."

"It's OK, sweetheart, let's clean it away," Johnny said, trying to keep both of them happy.

"It's your favourite meat and potato pie," Kylie said excitedly.

Michelle gave him a withering glance and stormed off.

Kylie rolled her eyes, whispering, "She's got them on her again."

"Sssssh," he whispered back. "Let's not cause any arguments."

Finishing the tidying up, he walked into the lounge, undid the button on his shirt and poured himself a whisky.

"Hadn't you better stop drinking?" Michelle complained.

"Yeah – when I'm dead."

He took his drink out onto the patio. He needed to chill out, but with all that was going on around him it was virtually impossible. He was drinking far too much and he knew it; at home and at work. He'd even got up in the night and taken a whisky. Jeez! What had happened to him? All he knew was that he felt trapped, unable to think straight any more. Wasn't he the one who had always believed in himself, vowing never to get married? And now look at him, in one hopeless rut.

Heated voices coming from the living room suddenly erupted, the stern harshness of Sylvia's voice. "Where is he? Where is the beast?" Walking back into the lounge, he came face to face with her.

"So you're the father?" she spat, sizing him up with a disgusted look.

"Who are you? And what the hell are you doing here?" he said, infuriated by this middle aged busybody.

"I'm her grandmother and I've come to take her home," Sylvia announced, standing primly in her Karen Millen suit, with firm-set hairstyle and over-made-up face.

"You've no right to come barging in here," he said bluntly.

She ignored him. "Come along, Kylie. We're going home."

"But Gran, I'm cooking dad some dinner."

"He is not your father," she said sternly. "Phil is your father."

"Would you mind leaving?" Johnny said, steering her in the direction of the door and trying to control his temper in front of Kylie.

"I'm not leaving without my granddaughter," she insisted, rushing back to the child and grabbing her hand.

"I don't want to go!" Kylie screamed.

Sylvia was furious. "How dare you take her without our permission?"

"I got Phil's permission."

"Well – you certainly haven't got mine or my daughters. You think you can just turn up and take her."

"I offered to look after Jane and the baby, but it was thrown in my face," he said firmly. "And I haven't just turned up – I've been trying to see my daughter for eleven years."

"Well, you won't be seeing her any more, I'll make sure of that."

"Try an' stop me. I'm her father an' if it means taking you to court, I will."

Sylvia had no reply to that. She attempted to drag Kylie to the door.

"I don't want to go – and I'm stopping here with my dad," she screamed.

"You little brat," Sylvia spat. "I shall remember this next time your birthday comes along."

"I don't bloody care," Kylie screamed back.

Sylvia stared at the child in horror. "What did you say?"

"Can't you see you're upsetting her? Just leave," Johnny demanded.

Sylvia stared at all three of them. "Don't think you've heard the last of this."

"No. I dare say I haven't," Johnny said. "But for now my kid stays with me."

He slammed the door on her and held his breath.

Michelle stood with her arms folded. "Why do you insist on hanging around the stupid bitch?" she exploded.

"Who are you on about?" he yelled back.

Michelle threw a thumb in Kylie's direction, "Her mother – who do you think?"

"Just grow up, Michelle," he hissed, walking past her. The amount of pressure was beginning to take its toll. He felt like he was in the middle of a tug of war, Michelle at one end, Jane and her mother, the other. He didn't know how much more he could take.

"Dad, I've ruined the dinner. It's burnt. Are you all right?"

"Yeah, fine," he said, trying to put on a brave face.

"Don't let Gran upset you, she's just a wicked old witch."

"Hey – who's upset, sweetheart?"

"You are. I can always tell." She waited until Michelle's back was turned. "It's her, isn't it?" she whispered curtly.

"Don't let Michelle hear you speak about her like that," he said firmly.

He took the plates through to the diner where Michelle was waiting. "Why didn't you just let her take the child?" she snapped.

"What concern is it of yours?" he hurled back.

"She's been here five days already," Michelle complained.

"I don't give a damn if she's here for another five days, that's my kid."

Michelle flung down the tea towel. "You're a selfish bastard. You'll be sorry for this."

"Sorry - for what?" he yelled after her as she stormed off.

Kylie was listening by the door. "She hates me, dad."

"No she doesn't hate you, angel," he said, in an attempt to console her.

"She does – and you know it. So why are you taking her side?"

"Listen Kylie, you sometimes have to bend the rules a bit. It's not always simple but you've gotta try."

"I don't like her an' I wish you'd never met her," she said, pulling a face.

That makes two of us.

"Hey – suppose we watch another video?" he suggested.

Kylie shook her head. "I'm going to my room. I need to be up early tomorrow if we're picking mom up."

He gave her a hug. "Night, sweetheart."

"Night, dad."

Jeezus! Why the hell did she always hear him arguing? If it wasn't with her mother it was with Michelle.

He took a shower, enjoying the peace and quiet of being on his own. If only he could just walk out, run off as he'd always done when the pressure had got too demanding. He dried himself and slung on a bathrobe. When he walked back in the room he caught Michelle with the photo of him and Donna.

"Who's this?" she demanded.

"Where d' you get it?" he snapped.

"I found it on the floor."

Like hell she had. "You've been in my frigging wallet."

"Is this her mother?" she yelled.

He ignored her question. "What the hell were you doing in my wallet?" he repeated.

"I needed a five-pound note," she said lamely, attempting to cover her tracks. "I only had a twenty."

"Keep outta my stuff in future," he shouted, snatching the snap back off her. "Or me an' you are gonna fall out big time."

"I asked you a question," she demanded, wagging her foot.

"Someone I knew some time ago, OK?" he replied bluntly.

"So why are you still keeping it?"

Good question. Why was he? It was all over between him and Donna. But why give Michelle the satisfaction of seeing him bin it?

Next morning he never spoke to her. He got up early and dropped Kylie back home.

Phil was already waiting when they arrived. "We can't have any more kids," he said glumly. "They've removed a lump from her ovaries. The tests have come back and thank God it's non-malignant, but she has to go back for regular check-ups."

"You have my number if you need me, Phil."

"I'm sorry about the trouble with the old battleaxe," Phil said. "She demanded the address, so there was little I could do about it."

He shrugged. "Ah, forget it." Giving Kylie a hug, he told her to look after her mom and baby sister.

He drove straight to work to find a pile of paperwork on his desk. Attempting to sort through it, he gave up. Life was crippling him. He couldn't take much more. He took the bottle of whisky out of his drawer and poured a large glass. Then he summoned Penny.

"I need you here – now," he yelled.

Sensing his urgency she quickly rushed to his office. "My God, are you all right?"

"She's doing my head in," he burst out. "She's doing my fuckin' head in!"

"Johnny, I'll get my keys and we'll take the back entrance," she said.

In five minutes they were heading off in her car. She drove to a quiet spot and parked. "You'll have to leave her, Johnny. If it's this bad there's no other way." She paused. "I think you know how I feel about things?"

"Cum' here," he said, pulling her close. "I guess I mucked up big time, huh?" He reached for her perfect soft breasts, bringing his head down to them. "Oh Jeezus Penny, you feel so good," he murmured, "So damned good."

CHAPTER SEVENTY-FOUR

Donna stood in the changing room, gazing at herself in an ivory satin bridal gown and unable to accept the fact that soon she would be married.

"You look simply beautiful," said the assistant fussing over her. "We can order it in white if you prefer?"

"Oh Dee, you look stunning," Sarah agreed.

The assistant helped Donna out of her dress. "It'll be here before you know it," she said.

They continued to look for bridesmaid dresses and then had lunch.

"Are you excited? I know I would be," Sarah said taking a bite out of a tuna and salad sandwich. "How's mother taking it? Has she warmed to the idea yet?"

"You know mother, she's too old fashioned to connect herself to the real world."

Donna broke off with a sigh. "If only father could have been here to give me away," she said regrettably. But of course he had gone, and she would never get the opportunity again.

"I'm sure he'll be looking down and giving you his blessing." Sarah's face lit up. "Dee,I have a date tomorrow night."

"You have?" Donna said, hoping for Sarah's sake that this time it would work out.

"He's taking me to dinner." She broke off with a smile. "Things could be looking up for us both."

Donna took a sip of cappuccino. "I hope so. It's funny, but I never imagined I could live anywhere except

London, and now I'm not so sure. I guess it must be a sign of getting old."

"You, old? Never," Sarah said.

"Sometimes I feel it." She paused for a second. "Sarah, am I doing the right thing?" she asked. "It's just I keep having doubts."

"Surely you're not having second thoughts, Dee?"

"I don't know. Alex is kind and considerate. He'd never do anything to hurt me. It's just... well I rushed into my last marriage, and look where that got me."

"Dee, if you're uncertain it's not too late to call it off. Maybe if you waited a few months – give things chance to settle down?"

Donna shrugged it off with a smile. "I'm just being silly," she said.

Darn it. She was getting married in a few weeks. Why couldn't she just feel happy about things?

She spent the following week with Alex in London. They went over the final wedding arrangements and Alex promised to put his apartment up for sale and look for something in a rural location.

Everything seemed perfect – and yet...

Why didn't she feel blissfully happy with the situation?

You're making a mistake. You'll regret it just like before.

Just shut the hell up.

"You look tired my sweet, I've obviously been working you too hard," Alex said, glancing at her like a forlorn puppy. "I'll go and make some tea." He hardly let her touch a thing and insisted on doing his own washing, ironing and tidying the apartment. Everywhere she went he wasn't far behind. Even in the kitchen he insisted on interfering. He was stifling her, couldn't he see that?

"At least let me cook you a meal, Alex," she complained.

"You'll have plenty of time for that," he promised, giving her an affectionate hug.

Over the week Alex did everything in his power to please her – he even bought her tickets for the theatre.

She couldn't help but feel relieved when it was time to return home. He was kind and sweet but she longed for her freedom and her own space.

Back home she sat quietly thinking in her bedroom, realising that once they were married there'd be no escape.

Maybe he did care.

Maybe he could give her security and a home but she simply didn't love him. Not only was she fooling him – she was fooling herself.

She thought long and hard before she picked up her mobile and called him. "Alex… " she began.

"Donna, did you get home safely?"

"Yes thanks." She hesitated. "Alex, you know I've always been honest with you…"

"This sounds very official," he joked, sensing this was bad news. "I hope it isn't going to take long, I've got a steak under the grill."

"Alex, I can't marry you."

There was silence on the line.

"Alex – did you hear what I said?" she repeated. "I'm sorry for putting you through this but I can't make this commitment – at least not so soon," she added, still wondering if she was doing the right thing.

There was little surprise in Alex's reply. "I've been very foolish and selfish," he said calmly. "I've known for some time how unhappy you were."

"You have?" she said.

"I can't hold you against your will, Donna, and if you're not happy, neither am I."

"You mean you're not angry with me?" she asked, holding back her tears.

"Of course I'm not angry. Frustrated and disappointed, but not angry."

"Alex, you're the most thoughtful and kindest person I've ever met and as a friend I love you dearly – you know that?"

"He's a very lucky man," Alex said.

"There's nobody else, you know that."

"Isn't there?" he said, more of a statement than a question.

She laughed it off. "What are you – a fortune teller?"

"No. But I do have a touch of sixth sense," he replied with a smile in his voice.

She thought no more of it. "Alex, thank you for everything."

"Look after yourself," he said.

She hung up. She'd never intended to hurt him. And then the tears began to fall.

★ ★ ★

"I've called off the wedding," she told Sarah on the phone the next day. "I don't know what I want any more." She trailed off with a sigh. "Maybe I should have married Alex."

"If you have the slightest doubt Dee, it's best to let things cool down and wait. What are you doing about work?"

"I haven't given it much thought."

"Dee, why not come and live with me for a while?" Sarah suggested. "Give yourself time to adjust to things?"

"Live in Birmingham? Are you mad?"

"I actually live in Solihull," Sarah corrected in an offended tone.

Birmingham, Solihull – what difference does it make?

Sarah decided not to push the matter any further. She knew better than to argue with her sister.

"How did your date go?" Donna asked.

"Fine – I'm seeing him again next week."

"So there could be a wedding in the family after all," she said attempting to sound cheerful.

"Give me a chance," Sarah chuckled. "I haven't seen what's on offer in his lunch box yet."

CHAPTER SEVENTY-FIVE

"It's Kylie," Phil began anxiously. "She's been in a road accident."

Johnny felt the blood drain from his body. "What's happened? Is she OK?"

There was a pause on the line.

"For crissake, Phil!"

"She's in a critical but stable condition. Jane's at the hospital with her."

"Which hospital?"

"Solihull."

He quickly wrote down the details, jumped in his car and raced over. Jane was waiting in the corridor outside the ICU when he arrived.

"The doctors are with her at the moment," she said, dabbing her eyes with a handkerchief. "She's unconscious, Johnny - she never came round."

"Oh Jeezus," he said, overcome with shock.

"We have to be ready for the worst, Johnny," Jane muttered in a low shaky voice. "If she doesn't make it..."

"Don't say she won't make it," he cut in sharply, cracking with emotion. "She's a tough kid. She'll pull through."

They held on to one another and Johnny led her over to a chair. "Where's the driver?" he asked.

"It's not his fault – he's just as shaken up as we are," she said, trying her best to console him. "Kylie was on her mobile and she stepped out into the road – whatever was she thinking of?"

"Why couldn't it have been me!" he cried, banging his fists.

Jumping up at the sound of the doctor's voice, they listened anxiously while he spoke. "Your daughter has severe concussion; we can't say exactly how bad it is until the MRI scans come through."

"She's gonna be all right, isn't she?" Johnny cut in anxiously.

He looked at them solemnly. "I have to warn you that your daughter may have permanent brain damage. There's also a possibility that she may have broken a vertebra in her neck."

Johnny stood too dazed for words.

"You mean she may never be able to walk again?" Jane murmured.

"As I've said, until the scans come through I can't tell you much more."

How could this be happening? His precious daughter and Donna were the only people he cared about.

"Try not to get too upset at this stage," the doctor went on to say. "The next twenty-four hours are the most critical."

" I just want her to pull through," Jane sobbed. "I don't care what else happens."

Johnny realised he had to be strong for her sake, if nothing else. Taking Jane to one side he gave her a comforting hug. "She'll make it," he murmured softly, "I know our daughter will make it."

Donna thought long and hard about what Sarah had suggested. What had she got here in the village? No friends, no excitement. She was fine when she had something to occupy her, but when she was alone she couldn't help but think things over. She was getting old, older than she'd ever imagined. Maybe she was going to be a grumpy old woman and stuck here permanently.

Donna Layton, you're becoming a bore – is that what you want?

What I really want is Johnny.

Bullshit. He's a loser. He'll never settle down and you know it.

But I love him.

No you don't.

Liar.

She picked up her mobile and rang Sarah. "I've changed my mind," she began. "Is the offer still open?"

"You mean moving in with me? Oh Dee, this is wonderful."

"Don't get too excited – it's only for a short time," Donna pointed out.

"Yes. Of course," Sarah replied shrewdly.

"Are you sure I won't be in the way – you know – with the boyfriend and that?"

"Of course not," Sarah said gleefully. "You've just missed a cracking job at my place. I wish you'd have rung me sooner. I could have spoken to my boss."

"As I've said, it's only a temporary arrangement until I get myself sorted."

"When are you thinking of coming?"

"I thought this weekend, if that's OK with you?"

"Splendid. Let me know the times of the trains and I'll arrange to pick you up at the station. Oh Dee – one other thing. You may have to bring some ear plugs. There's a student in the flat above learning to play the violin."

"Oh great, I thought you said it was peaceful where you were?"

"It is, usually."

"I hope I'm not going to regret this," Donna said scathingly.

"You won't, I promise."

CHAPTER SEVENTY-SIX

The sight of Kylie wired up to some machine with tubes down her mouth and her head encased was too much for Johnny. Suppose she never came round? Suppose he never had the chance to tell her she was the most important thing in his life?

In the two days he'd spent there, Kylie had never shown any sign of regaining consciousness. He'd hardly moved from her bedside, watching, waiting, hoping and praying that she might just bat her eyelids, anything.

"Kylie, can you hear me, angel? I love you, sweetheart, I love you," he whispered, squeezing her hand.

"Go home and get some rest," Jane said wearily. "I'll stay here and let you know if there's any change."

How could he rest when she lay critically ill – maybe she'd never gain consciousness? He was emotionally screwed up inside.

He hadn't washed or changed and realised he must be looking a physical wreck as well as feeling one.

"What's it been like for her, with us at each other's throats?" he said, fighting to keep the frustration out of his voice. "If it isn't us it's… " he trailed off, not intending to let Jane know what a disaster his own marriage was.

"I know it hasn't been easy for you, Johnny," Jane began with a lump in her throat. "But if she… I mean when she finally pulls through, things will be different, I promise," she said, realising he was going through just as much pain.

He gave her a smile as if to say thanks, the same smile

that had once made her heart race. She could see why she had fallen in love with him. It didn't make her want to run into his arms, but she was thankful that he cared for their daughter and she was determined that from now on he'd play an important part in bringing her up.

Pacing the room anxiously, he glanced at the 'no smoking restriction on the wall. He needed a cigarette but he was hesitant to leave in case Kylie came to.

"I thought I'd let you know I've seen the head teacher," Jane began, trying to take their minds off things as they waited. "The boy in question is being cautioned."

"Cautioned..." he repeated heatedly. "Is that it?"

"At least it's a start." She broke off and struggled to make conversation. "How's married life?"

"Fine," he shrugged.

"I never thought you'd be the type to settle down," she said with a faint smile.

He was eager to get away from the conversation. "I'm going for a quick fag. I'll only be a couple of minutes," he said.

On his way back he grabbed two plastic cups of coffee from the vending machine and took one to her. "You look as if you could do with this," he murmured.

"Thanks."

"Mr and Mrs Ricci?" a nurse interrupted.

"I'm Mr Ricci," Johnny said, jumping to his feet. "And this is Kylie's mother."

The nurse gave a faint smile. "Well, the results are back and you'll be pleased to know that apart from the concussion there's no permanent brain damage."

"Oh, thank God," Jane breathed.

"But suppose she never regains consciousness. What then?" Johnny asked.

"I'd try not to worry too much," the nurse said. "The body has ways of repairing itself and sleep is a part of the natural process."

Johnny wasn't so sure. He imagined all sorts of things. He'd heard of people being in comas for years.

"I'm afraid the scan shows a fractured vertebra in her neck."

"Does this mean she'll never be able to move again?" Jane muttered, stricken by the news.

"It's a hairline fracture, which isn't as bad as a break. But your daughter will need to be hospitalised and kept in traction for a few weeks. Try to get some rest – both of you."

Nodding wearily at the nurse as she left, Jane turned to Johnny. "You look exhausted," she said. "I wish you'd go home and get a good night's sleep."

He shook his head. "She's our kid, Jane, no matter what's happened between us."

They sat and waited, Johnny in silent prayer. He was far from any saint. He'd done some bad things in his time, but he prayed to God that Kylie might somehow pull through.

He must have dropped off at some point through sheer exhaustion. The next thing he heard was a faint voice calling out. At first he thought he was dreaming, but then Jane rushed to her side. "Kylie sweetheart! It's all right, darling, it's all right."

"Dad," she murmured.

"I'm right here, angel." Leaning over, he kissed her on the cheek. He wasn't supposed to cry – men never cried. Wiping a tear he whispered faintly, "Thanks."

Michelle was waiting when he got back. "So you finally

decided to show your face?" she threw at him the minute he walked through the door.

"Just shut it," he said, his voice dangerously low.

Michelle didn't let it rest. "I've been waiting here like a bloody fool while you disappear for three days with that woman. You're lucky I didn't catch the pair of you at it."

"At what?" he snapped.

"You know very well what."

At that moment he felt like strangling her. "In case it may have slipped your attention, I had more important things on my mind."

"Like making out you were upset," she snorted. "Like, oh my precious daughter's hurt herself... Mummy what shall we do? Oh I know, we'll have a shag while we're waiting."

"You're off your flaming rocker," he snarled.

Marching past her, he went straight up to his room, locked the door and pulled down the shutters. He lay on the bed and in no time he had fallen asleep. When he woke, Michelle had gone to keep fit.

Peace at last.

He fixed himself some food and walked into the lounge and turned on the TV. Then he sent Penny a text. If he was going to get blamed for something he'd never done, he might as well do it.

Missin U

Need a woman 2 keep me company. Johnny

A few minutes later a text came back.

Missing U 2

How's your daughter? P

As the texts continued, the contents became more intimate. Finally, he called her.

"I gotta see you," he insisted.

"It's not that easy – what do I tell...?"

"Shove a sleeping pill in his cocoa," he cut in briskly.

"What about your wife?"

"What about her?"

"Give me a few minutes and I'll be there."

They met up in the secluded lane they normally used and she parked her car and came over to him. Within seconds they were at it like rabbits.

And that's how his life continued.

CHAPTER SEVENTY-SEVEN

Donna arrived in Birmingham, and after a week there was still no sign of work on the horizon. What she really wanted was her own little tea room somewhere out in the country, but that would have to be put on hold for a while. Glancing down the Evening Mail she spotted two possibilities. One was working for an accountant, which she decided to pass on, remembering her last experience. The second was at a care home that was advertising for a girl Friday to manage the phones and help out with orders. She wasn't all that impressed, but as it was only for a short time she decided to give them a ring. The woman hastily told her to come along.

An hour later she was making her way into a building, feeling herself being dragged into what could only be described as a time warp. There were shelves upon shelves of documents; she'd never seen so much paperwork. Her first reaction was to get out of there as fast as she could.

"Ah, you must be Donna?" a voice said, peering at her from behind a small gap in the shelf.

"Yes but… "

"Come along, luv – bring those invoices with you, the ones marked A to L."

Before she knew it she was being led through to a small dingy looking office clustered with more paperwork. Two women glanced up when she walked in.

"Where shall I put them?" she asked.

"Just plonk 'em anywhere, luv - I'm Barbara, by the way. And this is Lynne and Irene. Janet's gone out for a fag, she'll be back in a minute."

Donna glanced at the large table piled high with invoices and documents. A phone was ringing somewhere beneath the rubble.

Barbara began shifting some delivery notes from a chair. "Ere – sit yerself down."

Presumably this was the interview, Donna thought, returning her friendly smile.

"You'll be answering the phones and helping out with enquiries, any problems you've only to ask Lynne. Any questions?"

"What about salary?"

"Didn't the agency mention it?"

"I didn't go to an agency."

"Oh course not," Barbara said. Donna couldn't help but notice her dirty, worn fingernails. She was roughly in her late forties, and by the looks of things hadn't had an easy life. Lynne was about the same age, equally rough, and wore glasses.

"So how soon can you start?" Barbara asked.

"I'll have to think about it," Donna said, not entirely struck on the idea. Although it wasn't as if she was going to be there long and they seemed an easy enough bunch to get on with. Definitely no chance of the grilling she'd had in her previous job.

"I've three others to interview, duck," Barbara said. "The closing date's this Friday so I'll need an answer by the end of the week."

Driving back from work, Johnny's mood was up and down. He'd tried being nice to Michelle and all she'd thrown back was he 'must be feeling guilty.'

Jeezus! Is there no pleasing the bitch?

He'd arranged with Jane to share the visiting hours between them. Tonight it was his turn, and he realised he'd have to move if he was going to make the hospital in time.

Pulling onto the drive he noticed a builder's van parked outside. He got out and walked into the house, only to find two workmen sizing up the back of the property.

"What's going on?" he called to Michelle, who was busy in conversation with them.

"Johnny!" She broke off and came rushing over to him. "I'm having an indoor swimming pool installed," she said, linking his arm. "The extension will come out somewhere by the end of the patio."

He noticed there wasn't a sign of any dinner. "An' who's the mug paying for this little lot?" he said.

She quickly covered her tracks and took him to one side. "We have more than enough money."

"I do, you mean," he said, raising his voice.

"Sssh," she murmured discreetly. "Please keep your voice down."

"If you think I'm working my balls off to pay for this lot you're very much mistaken," he hissed.

He shook her hand off and turned to the workmen. "Sorry, there's been a misunderstanding," he said, "I'll let you know if and when we need anything doing."

He bungled them out of the door and quickly turned on Michelle.

"What the hell are you playing at?"

"How dare you?" she screamed. "You're complaining of wasting money and you go out and buy yourself a bloody Audi!"

"So? I'm entitled. I work hard enough for it."

"Why do you need another car?" she yelled back. "You already have the company one."

Why should he feel guilty? He'd always dreamed of

owning a flash sports car. It was the only pleasure he had in life, and the only thing that really belonged to him.

"You're pathetic!" she screamed.

"I'm pathetic – try looking at yourself," he retaliated. "I'd be happy to live in a two-bed semi. But your father has to stick us in this lot. And why a swimming pool, of all things?"

"For when we entertain," she yelled back. "Oh – I forgot," she said scathingly, "Most of your entertainment's spent up other women's arses."

He stared at her, his jaw set firmly in anger. "Fine - I want a divorce."

"Well, I'm not giving you one, you good for nothing bastard!" she screamed at him.

"We'll see about that," he spat, storming past her.

Picking up a meat cleaver, she let out a scream and lunged for him. He only just managed to duck out of the way, the sharp blade catching his hand. "Fuck you!" he yelled heading for the door.

"That's right!" she screamed after him. "Wherever there's a problem just make for the drink."

Who cared? It was his life.

He spent an hour or so with Kylie, reading her a book and talking about what they would do when she finally came out. Before he left a nurse gave him an anti-tetanus injection and insisted on putting a bandage on his hand, telling him to be more careful when chopping wood.

Driving back he decided to call in on Rose and see if there was anything to eat. Just lately he'd been going there regularly for meals.

She opened the door, and glancing through he could see she was not alone.

"Come on in, you silly beggar," she called after him.

A stout woman with brownish hair lifted her bifocals and took a good look at him. "You must be Johnny," she said, grabbing his hand. "You're very handsome – isn't he handsome, Maria?"

With a limp smile he tried to retrieve his hand, but she held on to it.

"Have you had an accident, my love?" she asked.

Rose came to the rescue with a plateful of spaghetti bolognaise. "The lad's starving," she said. "Goodness knows what his wife feeds him."

Eager to get away, Johnny mumbled his thanks to Rose and left shortly afterwards. After sitting in his car for a while, he decided it was too early to go home. Why have the crap nagged out of him? Instead he called in at Catherine's.

"How's Kylie?" she asked.

"She's coming along fine," he said, making himself comfortable in a chair and taking out his cigarettes.

"Sorry, Johnny, cigarettes are not allowed in here."

"Who's gonna know?" he said.

"I'll know when my walls are discoloured and filthy," she complained.

Following her out to a small garden area, he lit up two cigarettes and handed her one.

"So apart from your daughter, how are things?" she asked.

He shrugged in silence and took a deep drag of his cigarette.

Catherine glanced at him with concern. "What happened to your hand?"

"Ah, just an accident," he mumbled.

"Are you sure everything's all right?"

He put on a smile. "Hey - what gives with the concerned sister act?"

Looking at him sympathetically she said, "I can read you like a book and I know when something's not right."

"Yeah, well it's not that easy when you're dragging a frigging ball and chain around."

Catherine read between the lines. "You could leave her, you know. It's not as if there are any kids to worry about."

He tossed his cigarette onto the ground. "She's crazy. She threatened suicide the last time, and she meant it, Cath."

"I wouldn't put it past her to try anything. She tricked you into marriage don't forget. If she's capable of that, she's capable of anything. You have to make the break, Johnny."

He looked downcast. "Yeah, I know."

It was almost ten thirty when he finally got to leave. He knew Michelle would be onto him like a screaming banshee when he got home. But when he crept in, she'd gone up to bed.

He settled down with a scotch and then made up a bed on the sofa. A few minutes later she crept down, standing over him. "I'm sorry what happened, Johnny... " she began. "I get all strung up and then I can't help it."

"Just get out of my sight," he warned, struggling to control the rage that was building up inside him.

Michelle knew she'd overstepped the mark. Her eyes glistening with tears, she said quietly, "I'm sorry about your hand – I never meant to hurt you... please Johnny, come to bed."

Wrapping the duvet around him, he turned over and ignored her. Eventually she went back upstairs.

PART 4

CHAPTER SEVENTY-EIGHT

"Ever been to a karaoke?" Janet asked, busy wading through a pile of delivery notes.

"No, can't say I have," Donna replied.

"You mean you ain't sung on one?" Janet shrieked with disbelief. "Bloody hell, you can't get me off the stage once I'm there." She was in her late twenties, the youngest of the bunch, wispy with mousy brown hair.

"Never mind your karaoke, I'm starvin," piped up Lynne. "Me stomach's beginnin' to think me mouth's been slit."

"Pity it ain't," Barbara muttered under her breath. Shrieking at the top of her voice she yelled, "Right you lot – whose turn is it to fetch the grub?"

Three pairs of eyes settled on Donna. She wasn't exactly thrilled by running their errands but at least it got her out of the office. Not that they were a bad crowd to get on with. The job was definitely different. Surprisingly not as boring as she had first thought. Barbara hadn't been joking when she had said the phone never stopped ringing. In the few weeks she had been there she hadn't had time to think about going out. Most evenings she was just glad to get back to the flat and put her feet up.

"Eh up," Barbara yelled, "here she comes."

Irene walked into the office and dumped her bags down on the floor with a puff. "Sorry I'm late, Barbara," she gasped, catching her breath. "I bust me dentures on a bag of scratchins last night. I've bin runnin' round like a blue-arsed fly trying to find someone to fix 'em... 'Ere look," she said, snatching them out of her mouth. "I've had to stick 'em together with superglue."

"Ugh!" squirmed Janet. "That's bloody disgusting, Irene. Put them back."

"There's this bloke in Yardley that fixes 'em, duck," Lynne piped up. "Just by... "

Donna waited impatiently. "Am I getting the food, or not?" she complained.

"OK girls – let's have ya," Barbara roared. Passing the order onto Donna she added, "If there's any dishy blokes throw 'em in an' all."

Who needed men, Donna thought, setting out for the bread shop. She certainly didn't. Her life had become considerably more comfortable without them.

Driving the Jaguar through the midday traffic, the radio blasting and Penny at his side, Johnny forgot about his cares for a while and concentrated on the present. It wasn't easy; the thought of having to go back to that house with Michelle ate away at him. It was almost like having to face a volcano, never sure when it was about to erupt.

He glanced at Penny, her long blonde hair blowing in the breeze, laughing and deliriously happy, and at that precise moment he felt happy as well.

"I'm leaving her," he said.

"When?" Penny asked with a broad smile.

"Just as soon as I decide where I'm going."

"I could always sell the flat and we could get somewhere together?" she suggested.

"It's not that simple. I've gotta work things out carefully," he said. "I've gotta go where she can't trace me."

"If you're separated for twelve months then she has to give you a divorce by law," Penny pointed out. "You know I'll always be there for you, Johnny."

Pulling up at the traffic light he gave her thigh a squeeze. "Yeah babe – I guess you will."

They were laughing and joking when he spotted Donna rushing across the road. On impulse he went to call her name. But she disappeared into a bread shop.

"Is something wrong?" Penny asked.

"It's just someone I once knew," he said, trying to gain control of the situation.

Gathering his thoughts he dropped Penny back at the office.

What was Donna doing in Birmingham? Maybe he was imagining things? Maybe it wasn't her? He hadn't got her mobile number any more, and in any case she probably wouldn't speak to him. He thought of ringing Sarah – but again he'd thrown away her number on account of Michelle finding it.

He racked his brains all afternoon trying to remember the number. Was it 07841 or 07814? He juggled the numbers around and rang them, first getting a grumpy old woman, the second – no reply.

Before leaving work he tried the operator, asking for the alarm company Sarah worked for. She would have left by now, so he decided to call her first thing in the morning.

After dropping in for a pint he finally made his way back to the house. Michelle smelt beer on his breath immediately. "Why didn't you come straight home?" she said harshly.

"What difference does it make?" he replied, switching on the telly in an attempt to drown her out.

"You were with her, weren't you?" she screamed at him. "I'll kill the bitch when I get hold of her."

"What the hell are you going on about?" he snapped.

Wagging a threatening finger at him, she screamed, "Don't come the sweet innocent with me. I know exactly what you've been up to. I followed you the other day. I'm having that bitch in the morning. She'll be sorry she ever crossed me."

Feeling like a naughty boy who'd been caught out, he lowered his voice. "Don't be ridiculous," he said, trying to calm her down. "Penny was just helping me out, that's all."

"Helping you out all right – you must think I'm a bloody fool."

He wasn't bothered what she thought. He was more concerned about Penny getting fired. "Make you look a fool?" he snorted. "You're managing that yourself."

There was only one way to tackle this, he thought, which was anything but easy.

"Come here," he said, pulling her close and attempting to soften her up. "You know I wouldn't do the dirty on you." Lifting her top he began kissing her nipples and running his tongue down her belly towards the magic spot, all the time trying to convince himself that it was Donna.

Oh Jeez! If only.

CHAPTER SEVENTY-NINE

Mick Brennan strode out of prison and took a deep breath. He was not a happy bunny.

He'd done five years of his six-year sentence and been discharged for good behaviour and he'd only been out of jail a few months when he'd got involved with a gang of crackheads. He was desperate for cash, and when they suggested robbing a store he didn't hesitate.

It seemed a straightforward enough job and it wasn't until one of them lost his bottle that things turned nasty. "Hand over the money – now!" the kid yelled, waving a gun in the shop assistants face.

The terrified woman opened the till, her hands shaking violently.

"All of it," he yelled. "Come on – hurry up." He began to panic and the gun went off accidentally, killing the woman. All four of them made a run of it.

They were all eventually caught and arrested and Mick along with the rest of them was sent down, charged with murder and being in possession of firearms.

Another eight lousy years slapped on him for a crime he'd never committed. It wasn't as if he'd pulled the trigger – all because of some headless junky. Well screw it! Things were gonna be different from now on.

He hung around outside the jail in Winson Green, figuring out his best move. He had hardly any cash. In fact he had hardly anything.

Sorting out some loose change, he caught a bus and made his way over to his mother's council flat. The curtains were drawn. He knocked the door but there was no reply.

"Anyone in there?" he yelled.

Sorting through his pockets, he eventually came up with a key.

He found his mother sitting in a chair, clutching a filthy cardigan around her wasted frame and muttering away to herself. She glanced up at him with sunken eyes. "What you doin' here? What d'ya want?" she said, raising her voice.

"I'm your son. I live 'ere – remember?" Walking over to the fridge he found it empty.

"You ain't no son of mine," she mumbled. "Never was, never will be."

"And whose fault's that?" he yelled at her. "It's not easy bein' brought up by a fuckin' druggie an' alkie!"

A dozen empty spirit bottles were on the worktop, along with a half-drunk bottle of rough cider.

"The place stinks like a piss pot," he hissed, glancing to see if any money was lying around. His mother continued to mumble away to herself, staring vacantly into space.

"I need some money!" he yelled, giving her a shake. "C'mon – where is it?"

She glanced up at him with a smile on her drawn face. "You're goin' to hell, my boy... oh yes... straight to Satan himself."

"Shut it, you stupid cow."

Pushing her to one side, he began rummaging through her belongings, turning out drawers and slinging them across the kitchen. Finally he came across what he was looking for – a rolled up bundle of notes.

"Watcha doin'?" she cried, rising unsteadily to her feet.

"Watcha stolen?" Her eyes stared accusingly at him. "Get out o' my place. Get out!"

"Mrs Brennan are you all right?" a concerned neighbour called through the letter box.

Pocketing the money, he rushed past the neighbour out into the street.

He had plans – big plans. While he'd been in jail he'd had plenty of time to think things over. Seven years, six months and three days to be exact. He and two other inmates had planned a bank robbery down to the very last detail, including forged passports. There was one slight problem - they needed a good driver, someone who could handle the wheel. He knew just the man.

He'd heard from a source that Ricci was working for a man called Gillespie. He vaguely knew the name. Word had it that Gillespie was making quite a profitable business – maybe it was time he helped himself to a fat slice? He grinned thoughtfully to himself. Ricci, his old buddy and partner who had ran out on him and left him to face the consequences. Well now he was out and ready to take control of things. It was time he took a little trip over there; pay 'em an unexpected visit.

He grinned to himself. Ricci and Brennan were about to go back into business. Only this time Ricci would do things his way.

CHAPTER EIGHTY

Penny was waiting when Johnny arrived in work the next day. She greeted him with her usual kiss. Pushing her to one side he said, "We need to cool things down. Michelle knows. I had the job of trying to convince her last night."

"Do you think she believed you?"

"By the time I'd finished with her – yes."

"You mean you had sex?" Penny asked in an outraged tone.

"That's what you usually do when you're married," he replied shortly.

Stepping out of the lift, Penny followed. "So when are you going to tell her?" she asked anxiously.

"I can't take any more risks at the moment," he said, doing his best to
call it off.

"You've no intention of leaving her, have you?" Penny asked, raising her voice.

"Ssssh," he said, glancing down the corridor to see if anyone had heard them.

"I put my fucking job on the line for you!" she screamed.

"Did I tell you to?" he hissed back. He wished they'd all disappear, the whole darn lot of them – all except the one woman he loved.

Walking into his office he slammed the door shut and, settling into his seat, reached for the bottle of scotch, pouring himself a hefty glass. Then he picked up the phone and asked the operator to get him the alarm company. A girl answered, telling him that Sarah had just left the office and was on her way to see a client.

"Can I help?" she asked.

"Thanks sweetheart, but this is a personal call," he said. "You wouldn't happen to have her mobile, would you?"

Scribbling the number down, he swiftly gave her a call.

"Johnny I'm driving, I can't talk at present," Sarah replied.

"I just need to know – is Donna in Birmingham?" he asked.

"I'll call you back later. We'll talk then."

"Just tell me – yes or no," he insisted.

"OK – yes," she replied shortly.

"Pull over for a second."

"I'm on my way to see a client," she snapped.

"Give me one minute, Sarah. That's all I'm asking."

"What, now?"

"I need to see her."

Sarah gave a sigh. "We've been through all this before. You know very well she won't see you."

"Not if we play it my way."

"She'll know we've been talking, Johnny. And I gave her my word."

"Listen, I've got a plan," he suggested diplomatically.

Pulling into a lay-by she stopped the car. "You've got exactly one minute to explain, and that's it."

Tucking into a hefty meal of burger, sausage, chips and beans, Mick hadn't felt this good in a long time. OK, maybe it wasn't steak but it sure beat the garbage he'd been served in prison.

Fuck it! Soon he'd have all the luxuries he'd ever wanted, he thought moping up the grease with a slice of bread.

He leaned back and let out a burp loud enough for the woman sitting at the table opposite to glance up at him over the rim of her tea cup.

"Boo!" he sniggered making her jump.

After sitting in the warmth and comfort of the café for three parts of an hour he finally made a move and caught a bus into the city. Lighting up a cigarette he hung around on the street for a while. Then he checked out the details he'd been given by an inmate and began making his way to a strip club in the town centre.

He eventually came across the brightly lit building. The sign immediately caught his eye: "GIRLS GALORE! EXOTIC DANCERS AND ESCORTS."

Breezing into the club, he was met by a black bouncer with dreadlocks who swiftly refused him entry.

"Tell your boss I'm 'ere on business," Mick said.

"Who wants 'im?"

"Just tell 'im Micky Brennan – I'm a friend of an old friend, so to speak."

He was told to hang on for a second while dreadlocks went and checked it out. While he waited he watched a busty stripper gyrate her tits on stage. He fancied some of that. He fancied it real bad. Prison had deprived him of many things, including the carnal pleasures of a woman. But soon he'd have plenty.

Just then Dreadlocks came back and led him over to a room where a stocky middle aged man in a tuxedo sat at a table.

"Ah Mr Brennan, do come in," he said. "If it's a good time you're after, then look no further. My girls are all groomed to a high standard, whether you fancy a touch of Oriental spice or... "

"I'm after a gun," Mick cut in bluntly. "I believe you can supply me with one?"

The man leaned back on his chair, surveying Mick with caution. He didn't strike him as a cop, but there again appearances could be very misleading.

"What makes you think I can get hold of firearms?" he asked.

Mick leaned over the desk towards him. "I bumped into an old friend of yours while I was in the nick," he said. "He reckons you met up a few years back an' he did you a favour. Does the Tasmanian job ring any bells?"

The man stubbed out his cigarette. A few minutes later he was being led down to a basement, where the man produced a sawn-off shotgun.

"Let me give you a word of advice," the man said. "You don't know me, we've never met, neither have you had any dealings with this club."

"What club?" Mick replied.

"Good. I'm glad we understand one another," the man said with a pat on the back. "Just be careful, Mr Brennan."

He intended to. Twelve lousy years in jail had taught him that. He felt more powerful with a gun, it made people respect you- Yeah, it could be very persuasive indeed, which brought him to the task of finding Johnny. But that shouldn't be too difficult. All he had to do was look up Gillespie.

★ ★ ★

"A girly night?" Donna said, not entirely impressed by the idea. "I'd rather spend a night in watching Corrie." She was curled up on the sofa with a packet of chocolate raisins.

"Come on, Dee, don't be a party pooper," Sarah said, doing her utmost to persuade her sister, and wishing she'd never got talked into Johnny's wild ideas.

"Please Dee – it'll be fun."

"How can you call a load of gossiping women having fun, especially if they're anything like the bunch I work with? And besides, I'm too old for those kind of nights."

"I keep telling you you're not old..."

Sarah bit her tongue. She was about to say she'd have every man in the place ogling her, then thought better of it.

"Please, Dee. The girls will be disappointed."

"Anyway I've nothing to wear."

"Put your jeans on. That's all I'm wearing."

"You won't get into a club wearing jeans," Donna pointed out.

"Who said anything about a club?"

Donna hesitated for a moment. Unknown to Sarah, she intended giving her notice in and leaving Birmingham at the end of the month. Maybe she owed her sister a night out if nothing else.

"OK, I'll think about it," she said. "But I'm not promising anything."

CHAPTER EIGHTY-ONE

Mick wandered onto the forecourt and inspected the Citroen, Gillespie hot on his heels. "Nice little car," he said in his usual banter. "And at a bargain price, I must say."

At four grand, Mick didn't think so.

"If you're interested we can slip in the office and discuss it?" Gillespie suggested, rubbing his hands together gleefully.

Mick followed him through. Once inside, he switched the notice round on the door and took out the gun.

"Good grief! There's no need for violence," Gillespie panicked. "I'm sure we can reach an acceptable agreement."

Mick kept the gun aimed steadily towards him. "Sure we can. Now open the safe, grandad."

"There's no money in there, I can assure you – it's all been taken to the bank."

"Nice try." Mick clicked the trigger and Gillespie sat rigid in his seat.

"Get off your arse an' get me the money – now!"

Gillespie stood up, his knees knocking together like castanets, and made his way unsteadily over to the safe. Whoever this maniac was, he clearly meant business.

"C'mon – open it up!" Mick shouted.

Taking a cigar out of the box, he helped himself to Gillespie's lighter, lit up and put his feet on the desk. "Nice cigars, pop," he said, taking a drag.

"Just take them – and the money," Gillespie panicked, throwing the cash at him.

Grinning, Mick shoved the money in his pockets.

"What else do you want?" Gillespie croaked.

"Let's just say I've met the organ grinder, now I'm waiting for his monkey."

"Johnny? What's he got to do with this?"

Mick took a generous draw on the cigar. "Hasn't he mentioned? We're old buddies."

Gillespie panicked. "Can't you go and sort this out somewhere else, instead of my office?"

"Don't fuck with me!" Brennan snarled, pointing the gun in his face. "Where is he? Where's the little toerag?"

"How should I know?" Gillespie croaked. "He left here almost twelve months ago."

Mick grabbed hold of him. "Get 'im now – or I'll shove this gun down your bleedin' throat."

"What are you looking so pleased about?" Penny asked, all signs of their earlier tiff now completely dispersed.

"I've got a good feeling about things," Johnny grinned, leaning back on his chair, hands clasped behind his head. "Today is the beginning of a new chapter in my life."

"Really?" Penny said in a pleasant tone. Placing the letters down she perched herself on the edge of his desk. "Has wifey finally agreed to a divorce?"

He hated it when Penny insisted on calling Michelle 'wifey'.

"Like hell she has," he said, grabbing his pen to sign.

She pondered at his desk for a minute. "Am I getting the vibes that this is where wham bam thank you ma'am comes in?" she asked.

He gave a weary sigh. "Penny, we both agreed we were taking a risk – right? And you still have your job."

"Don't act as if you're doing me a favour," she snapped.

"I'm not acting anything," he said tedious of arguing. "Look, I like you Penny – you know that."

She gave a brittle laugh. "You like me – wow! And there was stupid old me thinking we had something going. Well thanks for nothing." She got up and stormed out of the office, slamming the door.

He held his head for a second before picking up the phone to call Sarah. "Are things still on for tonight?" he asked her.

"Yes. Everything's going according to plan, trust me."

"How did you manage it?"

"With great difficulty I can assure you. Be there at seven thirty – and don't be late."

"Try an' stop me."

He put down the phone with a smile.

He had it all planned. Little did Donna know that tonight he was meeting her. He intended telling her everything. If he could just persuade her, make her understand. And then somehow he'd leave Michelle. Go abroad, to some place where no one would find them. It could work. It had to work.

"Mr Ricci, I have a Mr Gillespie on line one," the receptionist said.

"Put him through."

Two seconds later Gillespie came screaming down the phone. "Johnny – thank God. I need you to come over here as quickly as possible."

"Hang on, Ronnie, I can't just drop everything. I'll catch up with you later this evening on my way home."

"I need to see you now," he insisted, his voice quavering with panic.

"Ronnie – are you all right?"

"Johnny there's a maniac standing over me with a gun."

Mick grabbed the receiver off him. "Just get your arse over 'ere, Ricci."

Holy Mary!

His past came back to haunt him. All the bad memories he'd tried so desperately to obliterate. And now he had no other choice than to face Brennan.

He grabbed his jacket and rushed out of his office. "Tell Louis I've had to slip out. An emergency cropped up," he called to one of the staff.

Mick was sitting at Gillespie's desk, an arrogant smirk on his face. "Nice Jag, Ricci. Things must be lookin' up."

A panic stricken Gillespie sat opposite. "What in Gods name is going on, Johnny?"

"Shurrup grandad," warned Brennan.

Johnny pinned him dangeriously. "What the hell are you doin' here,"

"That's a nice way to treat your buddy." Mick began to show signs of impatience. Things weren't going as well as intended. "I've got a little proposition ya may be interested in."

"You can shove your propositions."

Mick stood up. "Ain't you forgettin' summat? You an' me are two of a kind, Ricci. Once a tealeaf, always a tealeaf."

"Just piss off."

Mick scowled and waved the gun at him. "I need a driver, an' you're comin' with me."

"Go screw yourself," Johnny hurled back.

Mick fired a shot at his legs, deliberately missing, and then another one. "C'mon– let's see ya dance," he sniggered.

Gillespie could hardly look. He was still shaking, but

he managed to reach for the panic button under his desk which went straight through to the station. Thank goodness he'd had the security system installed.

Mick continued firing at Johnny's legs. "Jumping Jack Flash is a g… g… gas," he sniggered with laughter. His smile drained and he pointed the gun at Johnny's head. "Get down on yer knees and grovel," he said in a nasty tone.

"Go to hell."

Mick clicked the barrel. "I said get down on your fuckin' knees."

Gradually Johnny stooped at his feet.

"Now lick my boots, Ricci. C'mon lick 'em."

Gillespie winced. "Oh my God, do you mind if I have a cigar to calm my nerves?" he said, playing for time.

"Sit down an' shurrup up!" Mick yelled at him.

Johnny seized the chance to grab Mick, pulling him to the ground and sending the gun spinning across the floor. They wrestled and fought violently, crashing into anything that stood in their way until Johnny pinned him down.

"You arsehole!" he spat. "I guess I've been waiting a long time to do that."

Mick managed to throw him off and scrambled for the gun. "You're gonna pay for this, Ricci," he said, holding the barrel to Johnny's head. "I'm gonna make you pay for every miserable lousy moment I've wasted in jail."

★ ★ ★

Following a tip off from an anonymous caller claiming to have heard gunshots, the DCI realised they were dealing with something a lot more serious than they had anticipated.

"Get the men over to Gillespie's place – now!" he shouted. "And remember we're dealing with an armed and dangerous man."

★ ★ ★

"Tell you what we're gonna do," Mick said, holding the gun to Johnny's head. "We're gonna walk outta 'ere an' you're gonna drive us over to Frankley in that smart car of yours."

"You're frigging nuts."

"Oh yeah – we'll see who's nuts - So let's start walkin."

Keeping an eye on Gillespie, who was reaching for his phone, he warned. "Just try it an' I'll blow your fuckin' head to smithereens."

Frog-marching Johnny out of the door, they headed across the forecourt to the Jaguar.

"Where're you off to tonight?" Janet asked as they took a break over a cup of tea.

"Oh, just out with my sister and friends," Donna replied. Just lately she had formed a close relationship with Janet – if anything it was Janet's humorous stories that helped pass the time. Checking her watch Donna found it was only two-thirty and there were still loads of invoices to sort through.

"Why can't they get a smoking area in the place," Janet complained. "I'm fed up with having to stand outside in the cold. Me bleedin' feet are like icicles."

"Maybe that's why they do it, to put you off."

"Yeah – well it ain't working. They can do what they bloody like but it'll be a long time before anythin' comes between me an' my fags."

Janet took Donna's empty cup and turning it upside

down said, "Ere look… you're gonna marry a dark haired man."

Donna smiled. "I didn't know you could read teacups."

"It's something me mom taught me." Glancing curiously at Donna she asked, "How come you don't have a bloke?"

"Who said I haven't?"

"Well have ya?"

"No. I was once married and that was a disaster."

"I've never heard you mention it."

"No. It's best forgotten."

Janet raised a curious brow. "And you haven't met anybody since?"

"I guess once bitten, twice shy," Donna said in a brusque tone.

"Bloody hell! How can you live without a bloke?" Janet gasped. "I'd be lost. Even if they are all tossers."

Donna thought briefly of Johnny. Why was she so hooked on him? Why couldn't she just forget?

"There was someone once," she began.

"So what happened?"

"I suppose we just drifted apart, as people do."

"I had this bloke," Janet said. "He tried it on in the kitchens where I worked, would you believe. So I stuffed an ice cube down his pants. I never saw anyone run so fast." She trailed off with a giggle. "Tell you what though – he wasn't short of dosh. I guess I missed my opportunity there."

They walked back to the office and Donna thought of the night ahead. She wasn't particularly bothered in going out but she couldn't very well let her sister down.

"How do you fancy coming along with us tonight?"

Janet shrugged. "Nah - Gotta wash me hair an' I've promised myself an early night. Maybe we can do it next month when I get paid?"

Donna smiled faintly. Hopefully by then she'd have left Birmingham and be planning her own business. But for now, she kept it to herself.

* * *

In a matter of seconds the police were screeching onto the forecourt. "Freeze. Drop the gun and put your hands up."

Mick had no intention of letting anyone or anything stand in the way of his plans.

Using Johnny as a shield, he pointed the gun at his head, warning, "Shoot an' he gets it."

Oh sweet Jesus.

Johnny's life flashed before him; the good and the bad. He thought of Donna and his beautiful daughter. Maybe he'd never see either of them again.

"You'll never get away with it," he muttered, trying to persuade Mick to hand himself in."

"Just shut the hell up an' get in the car. C'mon, do as I say."

An armed officer opened fire just as Mick was about to climb in. The bullet struck him in the side. "Drive! Fuckin' drive!" he screamed.

With the gun pointing at Johnny's head, he had no alternative but to screech off the car park.

"I gotta get help," Mick muttered, trying to stop the blood pumping out of the wound. "There's this chemist on the other side of town. I need you to get me the stuff."

"What are you hoping to achieve from all this?" Johnny

asked, glancing sideways at the gun while attempting to concentrate on the road.

"I got plans for a bank job," Mick rasped. "You're either in or out, so take your fuckin' pick."

Johnny shot him a hostile glance. "It seems I don't have a lot of choice."

"Keep your eyes on the road," Mick warned. Keeping the gun aimed steadily at Johnny, he clutched his side.

"Six lousy years I spent in prison," he snarled. "Six fuckin' years, while you pissed off without a second thought. Well now you owe me."

"I owe you nothing," Johnny spat.

Glancing in the mirror, he spotted a police car on their trail. "It's finished. Give yourself in."

"Shut the fuck up an' do as I say." Blood was spurting out of the wound like a fountain and his side was killing him. Taking a quick look back he snarled, "They're catchin' up – put yer foot down an' lose 'em."

"What d'you think this is – Mission Impossible?" Johnny screamed, the car hitting over the ton.

"Do it – fuckin do it!" Mick screamed. He was beginning to feel faint and light-headed. Christ, what was going on? He hardly had strength to hold the gun.

"What do you mean – you don't know where he is?" Michelle snapped down the line to the receptionist.

"All we know is it was an emergency," the girl told her.

"Emergency?" Michelle asked, tapping her manicured fingernail with annoyance. "He must have said where he was going?"

"He said nothing, Mrs Ricci."

"Is Penny with him?" she asked, her nostrils flaring.

"No. Penny is with Mr Phelan. Are you sure I can't help you?"

"No. It doesn't matter. Maybe you'll get Mr Ricci to call me when he gets back.

"Yes, Mrs Ricci."

She slammed down the phone with rage. She had tried calling his mobile, with no answer. Pacing up and down, she swiftly jumped to her own conclusions. There was no other explanation. He was with a woman, as usual. He'd be sorry, very sorry indeed.

Police cars with their beacons flashin, signalled for Johnny to pull over.

Mick gave an eerie gurgle. What was all the noise? What the hell was going on? And why were they stopping? Had they reached the pharmacy yet? Fuck! Who cared?

The gun slid out of his hand and he slumped forward. Blood began to trickle steadily down the car seat and onto the mat.

★ ★ ★

A crowd had gathered at the scene. Johnny, surrounded by police, sat at the wheel, his face buried in his hands.

"Are you all right, sir?" asked an officer.

He nodded in silence.

One of the officers opened the passenger door and checked Mick out.

"He's dead," he said. "Looks like he bled to death."

Watching as they extracted Mick's body from the car, Johnny leaned back and gave a sigh of relief. Thank God, the nightmare was finally over.

"We'll need to take a statement from you down the station," the chief told him. "Then I'll get one of my officers to run you home."

One last glimpse at Mick just to make sure, and then he was escorted into the police car.

CHAPTER EIGHTY-TWO

It was almost seven o'clock before Johnny was finally dropped off. A distraught Michelle rushed to the door and was horrified to see Johnny getting out of a police car.

"What happened? Where's the Jaguar?" she screamed, hardly giving him chance to get inside the house.

"I met up with an old pal," he said with irony.

"How could you get into a brawl?" she screamed unsympathetically, glancing at his blood splattered jacket and black eye.

Like it was his fault?

He didn't bother to argue back. He was totally past caring what she thought.

"You'd better sort yourself out. I don't want daddy catching you like that."

"Screw daddy!" he hit back. "Have you given one bit of thought to what I've been through?"

"If you will insist on playing dangerous games that's your problem," she said curtly. "Heaven help you when daddy finds out about the car."

He heard her slamming things about in the kitchen.

"Your tea's dried up, so you'll just have to make do with whatever's there," she shouted on her way out.

Go to hell.

As soon as she'd left, he gave Sarah a call.

"Where are you?" she said sharply, taking the call outside the pub. "I've been trying to call you all afternoon."

"I ran into a spot of bother."

"You do realise you're supposed to be meeting my sister at seven thirty?"

He checked his watch. It was seven twenty five.

"I'll be there in forty minutes," he said.

"You'd better not let me down, Johnny," she said abruptly. "Do you know the trouble I've had trying to persuade her?"

Did she think for one minute he was going to let an opportunity like this slip by?

Swiftly he got himself ready. He took a quick shower, sprayed on some deodorant and jumped into his casual clothes.

"Holy mother," he muttered, glancing at his split lip and bruised eye, which had now turned a nasty purple. She'd just have to accept him the way he was. At least he was still alive. Putting on his shades, he rushed out to his Audi and sped off.

Feeling uncomfortable with the arrangements, Donna checked her watch yet again.

"I thought we were all meeting at seven thirty?" she said.

"There's been a slight change of plan,"Sarah replied, glancing around the bar to see if there was any sign of Johnny. "We've now arranged to meet just after eight."

"You're very quiet considering we're on a night out."

Sarah put on a smile. "Let me get you another drink."

"No thanks. I'll wait until the others get here."

"They shouldn't be long," Sarah said, doing her best to sound as if she meant it. "I'll just pop out and give them another call."

"I'll come with you," Donna said, standing up.

"No, you wait here just in case we miss them."

"How do I know who I'm supposed to be looking for?"

"Just trust me for once."

It was packed, and she felt conspicuous as she sat on her own. She decided to get another drink and squeezed up to the bar.

"Hi gorgeous," slurred a burly middle-aged man in a suit, breathing alcohol over her. "Can I get you a drink?"

"No thank you," she replied shortly.

He continued to pester her. She was about to give him his answer when a voice said, "Lay off - the lady's with me."

Oh my God!

She turned around and there stood Johnny. "Hello Donna," he said.

"Um... hi."

For the first time she could remember, she felt shy. She realised that this was all Sarah's doing. There was no girly night.

"What you having to drink?" he asked.

He ordered a beer and a wine and led her over to a quiet corner. "Hey, you look great," he said.

"Thanks. What happened to your face?"

"I figured I was too handsome," he smiled.

She gave a nervous laugh.

"I've missed you. Jeez! I've missed you," he said.

"Me too."

They made light conversation over drinks, talked about old times.

"Remember when we first met?" she said.

"How could I forget - you were a bitch."

"You weren't much better yourself." She began to laugh for no apparent reason; he always had the same effect on her. "What about the night at the club when Eddie hit you?" Now she was giggling hysterically.

"Hey, that's not so funny," he said.

She glanced at him, lost in his dark eyes. He still had that boyish look and that wisp of hair that sent her crazy.

He gave her hand a squeeze and looked directly into her eyes. "So you finally got to leave him?"

She gave a nervous giggle. "Yes, finally."

They both began to talk at the same time.

"Sorry," she said. "What were you about to say?"

"Donna," he began solemnly. "There's something I haven't told you. I guess I haven't been exactly honest… "

She took a huge gulp of wine. Somehow she had the feeling she wasn't going to like what she was about to hear.

"I'm, um… married."

"Married?"

Oh God! She glanced at the gold band on his finger and her world collapsed. "You dragged me here to tell me you were married?" she screamed at him.

"If it means being with you then I promise I'll leave her. I've got it all worked out – we can be on the other side of the globe an' no one's gonna know any different."

"I may be a lot of things, but I'm certainly not a home wrecker," she said bitterly about to stand up. But he pulled her back. "I wanna show you something," he said. Reaching into his wallet he took out the photo – a little torn and worse for wear, but still recognisable.

She glanced at it and was drawn into that moment. "You've kept it all this time."

"Yeah - I had this crazy idea that as long as I had it somehow we'd eventually be together. Soulmates, remember?"

It all seemed such a long time ago, yet she could still visualise that magic moment.

"Jeezus, Donna, what happened? Why has it ended up

like this?" He brought his lips down on hers, capturing her in the moment.

"I... must go," she said, attempting to push him away, but she was just as lost in the moment as he was.

Inevitably they ended up back at a hotel. Nothing had changed. There was still that electrifying chemistry between them. Perhaps even more so. Their once impetuous lovemaking had now mellowed into a deeper understanding of each other's needs.

"Are you happy?" he asked her.

"Are you?" she whispered.

"More than I've been in a long time," he whispered back. They rolled together in bliss.

First thing in the morning, Donna knew exactly what she must do. She hardly slept a wink all night. It was six o'clock when she finally crept quietly out of bed and scribbled the note – short but to the point.

Johnny, thanks for a wonderful night. You will always be part of me no matter what. I wish you all the luck and happiness in the future, and I sincerely mean that.

Love you always.

Donna. X

She left the note by his bedside and crept quietly out.

CHAPTER EIGHTY-THREE

Johnny woke and automatically reached for Donna. He gathered his senses and jumped up out of bed. How could she just walk out on him? There was so much he wanted to say. He loved her, but somehow he'd never got round to telling her.

He spotted the note at the side of the bed, read it twice and then tried calling her mobile, but it was switched off.

And then he remembered Michelle. Checking his mobile, he found he had five missed calls from her. "Answer your phone, u bastard!" she demanded.

She was already at the nursery when he managed to get hold of her. "Where the hell have you been all night?" she screamed down the line at him.

"Michelle – we have to talk."

"We'll talk all right, you bastard! You couldn't give a sod so long as you get your end away!"

"The feeling's mutual, so lets just call it a day before we tear each other apart," he snapped back.

Even now she still had no intention of letting go. "If you carry on sleeping with whores I swear I'll start making your life hell."

What did she mean by start? She'd been making his life hell for the past eighteen months.

"We'll discuss this later," she said sharply and hung up.

No chance, sweetheart, because he wasn't going to be around later. He'd endured enough over the months and he was tired of fighting; tired of the whole damned lot. She could threaten him as much as she liked. He had his life and if she was foolish enough to end hers then that was up to her.

Checking himself out of the hotel, he headed back to the house to collect his belongings. He had a plan, and he was about to put it into action.

"How could you have allowed this to happen?" Donna screamed, pacing up and down Sarah's flat.

"I swear I didn't know anything, Dee. Do you think for one minute I'd have agreed for him to see you if I'd have known?"

"He's a no good son of a bitch," she screamed. "I did warn you what he was like and you wouldn't listen."

"Just forget about him, Dee."

"I'm trying, but people keep interfering," she snapped back.

They were both silent for a moment before Sarah said, "I'm having my mobile number changed."

"And what's that going to achieve? He's got your works number." She paused for a second before saying, "I'm leaving Birmingham, Sarah."

"Why spite yourself for him?"

"It's not just because of this. I've been meaning to tell you. I'm going to open up a tea room, maybe somewhere in the country."

"You really mean it, don't you?"

"I've been planning it for some time," Donna replied. "I'm giving a weeks notice at the care home. And if he should call I'm not here. Do you understand, Sarah? There's no way I ever want to see him again."

It only took one spark, and within seconds the inferno roared through the corridors, igniting anything that stood in its way. The blast shook the building, shattering glass and spreading rapidly towards the nursery.

Michelle's first reaction was to try and lead the children to safety, but the corridor was ablaze and there was no escape. She grabbed a chair in an attempt to smash it against the double glazed window with no effect. She stood helplessly, screaming at the window, while outside an anxious crowd had gathered and fire crew formed a barrier to hold back hysterical parents.

Louis fought his way through the barricade. "My daughter's in there – you have to get her out!" he yelled.

"We're doing all we can, sir. Please stand back."

"You have to get my daughter!" he screamed at them. "For God's sake – get my daughter!"

★ ★ ★

"Mrs Ainsworth?" said a voice urgently. "I'm speaking on behalf of the Little Angels nursery. I'm afraid there's been a fire."

"Oh my God! My two babies are in there!" she screamed down the line. This couldn't possibly be happening. She was having a nightmare, and any minute now she would wake up.

"The fire crew are doing all they can," the voice on the end of the phone told her. "I suggest you get over there immediately."

She hung up, numb with shock, and ran out to her car. Grabbing her mobile, she tried to call Chris. "For God's sake pick up and answer your damned phone," she cried hysterically.

Tears streaming down her face, she sped off to the nursery.

Michelle kept the children huddled together, protecting them as best as she could as falling debris capsized around them.

"I want my mummy!" one child screamed. The other children followed suit and began screaming.

"Hush, children," she cried, trying to control the fear in her voice. "The firemen are going to help us. Everything is going to be all right, you'll see."

There was a loud blast as the windows blew out, sending shards of glass smashing to the ground and the children scattered with screams of terror. She prayed silently in the hope that someone would come and rescue them quickly.

"Get back, sir. You can't go in there."

"I have to get my daughter," Louis demanded, scrambling for the entrance. Two of the fire crew held him back. "It's all under control, sir. Now will you just let us do our job?"

Angie walked round in a trance amongst the rest of them. A woman grabbed hold of her. "Please help me find my kids," she cried.

Angie carried on walking in a daze, tears streaming down her face as she searched for her own children. "Oh God, please let them be all right," she prayed to herself.

She tried yet again to contact Chris and this time his apprentice answered. Almost breaking down she screamed, "Get Chris... please get Chris, quickly!"

One by one the children were all led to safety, until there was only Michelle left. She was about to be rescued when the ceiling collapsed and a large timber came crashing down on top of her. Her legs were crushed beneath the timber and she was fighting for breath in the thick fog of smoke. "Help me … please help me… " she whimpered.

"One of our men's still in there," shouted a fireman. "It's about to blow up at any second."

There was a sudden loud explosion and flames belched out of the building with a mass of black smoke. In the thick haze one of the fire crew came staggering from the building carrying a young woman.

Louis rushed forward. "Michelle - my dear Michelle," he cried. Sobbing, he cradled her in his arms.

"Daddy… " she gasped in her dying breath. "Please… tell Johnny… I'm sorry and I love him." She closed her eyes. There was nothing more anyone could do.

Angie eventually found her two children huddled together and frightened. "Mommy we want to go home," they cried.

"Thank God," she whispered, hugging them. "Thank God you're all right."

Johnny packed his belongings and grabbed his passport. He was about to walk out of the house when his mobile rang. He was in two minds whether to ignore it, but spotting Chris's number he changed his mind.

"Yeah?" he said abruptly.

"Ricci, there's been a fire at the nursery, I think you'd better come quickly – it's Michelle… she's… "

"She's what?" he said in an agitated tone.

"She's dead, mate."

CHAPTER EIGHTY-FOUR

There was a massive turnout for the funeral. The whole of Phelan Foods attended. Johnny stood silently at the graveside in a black suit, black shirt and white tie, trying to look as sombre as possible. Inwardly he gave a sigh of relief.

Free at last.

Louis stood beside him, head lowered and overcome with grief. Johnny knew he should be feeling some kind of anguish but there was nothing. He almost felt guilty for feeling the way he did, but two years of misery was enough for anyone to cope with.

"I'm so sorry," said a voice he didn't even recognise. A woman offered her condolences. It turned out she was one of the packers from the factory. "It must have been terrible for you," she said. "One minute you're with someone, the next they've gone."

He managed a weak smile.

Louis eventually spoke as they headed out of the cemetery. "What will you do about the house?" he asked. "It was a present for you and my daughter, so whatever you decide is entirely up to you."

"I'm going away for a while," Johnny said. "When I come back I'll deal with it then."

There was a moment's silence before Louis spoke. "I know about the baby – believe me I had no idea."

"I tried my best for your daughter, Louis, but apparently it wasn't good enough," he said.

Louis gave him a pat on the shoulder as if to say he

understood. "You're good at your job and I want you to stay on with the company?"

"Thanks, but I'm thinking of leaving Birmingham," he said. "I figured it's time I made a fresh start an' put things behind me."

"Oh?" Louis said, glancing across at Penny. "I was under the impression that you would settle down here."

"Nah. I got other plans."

"I'll arrange for the house to go on the market and settle with you in due course," Louis said.

Johnny nodded in silence. It didn't seem as if the money belonged to him. In fact he didn't want the money, or anything that belonged to her. It had a bad feeling to it. He could almost sense Michelle's presence watching over him – nagging him, as she always had.

"I thought you should know that her dying words were she was sorry and that she loved you."

Yeah – she probably did, in her own twisted way.

"Are you coming back to the hall?" Louis asked. "I've put on a buffet and there's a bar."

"If you don't mind I've gotta push off," he said excusing himself.

He was about to turn when Penny rushed up to him, all smiles. "I suppose I should say I'm sorry," she began. "Although under the circumstances they're hardly the appropriate words to say." She looked all demure in a little black dress, her eyes sparkling brightly. "At least you can put this behind you and move on with your life," she added with a smile.

"Yeah - that's exactly what I'm gonna do," he murmured quietly.

She gave him another one of her pearly white smiles. "So what are your plans?"

"I'm leaving Birmingham."

She looked shocked. "Leaving?"

"You're a good kid, Penny, and I dunno what I'd have done without you, but I've gotta move on," he said, trying to break it to her as gently as possible.

Kissing her chastely on the cheek, he walked off and never looked back.

Racing over to the house he picked up his stuff. Before he left he called Donna yet again. He finally got an answer from Sarah.

"Is Donna there? I need to speak to her."

"Stop harassing her, Johnny. You've been nothing but bad news. Do us both a favour – stay out of our lives."

"Let me speak to her, now!" he demanded.

"She never wants to speak to you or see you again. Those were her words," Sarah snapped. "You know, I really had you down as a nice person, and all along you were playing with us. Well, goodbye Johnny. Find some other fool to work your magic on."

"Stop messing around and put her on the phone – now!" he yelled, losing his rag.

Donna snatched the mobile. "What do you want, Johnny?" she said abruptly.

"We have to talk."

"We said all we had to say last week," she said, her heart racing.

"So it's time we did something about it. I lost my wife – did you know?"

"Yes. I heard and I'm sorry," she said curtly.

"I waited six weeks for you to call me back. I eventually gave up and got married. I never intended it that way, Donna."

"Six weeks – wow! You certainly don't waste much time, do you?"

"Come on, Donna, you know how I feel."

"Do I?"

"I'm leaving Birmingham. In fact I'm leaving England, and I want you to come with me," he said.

"It's too late. I'm on my way back to Norfolk. My train leaves in twenty minutes."

"Donna, listen… "

"Goodbye, Johnny."

Bang – the line went dead.

Damn!

Racing out to his car, he swiftly sped off.

"Poor Johnny," Angie said, thinking back to the fire and feeling relieved it was all over. "To lose his wife like that. He must be feeling devastated. Why don't you invite him round to dinner this evening?"

"I think Johnny's OK, believe me," Chris replied.

"How can you say that?" Angie said firmly.

"Because as you once said, he's a tough cookie."

"Even so, you could show a little consideration."

Chris helped peel the potatoes. "Didn't I mention – he had to get married. Or at least that's what he thought at the time."

Angie glanced at him. "Michelle was pregnant?"

"Nah, it all turned out to be a hoax. She conned him into marrying her."

"You're kidding?"

"They used to argue something rotten."

"And I thought they were happily married. Well, that's what Michelle led me to believe."

"Put it this way, I don't think he'll be grieving for too long," Chris said. "He's probably got some woman lined up at this very moment."

He only just made it. The train was drawing in as he

raced down the steps. He spotted Donna and Sarah hugging one another.

"Donna!" he shouted, rushing towards her.

"Oh no, here comes trouble," Sarah sighed. "What are you going to tell him?"

"Leave it to me. I'll call you later when I get to mother's."

Donna turned to face him, her heart beating rapidly.

"You weren't thinking of running out on me, were you?" he said.

She was about to pick up her case. "I'm leaving you to get on with your life, so I can get on with mine."

"And suppose I don't want you to go?"

"Stop it, Johnny – just stop it."

"Just say you don't feel the same and I'll go," he said, gazing intently into her eyes.

"I don't know how I feel. You're screwing up my life. I can't take much more."

"Donna, we can make this work!"

She gave a brittle laugh. "I don't believe anything you say any more. You're full of lies, Johnny."

"Donna, listen. You were married and I was just a kid. Things have changed."

"It's hopeless," she cried. "Whenever we arrange to see each other something bad always happens."

"Don't you see it's fate? We were meant to be together."

"I… I don't know."

"Look at me, Donna, look at me!" he said, grabbing hold of her shoulders and staring at her with those intense dark eyes. "I love you," he said. "I guess I've always loved you from the moment I first saw you."

"I love you too, but it's hopeless," she whispered.

He held her tightly in his arms. "I love you, I love you," he kept repeating.

As the train pulled out it left two people standing on the platform, locked in each other's arms. For the first time she could remember, she felt it was where she truly belonged.

"Marry me," he whispered. "I can't cook, I'm hopeless at keeping things tidy, in fact I'm pretty useless at most things, but... "

She silenced him with a kiss. She didn't care what he did or where they lived, she had all she'd ever dreamed of right there in his arms. "Yes," she replied, without a moment's hesitation. "Yes. Yes."

"Come on," he said, picking up her case and taking her hand.

"Where are we going?" she giggled as they walked off.

"We're taking a couple of weeks' break. Call it a pre-wedding honeymoon," he said.

Leading her out to his car, he flung her case in the boot and they climbed aboard. "Donna," he began. "There's something I never mentioned... "

"Oh no, Johnny."

"Hang on," he smiled. "I think you'll like this. I have a daughter, Kylie. She's coming up to fourteen, and she's gonna love you."

"How can you be so sure?"

"Trust me," he winked. "She has her father's good taste."

They glanced at one another and burst out laughing, knowing that nothing and no one would separate them, ever again.

The End

ND - #0053 - 270225 - C0 - 203/127/27 - PB - 9781861510365 - Matt Lamination